Women's
Wiles

Women's Wiles

Edited by
Michele Slung

AN ANTHOLOGY OF MYSTERY STORIES
BY THE MYSTERY WRITERS OF AMERICA

Harcourt Brace Jovanovich
New York and London

Printed in the United States of America

Library of Congress Cataloging in Publication Data

Main entry under title:
Women's wiles
1. Detective and mystery stories, American.
I. Slung, Michele B., 1947–   II. Mystery
Writers of America.
PZ1.W6849 [PS648.D4]   813'.0872   79–1835
ISBN 0-15-198421-2

First edition

B   C   D   E

"The Two Sisters," copyright © 1976 by Joyce Harrington. First published in *Ellery Queen's Mystery Magazine*. Reprinted by permission of the author.

"Second Chance," by Edward D. Hoch, copyright © 1977 by Davis Publications, Inc. First published in *Alfred Hitchcock's Mystery Magazine*. Reprinted by permission of the author.

"The Greek Refrain," originally published as "The Strange Adventure of Charles Homer," copyright © 1967 by Frank Sisk. First published in *Ellery Queen's Mystery Magazine*.

"Mom Knows Best," by James Yaffe, copyright © 1952 by Mercury Publications, Inc. First published in *Ellery Queen's Mystery Magazine*.

"The Candle Flame," copyright © 1975 by Lawrence Treat. By permission of the author and the author's agent, Robert P. Mills, Ltd.

"The Kitchen Floor," by Dorothy A. Collins, copyright © 1978 by Davis Publications, Inc. First published in *Alfred Hitchcock's Mystery Magazine*.

"The Girl Friend," by Morris Hershman, copyright © 1957 by Flying Eagle Publications, Inc. Reprinted by permission of the author.

"Double Jeopardy," originally published as "Death Threat," copyright © 1978 by Susan Dunlap. First published in *Ellery Queen's Mystery Magazine*.

Contents

Acknowledgments

This anthology could not have been possible without the co-operation of Eleanor Sullivan, Constance DiRienzo, Bill Pronzini, Patricia McGerr, and Gene Stone of Harcourt Brace Jovanovich.

*Women's
Wiles*

Introduction

When I was a young girl, I was unable to work up any enthusiasm for earnest biographies that told me how Madame Curie discovered radium or how Jane Addams founded Hull House. Instead, I spent much of my time figuring out how to be Nancy Drew. Sadly, roadsters were already collector's items, but I did have two friends who never argued about taking the subordinate roles, and so off we would go, looking for whispering statues, hidden passages, lost wills, and buried treasure. (Corpses, the hard currency of adult detective fiction, did not yet play a part in my make-believe.)

If I sat down to a game of *Clue,* I had to be Miss Scarlet or I would sulk. Having pleasant, fairly reasonable parents did not stop me from wondering what Lizzie Borden had done with those bloodstains, and my standards for conversation with male adolescents were based on the repartee sustained by William Powell and Myrna Loy. I found *Busman's Honeymoon* every bit as erotic as *Peyton Place,* and I could never take a train ride without positioning myself near elderly ladies who seemed likely to vanish.

To this day—thank goodness—I have not met up with a corpse. But I have been allowed to join the Mystery Writers of America, an organization that supports the dictum, "Crime doesn't pay—enough." With such a sinister conspiracy (of the imagination), who can tell what may happen? And please remember that, with this 33rd of the annual anthologies coming from the MWA, you're holding in your hand a blunt instrument.

Now, even though I've established the fact of my having crime on the mind, some of you still may ask, What's a nice woman like you doing in a book like this? To say a few words about the liberating qualities of suspense: It's not only that a loaded gun (or a vial of poison) is a great equalizer, or that woman's intuition triumphs over brawn every time, or even that the female of the species may be, as reputed, more deadly than the male, but simply that the mystery genre is an equal opportunity employer. For ever since the mystery story began to assume a definite shape in the nineteenth century, and ever since it started to fulfill the public's distinct expectations, it has admitted women into all of its precincts.

That women can be successful mystery writers goes without saying, and a number of notable American women authors have served over the years as president of the MWA. That women can be detectives is rather remarkable, considering that they sleuthed in early crime stories long before their real-life sisters were able to have active or interesting careers. (Almost from the beginning, there have been professional female investigators in the pages of fiction, as well as amateur ones.) That women can be victims does not make the genre an accomplice to sexist practices, for just as many male cadavers have set the mechanisms of whodunits into motion. The existence of the female villain proves that mystery writers have not oppressed their feminine characters with the restrictions of sugar-and-spice behavior. (After all, it was a woman—*the* woman, Irene Adler—who outsmarted Sherlock Holmes.)

Certainly mystery stories can be unreal or melodramatic—so can a lot of mainstream fiction—and the conflicts of a genre situation are resolved by mayhem more often than they are in everyday life. However, in this particular type of escape fiction, one can escape only so far from the potential for violence and the demands for justice that exist in the society around us. Each of the following stories, chosen with elements of woman-ness in mind, contain shadings of the violence/justice duality central to both fact and fiction. Not all are straight tales of homicide, or femicide; some are humorous, some fantastical, some philosophical, and some, for want of a better word, are educational.

There is no longer a strictly designated distaff geography; a woman's place can be behind a desk or behind bars. However, she will always have a home in the mystery story.

Michele Slung

The Two Sisters

Joyce Harrington

The sisters were inseparable.

They lived together, in a suburban apartment where each had her separate room of equal size. They rode to work on a bus crowded with other suburban commuters, but they always found a seat together. They worked together, in a travel agency where together they plotted exotic tours for finicky travelers to places the sisters had never seen. Once a year they took a cut-rate cruise, together, to a sunny island where they drank rum drinks chunked with tropical fruit and lolled on the beach in outrageous bikinis. They hoped to find husbands.

It wasn't easy. The sisters had high standards. They vowed to each other that they would never accept second-best. But the best was elusive and hard to define. He must be handsome, of course, but where was the dividing line between handsome and not handsome? He must be rich, but how rich was rich enough? He must be kind, considerate, and intelligent.

They agreed that a doctor would do nicely, and in a pinch a dentist, although there was something not quite pleasant about the thought of hands that probed anonymous mouths all day. Lawyers were in, and salesmen were out. Stockbrokers were ideal. University professors were undoubtedly nice, but poor.

Engineers were acceptable, providing they were not vulgar. Artists and writers of any kind, however rich and handsome, were likely to be unstable. Best of all would be a young man, or rather two young men, of independent means who recognized the fragile beauty and sterling virtues of the two sisters.

The sisters made the most of the miniature style of beauty they shared. They were equally small and identically slender, and possessed similar heart-shaped faces. Marjorie, the older by two years, accented her gamine quality by wearing her dark hair cropped short in springing curls, while Audrey allowed hers to swing in a dark curtain to her shoulders.

Assiduously, they developed all the talents they calculated they would need when they at last became mistresses of fine houses, neighboring, of course, in the most exclusive suburb. They played golf and tennis, learned gourmet cooking, studied antiques and wine, took part in amateur theatricals, and spoke disparagingly of everyone they knew.

Once, when Marjorie was being eagerly pursued by a young accountant and seemed on the point of capitulation, Audrey saved her by a few cutting words.

"He's nothing but a glorified bookkeeper. You might as well marry a computer. Computers never get rich. They only count other people's money."

Marjorie, brought to her senses, quickly totted up the debits and credits and arrived at a minus balance. Her accounting suitor had sweaty palms and bowled on the company team. No, he would never do.

Again, when Audrey was being showered with expensive gifts by a distinguished-looking although middle-aged pencil manufacturer, it was Marjorie who found out the awful truth.

"He already has a wife."

"He'll get a divorce, I'm sure he will," Audrey asserted. "He's very rich."

"Better make sure," cautioned Marjorie.

But although the pencil magnate proposed setting Audrey up in a luxurious apartment and promised undying love and a place in his will, he did not propose to divorce his wife and put Audrey in her place. Regretfully, Audrey wrote him off. She kept the mink jacket, the diamond wrist watch, and all the other tokens of his esteem.

The years passed in double dates and disappointment. The shifting population of the suburban apartment complex seemed to grow younger and younger. The few friends they had made among the apartment dwellers had long since married and moved to neat suburban split-levels where they raised children, puppies, and tomatoes, and worried about the mortgage. A

dreary life, the sisters agreed, and after a few years they stopped
sending cards at Christmas.

One summer the sisters noticed they were no longer in-
cluded in the splashing frolics in the apartment's pool. They
knew none of the playful young creatures who swam and ducked
each other and shrieked with merriment in the bright chlorined
water. If they noticed the giggles and whispers that greeted their
approach to the pool, they did not comment even to each other.
Someone labeled their mailbox: The Weird Sisters.

Audrey was furious and complained to the management.

Marjorie shrugged and said, "At least they know some
Shakespeare."

That was the summer Marjorie began pulling gray threads
out of her gamine curls and Audrey took up needlepoint. It was
that summer, too, that a whole month went by without a single
date. The sisters did something they had never done before.
They stopped at a cocktail lounge after work and sipped two
whiskey sours apiece before boarding their suburban bus.

They had never been in a bar unescorted and they felt conspicuous. They sat nervously at a tiny table in a dark corner and
chattered over their drinks of the day's happenings at the travel
agency. But although they kept their eyes studiously averted
from the crowd of noisy men at the bar and their mouths moved
in a semblance of conversation, their ears remained attuned to
the babble of the drinkers.

When the bartender approached their table with two more
drinks on a tray and said, "Compliments of the gentleman at the
end," the sisters turned startled to see a grinning florid face nodding on top of a pair of beefy shoulders in a loud plaid jacket.
The sisters shook their heads primly, paid their bill, and left.

But they returned the next day. And the next. Soon it became a habit with them to stop after work at one cocktail lounge
or another. Faces became familiar and some even acquired
names. Summer sweltered moistly into fall, and still no one
called to take them out to dinner or even to a movie.

"Everyone must be out of town," said Audrey.

Marjorie mulled over her address book, crossing off names

of those who had proved unworthy, or had got married or moved to jobs in distant cities. When she finished, she threw the little book in the wastebasket and lay on her bed and cried.

In September the Riverside Players began rehearsals for their fall season. The first play was to be *The Royal Family,* and the sisters attended tryouts. Audrey preferred to work backstage and volunteered to do costumes. Marjorie was confident she would be asked to play one of the young women's parts. The sisters were relieved that the long dull summer had ended and their evenings and weekends would now be filled. The director asked Marjorie to read the part of Fanny Cavendish, matriarch of the play's theatrical clan.

"But she's seventy years old!" protested Marjorie.

"There's no one else who can do it," said the director. "It's a terrific role."

"But I'd really rather play Gwen or even Julie."

"Fanny's the best part in the play. You'll have a ball."

"I will *not* have a ball! Count me out."

Marjorie brooded for a week, while Audrey sketched page after page of luscious 1920's costumes. Marjorie glanced over the sketches without enthusiasm.

"Who have they got to play Fanny?" Marjorie asked.

"Nobody yet. What do you think of this gown? Plum satin with just a hint of a train. And this one? Champagne lace over an apricot underdress."

"Sounds like fruit salad to me."

But when the director called at the end of a week to appeal to Marjorie as an old trouper and one of the founding members of the group, she agreed reluctantly to do her best with the help of makeup and silver hair spray. "At least it's an important part. But you've got to give me a young one later on," she insisted.

"I'll try. But, Marj, it's time you got out of the ingenue routine."

"Perhaps you're right. Well, I'll see you at rehearsal."

Rehearsals did not interfere with the sisters' habit of stopping at their favorite cocktail lounge after work. There was plenty of time for their usual two whiskey sours and a quick meal at home before they had to appear at the playhouse in the old church. One day, when Audrey stayed home with a mild case of flu, Marjorie found herself seated at their tiny table alone. So accustomed had she become to the routine, she felt neither conspicuous nor promiscuous, as she might have done a month ago.

The bartender brought her usual drink and inquired after Audrey. Then he left her alone. Marjorie opened her script and mumbled over Fanny Cavendish's lines while she sipped her whiskey sour. She was deeply immersed when a hesitant voice disturbed her mood.

"Do you—ah—would you mind if I—ah—sat down here?"

She looked up and saw a lanky gray-haired man bobbing before her like a small boy begging for a cookie. His face was boyish, too, despite its lines, and his mouth was curved in an engaging small-boy smile. She quickly categorized him as "not worth bothering with" and "probably married" and was about to utter a freezing "Yes, I mind very much." But his smile widened to a grin and his gray eyes crinkled in a most beguiling way.

"Please don't think I'm trying to make a pickup. I'm new in town, and I saw you studying a script. I used to be interested in little theater, a long time ago. My name is Norman Jolly."

Norman Jolly waited politely for Marjorie's permission to sit down. After a moment's hesitation she gave it and introduced herself. What harm could it do? The Riverside Players were always looking for new recruits.

"*The Royal Family!*" he exclaimed, when she showed him her script. "That certainly brings back memories! I once played Tony Cavendish and thought I was a new John Barrymore. But you're much too young to play Fanny."

Marjorie glowed. "I'm only doing it as a favor," she explained. "There are no older women in the group."

They sipped their drinks and Norman Jolly told her briefly of his life—his years as a high-school science teacher, his two children now grown and married, the death of his wife a year ago.

"I moved here to be near my daughter," he said. "And I

opened up a little hobby shop to occupy my time. It doesn't make much money, but it's fun. If I want to close up and go fishing, I just put a sign in the window. But I need to get involved in something else. My daughter has her own life. She doesn't need her old father hanging around all the time. Do you think—?"

"Would you like to come to rehearsal with me?" asked Marjorie.

"Now that's a fine idea. Maybe I could make myself useful." Norman Jolly grinned that appealing little-boy grin. "And here's another good idea. Have dinner with me."

"All right," said Marjorie. "All right, I will."

Marjorie excused herself and went to the telephone. Audrey was better but still weak, and thought she would skip rehearsal. The costumes were being worked on and there was no urgent reason for her to be there.

"Then I think I'll grab a bite to eat downtown and go directly to the playhouse," said Marjorie.

Audrey asked no questions and Marjorie volunteered no information about Norman Jolly.

When she returned to the table, Norman had paid the bill and was ready to go. He took her arm protectively, and Marjorie felt surprisingly warm and sheltered.

"Where shall we go?" he asked. "I'll leave it up to you."

In years past, when asked that question, Marjorie always chose the most expensive restaurant in town. Now she considered carefully.

"We can't make an evening of it," she said. "I have to be at rehearsal by eight o'clock. Let's go to Maude's—home cooking and not too expensive. I hope you don't mind plastic tablecloths."

"I'll be too busy looking at you," said Norman Jolly.

Marjorie was confused by this transparent gallantry. Wordlessly, she allowed him to lead her to the parking lot, and his opening of the door of his battered old car seemed to her a kind of courtly ritual. He insisted that she fasten her safety belt. She did, and felt safe.

Dinner at Maude's was plain and nourishing. Norman, it seemed, was fond of lemon meringue pie and Maude made her own. Norman had two slices and complimented Maude graciously on its lightness and true lemon flavor. Maude beamed on both of them and Marjorie felt something she had not felt for a long time—pride in her companion.

At rehearsal Marjorie was swept immediately into scene blocking and left Norman on his own in the small auditorium. Once or twice, when she glanced from the stage, she saw him chatting with the director. At another time she caught a glimpse of him backstage, studiously examining the lighting board. When the rehearsal was over, she found that Norman Jolly had become a member of the group, had paid his dues, and was going to be the lighting technician for the show. She felt an odd satisfaction, and an even odder anticipation.

It was the habit of the group to gather after rehearsals at an all-night coffee shop where they pushed three or four tables together and spent an hour talking over the night's work and relaxing. Marjorie noticed how easily Norman fitted into the group.

In the ladies' room one of the young girls, the one who had got the part that Marjorie had had her heart set on, said, "Norman is really nice, isn't he? Where did you find him?"

Marjorie felt a flare of something that could only be jealousy. "He is nice. Finders keepers," she replied and smiled to show she was joking.

"Oh, don't worry," said the girl. "He only has eyes for you."

Marjorie went back to the table with a lighter heart than she could ever remember.

Later, when Norman drove up the winding drive to her apartment building, Marjorie debated whether or not she should ask him in. Audrey would probably be in bed, but if she weren't she wouldn't be in the right mood to meet Norman. But Norman forestalled her.

"Thank you for a grand evening," he said. "And thank you for bringing me to the Riverside Players. It'll be good to have something to do with my evenings. Who knows, I may even tread the boards again, although it's been over thirty years and I probably won't know upstage from down. May I meet you again tomorrow night?"

"But there isn't any rehearsal tomorrow night."

"I know. We can have the whole evening to ourselves."

Marjorie thought quickly. If Audrey were well tomorrow, she would be back on the job and ready to resume their cocktail routine.

"Call me at work tomorrow. Here's my number."

Norman took the scrap of paper and tucked it into his bill-fold. Marjorie noticed how slim the folded leather was and her heart constricted. He took her hand, patted it, grinned, and got out of the car. Again the ritual with the door, and Marjorie felt as if she were wearing hoop skirts as he helped her get out. He escorted her to the door of the building, and from the vestibule she watched as he waved, blew her a chaste kiss, and drove away.

The next morning Marjorie rode the bus alone. Audrey was still weak, and since it was Friday she thought she might as well take a long weekend to rest up. The sisters had seniority at the travel agency and never worked on Saturdays.

Marjorie hummed little tuneless hums softly to herself as she made out itineraries and wished customers happy traveling. Each time the phone rang she picked it up expecting to hear Norman Jolly's voice. When she realized that she was impatient for his call, she stopped humming and began belatedly to take stock. He wasn't handsome, although he had a winsome charm. He certainly wasn't rich. And he was much, much older than she. How much? Fifteen years, twenty years? It was hard to tell. His eyes were so young.

Suddenly Marjorie realized that it didn't matter. None of it mattered at all. This was certainly a day for realizations. She began humming again as she sent a honeymoon couple to Montreal.

When Norman finally called, Marjorie had already eaten her lunch—cottage cheese and fruit salad which she'd had sent in. She didn't want to take the chance of being out when he called.

"Hi," he said. "Sorry to be so late, but I've been baby sitting."

"Baby—?"

"My daughter had to go to the dentist and her usual sitter got sick. That little hellion of hers certainly kept me hopping. I took him over to the hobby shop and let him run the trains, but I had to watch him every minute."

"How old is he?"

"Three. Now about this evening. I'd like to pick you up after work and take you out to meet my daughter and her husband. You'll like them. Susie's already cooking up a storm."

"Just a minute. I have to answer the other phone."

Marjorie pressed the hold button and took a deep breath. Norman Jolly was a grandfather! Why hadn't she thought of that possibility? If she—if they—could she face being a grandmother before she was a mother? Suddenly she felt like laughing. After all the years of having no family but Audrey and no security but what she could grab for herself, here she was being plunged up to the neck in a complicated tangle of relationships.

What if she and Norman did get married? What if they had a child? It wasn't impossible. That child would be the uncle or aunt of Susie's child. Susie who was cooking up a storm to lavish on the new lady in her father's life. Oh, it was funny! Funny and warm and very, very appealing. Marjorie punched down the button that reconnected her with Norman.

"Norman? Are you still there? Of course I'll come. Meet me in the same place. I think I'll need a little reinforcement."

"Okay. I told Susie and Bob all about you and they're dying to meet you. They think it's wonderful that you were kind enough to take me along to rehearsal. And so do I. See you later."

But, Marjorie reflected as she hung up the phone, you didn't tell them *all* about me. You don't know about Audrey yet. You'll have to meet Audrey and I can just hear her now: "A retired schoolteacher! Living on a pension, I suppose. What a grand life you'll have. And he's so *old*. Well, at least we can be thankful you'll be a young widow. A poor young widow."

Marjorie straightened her back and did her best to forget about Audrey. She really ought to call her and tell her she wouldn't be home for dinner. But not right now. Marjorie hummed through the rest of the afternoon and at closing time hurried blithely down the street and around the corner.

Norman was waiting for her at their table. Hers and Norman's. Hers and Audrey's? It flitted through her mind that she had not yet called Audrey. Later. Right now Norman was rising and bending over her, smiling in his crinkly way and wrapping her in the warmth of his welcoming words.

Later there was no time. Norman was bounding with eagerness to take Marjorie to his daughter's home. They each had one drink—Norman gulped his down—and off they went, Norman full of anecdotes about his grandson, Brian. Marjorie was caught up in his enthusiasm and laughed wholeheartedly at his enjoyment. Somewhere small doubts niggled. What if Susie doesn't like me? What if this Brian child is a pest and I don't like him? But she brushed the doubts away in the extraordinary pleasure of Norman's company, in his undisguised joy in having Marjorie by his side.

The evening was a huge success. Susie was a tall awkward girl with fly-away hair, a face full of freckles and a wide full-lipped grin. She took Marjorie into the kitchen—"for company," she said—and put her to work shredding lettuce. She spoke seriously of her mother's long illness and gaily of the fun Brian had with his grandfather.

"Dad was lonely up there all by himself. I think he's done the right thing in moving here. And I'm glad he has his own place. Much as we love him, it wouldn't be good for him to live with us. He needs to make new friends. I can't tell you how excited he is about the Riverside Players. And about you, Marjorie."

Marjorie blushed with pleasure. How absurd, she thought. I haven't blushed since I was seventeen.

At seventeen, Marjorie, in her last year of high school, had been wakened one morning with the news that her parents had been killed in a highway accident. The memory was a dim one, hardly ever dredged up, of a gruff-voiced state trooper standing in the gray dawn at the door of the house. He wouldn't come in, but he stated his message and asked if he could call someone to help her.

Aunts had taken over, arranged things, sold the house, and Marjorie and Audrey were taken to live first with one and then the other until the insurance money ran out. Then it was politely suggested that they find other accommodations. Marjorie had by then gone to work for the travel agency, and when Audrey finished school a place was found for her too. It was all so long ago, so numbed by time. When had it not been numb, and why should it come back so painfully now?

". . . been carrying on like a moonstruck puppy. Marjorie this and Marjorie that. And I'm glad for him." Susie laughed. "I guess I sound like a matchmaker, don't I? It's just that I haven't seen him happy in a long time. And I want you to know that however it turns out, I'm grateful to you for bringing him back to life."

Marjorie searched for words and was saved from answering by the entrance of Bob and Norman.

"It took a while, but Dad said it had to be a whiskey sour. I hope it's all right. We collaborated."

Bob presented the tray with a flourish and Marjorie took the glass gratefully. She sipped and pronounced the drink very good, but everyone laughed at the involuntary pucker that belied her words.

"Well, it is a bit on the sour side," she admitted.

"If you're going to hang around with us plain folks, you'll have to say what you mean." Norman put his arm around her shoulder and tipped her face up to meet his twinkling eyes. "And mean what you say."

The evening passed swiftly. When it was over and time to go, Marjorie could not have said what had happened to make her feel so different, so vulnerable. They had eaten Susie's fine meal, talked, laughed, and teased each other. Brian had appeared in his pajamas and attached himself to his grandfather's leg. He'd nodded solemnly at Marjorie and handed her his "Bun-Bun," a bedraggled rabbit with droopy fleece ears.

"Even Brian thinks you're special," announced Norman. "Back to bed, old man." Norman and Marjorie had tucked him back into his crib, and slipped "Bun-Bun" into the small curve of his arm.

A perfectly ordinary evening, with perfectly ordinary people. Yet never before had Marjorie been so relaxed, so much at ease. With other men there had always been a tension, a sizing up, a fear of losing out on a good thing, or, worse yet, of encouraging a hopeless entanglement. With Norman there was only a warm acceptance and an ever-increasing feeling of well-being. Either Norman was different from anyone she'd ever known, or Marjorie had changed. Perhaps a little of both.

In the car going home, Marjorie suddenly sat bolt upright out of her peaceful reverie.

"My God! I forgot to call Audrey!"

"Who?"

"Audrey. My sister. I meant to tell her I wouldn't be home for dinner, and I forgot."

"Will she be worried?"

"I don't know. She must be sleeping now. She hasn't been feeling well."

"You never told me you had a sister."

"I haven't had a chance," Marjorie evaded. "Please hurry, Norman. I'll feel terrible if she's waiting up for me."

Norman's old car sped through the deserted streets. Marjorie sat silent and worried beside him.

When they neared the apartment building, Norman said, "Would you like me to come in with you and help you explain?"

"No," Marjorie answered quickly. "If she's upset, it wouldn't be a good time for you to meet her, and if she's asleep I don't want to wake her up. She'll probably be at rehearsal tomorrow."

Marjorie glanced up at the front of the building. There were no lights showing from her windows. She felt enormously relieved that she would not have to invent an explanation.

"I feel like a teenager out after curfew," she said.

"You look about sixteen right now," said Norman as he stopped the car.

Marjorie laughed a small self-conscious laugh. "It's the dim light. It'll do it every time."

Norman smiled and looked straight into her eyes. Marjorie tried to look away, but was held by what she read in his gaze— peace, a safe harbor, honest affection, love. Love? Marjorie shivered. Norman reached for her and Marjorie sank into his arms. He kissed her gently, and tears welled behind her closed lids. "I've come home," a voice within her exulted. "At last I've come home."

"Tomorrow afternoon. Two o'clock." Marjorie could say no more.

"I'll be there." Norman leaped out of the car and opened the door for her.

"Good night," she said.

Norman seemed about to say something more, but instead he smiled, shook his head, and got back into his car.

Marjorie tried to open the apartment door quietly, but the key sounded like the crack of a pistol. She tiptoed into the dark apartment.

Audrey's voice stopped her in her tracks.

"Are you doing social work for senior citizens these days?"

"What?"

"Who's the 'ancient mariner'? I sincerely hope he's a wealthy old eccentric who drives a beat-up old car and keeps all his money invested in gilt-edged stocks. Just be sure he's not too tight to spend some of it on you."

"Audrey, it's not like that. Norman is—"

"Norman! What kind of name is Norman? The only Norman I ever knew was a cross-eyed kid who delivered newspapers."

"Audrey, please. Not now. I'm very tired." And suddenly she was very tired. Tired of the shallow self-interest by which they had guided their lives together; tired of the wasted years of picking people apart, of magnifying the faults of others and ignoring their virtues. But Audrey was not ready to let her off. She switched on the light and glared at Marjorie across the room.

"Why didn't you call me? Have you any idea how worried I was? I was just about to call the police. I've been standing by that window for hours wondering what to do."

"You didn't have to do that, Audrey. I can take care of myself."

"Take care of yourself! What did I just see out there? Do you call that taking care of yourself? Tell me that gray hair was just a trick of the moonlight. Tell me that old junk heap was a Cadillac in disguise. Go on, tell me."

"It's worse than even you can imagine," Marjorie flared. "Norman Jolly is a retired schoolteacher *and* a grandfather. And if he asks me, I'm going to marry him. Now I'm going to bed."

The next morning Audrey was subdued. The sisters breakfasted and scarcely a word passed between them. It was Marjorie's turn to do the laundry and she fled to the basement, leaving Audrey morosely pushing the vacuum cleaner. When she returned, Audrey was studying fabric swatches and comparing them with her costume sketches.

"Norman will be at rehearsal this afternoon."

"Will he?"

"He's going to do the lighting. Audrey, when you meet him, you'll understand."

"Will I?"

"Audrey, he's different. He's made me see things differently. I'm happier than I've ever been."

Audrey stared at her sister for a long moment. At length she said, "How nice."

The wedding was planned for the Saturday following the last performance of the play. Marjorie scheduled their honeymoon trip herself. First to Colorado to visit Norman's son and his wife, then on to San Francisco, which Marjorie had never seen but had always wanted to visit.

Audrey said, "I guess I'll be taking our winter cruise alone."

"Why don't you try something new for a change? Go skiing in Vermont. Or look, here's a tour of Mexico that might be fun." Marjorie waved a brochure.

"Old habits die hard," said Audrey. "I don't want to go alone."

Rehearsals went smoothly and the director complimented Marjorie on her characterization.

"You're positively regal, old girl. I don't know how you've done it, but you've brought more depth to this role than I suspected you had in you. You're going to be a grand old lady one of these days."

Marjorie smiled and Norman beamed. Audrey went silently about her work of making last-minute alterations and adjustments to the costumes. She had met Norman with reserve and had avoided him as much as possible.

"I think your sister resents me," Norman said during a break in rehearsal one evening. Audrey was sitting in a dark corner backstage gazing blankly at nothing.

"Maybe," Marjorie whispered. "She hasn't been feeling well. Headachy and not sleeping. But she's been to the doctor and he's given her some sleeping pills. She'll be all right."

After her first outburst Audrey had said nothing further against Norman. She seemed to be struggling with some inner turmoil but was not inclined to talk about it, and Marjorie attributed it to disappointment with Marjorie for planning to marry so unworthy a person as Norman Jolly. Marjorie wished her sister could see Norman as she did, but she didn't press the issue.

Late one night, after the final rehearsal, Audrey said, "I don't suppose you two would consider moving in here?"

Marjorie glanced sharply at her sister. Audrey's face was haggard and her eyes looked bruised. She seemed to have lost weight. Marjorie worded her answer carefully.

"Norman has a house, Audrey. He's converted the garage into his hobby shop. I can't ask him to leave it."

"No, of course not. And I can't afford this place by myself."

"Have you thought about advertising for someone to share it with you?"

"I won't share my home with just anyone off the street." Audrey's voice cracked with suppressed pain. "We've been together since we were children. Do you think you can just walk out and expect me to get used to some stranger overnight?"

"I'm sorry, Audrey. I didn't think—" It was on the tip of her tongue to ask Audrey to move in with her and Norman. His house was small, but surely big enough for three. But she couldn't do it without consulting Norman.

"Never mind," Audrey said. "I'll just have to move into some dreary furnished room somewhere."

"Don't be silly. I don't need the furniture. You're welcome to it. And you'd be better off in a smaller apartment closer to town. You know we don't fit in here any more."

"It isn't just the apartment. It's—well, I'll be alone. We've been together for so long. I don't know how I'll like living alone."

Marjorie felt an enormous wave of sympathy for her sister. She had hoped that the example of her own newly learned capacity for love would work a miracle for Audrey too. She put her hand on her sister's shoulder, feeling the quivering tenseness there.

"No one has to be alone, Audrey. You have to learn to let people into your life."

"So you say." Audrey opened a kitchen cabinet and took down her vial of sleeping pills. "Good night, dear sister."

The play opened to a rousing success and ran its full three weekends to packed houses. On the final night the director threw a party at his house and surprised everyone by producing a three-tiered wedding cake.

"Since our young lovers are going to sneak out of town

right after the wedding, we're having the reception before the fact. I hope it's not bad luck."

Norman and Marjorie cut the cake, a ragged chorus sang "Here Comes the Bride," and someone handed Marjorie a wilted bouquet of paper flowers which Marjorie threw directly at Audrey. Audrey caught it and smiled a tentative cautious smile as if her face were made of china and might crack. After that Audrey joined the festivity, talked and laughed, drank perhaps a little too much, and seemed as cheerful as anyone else. The party straggled off into the sunrise and Audrey was among the last to leave. Marjorie was glad to see her enjoying herself.

The wedding was set for Saturday. In the intervening week Marjorie shopped, packed, and made final arrangements. Audrey helped her with good grace, and bought a new dress for herself as maid of honor. The ceremony would take place in the minister's study. Susie's Bob would be best man.

"I'm glad you're feeling better," said Marjorie.

"Yes, I am," said Audrey, "and I hope you and Norman will be very, very happy."

On the Thursday evening before the wedding, Norman had one final business trip to make. He had learned of a collection of HO trains that was for sale in a small town about 200 miles to the north. After prolonged negotiations by telephone, the owner had agreed on a price and Norman planned to drive up Thursday night, pick up the trains on Friday morning and be back by Friday afternoon.

"Let me cook dinner for you before you go," said Audrey.

Marjorie was delighted that Audrey had come round, and Norman needed no urging to accept. "But I'll have to leave right after dinner. It's a four-hour drive and I don't want to get too tired."

"That's all right," said Audrey. "Marjorie and I have lots to do before the big day."

On Thursday afternoon Audrey left work early.

"I need to do some shopping," she said. "And I want everything to be perfect. You're not to lift a finger, Marjorie. This is my treat for you and Norman. He really is a nice person."

Marjorie's happiness was complete. If Audrey could only realize how wrong-headed they both had been, if she could only be a little less calculating, she might find such happiness for herself. And it looked as if she was on the way.

When Norman and Marjorie arrived, Audrey was busy in the kitchen. The dining table was set with candles and a small centerpiece of sweetheart roses. Audrey popped her head out. Her cheeks were flushed and she was smiling.

"Just sit down and relax, folks. I'll bring you a drink in a minute. Something different. A Negroni."

"I don't know if I ought to drink," said Norman. "I've got a long drive ahead of me."

"Oh, just one. It won't hurt. And then we have Chicken Kiev and fresh asparagus. A light meal so it won't make you sleepy."

Audrey disappeared back into the kitchen.

"I can hardly believe the change that's come over her," said Norman.

"Yes. Isn't it wonderful! And she's found a nice apartment downtown. She'll be near everything. Promise me, Norman, that we won't shut her out of our lives. She dreads being alone."

"She'll have more family now than she's ever had."

"Here we are," said Audrey. She carried two pinkish drinks in her hands. "Here's yours, Marjorie, and this is yours, Norman. They're a little bitter-tasting, but that's the Campari. Have you ever tasted Campari, Norman?"

"No, I don't think I ever have."

"Well, I have to get back to the finishing touches." She skipped back to the kitchen.

"Not bad," said Norman after the first sip.

Back in the kitchen, Audrey put some butter over a slow flame to melt. The salad was ready, the asparagus almost done. The chicken was perfect. And for dessert, a lemon meringue pie—Norman's favorite.

Audrey smiled as she tidied up the kitchen. She washed the paring knife and put it away. She wiped the counter clean. And she placed the vial of sleeping pills back in the cupboard.

There were still two left. She could get some more tomorrow.

"Maybe I'm marrying the wrong sister," said Norman an hour later. "Anybody who can make a lemon meringue pie like that one deserves to be kissed."

He rose from the table and did just that. Audrey laughed and said, "Be careful, Marjorie, or I'll steal him away from you."

"I hate to eat and run, girls. But I really should be on my way." Norman took Audrey's hand. "Thank you, Audrey. I know it's been difficult for you, but you're not really losing your sister. We'll have lots of happy times together."

"I'm sure we will," said Audrey, smiling warmly.

Marjorie went with Norman to the door and Audrey began clearing the table. The sisters washed the dishes together.

"Just two more nights," said Audrey. "Then you'll be gone."

"I'm so tired," said Marjorie. "Can't keep my eyes open. I can finish the packing tomorrow. I think I'll go right to bed."

"Must be all the excitement," said Audrey.

Marjorie woke early. It had always been her habit to shower and put the coffee on before waking Audrey. This morning was no different. She plugged in the coffee pot and switched on the radio. The announcer's voice filtered through her thoughts of tomorrow and all the days to come.

". . . in a highway accident late last night. Witnesses said the car began swerving in and out of its lane before crossing the median and crashing head-on into an oncoming trailer truck. It seemed as though the driver had suffered a heart attack or fallen asleep at the wheel. Dead at the scene was Norman Jolly, 55, of this city. The driver of the truck is listed in fair condition at—"

A numbness enveloped Marjorie like a freezing shroud. She could only breathe in shallow gasps. Her lips framed a name, but she could make no sound. Her legs felt huge and leaden, her head seemed to be floating to the ceiling. She shivered spasmodically and fell to the floor. Far away the telephone rang . . .

The icy shroud covered her face and cold wetness trickled down her neck.

"Marjorie! Marjorie! Can you get up?"

Hands plucked at her. The voice commanded her attention.

"Marjorie! Can you make it to your bed?"

Her own arm moved and her hand pulled the wet towel away from her face. She scrambled clumsily to her feet.

"That's the way. Easy does it. Susie just called and told me. Oh, Marjorie, it's terrible! She's been down at the morgue. She wants you to call her."

"No." Marjorie lurched toward her bedroom, stumbled past her suitcases, and fell onto her bed.

"That's all right then, dear. Just lie down. I'll take care of you."

"Audrey?" Marjorie's voice was faint and muffled in her throat. "Don't leave me."

"I won't leave you."

"Audrey? Can I have one of your sleeping pills?"

The sisters are inseparable.

They live together and work together. They wear each other's clothes and cook neat little meals for each other. Once a year they take a cruise together. And if one runs out of sleeping pills, the other will share hers.

But sometimes Audrey's eyes glitter and her jaw juts at the memory of things past. And sometimes Marjorie's eyes widen and swim with wonder at the memory of things that might have been. These memories they do not share. There are some things that cannot be shared with anyone.

Second Chance

Edward D. Hoch

Their meeting was one of those bizarre things that happen only in real life. Carol Rome was home from her assembly-line job at Revco with the beginning of an autumn cold, running just enough of a fever to prefer the quiet warmth of her apartment to the constant chatter of her co-workers. She'd heard the door buzzer sound once but decided to ignore it. What was the point of being sick in bed if you had to get up and answer the door?

She had almost drifted back into sleep when she became aware of some scrapings at the apartment door. Then, with a loud snap that brought her fully awake, the door sprang open. Through the bedroom door she saw a tall, dark-haired young man enter quietly and close the jimmied door behind him. He looked to be in his late twenties, not much older than Carol herself, and he carried a black attaché case in one hand. The iron crowbar in his other hand had no doubt come out of it.

The telephone was next to the bed and Carol considered the possibility of dialing for help before he became aware of her. She was just reaching for the phone when he glanced into the bedroom and saw her.

"Well—what have we here?"

"Get out or I'll scream," she said.

He merely smiled, and she was all too aware that he was still holding the crowbar. "You wouldn't do that," he said. "I'm not going to hurt you." His face relaxed into a grin. "That is, not unless you'd like me to."

"Get out!" she repeated.

"You should get a stronger lock on that door. In this old building they're awfully easy to pop open."

She was becoming really afraid now, perhaps because he wasn't. "Look, my purse is on the dresser. There's about twenty dollars in it. That's all I've got."

He continued grinning at her, making no move toward the purse. "You're sort of cute-looking, you know. What're you doing home in bed in the middle of the day? Are you sick?"

"Yes."

"Too bad. I buzzed first. If you'd answered the door I'd have said I was an insurance claims adjuster looking for somebody else. That's why I'm dressed up, with the attaché case and all. I wouldn't have come in if I'd known you were home." The grin widened. "But I'm glad I did."

She took a deep breath and lunged for the telephone.

He was faster. He dropped the crowbar and grabbed her, pulling her half out of the bed until they tumbled together to the floor in a tangle of sheets and blankets.

His name was Tony Loder and he'd been ripping off apartments for the past two years. He didn't need the money for a drug habit, he was quick to inform her. He just liked it better than working for a living.

"Aren't you afraid I'll call the cops?" she asked, rising to get a cigarette from her purse.

"I guess you'd have done that already if you were going to."

"Yes," she agreed. "I guess I would have."

"What about you? How come you're living alone?"

"My former roommate moved in with a guy from the plant. Besides, I like living alone." She sneezed and reached for a Kleenex. "I hope you don't catch my cold."

"I don't worry about colds." He was staring at her with the same intensity as when he'd first discovered her in the bed. "Do you have a man around?"

"Not right now. I was married once, five years ago."

"What happened?"

"He was dull. He wanted to buy a house in the suburbs and raise kids. I don't think I could live like that. As soon as I realized it I got out."

"What do you do at this plant? Anything connected with money? Are you in the bookkeeping department?"

Carol laughed. "Sorry. I'm on an assembly line with twenty-three other girls. We run wire-wrap machines. Do you know what they are?"

"I don't want to know. It sounds too much like work."

"I'll bet you do as much work breaking into places as I do working on the line."

"It'd be a lot easier if I had a partner, that's for sure."

"How come?"

He shrugged. "I could do different things. I wouldn't have to jimmy doors for a living."

He left her after an hour or so, promising to phone. And he did, the following evening. She began seeing him almost every night. There was something exciting about having a burglar for a lover, something that kept her emotions charged all during the day. It was a life worlds apart from the dull, plodding existence she'd known during her brief marriage to Roy. Listening to Tony's exploits, she was like a child hearing fairy tales for the very first time.

"I almost bought it today," he'd say, rubbing the back of her neck as he sipped the martini she'd prepared for him. "An old lady came home too soon and caught me in her house. I'd phoned to tell her I was from the social-security office and she had to come down about some mix-up. Old ladies living alone always swallow that one. But after she left the house it started to drizzle and she came back for her umbrella."

"What'd you do? You didn't hurt her, did you?"

"I had to give her a shove on my way out and she fell down, but she wasn't hurt bad. I could hear her screaming at me all the way down the block."

In the morning paper Carol read that the elderly woman had suffered a broken hip in the fall, and for a moment she felt sick. That evening she confronted Tony.

"It wouldn't have happened if I had a lookout to honk the horn when the old lady came back. I didn't *want* to hurt her!"

She believed him and calmed down a little. "A lookout?"

"How about it, babe? You could do it."

"Me?"

"Why not?"

"No, thanks! I'm not going to end up in prison with you! I like my freedom too much."

She was cool to him the rest of the evening and he said no more about it.

When he phoned the following evening she told him she was sick and refused to see him. She spent a long time thinking about the old woman with the broken hip and even considered sending flowers to the hospital. But in the end she did nothing, and a few days later she saw Tony Loder again. Nothing more was said about the old woman or his need for a lookout, and he no longer told her his detailed stories of the day's activities. She was almost afraid to hear them now.

Around the end of October, half the girls on her production line were laid off, including Carol. Standing in line at the unemployment office she thought about the bleak Christmas season ahead, and about Tony's offer. It meant money, and more than that it meant excitement. It meant being with Tony and sharing in a kind of excitement she'd dreamed of but never really experienced.

That night she asked him, "Do you still want a partner?"

The first few times were easy.

She sat in the car across the street from the house he was hitting, waiting to tap the horn if anyone approached.

No one did, and for doing nothing he gave her a quarter of his take. It amounted to $595 the first week—more than she'd earned in a month on the production line.

Once during the second week Carol honked the horn when a homeowner returned unexpectedly from a shopping trip. Then she circled the block and picked Tony up. He was out of breath but smiling. "Got some jewelry that looks good," he told her. "A good haul."

"Sometime I want to go in with you, Tony. Into the house with you."

"Huh?"

"I mean it! I get bored sitting in the car."

He thought about that. "Maybe we'll try it sometime."

His voice lacked conviction but that night she pestered him until he agreed. The following morning they tried an apartment house together, going back to his old crowbar routine. She worked well at his side, but the haul was far less than in private homes.

"Let me try one on my own," she said that night.

"It's too dangerous. You're not ready."

"I'm as ready as I'll ever be. Were you ready the first time you went into a house alone?"

"That was different."

"Why? Because you're a man and I'm a woman?"

He had no answer to that. The next morning they cruised the suburbs until they found a corner house with a woman in the front yard raking leaves. "Pull into the side street and drop me off," Carol said. "She'll have the door unlocked and her purse just sitting around somewhere."

"What if someone's home?"

She shook her head. "Her husband's at work and the kids are at school. Wait down the block for me till I signal you."

"All right, but just take cash. No credit cards. That way if you're grabbed coming out it's your word against hers."

She got out of the car halfway down the block and walked back toward the corner house, feeling the bright November sunshine on her face. She was wearing slacks and a sweater, and her hands were empty. The money, if she found any, would go into her panties.

The woman was still in the front yard raking leaves, with the corner of the house shielding Carol's approach. The side door was unlocked as she'd expected, and she entered quietly. It was even easier than she expected—a big black purse sat in plain view on the kitchen table. She crossed quickly to it and removed the wallet inside, sliding out the bills and returning the wallet to the purse. She moved to the living room doorway to check on the woman through the front window, and had an unexpected bit of luck. There was a man's worn wallet on top of the television set. She pulled the bills from it and added them to the others.

Only then did she realize the wallet meant there was probably a man in the house.

She started back through the kitchen and was just going out the door when an attractive red-haired man appeared, coming up the steps from the basement. "What are you doing here?" he demanded.

She fought down the urge to panic and run. He could easily overtake her, or get the license number of Tony's car. "Is this the place that's giving away the free kittens?" she asked calmly.

"Kittens? We don't have any kittens here."

She edged toward the door. "I know it's one of these houses."

"There are no new kittens in the neighborhood. How come you opened the door?"

Carol ignored his question. "Is that your wife raking leaves? Maybe she knows about them." She hurried outside and down the steps, walking purposefully toward the front yard.

The woman was still raking and she didn't even look in their direction as Tony pulled up and Carol jumped into the car. "My God, there was a man in the house! Let's get out of here!"

"Is he after you?"

"He will be as soon as he checks his wallet. I told him I was looking for free kittens."

Tony chuckled and patted her knee. "You're learning fast." He turned the car down another side street to make certain they weren't being followed. "How much did you get?"

She thumbed quickly through the bills. "Forty-five from her purse and fifty-three from his wallet. Not bad for a few minutes' work."

"From now on you get half of everything," he decided. "You're a full partner."

His words made her feel good, made her feel that maybe she'd found her place in life at last.

With the coming of winter they moved their operations downtown to the office buildings. "I don't like leaving footprints in the snow," Tony said.

Large offices occupying whole floors were the best, because Carol could walk through them during lunch hours virtually unnoticed. Mostly she looked for cash in purses or desk drawers. If anyone questioned her, she always said she was there for a job interview. Once Tony dressed as a repairman and walked off with an IBM typewriter, but both agreed that was too risky to try again. "We've got to stick to cash," he decided. "Typewriters are too clumsy if someone starts chasing you."

But after a few weeks of it Carol said, "I'm tired of going through desk drawers for dimes and quarters. Let's go south for the winter, where there isn't any snow to show footprints."

They didn't go far south but they did go to New York. They found an apartment in the West Village and contacted some friends of Tony. "You'll like Sam and Basil," he assured Carol. "They're brothers. I met them in prison."

Somehow the words stunned Carol. "You never told me you were in prison."

"You never asked. It's no big secret."

"What were you in for?"

"Breaking and entering. I only served seven months."

"Here in New York?"

"Yeah. Three years ago. And I haven't been arrested since, in case you're wondering. That was just bad luck."

She said no more about it, but after meeting Sam and Basil Briggs in a Second Avenue bar she was filled with further misgivings. Sam was the older of the brothers, a burly blond-haired man of about Tony's age. Both he and the slim, dark-haired Basil seemed hyped up, full of unnatural energy. "Are they on heroin?" she asked Tony when they were alone for a moment.

"No, of course not! Maybe they took a little speed or something."

"I don't like it."

"Just stay cool."

Basil went off to make a phone call and Sam Briggs returned to the table alone. He ran his eyes over the turtleneck sweater Carol was wearing and asked Tony, "How about it? Want to make some money?"

"Sure. Doing what?"

"A little work in midtown."

"Not the park."

"No, no—what do you take us for? Hell, I'd be afraid to go in the park at night myself! I was thinking of Madison Avenue. The classy area."

Tony glanced at Carol. "We've been working as a team."

"You can still work as a team. She can finger our targets."

"What is all this?" Carol asked. The bar had grown suddenly noisy and they had to lean their heads together to be heard.

"Most guys get hit when they're all alone, on some side street at two in the morning," Sam explained, eyeing her sweater again as he spoke. "But I got a spot picked out right on Madison. We hit middle-aged guys walking with their wives earlier in the evening—nine, ten o'clock."

"Hit them?" Carol asked.

"Roll them, take their wallets. And their wives' purses. We're gone before they know what happened!"

"Aren't there a lot of people on Madison Avenue at that time of night?"

"Not as many as you'd think. I got a perfect corner picked out—there's an empty restaurant there and when the offices close down it's fairly dim."

"What do I have to do?"

"Go halfway down the block, pretending to windowshop or wait for a date, and watch for a likely prospect. If a couple come by talking, listen to what they're saying. If they sound right, just point your finger and we do the rest."

Carol was silent for a moment. "There won't be knives or anything, will there?"

"Hell, no! What do you take us for?"

She turned to Tony. "Do you want me to?"

"We've got to live on something."

"All right," she decided. "Let's do it."

Two nights later, on an evening when the weather had turned unusually mild, Carol and Tony met the Briggs brothers at the corner of Madison and 59th. Carol was wearing a knit cap to hide her hair and a matching scarf to muffle the lower part of her face.

"It's just after nine," Sam Briggs told her. "Look for couples with shopping bags, maybe coming from Bloomingdale's, tourists heading back to their hotels. If the man has both hands full it's easiest for us."

The three men hovered near the corner, glancing into the empty restaurant as if surprised to find it closed. Carol walked up the block toward Park Avenue, letting one man pass who was carrying only a newspaper. She'd been strolling back and forth about five minutes when she spotted a couple crossing Park in her direction. The man, stocky and middle-aged, carried a shopping bag in his left hand and a briefcase in his right. The woman, obviously his wife, carried a tote bag along with her purse.

Carol followed discreetly along behind them, listening to their conversation until she was certain they weren't police decoys. About fifty feet from the corner, she signaled a finger at them. When the couple reached Tony and the Briggs brothers at the corner, Sam Briggs walked up to the man and asked for a match. Before the man and woman realized what was happening, Sam punched the man in the face, knocking him backward into Basil's arms. Tony grabbed the woman as she started to scream and yanked the purse from her hand. Basil had pinned the man's arms while Sam went for his wallet.

Then, throwing the man to the sidewalk, they scattered in opposite directions. Carol, walking quickly back to Park Avenue, ducked into the lobby of a hotel and pretended to use the pay phone near the door.

The whole thing had taken less than a minute.

They tried it again three nights later in almost the same location. This time the man tried to fight back and Sam Briggs gave him a vicious punch in the stomach. The first time they'd gotten $214 plus some credit cards they'd promptly discarded. The second time they realized less—only $67 from the man and $16 from the woman.

"Everybody carries credit cards now," Sam Briggs complained later over drinks in his Village apartment. "What good are credit cards to us? By the next day the computer knows they're stolen."

"Let's go after something big," his younger brother suggested.

"Like what—a bank?"

"Count me out," Carol said, afraid they might be serious. "I'm having nothing to do with guns."

She went to the kitchen to make some coffee and she could hear Tony speaking in a low tone while she was gone. Later back at their own place, he started in on her. "You got this thing about guns and knives, but sometimes they can actually *prevent* violence."

"Oh yeah? How?"

"Remember that first time you went into a house alone? Remember how the man came up from the basement and surprised you? Suppose he hadn't believed your story about the kittens. Suppose he'd grabbed you and you'd picked up a kitchen knife to defend yourself. You might have killed him. But if you'd been carrying a weapon he wouldn't have grabbed you in the first place."

"I don't buy that sort of logic, Tony."

"Look, you saw Sam Briggs punch that guy tonight. You're part of it! Suppose there's some internal bleeding and the guy dies. The simple act of carrying a gun or knife isn't all that much worse than what we're doing already."

"It's worse in the eyes of the law."

He sighed and tried again. "Look, Carol, Sam and Basil have an idea that can make us a lot of money all at once. We won't have to go around mugging people on street corners. The thing is foolproof, but we need you to hold a gun on two people for about ten minutes."

"In a bank?"

"No, not in a bank. This is far safer than a bank."

"Why can't you do it without me?"

"We need a woman to get in the place before they're suspicious."

"Where?"

"I want Sam to tell you. It's his plan."

"I don't like that man, Tony. I don't like the way he looks at me."

"Oh, Sam's all right. He's a little rough at times."

"He's a criminal!"

"We're all criminals, Carol," Tony reminded her.

She took a deep breath. "I've never thought of myself as one," she admitted. "Maybe because I've never been arrested."

"How about it? One big job and we can live like normal people for a change."

"Maybe I don't want to live like a normal person, Tony. I guess I've always been bored by normal people. I was married to one once, and it bored the hell out of me."

He put his arms around her. "How about it? One big job? I promise it won't be boring. You'll never be bored with me."

"One big job . . ." She remembered them saying that in the movies, and they always walked into a police trap. But this wasn't the movies, and she knew she'd go along with whatever they wanted of her. She'd go along with it because Tony Loder had made her feel like a real person and not just a cog in some insensitive machine.

The plan was simple.

Sir Herbert Miles, the wealthy and successful British actor, maintained a luxury apartment with his wife on Central Park South. They were going to rob him of cash and jewelry, using Carol to penetrate the elaborate security precautions in the building's lobby. "You see," Sam Briggs explained, sketching a rough diagram on a sheet of paper, "they have a guard at a desk just inside the door. He monitors the elevators and hallways with a bank of closed-circuit TV screens. And nobody gets by him unless they're a resident or a guest who's expected."

"Then how do I get by?"

"There's a night elevator operator as added security, and from eleven o'clock on he sells the following morning's newspapers. All you do is walk through the revolving doors about eleven-fifteen and ask the man on the desk if you can buy a copy of *The Times*. He'll say sure and send you back to the elevator operator. That's when you take out your gun and cover them both. Make them lie on the floor. We come through the door, take the elevator up to the penthouse, and rob Miles and his wife. In ten minutes we're back downstairs. You stay in the lobby the whole time."

"Why can't we just tie up the two guards and leave them?"

"Because another resident might come in and find them while we're all upstairs. This way if anyone else arrives you cover them with the gun too."

"I couldn't bring myself to shoot anyone."

"You don't have to shoot anyone. Just hold the gun and they'll behave. Nobody wants to get shot."

Sam gave her a .38 revolver of the sort detectives carried on television. It held five bullets and he showed her how to load and fire it. "That's all you need," he said.

"Will you all have guns too?"

"Sure, but nobody'll need to use them."

That night, in bed with Tony, she started to tremble and he held her tight. "It's going to be all right," he whispered reassuringly.

She was a long way from the assembly line at Revco.

The uniformed guard glanced up from his newspaper as she entered. Behind him a half-dozen TV screens flickered their closed-circuit images. "Can I help you, Ma'am?"

"Someone said you sold tomorrow's *Times* here."

He nodded and motioned around the corner. "The elevator man has some."

She walked down two steps and saw the second uniformed man already folding a paper to hand it to her. The gun came out of her purse. "Not a sound!" she warned.

The man behind the desk turned toward her and she shifted the pistol to bring him into range. "You too—get down here and lie on the floor! Quickly!"

"This building is robbery-proof, girlie. You won't get away with it."

"We'll see. Both of you stay down there. Don't even lift your heads or I'll shoot!"

As soon as they saw the empty desk, Tony and the Briggs brothers came through the revolving door. They were wearing stocking masks, and she wasn't too happy about being barefaced. Still, the knit cap and scarf helped hide her features. "Ten minutes," Tony said as he went by her.

She watched the floor numbers as the elevator rose, keeping the gun steady on the two guards. "Who are they after?" the elevator man asked.

"Shut up!"

Eight long minutes later she saw the elevator start down from the top floor. No one else had entered the lobby and she was thankful for that. When the elevator stopped, Sam Briggs was the first one off, carrying a bulging plastic trash bag in one hand. The other two were behind him. "Let's go!" he told her.

"Don't follow us," she warned the two guards. "Stay on the floor!" Then, as she backed toward the door, she asked Tony, "How'd it go?"

"Great! No trouble."

Basil had left the car on one of the secondary roads in Central Park, with a phony television press card on the windshield in case anyone got curious. They broke onto Central Park South, running across toward the low park wall. Carol was in the middle of the street when she heard a shouted command.

"Police! Stop or we'll shoot!"

At the same instant she saw the police cars, realized both ends of the street were blocked off. "The guard must have pushed a silent alarm," Tony gasped at her side. "Forget the car and run for it!"

She heard a shot and turned to see Basil with his gun out. Then there were three more shots close together and he spun around and went down in the street.

She kept running, afraid to look back.

There were more shots, and the stone wall of the park was before her. She went over it fast, her legs scraping against the rough stone. Tony was somewhere behind her and she turned to look for him.

"Run!" he screamed at her. "Run!"

She saw the blood on his face, saw him reaching out for her as he ran toward the wall, then his whole body shuddered and he went down hard.

She ran on, deep into the park, until the breath was torn from her lungs in pulse-pounding gasps and she sank to the frozen earth and started to cry.

God! Oh, God!

Tony was hit, probably dead. And the others too.

After a long time she picked herself up and after walking for what seemed hours she managed to reach Fifth Avenue, at 66th Street. She hailed a taxi and took it downtown, getting out a block from the apartment in case the police tried to trace her later. She circled the block twice on foot, mingling with the late strollers, until she felt it was safe to go in. Then she collapsed onto the bed and pulled the blankets tight around her, trying not to think.

She must have lain there an hour or longer before she heard a gentle knock on the door. Her first thought was the police, but they'd have been less timid. She got up and listened at the door. The knocking came again and she could hear breathing on the other side of the door. "Who is it?" she asked softly.

"Me!"

"Tony!" She threw off the bolt and opened the door.

It was Sam Briggs. "Let me in!"

"I—"

He pushed her aside and closed the door after him. "I thought they got you too."

"No."

"Basil and Tony are both dead. The cops were right on my tail but I lost them in the park."

"You can't stay here," she said. "I want to be alone."

"Come on! There's only the two of us left now. Tony's dead!"

She turned away from him. "What about the money?"

"I dropped the bag when I was running. I had to save my skin!"

She didn't know whether to believe him, but it didn't really matter. "You'll have to go," she repeated. "You can't stay here."

"I'm afraid to go back to my place. They'll be looking for me."

"I'm sorry."

"To hell with you! I'm staying!"

She walked casually over to her coat and slipped the pistol from the pocket. Pointing it at him, she said, "Get out, Sam."

His eyes widened. "Hell, Carol, we're partners! I always liked you, from the first time I saw you."

"I was Tony's partner, not yours. Get out!" The gun was steady in her hand.

He smiled. "You wouldn't use that."

"Wouldn't I?" In that instant she wanted to. She wanted to squeeze the trigger and wipe the smile off his face for good. He had caused Tony's death and now he was standing grinning at her.

But he was right about the gun. She wanted to use it, but she couldn't.

"You can sleep on the couch," she told him. "Just for tonight." She went into the bedroom and closed the door, taking the gun with her.

In the morning he was still asleep as she dressed quickly and left the apartment. She bought a paper at the corner store and read about the robbery: "ACTOR'S PENTHOUSE ROBBED AT GUNPOINT—POLICE SLAY TWO FLEEING SCENE." The dead were identified as Tony Loder and Basil Briggs, both exconvicts.

She put the paper down.

So that was Tony's epitaph, after all the things he'd been. Not lover, nor dreamer, nor even thief. Only exconvict.

She started reading again. The police were seeking Sam Briggs, brother of the slain man, and an unidentified woman, who were believed to have fled with an estimated $80,000 in cash and jewelry.

So Sam had lied about dropping the bag. He had it stashed somewhere, probably in a locker at the bus station.

She thought about going back to the apartment and confronting him, pointing the gun at him again and demanding a share for her and Tony.

But Tony was dead, and she'd shown Sam last night that she wouldn't use the gun.

She went to a phone booth and dialed the police. When a gruff voice answered she said, "You're looking for Sam Briggs in connection with last night's robbery. If you hurry you can find him at this address."

After that she took the subway to the Port Authority Terminal on Eighth Avenue and caught the next bus home.

They were hiring again at Revco and they took her back without question. She had her old spot on the assembly line, with many of the same girls, and when they asked where she'd been she only smiled and said, "Around."

She learned from the New York papers that Sam Briggs had been arrested and the loot recovered. The unidentified woman wasn't mentioned. Even if Sam had given them her name, he didn't know where she came from. After a month she stopped worrying about being found. Instead, she felt that by some miracle she had been given a second chance.

For a time she was happy at work, and she thought of Tony only at night. But with the coming of spring, boredom set in once again. The routine of the assembly line began to get her down. She tried going out drinking with the other women on Friday nights but it didn't help. There was nothing in their bickering conversations or the half-hungry glances of their male friends to interest Carol.

One morning in May she phoned in sick, then dressed in a dark sweater and jeans and went out for a drive.

She parked near an apartment house in a better section of town and walked through the unguarded lobby. An inner door had to be opened with a key or by a buzzer from one of the apartments. She pressed three or four numbers until someone buzzed the door open, then took the elevator to the third floor.

Tony had told her once never to go up too high, in case she had to run down the fire stairs.

She used the knocker on a door chosen at random and nobody answered. Taking a plastic credit card from the pocket of her jeans, she used it on the bolt the way Tony had shown her. She was lucky. There was no chain, no Fox lock. In a moment she was inside the apartment.

It was tastefully furnished in a masculine manner, with an expensive TV-stereo combination and a few original paintings. She saw a desk and crossed to it.

"Hello there," a male voice said.

She whirled around, tensed on the balls of her feet, and saw a man standing there in his robe. His dark hair was beginning to go grey, but his face still had a boyish quality. He was smiling at her. "This is my first encounter with a real live burglar. Are they all as pretty as you?"

"I'm no burglar," she said, talking fast. "I must have gotten the wrong apartment." She turned and started for the door.

"Not just yet!"

"What?"

"I want you to stay a bit, talk to me."

She was reminded of that day last year when she'd been home in bed. "Are you sick?"

"Only unemployed. I lost my job last month. It's sort of lonely being unemployed. I'd find it interesting to talk with a burglar. Maybe I can pick up a few pointers."

She moved a step closer. "Are you going to call the police?"

"I'd have done that already if I was going to."

"Yes," she agreed. "I suppose you would have."

She sat down in a chair facing him.

"Tell me what it's like breaking into apartments. Is it exciting? Can you actually make money at it?"

"It's like nothing else in the world," she said.

He smiled again and suddenly she knew that this was her real second chance, now, with this man whose name she didn't even know.

And maybe this time it wouldn't end the same way.

Frank Sisk The Greek Refrain

The bronze plaque glinted like gold in the noonday sun. Recessed in the high wall of red brick, it was large enough to be read 20 feet away. Sitting at the wheel of my shabby two-door sedan, I read it with an uneasy sense of wonder. I even tried the sibilants aloud: "Surcease Isle."

The entrance was guarded by an iron gate wrought into scrolls and fleurs-de-lis that formed a black garland around two rampant white lions. Beyond the gate a concrete road glistened as if bleached between borders of rich green grass. Heroic formality—this was the general aspect of Surcease Isle. For a moment I was almost afraid to honk my horn, but only for a moment.

The single intrepid summons immediately produced the gatekeeper. He could have been hiding behind the rampart to which the gate was hinged. He was a huge man with a curly black beard; at his heels capered a small Scottish terrier.

"I'm here to see Miss Goodis," I said.

"Das Geschaft, vat iss?" said the gatekeeper in the burliest gutturals I've ever heard.

"A luncheon appointment is das Geschaft," I replied civilly. "I'm a lawyer—Charles Homer."

"Das Mittagessen, ja. Das Tor I open now up, Herr Homer." And he began to fit into the heavy padlock a key at least eight inches long. The little terrier barked with delight. "Be shtillen, Harold," the gatekeeper growled; and the terrier, lowering its muzzle as if understanding the pain of rebuff, skulked a pace backward.

Finally the outsize key did its work and chains rattled free, and in another moment the enormous gate swung slowly inward to the right.

I shifted the car into first and moved cautiously ahead,

offering a half salute to the keeper and a winking tch-tch to the downcast Harold. Then my attention was wholly occupied by the enchanting vista that spread before me.

The main house, reputedly constructed of yellow Sienna marble, crouched on a terraced eminence half a mile up the gleaming road amid a sheltering grove of Babylonian willows. Here and there the façade shone like butter through the pale-green lace of leaves; and the roof, rising above the pendulous branches, displayed its red tiles to the blue sky like a banked fire.

For years I had been hearing of this place. Now seeing it for the first time it was as though each item of interest had been foretold in my most fanciful dreams.

There were the fabled water lilies, big as dinner plates, floating in the artificial pond beside reflections of the pink roses which climbed round four fluted pilasters. Here a swan and luscious Leda became one as a bronze fountain whose silvery spray eternally caressed the stone breasts of naked dryads. A grotto of myrtle and bittersweet parted briefly on my approach to disclose a piping Pan clothed only in a hand-held bunch of grapes.

Everything about the place was incredibly rich and yet expected. Twice at a distance I sighted deer browsing on carpets of purple clover, and once a big-horned goat with whiskers the color of cornsilk peered at me (wistfully, it seemed) from a break in a green hedge. I'm in another world, I thought, where reality is half hallucination.

But truth compels me to say that Surcease Isle was not really out of this world and it was not an island at all. According to the deed on file in the town clerk's office, it was 76 acres of gently rolling pasture and woodland near the southern tip of one of the Finger Lakes.

It was known to the natives as the Goodis Estate. They usually thought of it in connection with Andrew Goodis, although at the time of this visit he had been dead at least ten years and his daughter Millicent was as fully and forcefully in residence as he had ever been. It was she, in fact, who named it Surcease Isle on succeeding, as the old man's only child, to the Goodis millions.

The natives regarded father and daughter as two of a kind, a most uncommon kind, and kept a respectful distance.

Andrew Goodis had been a steel baron when such Gothic nomenclature was significantly current. His withdrawal from the hard realm of business, he used to say, was ordained the day he saw an up-and-coming young steel executive drinking cocktails in the Detroit Athletic Club with a union leader. Thereafter the old man had devoted himself somewhat quixotically to blooded horses, skittish blond women, thoroughbred hunting dogs, and his beloved daughter—allegedly in that order. Unlike Millicent, he had spent more time abroad than at home. He is reported to have once said, apparently without tongue in cheek, that he found Paris infinitely more entertaining than Pittsburgh. He died at his grouse-shooting lodge in Scotland.

Taking over the reins and leashes, Millicent at 25 wasted no time following in her father's wide-ranging footsteps as closely as the difference in sex would permit. She liked blond men but she was not averse to brunets either. She required brawn, not brains.

Sometimes her notoriously transitory interest in a certain man lasted long enough to result in marriage. The count now stood at four husbands, perhaps five. This ambiguity revolved around doubt in many quarters as to whether her liaison with Burton Dray had ever been sanctified or notarized.

Dray, a second-string linebacker for the Giants, had left his post six months earlier with the publicized intention of becoming, as the sports writers put it, the fifth Mr. Goodis.

His red foreign sports car had been observed one evening to enter the gateway of Surcease Isle. Two evenings later other anonymous observers saw the same rakish car issue from the walls with Millicent and Dray in the front buckets and a prize-winning Irish setter sitting aloof in the back.

Within a week spectators at a gymkhana in Pinehurst noted the couple attending; and within two more days they (or at least Millicent) were reported to have shifted to active participation at field trials for pointers and setters in Augusta.

A month passed then before Millicent, alone, was seen and interviewed by reporters at Kennedy International a few minutes before boarding a plane Zurich-bound.

Where was her supposed spouse?

Obviously not present, admitted Millicent grandly. After all, many arrangements fall unhappily short of expectations.

Not much aghast, the scandalmongers desired to know if a divorce were imminent.

Millicent merely acknowledged that ties had been severed, most amicably on both sides, which obtuseness disposed one newshawk to inquire if a marriage had actually taken place. And if so, where—among the Carolina jumpers or the Georgia scenters?

Millicent was said to have smiled mysteriously at this insolence. "You would not have me compromise myself," she murmured, then vanished into Swissair.

Apparently Burton Dray had also vanished but in another direction. At any rate, on the day of my visit to Surcease Isle he was still absent from his accustomed haunts. I hoped his case was not a precursor of the matter that was bringing me here.

It was exactly 12:15 when I parked the jalopy under the friezed portico and, attaché case in hand, mounted the eight marble steps which led to the entrance door—an impressive slab of black mahogany into which was carved a nude archer (Heracles, as I learned later) drawing a powerful bow whose arrow was aimed in the general direction of an ivory doorbell button. I gave the button a decisive push and half turned to view the Corinthian columns that supported the portico. It didn't really surprise me to see a mule leaning against one as if preparing to scratch the side of his belly.

The only thing about Surcease Isle that kept me continually astonished was the fact that it was only about 20 miles from Ithaca, New York, where at this moment the mundane citizenry were engaged in the production of shotguns, salt, cement, men's shirts, and ladies' underwear. And where at this moment the part-time stenographer in my cramped law office was taking advantage of my absence by phoning her Cornell University bedmate to discuss his major, which was purebred sheep in general and Dorset rams in particular.

As I stood there exchanging speculative glances with the itchy mule, I suddenly felt a void nearby and again with a half turn, perceived that the heavy door had been opened wide by a man as black as itself.

"Monsieur Sharl Omay, is it not?" he asked in a voice as rich as the red velvet jacket and pantaloons that clothed his lank frame.

"It never sounded better," I said.

"The mademoiselle is expecting of you, monsieur. If you please to follow me."

So it was still mademoiselle despite four or five husbands, I thought, as I followed the plush majordomo back into a large hall. The ceiling arched at least 30 feet above my head and was ornamented with arabesques of fruit and foliage inhabited by repetitions of the same unicorn and phoenix. Mademoiselle and père liked it gaudy, I mused, passing a Gobelin tapestry. The letter G (for Goodis, obviously) recurred as a cartouche on such things as lamp standards, cabinets, and door panels.

At a door that was open the majordomo stepped aside and bowed me into a room abloom with splashes of red, green, and gold. "Attend here comfortably, monsieur," he said. "A moment will transpire before the mademoiselle arrives."

It was hardly a room to feel at home in. The decor was too dazzling. The mantelpiece alone, constructed of a peach-colored marble, was worth an hour's rapt study. A mask of Dionysius dominated its center with ormolu garlands streaming from either side of his head. Above was a two-paneled mirror framed in gold which served as a foundation for a carving of Hades seizing a voluptuous Persephone while a band of satyrs looked on from the sanctuary of a wood.

"Mister Charles Homer." The voice, a vibrant contralto, might have issued from the Theban glade above the mantelpiece. "But may I call you Charles?"

Slowly turning, I beheld Millicent Goodis in the flesh. And I use the term advisedly, for flesh consummate, flesh alive and pulsing, flesh perfected in lithe yet lush harmonies—this was the essence of impact at first sight.

She was 35 or so, but the years had brought her to an ideal maturity—not of ripeness but of still ripening. She wore her glistening black hair in a severe style which enhanced the luminous quality of her brown eyes and the flawless white delicacy of her face. She was dressed in a white silk blouse that plunged and rose and black satin trousers that clung tenderly tight to each exquisite curve from waist to ankle.

Yea, Millicent Goodis was every inch a magnificent mammal.

I might have gaped at her interminably like a transfixed bumpkin if something directly to her right, something quite enormous and of another species, had not beckoned the corner of my eye for attention. Even so it required a profound effort of will to shift my line of vision from beauty to the beast. And beast it was—a canine type of brindle hue that stood taller than any of its kind in my acquaintance and must have weighed close to 200 pounds without the collar, a huge leathern device with cruel iron brads.

"May I ask once more," said Millicent Goodis in that dusky voice, "may I call you Charles, Mister Homer?"

"Yes," I said. "Yes, of course. And what do you call that?"

She laid a slender-fingered hand on the animal's great skull and it looked up at her worshipfully. "This is Michael, a rather recent acquisition. Isn't he superb?"

"Of his kind, yes. And just what kind is he?"

"He's an Irish wolfhound, aren't you, Michael?"

Michael appeared to nod assent.

"Gentle and intelligent, looks like," I said fatuously. "Big as he is."

"Gentle indeed," said Millicent Goodis with a faint smile, "but not too intelligent. I don't believe the lower orders should be too intelligent, do you, Charles?"

"I haven't ever prepared a brief on the subject."

"A brief? Oh, yes, that's a legal term, isn't it? And of course you're a lawyer, Charles. I'd forgotten for the moment.

Most lawyers I meet run so grossly to age and adipose tissue that I find it difficult to associate a young and attractive man with the profession."

Needless to say the flattery dazzled me, but before I could expose my susceptibility with some stammering foolishness, the black majordomo rolled a service cart into the room and headed toward a set of French doors.

"It's such a lovely day," said Millicent Goodis, "that I felt we should take lunch on the terrace. You do approve, don't you, Charles?"

"Utterly," I said.

Closely squired by the hound, she approached me and slipped her arm in mine. Her delicious propinquity, combined with a subtly rapacious perfume, sent an enervating tingle in radial formation from the solar plexus to all parts of my body. I felt as though I had been suddenly deprived of the simplest volition and given in its place a euphoric desire to bask forever in her lovely presence. Happy slaves must have felt this way, and animals well cared for.

I accompanied her to the sun-filled terrace with no less devotion than Michael.

"And what have you provided for us, Anatole?" she asked, addressing the majordomo. "Champagne?"

"Mais oui, mademoiselle." He held aloft a magnum swathed in spotless white and sweating cold beads of moisture. "A Veuve Clicquot of a very good year." He deftly twisted the restraining wire and released the cork with a hollow pop. "Permit me," he said, pouring a glass half full and holding it out to Millicent Goodis.

She drank it and handed the glass back to Anatole with a commendatory smile. He filled it to the brim this time and then did the same for me.

"A glass of champagne is the best way to begin a friendship," said my hostess by way of toast, "and the only way to end one."

"If end it must," I added.

"But everything must end, Charles. Naturally."

"May I call you Millicent?"

"Do. And do be seated."

The table was set for color photography. Smoked salmon with the tone and texture of pink rose petals lay luxuriantly over green hillocks of lettuce; black olives, nestled gleaming against stalks of pale celery hearts; a white cheese redolently mottled with age sat against a double stack of wheaten crackers; black caviar shimmered in one silver dish, a carmined bisque of lobster in another.

The presence of my attaché case seemed awkward, yet as I placed it out of sight beside my chair it reminded me that I had come here for business, not for pleasure.

"Millicent," I began, savoring her name in spite of myself like a magic incantation, "Millicent, Millicent."

"Yes, Charles?"

"Millicent, this—this champagne is delectable."

"It rather suits any occasion, doesn't it?"

"I'm beginning to think so."

"And you're thinking something else too, aren't you?"

"I am? Well, perhaps so." I looked across the table into the unknown depths of her lustrous eyes and was all but lost to reason.

"I believe I can even read your mind, Charles."

"I hope not." I finished the champagne thirstily. "Or rather, I hope so."

"You are thinking how much nicer it would be to lavish this interval on pleasant inconsequentialities than to discuss the matter which brought you here."

"You are endowed with uncanny insight as well as with enchanting beauty,"* I said with uncommon felicity.

She gave me a curious look of approval and then turned to the majordomo, who had practically dematerialized himself against the backdrop of a tall boxed plant that dripped a profusion of scarlet flowers. "Anatole, refill our glasses, please."

He detached his black-and-red image from the floral camouflage and complied in dignified silence with the mademoiselle's request.

"You may withdraw for the nonce," Millicent said, and Anatole backed off and disappeared through the French doors.

"You're accustomed to good service, I see," I said.

She raised a quizzical eyebrow. "It's a birthright, Charles. I expect it."

"I see."

"But I don't always get it." She raised her glass and looked amusedly at me over the sparkling brim. "Right now, for instance, I would give much to obtain a moment's beguilement, but I realize I must first help you to dispose of a most urgent problem."

"Urgent?" I asked.

"That was the word you used on the phone yesterday."

"That's right." I raised my glass. "Let's drink to a speedy solution."

"By all means."

We drained our glasses simultaneously.

"Now," I said, "I regretfully come to the matter of Patrick O'Dell."

The wolfhound began to bark furiously.

"Silence," Millicent commanded, "or I'll have Anatole confine you to the cellar."

The animal whimpered pitifully for a moment, then subsided.

"What brought that on?" I asked.

"Probably the name of Patrick O'Dell."

"Incredible. Does the dog know Pat, by any chance?"

"The real question, Charles, is whether I knew Patrick O'Dell, isn't it?"

"Yes, I'm afraid it is, Millicent."

"What makes you so interested in the answer?"

"Well, as I told you on the phone yesterday, I need the information for a client."

"Is the client's identity to remain a secret?"

"Not necessarily. Her name is Norma Confrey. She's a cousin of mine."

"And what is her relationship to Patrick O'Dell?"

The dog started a deep growl and stifled it.

"They're going to be married," I said. "That is, if I can find him."

Millicent poured more champagne for both of us, then said, "How is it, Charles, that you connect my name with Patrick O'Dell's?"

"I'm not exactly the original maker of this connection. The idea came from Norma." Draining off half the wine—the glasses had been refilled—I reached for my attaché case. "When Pat turned up missing six days ago, Norma went to his apartment. She had a key because it is soon supposed to be their apartment and she was shifting the furniture in her spare time."

"Naturally," said Millicent, not too enigmatically.

I opened the case in my lap and next resorted to the remainder of the wine. "Among Pat's personal papers, Norma found a note purportedly written in your hand and at least signed by you. I checked the signature against the one that appears on several county documents—it's yours all right, Millicent, or a beautiful forgery."

"And what did I say in this note to Miss Confrey's precious Pat?" asked Millicent with a teasing note of challenge.

The hound groaned audibly for a split second.

"You invited him to visit you at his earliest convenience for the purpose of renewing the brief but inspiring—these are your own adjectives—relationship begun so fortuitously at Hialeah."

"That's the race track?"

"That's the race track."

"Is your Patrick O'Dell a jockey?"

"He's a veterinarian. Quite a good one, I guess. He had never been to Hialeah in his life until a month ago and then he was called in to consult about a suspected bone disease in a horse."

Millicent again poured champagne. The bottle, like those self-replenishing vessels in Oriental myths, seemed full as ever. A slightly intoxicated thought rambled past my preoccupied mind: how endless a magnum is.

"You have the alleged note in your possession, Charles?" Millicent was saying.

"Yes. An azure rag-paper engraved with your crest. The

G. Right here." I extricated the letter in question from the *Goodis, Millicent* folder in my attaché case. "Your salutation is most affectionate. It almost makes me jealous. 'My dearest Pat,' you begin—now that's strange, that's very strange."

"Not really, Charles. At times I can be extremely affectionate."

"I mean the page is blank." I spoke exclusively to myself as I turned the notepaper from one side to the other. "Not the trace of a single word. Not even the crest. Nothing."

"Perhaps I write my billets-doux with invisible ink." Her laughter was musical but triumphant. "So much for the insidious horse doctor, Charles."

To cover my bewilderment I took a deep draft of wine. Instead of clearing the fog gathered behind my eyes it thickened it a bit. Across Millicent's lingering laughter I detected a braying counterpoint.

I got to my feet somewhat unsteadily and saw the itchy mule standing big-eared and open-mouthed 30 feet off in an azalea bed. It wore, I noticed, a halter of woven jute. That's what makes it itchy, I thought, but I must have expressed the thought aloud.

"Itchy. Who in the world are you talking about, Charles?" Millicent was also on her feet. "Are you feeling well?"

"I'm not sure. The champagne seems to have hit me."

"I think you should lie down then." She set her glass aside, took me by the elbow, and led me to a nearby lounge chair with a depressible back. Her cool hand was a balm to my clammily knitted brow, and I was about to surrender myself to gentle delirium when something prickly hot stabbed the back of my right hand. I came bolt upright.

"What ails you, Charles?" Millicent exclaimed, with just the hint of annoyance.

"Something—" Michael the wolfhound, at her side, caught my eye with his lolling bologna of a tongue and I realized at once that *that* was what had touched me, licking voraciously (?) or amiably (?). "I'm out of kilter somehow. Forgive me. Doesn't the wine affect you at all?"

"Not noticeably. May I get you some more?"

I said Yes when I meant No. I tried to amend the mistake by shaking my head vigorously, but somehow I nodded it idiotically instead. At the table Millicent tilted the infinite magnum over the glasses. I recovered my ability to speak only when the fingers of my dog-kissed wet right hand received the crystal stem that bore the vinous blossom.

"Another thing. Please. Please?"

"Of course, my comely lawyer."

"Case. The attached, the attacked, the attaché. You understand. Please?"

"Yes." She loomed, a divine translucence, above me. "But why?"

"A dossier," I muttered, drinking the wine in spite of myself. "Contains dossier. On you. Your husbands, others, Durton Bray."

"You mean, Charles, you have been doing research into my past?"

"Background. Legal routine. Questions arise. Where do the men go? Ask myself. Ask yourself. Now. Where?"

"Do you know the answer?"

"No."

"Anatole." Her low voice, suddenly raised, stabilized my spinning faculties.

The black man soon appeared, also looming; and the white-fanged, hot-tongued hound.

"I know they don't come home again," I said. "That much I do know."

"Cremate this attaché case, Anatole," said Millicent in a voice as suddenly strange to me as my own. "Now."

"Oui, mademoiselle."

"We," I said in a final struggle against utter incoherence. "We must not mis. Under. Stand? Please."

My last conscious thought was: how odd it is that Miss Goodis (which at this moment manifested itself on my fading mental retina as "Miss Goddess") does not find my speech blockage odd . . .

I slid expansively beneath a soft slow avalanche of snowy sheep. The face of my part-time stenographer passed severally

by, pursued by a recurring ram with horns the size of cornuco-
pias. I tried to shout a warning but couldn't pronounce her
right name, which was Hattie; it persisted in being enunciated
as Penelope . . .

When I regained consciousness I was panting desperately
and for some reason was lying on my belly. I opened my eyes
to look at my hands stretched out in a strange fashion on the
lounge's brocade pattern. But my hands were not hands. They
were sable-furred paws. My jaw fell and I emitted an astonished
bark.

An answering bark nipped at my muffled ears. Raising my
protuberant muzzle, I turned an abashed eye on the Irish wolfhound and saw, truckling in its superstructure, the missing
Patrick O'Dell. I wanted to say "I'll be damned," but the words
came out in three short yelps. Pat replied in kind.

"The collar, Anatole." It was Millicent Goodis' enchanting
voice, threaded this time with a strident note of command.
"Quick—before he fully orients himself."

The majordomo came toward me with a chain choke collar. As he began to slip it over my head, I reacted with a new
instinct and bit him viciously in the wrist and then leaped from
the lounge and scampered across the terrace tiles to the lawn.

The itchy mule was still loitering in the azalea bed and it
grinned as I approached. Burton Dray, of course—I recognized
him from his pictures in the newspapers.

I trotted to the driveway with Burton Dray lumbering
along beside me. But as we neared the gate I saw the bearded
keeper approaching us with a bull whip coiled around his great
forearm. He had been notified of developments, presumably by
phone, from the mansion.

I wasn't a large dog but I realized I was not small enough
to squeeze through the openwork of the gate, even if I were
willing to risk a laying on of the lash. So I veered off the road
and into the higher grass that bordered it. Promptly I knew the
move had been a mistake. The grass was so thick and wiry that
it considerably hampered my gait.

Casting a glance over my haunches, I saw that the gatekeeper had also left the road and was covering a vast amount

of ground on his piledriver legs. He was already uncoiling the whip. In a matter of seconds he would be able to snap my legs out from under me with a flick of his wrist.

It was then that Burton Dray, behaving more like a first-string guard than a second-string linebacker, charged past me and took the keeper out of action with the most bone-crushing block I've ever seen.

A happy yip greeted the downfall. It came from Harold the Scottish terrier who came plowing, chin up, through a patch of dandelions. With my canine insight I saw that Harold in reality was a sandy-haired man with a freckled face and a Puckish mouth. In my dossier there had been a rumored romance between Millicent Goodis and a man later apprehended for poaching on Andrew Goodis' game preserve in Scotland. Perhaps this was the man.

The poacher, as I recall, had vanished from the view of family and friends after his fine had been paid by an anonymous benefactor. But regardless of Harold's origin, he had the true poacher's ability to find a hole in a fence and he led me to it.

As I prepared to leave I indicated that my freckled friend should join me, but he shook his head sadly and managed to draw attention to his collar. Then it all came back in a flood of memory.

It was the collar that held them in thralldom. When they made too deep an obeisance before their lovely enchantress, she slipped the collar over their heads and around their throats and they were held evermore in a bondage they could not break by themselves.

Even the hole in the fence did not represent freedom to Harold. He was held by an invisible leash that prevented him from moving outside to the mundane but wider avenues of the world and assuming his true identity.

It came back to me with enormous force now because, with slight variations, it had happened once before, in another age, when I was known only by my surname and the Goodis Estate, floating in the waters of Oceanus, was called Circe's Isle.

Mom
James Yaffe Knows Best

My mother always wanted me to be a professional man. It didn't matter to her what kind of profession. Any kind would do, as long as it was really "professional," and absolutely not "business."

"Your uncles are in business, your cousins are in business, your Papa was in business, and none of them ever made a cent of money," Mom always said. "Except your Uncle Max, and he don't count, because God forbid you should ever turn out to be such a physical and nervous wreck as your Uncle Max and your Aunt Selma."

And so, even when I was a small boy in the Bronx, Mom saw to it that I got some professional training. She gave me chemistry sets for my birthday; she made me take violin lessons; she even encouraged me to work my childish charms on a distant cousin of ours who was a lawyer. And finally Mom got her wish. Today I am a professional man. But I'm afraid this fact has never given Mom any satisfaction. You see, she didn't exactly expect me to become a policeman.

From the very beginning she raised objections. All sorts of objections, every day a new objection—but most of them were smokescreens. Her antagonism to the life of a policeman really boils down to two points. One: the work is dangerous. "All those gangsters and dope fiends and bookies and hatchet murderers and other such *goniffs* you have to deal with," she says. "Isn't it possible that you could get hurt some day?"

Two: she thinks the job is beneath me. "Always it was my ambition that you should take up something that needs a little intelligence and brainpower," she says. "But this detective work, this figuring out who killed who, and playing cops and robbers like the kiddies in the park, this is no work for a grown-up man. For all the brains it takes, believe me, you might as well be in business with your uncles."

And there is simply no way of talking Mom out of this opinion, of convincing her of the dignity and difficulty of my profession. Even though I've done pretty well for myself, even though I'm in plainclothes now and chief assistant to Inspector Slattery, Mom still makes fun of me. And with justice. Because to tell the truth, this cops and robbers business *is* child's-play—for Mom. Figuring out who killed who *is* an easy job—for Mom. With her ordinary common-sense, and her natural talent for seeing into people's motives and never letting herself be fooled by anybody (this talent comes from her long experience with shifty-eyed butchers and delicatessen store clerks), Mom is usually able to solve over the dinner table crimes that keep the police running around in circles for weeks.

In fact, I might even go so far as to say that my chief value to the Homicide Squad lies not in the strenuous investigating, manhunting, and third-degreeing that I do all week, but in the revealing conversations I have with Mom every Friday night, when she invites my wife and me up to the Bronx for dinner.

Take last Friday night, for instance.

Shirley and I got to Mom's apartment at six. Mom gave us the usual glass of wine, and we sat down to the usual roast chicken dinner (which is really unusual, because who can equal Mom's roast chicken?). For a while, the conversation ran along the usual lines. Mom told us about the ailments and scandals of everybody in the neighborhood. Then she gave Shirley advice on how to shop for groceries. Shirley is a Wellesley graduate with a degree in psychology, so naturally Mom is convinced that she's incapable of understanding the practical affairs of life. Then she lectured me on wrapping up warm in this damp weather. Finally, after bringing in the noodle soup, she asked me: "So how is the work going, Davie?"

"Nothing very interesting, Mom," I said. "Just an ordinary everyday murder case. Three suspects. One of them must be guilty. It's just a question of working on them long enough, till the guilty one cracks."

"And so far he didn't crack yet, the guilty party?"

"Not yet, Mom. But he will, all right. We'll sweat it out of him."

"And out of yourselves, while you're at it!" Mom gave a sigh. "This third degree, it's harder on the policemen than it is on the crooks. If you men only would stop a minute and use your heads, look at all the *tsouris* you'd save. Believe me, there isn't a single one of you that don't need a mother to look after you."

"It's not a question of using our heads, Mom. It's patience, pure patience. I'll tell you about the case, and you can judge for yourself. You see, this girl was killed in a hotel downtown. A sort of high-class low-class hotel, if you know what I mean. Very sporty, expensive crowd. Stage people, gamblers, radio and television people—a pretty flashy assortment. And blondes. The place is full of platinum blondes. With no visible means of support. Maybe they call themselves dancers—only they haven't stood on a chorus line for years; maybe they say they're models —only they never get any closer to a magazine cover than a million other readers.

"That's what this dead girl was. A genuine platinum blonde, who used the name Vilma Degrasse. Usual career— quit high school at sixteen to go on the chorus line. Quit the chorus line five years ago—to move into the hotel. Been living there ever since, in two rooms on the fifth floor. Her and a steady stream of admirers. All male—"

"And to make a long story short," Shirley cut in, "last night one of them killed her."

Shirley is always taking it on herself to make my long stories short. This doesn't bother me much—when I married Shirley, I knew I was getting a superior-type woman—but it never fails to get a rise out of Mom.

She rose now. "Well, well, isn't that interesting?" she said, turning to Shirley with a sweet polite smile. "So you're working on the case too, are you, Shirley dear?"

Shirley smiled right back at Mom, just as sweetly and politely. "Not at all, Mother. I'm just trying to help David cure himself of his terrible habit of talking on and on and never getting to the point. It's something he picked up in his childhood, though goodness knows from whom."

"Now here's our three suspects," I interrupted quickly, as

I saw a gleam coming into Mom's eye. "At ten o'clock last night the girl was escorted into the lobby by a gentleman—middle-aged banker of this city, named Griswold. Very unhappy about having his name mentioned in the papers. They were seen coming in by the clerk at the desk and by the elevator girl. The clerk is a gray-haired, seedy old man named Bigelow. The grumpy type. When I questioned him this afternoon he complained every two minutes about how he'd been standing on his feet behind that desk for four hours, and how the management don't even allow him to have a radio to help pass the time, and how the Assistant Manager is always poking around to make sure the clerks don't hide any magazines or newspapers under the desk, and so on and so on. And all the time this Bigelow was blowing beer fumes into my face. Unpleasant character, but just the same I think he's telling the truth. No apparent reason to lie.

"The elevator girl is Sadie Delaney, a talkative dark-haired Irish girl. Not married yet, built on the large side, but very cheerful and hearty, always doing special favors for people in the hotel. A good witness, too—cooperative and bright.

"So anyway, Sadie took the Degrasse girl and old Griswold up to the fifth floor, said good night to them, and rode down again. She passed the time with Bigelow about ten minutes, then she got a buzz from the fifth floor. She went up and found old Griswold waiting for the elevator and looking very mad. She took him down and said good night again, but he didn't answer her. He went stamping out of the lobby—"

At this moment there was an interruption as Shirley finished her noodle soup. "Oh, Mother, that soup was delicious," she said. "It's such a pleasure to taste your cooking. You know, that's really what you do *best* in the world."

"Thank you, with kindness, darling," Mom said. "But that's how it was with all the girls in my day, so I can't take any special credit. Even if we was too poor to go to college, we always learned something useful. We didn't fill our heads with a lot of *meshuggene* ideas that are no good to anybody—like so many of the young girls nowadays."

I saw that Shirley was getting ready to answer this, so I took a deep breath and hurried on with my story:

"A minute later, enter Suspect Number Two. This is Tom Monahan, the hotel handyman. He was just going off duty, but he told Sadie that Miss Degrasse had called him earlier that day to fix a leak in her bathtub, and he was afraid she'd be mad if he didn't do it before she went to bed. So Sadie rode him up to the fifth floor and rode down again. No sooner did she get down than she heard another buzz from five. She went up again and found Tom. He said he had knocked on the girl's door, got no answer, so he figured she was asleep already. He'd fix the bathtub tomorrow. Down he went with Sadie, and straight home from there.

"Now Sadie and Bigelow chatted for about twenty minutes in the lobby. They talked about the big prizefight which was on that night, and how brutal it was, and what a beating the champ was taking. Their chat was interrupted by Suspect Number Three.

"This is young Artie Fellows, playboy about town, theatrical angel, and general no-good, who's been showing up to see the Degrasse girl a lot of nights this last month. He was in evening clothes. Just left a party at the home of his young fiancée that he's going to marry in June. Sadie rode him up to the fifth floor and left him there. Five minutes later, the buzzer started ringing loud and long. She rode up again and found Fellows looking green. He told her he'd just entered the girl's apartment with his key—the key she gave him—and found her lying dead on her bed. Well, the house dick was called, and a doctor and the police, and it was finally decided that somebody stunned her with a blow on the back of the head, administered by a bronze candlestick, her own property. And then, when she was stunned, this somebody smothered her to death with a pillow. We found the pillow on the floor next to the body. It was all rumpled up, and there were teeth marks and saliva stains to show what happened."

"Somehow," Shirley said, "I find it hard to feel much sympathy for a cheap unrefined girl like that. Usually such people get what they deserve."

"Not always," Mom said, in a musing voice, as if she were talking to herself. "There's plenty people running around in this world that maybe ought to get themselves smothered. Not enough to kill them maybe—just a little bit smothered, to teach them a lesson." Before Shirley could say a word to this, Mom turned to me very calmly and said, "So go on with the case, please."

"Well, the first thing we did, of course, was to question the three men. Here's what they tell us: Griswold was cagey at first, but finally he came out and admitted that he and the blonde had an argument after they got into her apartment. She told him she was through with him, she'd found another gentleman friend who was younger and richer—young Fellows most likely. Griswold says he was mad when he walked out, but claims he didn't kill her. Says he left her very much alive, turning on her television set to listen to the big prizefight. She was a great sports fan, especially if there was lots of blood. Well, so much for Griswold.

"For a while the handyman Tom Monahan looked like our murderer. We discovered a funny thing. There was absolutely nothing wrong with the bathtub in the Degrasse girl's apartment. So finally Monahan came out with the truth. He and the blonde were carrying on a little flirtation—he's a big husky good-looking fellow, and she wasn't what you'd call particular. Monahan made up that bathtub dodge as an excuse to go up and see her. But he sticks to his story about knocking on the door and getting no answer. Incidentally, we asked him whether he heard the television going inside the room. He says he didn't notice.

"As for Artie Fellows—he still claims he came into the room and found her dead. What's more, he corroborates Griswold's story about the television. The television was on full blast when he came in, he says. In fact, this struck him as an especially gruesome touch, what with that blonde lying dead on the bed.

"So that's the set-up, Mom. It's got to be one of those three. It can't be anybody else who lives in the hotel, because we've checked up on everybody—it's a small hotel, not many tenants, and they've all got alibis. And it can't be anybody from the outside, because the clerk and the elevator girl didn't see anybody else come in or out. In other words, it's strictly a rou-

tine job. Griswold, Monahan, or Fellows, take your choice.
Eeny-meeny-miney—!"

"You forgot Moe," Mom said.

This remark struck me as slightly senseless, but I gave Mom
a sharp look anyway—because her senseless remarks have a
way of turning out to contain more sense than you'd expect.
"What do you mean by that?"

"Never mind what I mean by that," she said. "Time for
the chicken."

I was forced to control my curiosity while Mom served
the chicken. When she finally got settled again in her place. I
reminded her where we had broken off in our conversation.

"So now you've got those three men in your police station,
is that it?" she said. "And you're beating them with rubber
hoses?"

"Mom, how many times have I told you, we don't use
rubber hoses. Modern police methods—"

"All right, all right, so you're psycho-annihilating them.
Whatever it is, I'm positive it don't make no sense. The way
you're handling things with this Platonic blonde—"

"*Platinum* blonde, Mother dear," Shirley said.

"So I said it." Mother gave Shirley a sharp look, then
turned back to me. "What's holding you up on this case, I'd
like to know? Why are you wasting your time with third de-
grees? A bunch of *schlemiels!* Why don't you arrest the one
that killed her?"

"Because we don't *know* the one that killed her! In a few
hours—"

"A few hours, phooey! A few years is more like it, the way
you're going. So stop using your fists and your lungs, and start
using your brains. That's the big trouble with the world today,
too many fists and lungs, not enough brains. Listen, I wouldn't
be surprised if you never even bothered to ask yourself the four
most important questions."

"What questions, Mom? We've asked a million of them."

"Eat your string beans, and I'll tell you. Conversation at
the table is fine, but a young man has got to have his daily
supply of green vegetables."

I blushed a little, as I always do when Mom treats me like a small boy in front of Shirley, but I obediently started in on my string beans. And Mom started in on her "four most important questions."

"The first question," she said. "This Tom Monahan, the handyman. Has he got a wife?"

"Mom, is that one of your mysterious questions? Why, that's the first thing we found out. No, he doesn't have a wife. So if you're looking for a jealousy angle, you'd better—"

"String beans!" Mom said, pointing her finger imperiously. "It's my turn now to do the thinking, please. If you don't mind, the second question. How come this Platonic blonde—"

"Platinum, Mother," Shirley said.

"Thank you, thank you," Mom said. "Such an advantage, isn't it, to have a daughter-in-law that speaks such good English and isn't afraid to let the whole world know about it. —So Davie, how come, I was asking, this *Platonic* blonde didn't have any lipstick on when she got killed?"

This question actually amazed me a little. "Mom, how did you know she didn't have any lipstick on? I didn't say anything about—"

"You said that the pillow she was smothered with had marks on it from teeth and saliva. But you didn't mention any lipstick marks. A lady gets a pillow pushed over her face, believe me, she's going to leave lipstick marks as a result from the experience. Unless she didn't have any lipstick on! So how come she didn't?"

"I don't know how, Mom. She was getting ready to go to bed, so I suppose she washed her lipstick off. Is it really important?"

"Only to smart people," Mom said, patting me on the hand with a sweet smile. "The third question. When this playboy found her body, this Artie Fellows, the television was going full blast, is that right? So tell me, please, what program was on the television then?"

"Mom, are you crazy? Who cares what program was on the television? It's a murder we're investigating, not the television schedule—"

"In other words, you don't know what was on the television then?"

"As a matter of fact, I do know. Fellows just happened to say so. A musical program, some concert orchestra playing classical music. He noticed it because the music was very soft and sad, and he says he'll always think of it as Vilma Degrasse's swan song. Very romantic, Mom, but will you tell me what the hell that's got to do—"

"Swearing I don't like," Mom said, quietly but firmly. "Such language you can use in your stationhouse with the other policemen, but in my home you'll talk like a gentleman."

"I'm sorry, Mom," I mumbled, avoiding Shirley's eye.

"Fourth and last question," Mom said. "This hotel where she got killed, it's not located in such a swanky neighborhood, is it?"

"Mom, what does it matter—?"

"Do you answer me, or don't you?"

"It's a mixed-up neighborhood. The block that this hotel is on is very swanky and modern-looking. But right around the corner is Third Avenue, with all those tenement houses and dirty little bars where the bums hang out. All right, Mrs. Sherlock, does that help you? Is that the significant piece in the jigsaw puzzle which makes everything else fit together?"

Mom smiled quietly, unperturbed by my sarcasm. "If you want to know—yes, it is."

My past experience with Mom was enough to make me start a little. But at the same time I just didn't see how she could possibly have solved the case on the little evidence I had given her. So I pretended to be unimpressed. "Well, let me in on it, why don't you? Which one of those men do you want me to book?"

"The answer to that," Mom said, with a smile of secret wisdom that infuriated me, "you'll find out in a minute."

"You mean, you really *know*—?"

"Why shouldn't I know? I know how people act, don't I? Just because it's a murder case, that don't mean people are all of a sudden going to stop acting like people. A girl like that Platonic blonde—"

"Platinum," Shirley murmured under her breath—evidently just for the principle of the thing, because Mom ignored her elaborately.

". . . a girl who all her life is around men, such a girl is very fussy how she looks when a man drops in. So how come, when you found her dead, she didn't have any lipstick on? When Suspect Number One, this banker, this Mr. Grizzly—"

"Griswold! Just as I suspected!" I cried.

But Mom ignored me and went on, "When he brought her home, she had lipstick on. He took her up to her apartment, she told him she wouldn't go out with him any more, she laughed at him and sent him away—do you think she took her lipstick off before he left? Believe me, it's impossible. When a woman is making a fool out of a man, *that's* when she wants to look absolutely at her best! So when Suspect Number One went away, she was still alive—with her lipstick on."

"Well—it sounds reasonable. So it was Suspect Number Two who did it, then. Tom Monahan! I had a feeling—"

"That's a lovely feeling," Mom said. "Too bad it don't have any connection with the truth. This Tom Monahan knocked on the door and asked her if he could come in and see her. A handsome young fellow that she was flirting with—listen, even if she already took her lipstick off for the night, you can bet she never would've let him through the door without putting it right back on again. But she *didn't* put it right back on again. So that means she *didn't* let him through the door. For some reason she didn't hear his knock—maybe because the television was on too loud. Anyway, he couldn't have killed her."

"And that leaves Suspect Number Three," I said. "Artie Fellows. I had a hunch it was him all along. Your lipstick clue won't work for him. He had a key to the apartment. She might've been in bed already, with her lipstick off, when all of a sudden he came barging in with his key."

"Maybe so," Mom said. "But you could get a big headache trying to prove it. You remember, I asked you that question, what was on the television when Suspect Number Three found the body? Earlier in the evening, when Suspect Number One went away, the girl turned on the big prizefight. But it was an hour later before Suspect Number Three showed up. The fight must be over by then—especially a fight that was so uneven. Like the clerk and the elevator girl said, the champion was taking a terrible beating. So the fight was over, but the television was still on when Suspect Number Three found the body. Why?"

"That's a tough one, Mom. Maybe because she wanted to watch the program that came on after the fight."

"Maybe, maybe not. So what program was she watching? A concert orchestra, playing classical music! Now I ask you, Davie, from everything you know about this girl—a chorus girl that never even finished high school—does she sound like the type that's interested in classical music? Not to me she don't. So why did she still have the television on? Only one answer. Because she was killed while the prizefight was still going, and naturally she couldn't turn off the television after she was dead. So there you are—it couldn't be Suspect Number Three, since he got there too late."

"But, Mom, don't you realize what you're saying? It couldn't be any of the three suspects, because you just proved it—and it couldn't be anybody else from outside, because the clerk and the elevator girl were watching the lobby—and we know it couldn't be anybody else in the building, because everyone has an alibi. In other words, it couldn't be anybody!"

"Alibi!" Mom gave a contemptuous little shrug. "Listen, Davie, when you get to be as old as me, you'll find out that the world is full of Alibi Jakes." ("Ikes," Shirley muttered.) "Nothing is easier than tripping up an Alibi Jake. People doing favors for other people, for instance. Take your Aunt Selma's cook—"

"For Pete's sake, Mom, what possible connection could there be between Aunt Selma's cook and—"

"For six whole months, every night, your Aunt Selma's cook sneaked out of the apartment to meet the delivery man from the grocery store. All the time your Aunt Selma's chambermaid knew it—but did she tell your Aunt Selma? Not a word. Every time your Aunt Selma rang for the cook, the chambermaid answered the bell. The cook is busy baking a cake, she said, or the cook has a spitting headache, or the cook is arguing over the phone with the butcher—or some excuse. Davie, you don't know servants like I do. As long as they're not mad at each other, they got a way of sticking together. Especially when it's a question of fooling the boss."

A small glimmer of understanding was beginning to come to me. "Mom, what are you getting at exactly?"

"You don't know yet? What a *nebbish* son I've got!"

"Well, if I'm not mistaken, you could be talking about— Bigelow the clerk and Sadie the elevator girl."

"A genius! A regular Dr. Einstein! Naturally that's who I'm talking about. You told me yourself, how this elevator girl is so obliging and good-natured, and always doing special favors for people. Well, there was twenty minutes *after* Suspect Number Two went away and *before* Suspect Number Three went up in the elevator, and during those twenty minutes this clerk and this elevator girl were supposed to be chatting together about the prizefight on television, how brutal it was and what a beating the champion was getting. But what I'd like to know is—"

I couldn't keep myself from blurting it out. "How did Bigelow know the fight was so brutal if he was standing behind his desk all night—since there's no television or even radio in the lobby? That's what you're getting at, isn't it, Mom? You're saying that after Tom Monahan left and before Artie Fellows arrived, Bigelow came out from behind his desk, took the elevator up to the fifth floor, and killed the Degrasse girl—and while he was killing her, he saw the prizefight on the television in her room! And all this time, Sadie stayed downstairs and watched the desk for him, and covered up for him because she's so good-natured!"

I was extremely pleased with myself for catching on so quickly, and it surprised me when Mom gave an annoyed sigh. "Good-natured," she said. "How good-natured can a person be? Is anybody *so* good-natured that they'd give a man an alibi for a murder? They might be willing to give him an alibi if he slipped away from the desk for *another* reason—but not for a murder."

"But, Mom, you yourself suggested—*What* other reason?"

"You told me the reason yourself," Mom said. "You just don't pay attention, Davie, not even to your own words. You explained to me how you questioned the clerk this afternoon, and how he complained to you every two minutes that he'd been standing behind his desk for four hours, and how he blew beer fumes in your face. So if he'd been standing behind his desk for four hours, and the Assistant Manager was always poking around to see he wasn't hiding anything under it, so where did he get a drink of beer?"

This question stunned me. I couldn't say a word.

"This is why I asked you about the neighborhood," Mom said. "And you told me just what I thought already. Around the corner is Third Avenue. Along Third Avenue is lots of bars. So this is how the clerk got his beer—he sneaked around the corner a few times to one of those bars. Chances are he does it every day—and chances are it's what he did last night, when he and the elevator girl were supposed to be chatting. And she gave him an alibi because she didn't want him to lose his job."

"Very clever deduction, Mother," Shirley said. "But what use is it to David? You know, he can't arrest a man for taking a drink during working hours."

"Oh, thank you very much for the information," Mother said, giving Shirley her most condescending smile. "But who wants to arrest him? Davie, don't it even pop into your head yet? If the clerk was off in a bar somewhere drinking beer, who's to prove where the elevator girl was?"

"Sadie? Why, she was in the lobby chatting with—" I stopped short, as the truth dawned on me at last. "Of course, of course! That conversation she had with Bigelow about the prizefight! It takes *two* people to make a conversation! The same question I asked for Bigelow also goes for Sadie. How did *she* know that the fight was so brutal and that the champion was taking such a licking? She must've seen it on television—on the blonde's television!"

"Finally you're talking like a slightly intelligent human being," Mom said, beaming with motherly pride, despite her sarcastic words. "While the clerk was away in his bar, this elevator girl went up to the fifth floor, knocked on the blonde's door, then went into the room and killed her. And incidentally, you can see now, why the blonde didn't bother to put her lipstick on when the elevator girl knocked. Because naturally she wouldn't care how she looked in front of an elevator girl."

"But what about the motive, Mom? What was Sadie's motive?"

"Motive? The easiest part. Why do you think I asked you if this handyman, Tom Monahan, was married? A good-looking unmarried Irish boy—a good-natured unmarried Irish girl—and a blonde who's coming between them. Listen, I'd be surprised if such a situation *didn't* end up in murder!"

Well, I spent the next few minutes apologizing to Mom for my skepticism—while Shirley put on a distant, faraway look, as if she were completely indifferent to what was going on, and not the least bit annoyed or jealous at Mom's triumph.

But one little thing still gnawed at me, and finally I came out with it. "Mom, I'm still puzzled about Bigelow, the clerk. He and Sadie both spoke about how brutal the fight was, just as if they'd seen it on television. We know now how Sadie got to see the fight—on the television set in the blonde's room. But how did Bigelow get to see it, Mom? —unless he was up in the blonde's room, too?"

"Davie, Davie, my little baby," Mom said, with a rather fond smile. "You forgot already where this Bigelow was for twenty minutes. In a bar drinking beer. And these days— though naturally I don't patronize such places myself—I hear that you can't get a beer in any bar without getting, along with it—"

"Television!" I cried. Then I jumped to my feet. "Mom, you're a mastermind! I'll call up headquarters right now, and tell the Inspector!"

But Mom's voice, quiet and firm, made me sink back into my seat. "Such *chutzpah!*" she said. "Nobody's calling up anywhere, or telling anything to anybody, till he finishes his string beans!"

The Candle Flame

Lawrence Treat

In all the times I've seen her I think she never smiled. Or showed anger.

She arrived at the back door on that hot sultry day when everybody with any sense was cooling off at the lake. She was wearing a long red velvet skirt that swept a broad swath in the sandy path to the cottage. Her embroidered bodice was a fine example of nomadic art, and her flowing costume could have held three of her. It seemed impossible that her frail flat-chested body could support the weight of that heavy velvet and those strings of beads.

"Yes?" I said. "You wanted something?"

For the few seconds before she replied, she gazed at me, and even now it is hard to describe her eyes. They were blue, they were white, they were colorless, and they seemed unable to blink or change expression. They were a child's eyes—porcelain eyes, with no appearance of depth.

"I heard you were looking for somebody to clean house," she said.

"Right. But my wife is down at the lake. She'll be back around six."

"Could I see the house first?" she said.

"Sure. My studio's separate. I take care of it myself, so there's just the living room-kitchen that you're looking at and a couple of small bedrooms. Not very much. It's nothing but a summer shack."

"I know," she said. She moved forward and appeared to study the room. "When were you born?" she asked.

It was a peculiar question, and later it occurred to me that it was even more peculiar that I answered it. "Nineteen thirty," I said.

"No. I mean what date?"

"October," I said. "The fourteenth."

"Libra," she said. Then she walked forward and touched the paperweight on my desk. "That's why you have the opal," she said. "It's your birthstone. And your wife? When was she born?"

"Same month as I was, but on the seventh."

"I'm a Virgo," she said, "so there won't be any problem. Just so you're not Scorpio."

She seemed about to leave, but before making up her mind she took a last look at the room and saw the sketch I'd made that morning. It was a quick drawing, only half finished, of a young girl. She picked it up and gazed at it rapturously.

"Oh, I *like* that!" she exclaimed. "It's *me!*" And she clasped it to her meager bosom. "May I borrow it? I have to be with it for a while."

"Of course," I said, flattered by her enthusiasm and watching her hug it, carrying it as she would a sleeping infant.

She seemed embarrassed, and she turned and looked at me with those pale, innocent eyes.

"I have to go to The Area," she said, as if she hated the necessity of explaining, "but you don't have to take me there unless you want to."

"Glad to," I said. "No trouble at all." And I felt noble and virtuous at giving her a ride.

I don't know when people first started calling that grassy peninsula "The Area." It had acquired the name long before Gerda and I had started coming to the lake, and by immemorial custom it was reserved for nude bathing. Nobody was sure who owned it. I tried once to check the title on the tax records and found that theoretically it didn't even exist. Perhaps that was why the police, otherwise so strict in petty law enforcement, stayed away from The Area.

When I returned to the house, Gerda was changing from her bathing suit, and I told her about the apparition that was due to work for us.

"What's her name?" Gerda asked.

"Amanda Pyle. She has strange, light-colored eyes, and her hair is blond-red, something like a pink grapefruit."

"What a romantic image!" Gerda said.

I had to go to town shortly before six, and when I returned to the house I saw Martin Fuller's beat-up bug parked nearby. I recognized his car by the variety of oversized flower decals that decorated its pockmarked hide. I pulled up alongside.

"Hi," I said. "What are you doing here?"

"Waiting for Amanda," he answered. "It seems she's decided to work for you."

"We certainly need her. Ever since Gerda hurt her arm, she's been desperate for somebody to help out."

"That's why Amanda came," Martin said.

That stopped me. Gerda needs someone, and Amanda divines or intuits or telepathizes, and comes to the rescue. Which was ridiculous.

"Oh," I said. "You mean somebody told Amanda about Gerda's arm and that she needed a housecleaner?"

"Well," Martin said. "I suppose so."

I felt stupid and wanted to apologize or change the subject and get back to normal. "Been waiting long?" I said.

"Ten or fifteen minutes."

"Why not have a swim with me?" I said. "I'm going to have a quick dip before dinner."

"I can't swim," Martin said.

"You? A big guy like you? How come?"

Martin gave me a sheepish grin. "Makes me unique," he said. "Everybody else swims, I don't." Then, becoming serious, he said, "When I was a kid I almost drowned, and I've been scared of the water ever since."

"Don't worry," I said. "You'll get over that. Maybe Amanda can manage it."

"I guess she will, eventually," he said. Which was a commonplace remark, and yet at the time I had the feeling that Martin meant she'd perform some kind of hocus-pocus, that she'd tell him he was no longer afraid of the water and could swim, and her saying so would make it so.

"Mmm. Well, I'd better bring my packages in."

Gerda told me later on that Amanda had walked into the house, tilted her head to one side while she studied Gerda, and announced that it was all right for her to work for Gerda.

"Just like that?" I said. "She told you she was going to work for you? She didn't wait to be asked?"

"I wanted somebody and she looked clean, so why wouldn't I give her a try?"

"Just like that?" I said again.

"Well, she said I had the right vibes—vibrations, I guess—so we went on to other things."

They were on the "other things" when I arrived. They were discussing when it was best to eat fiddleback ferns and whether purslane should be creamed or merely sautéed. It was clear that they were kindred souls, even to the point of finance.

I heard the bargain being made. Amanda was about to leave when Gerda mentioned money. "I forgot to ask you how much you want. I suppose three dollars an hour, like everybody else."

Amanda objected. "Oh, no. I couldn't take more than two. Two is Yin and Yang, and three would be triad."

Gerda looked surprised, but she recovered quickly. "Oh, yes," she said. "That will be all right."

I quote the exact conversation, to prove that there was nothing sinister. Nothing.

I was in my studio the following morning when Amanda arrived, and I didn't see her until I came into the house for my second cup of coffee. She was standing at the sink. Despite the bright sunlight a lighted candle was burning on either side of her. She was using my favorite eggcups as holders, and she was slowly washing a coffee cup in a basin of water. Later on, when Gerda and I redid the dishes, she told me Amanda had put a white lily in the basin instead of soapsuds.

"It was quite beautiful," Gerda said.

At the time, however, I was overwhelmed by the sight of Amanda and her candles. "What!" I exclaimed. "What the——"

But Gerda put her finger to her lips and murmured a "Shh!" Amanda appeared not to hear. I think she was in a trance.

At lunch, after Amanda had left, I asked Gerda how things had worked out. "Well," Gerda said, "she did about ten cents' worth of work. Not much more."

"Did you complain?"

"In a way. She said she'd do better next time."

She did. Or at least Martin did. He brought her to the house and came in with her. "Martin is going to help me," Amanda announced. "It won't cost extra, he'll do a couple of things."

What he did was wash the kitchen floor, run the vacuum cleaner, sweep and clean the porch, and shake out the rugs.

"Twenty dollars' worth of work, easily," Gerda told me.

The next time, however, Amanda came alone. Perhaps in apology for her incompetence, she presented us with a loaf of health bread that she'd baked.

At almost every visit she brought something wild that she'd made or gathered, and she spent the first half hour or so, at our expense, telling Gerda how to prepare it. As the result, I found myself drinking sumac tea, eating pigweed or lamb's-quarters, and having wild sorrel salads and soups. Once Amanda arrived with a basket of mushrooms, and Gerda and I were shocked to see a couple of amanitas mixed in with some edible species.

"Amanda!" Gerda said. "Throw them out. Those white ones—they're a deadly poison."

"I know," Amanda said serenely. "I wasn't going to eat those. White is wrong."

"Amanitas," Gerda said sternly, "are poisonous."

"I'm careful," Amanda said, "and I know where to look. The ones that grow in circles are good to eat, and so are the ones that grow in clusters, but when they're alone and dressed in white they represent pride and vanity. I wouldn't dream of eating them."

"That's nonsense," Gerda said firmly. "Inedible ones can also grow in circles and clusters. That's no way to identify. You have to know a mushroom the way you know an aster or a rose."

Amanda didn't answer, and I'm not even sure she listened.

After a few weeks Gerda's arm had regained its normal strength, but it was not in her nature to fire anybody, particularly someone like Amanda.

"We're friends," Gerda said. "She tells me all kinds of

things. How she came to the lake, for instance. She was in a commune, and she was on her way to town one day when Martin's name popped into her mind. She knew him from some yoga classes that they'd both gone to, and they'd kept up with each other in a vague sort of way. When she got back to the commune, she found out that Martin had phoned her, so she called him and he said to come up here. Naturally she did."

"Naturally," I said.

She worked for us on Mondays and Fridays. Sometimes she brought Martin, and when she did he polished up the house until it was spic and span. Otherwise she left behind her a faint scent of incense, a couple of burnt-out candles, and a stack of dishes to be rewashed. We were therefore surprised to see her arrive one Tuesday morning.

"Bob's coming," she said, "and I need money to buy him a present. Shall I start in the bathroom?"

"That will be fine," Gerda said. "Who's Bob?"

Amanda went to the refrigerator and took out an egg and some of her barley bread for breakfast. "He's very special," she said. "He's coming from California and I have to fix the room for him."

"What about Martin?" Gerda asked.

"Oh, Martin will understand. Bob's special, you see. He's been to India and he studied under the Master." From the way she spoke you could tell that Master was spelled with a capital M. "Bob has Power." And that was spelled with a capital P.

"Amanda," Gerda said, "I don't like to interfere, but I'm a little older than you are, and I'd like to give you some advice. Martin's been sweet to you, he's helped you and he's been a good friend and you have certain obligations toward him, so it's not fair to push him out and take somebody else, just like that."

"I'm not pushing him out," Amanda said. "I wouldn't dream of such a thing."

"Do they know each other?" Gerda said.

"They know each other through me. I think of both of them at the same time, and in utter harmony."

"But when they see each other, maybe there won't be

quite that much harmony. Thinking doesn't always make things so."

Amanda turned slowly and fixed Gerda with her pale eyes. "I'd do anything that either of them asked me to," she said. "We're unity. We're not external, we're internal." Then she ate the egg and barley bread.

Later, after she'd meditated in the bathroom and then left with her $4 and breakfast on us, I teed off on Gerda.

"That little chit conned us," I said. "What did she do for her four dollars? What does she think we are?"

"She thinks we're lost in desire. She's a little sorry for us, and she uses us."

"I don't like to be used. I'm not a usee."

"Neither am I, but I'm learning things. Peter, what do you know about communes and long-hairs and acid freaks? What do you know about Amanda's young world?"

"I know plenty about her generation. First it went in for love and then it was acid and then the Jesus freaks and now I guess it's something else. These kids are looking for something. Sure. They haven't found it and I don't think they're on the right track, but they're having a hell of a good time and I'm glad they are, because by and by they'll settle down and have children and be good citizens and read the classics, just like you and me."

"You're old-fashioned," Gerda said, "and you're jealous of people like Amanda, and so am I. I envy Amanda and her two men, although I don't think it will work out, and that's why I said what I did. But deep down, Peter, I hope she gives it a try."

"If she does," I said, "it's going to be murder for one of them."

"Literally?"

"Of course not. They're gentle people. Amanda is one of the kindest and gentlest people I've ever met. But look at the way she leads Martin around. And us."

"You're sarcastic," Gerda said, "but wait and see."

"Martin's too nice a guy to be led around, and one of these days he'll see what's happening and he'll turn on her."

"And do what?" Gerda said. "Beat her up? Walk out on her? What?"

"I don't know. All I'm saying is that there's a limit. She puts things over on people, she does it all the time. Take yourself, for instance—has she ever really cleaned this place? Has she ever done a decent morning's work?"

"If she had," Gerda said, with her usual illogic, "my arm wouldn't have gotten better so fast. It's as if I had to cover up for her and my sprained arm was no excuse, so it had to get better and it did. All the things I've learned from her!" Gerda started laughing. "She's so pathetic that you feel sorry for her and you never realize what you've done until it's all over. Peter, how many pictures have you given her?"

"None," I said, grinning, "but she took two."

To nobody's surprise, neither mine nor Gerda's, Amanda failed to show up on her next cleaning day. "I guess that's the end of that," Gerda said. "No more groundnuts or crowberries, and no more barley bread. From now on we'll have to go to the corner store and buy our food like everybody else."

"But we can't let her go," I said. "I'm too damn curious about what's happening with Martin and Amanda and this Bob guy. How about going down to The Area and looking for them?"

It was a long time since Gerda and I had been there, and the initial impact was strange, almost shocking. The flat, grassy area was covered with dogs and naked bodies, small dogs and big dogs and thin bodies and fat bodies, lounging, sunning themselves, talking, or doing nothing. Two or three long-hairs were doing yoga exercises, and a small group was intent on watching a chess game. Some children were playing in the couple of feet of sand that had been imported long ago in an attempt to make a beach.

We found our threesome easily enough. They were lying in a circle, with their feet touching each other at the center. Martin, big and powerful, an athlete in perfect condition; Amanda, like a slender stick of flesh; and Bob, an undernourished little spider, all hair, hairy body and bushy beard with a stubby little nose poking out of it as if coming up for air. When I spoke, they sat up.

Amanda made a feint at introducing us. "This is Bob," she said.

"I've heard of you," I said.

Bob's squeaky voice surprised me. "Many have," he said.

Gerda tried to break the embarrassment by discussing edible wild plants with Amanda, but Bob's treble cut her off.

"Let's not talk about food," he said. "This is our day of fasting."

"Amanda fasting?" Gerda said. "She needs all the nourishment she can get. Just look at her."

"Her nourishment is of the spirit," Bob said. "She has a calm center."

I coughed. Gerda said, "Well, well!" Martin looked uncomfortable, and then pandemonium broke loose in the form of a dog fight.

They were big dogs, a German shepherd and a Doberman pinscher, and they battled in a snarling whirlwind of fury. Everybody near them jumped and ran off shrieking, except for a couple of brave young guys, probably the owners, who tried gingerly and ineffectually to separate them.

I grabbed Gerda's hand, ready, in case the tornado came our way, to pull her behind me in a gesture of protection. Bob, however, climbed to his feet, rising slowly, using some trick of elongating himself so that he seemed tall, despite the fact that he barely topped my shoulder. I was amazed to see him walk deliberately toward that whirling ball of canine destruction.

He was nude and unprotected against claws and teeth, while a pair of enraged animals were snapping and biting at each other and anybody near them. But Bob walked straight up to them, held out his hands, and said something no one could hear. Maybe he spoke, maybe he whistled, or maybe he exuded some power of silencing. In any case, the dogs stopped abruptly, withdrew, then faced each other growling. Bob held out his two hands and each of the dogs crept up to him, tails between their legs, and licked his outstretched fingers.

For a moment there was silence. Then you could hear the rising babble of astonishment, and a few sentences carried to where we stood—words of admiration, almost of awe.

Bob paid no attention to anyone. He said something to the dogs in a low voice, and they did not follow as he returned to us.

"That was wonderful," Gerda said. "What did you say to them?"

Bob didn't deign to reply. He reached out for Amanda's hand. "Let's go for a dip," he said.

She followed obediently, and we watched them walk toward the water, walking slowly until they reached the edge, where they seemed to explode and go splashing in. Martin gazed at them sadly.

"Does he do that kind of thing often?" I said. "Pull miracles, that is?"

"No, that's the first time I've seen anything like that."

"It's going to be tough on you," I said. "From now on he's a hero, whereas you——" I didn't finish the sentence.

"He's not a hero," Martin said. "You need an awful lot of ego to be a hero."

"You think he has none?" I said. "I think he has nothing but."

Martin shrugged. I felt that he agreed with me, but was afraid to say so. The subject seemed to be unpleasant to him, so I switched.

"Why don't you learn how to swim?" I said. "You're a good athlete, it ought to be easy for you."

"Amanda said she'd teach me when she thinks I'm ready for it."

"You'll be ready as soon as you try," I said. "How can *she* know when you're ready?"

"Don't," Martin said.

Don't talk about it any more? Don't destroy my confidence in Amanda and her way of life? Don't make problems for me? Don't—what?

We saw the three of them in town later that week. They were barefoot. Amanda was walking in the center, and her light cloak was thrown around both her escorts. It circled Bob's narrow shoulders and made him and Amanda as one, but on Martin's side the cloak was too short and too small to cover him, so it hung precariously from Martin's midriff and threatened to fall off at every step.

"Yin and Yang," I said to Gerda, "and three would be triad. I wonder whether she'd work for three bucks an hour now, if you offered it."

"Martin will leave her," Gerda said. "He has too much sense not to. He'll find himself a good healthy wench to love him, and he'll love her in turn."

"Sure," I said. "To the end of his days."

We were wrong.

The first we heard of the event was from one of our neighbors, who phoned to find out if we knew. Gerda answered the phone, and the shock in her voice made me gasp.

"What!" she exclaimed. "Martin? Oh, no! Not Martin. What happened?" She listened for a minute or so, then put the phone down gently. "Martin drowned," she said to me. "He went rowing with Amanda, and he fell out of the boat and drowned."

"But he was so scared of the water," I said. "What made him go? And how do you fall out of a boat? Only fools stand up, and Martin was no fool."

"You think not?" Gerda said. "You kept saying he was. Remember?"

The full account appeared in the local paper. It said that Martin Fuller, 22 years old and a part-time carpenter, had been drowned in a tragic accident. According to Miss Amanda Pyle, who had been with him, he had stood up in the boat, for reasons she was unable to explain. He either lost his balance or became dizzy, and he toppled and knocked over the oars in his fall.

Mr. Fuller, the story continued, weighed about 200 pounds and Miss Pyle barely half of that. It was obviously beyond her strength to dive in and rescue him, and it was all she could do to paddle the boat with her hands and reach the floating oars. By that time it was too late for her to do anything to help Mr. Fuller. She rowed ashore and notified the first people she saw, who called the police. The body was recovered several hours later.

Amanda came to work for us the following Thursday. She seemed calm and collected, and at first she made no mention of the tragedy. She had a wreath of daisies in her hair. She removed the wreath ceremoniously and placed it on one of the two towels she took from the linen closet. She took the other towel into the bathroom, and presently we heard the shower going.

"What the hell is she doing in there?" I said to Gerda.

"Apparently she's taking a shower," Gerda said acidly. "But don't ask her any questions for a while. If she doesn't tell me anything, I'll ask later on."

"I don't like it," I said. "The least she ought to do is look sad and tell us about Martin. But she's so calm and quiet."

"Wait and see," Gerda said.

I waited patiently while Amanda came out of the bathroom, found two candles, and set them up on either side of the sink. She put them in my eggcups, as she always did, then lit the candles and went through her usual vague motions of washing. This time, however, it was all too much for me to take, and I marched over to the sink and blew out the candles.

"In case you're wondering why I did that," I said, "those are my eggcups, and I like to use them as such."

"I'm sorry," Amanda said meekly. "But when you're with a candle flame, you are the candle flame."

"What does that mean?" I asked.

"I hoped you'd understand," she said. "You're upset about Martin, aren't you?"

"You bet I am."

"You don't have to be," she said. "He's no longer lost in the darkness. He's part of us now."

Gerda interrupted what might have become a rather nasty and probably futile interrogation by me. "Amanda," she said gently, "tell us what happened."

"It was wonderful," Amanda said. "Martin finally conquered his fear of water, and with it he conquered all fear. He *asked* me to go rowing with him, and when we were in the center of the lake he said he was no longer afraid of the water, and he stood up in the boat and he was smiling. When he swayed, I tried to reach out to support him and keep him from falling, but there was a force between us. There was an energy that kept me from reaching out, and suddenly I knew that his time had come, this was his karma, and I was privileged to be there at the time. I was so happy!"

"Happy?" I exclaimed. "When he's dead?"

"You don't understand," Amanda said. "You're like the police. They didn't understand either. They kept asking me whether I'd pushed him."

"Did you?" I said.

"I can't stay here when people keep thinking that. Don't you see, Martin and I were one. For a wonderful instant we were joined as can only rarely happen between people. We found ourselves in a perfect circle."

"And now you're leaving The Area?" I said.

"Yes."

"With Bob?"

"Oh, no. With a friend of mine. You don't know him, but he's Gemini, and Bob, while he's wonderful, he's Pisces. So you see, Bob couldn't go with me."

"Well, I hope it works out," I said, "and that the tragedy—"

"Please, don't call it a tragedy. It was the way of life, it was good that it happened and good that it happened with me. Some other people might have tried to interfere." Her pale eyes gazed upward, where police and other unbelievers like myself couldn't possibly reach her.

"Tell me just one thing more," I said. "Why did he stand up?"

"Because I wanted him to."

"Oh," I said.

I watched Amanda cross the room and take the daisy wreath from the towel on which she'd placed it when she'd come in. She adjusted the wreath carefully and then she left, with her long velvet skirt trailing along the path. She did not look back.

As soon as she was out of sight, I walked over to the towel and examined it. Her wreath had left a faint, lightcolored ring that seemed to give off tiny shafts of light.

"It looks like a halo," I said, dumfounded.

Gerda smiled. "Yes," she said. "Didn't you see her draw it?"

"Sure," I said sarcastically. Then I bent over and touched the wet towel, and the yellow pollen came off on my fingers.

"Halo?" I said. "Halo?"

The Kitchen Floor

Dorothy A. Collins

He wiped up the egg yolk with his toast, washed it down with the last of his coffee, and glanced sourly at the cane propped against the dinette table.

"How much longer you gonna go stumping around on that thing?"

Mildred stared at him, thinking of the vicious shove he'd given her the week before that had sent her sprawling, her ankle twisted beneath her.

"Another week or so, I imagine," she said levelly. "As soon as I can put my full weight on the foot."

He grunted and pushed himself back from the table. "Big deal," he said. Without looking at her, he put on his coat and left the house.

When she heard the door slam behind him, she relaxed her tense shoulders and sat quietly for a moment, savoring the emptiness of the house. Then she rose awkwardly, favoring her left foot, and carried the dishes to the sink, washing them in hot sudsy water, drying them, and putting them away carefully in the cabinet. She poured herself another cup of coffee and sat down at the table again. From the drawer beneath the table she took a pencil and a 3x5 memo pad. This was ordinarily her favorite time of day, the house quiet and awaiting her ministrations, the clean white pad ready for her daily list of chores and reminders, the freshly sharpened pencil at the ready. Today, she was tense and abstracted, and the homely little routine afforded her no pleasure. She sighed and began writing in her small neat hand:

S
M
V

Here she frowned. Better not attempt any vacuuming yet. Changing the sheets and polishing the mirrors were simple enough tasks, but vacuuming involved too much walking, too much bending and stretching. Although the ankle was no longer painful, Dr. Vincent had told her to keep her weight off it as much as possible and she couldn't run the risk of straining it. She erased the V and continued writing.

L

I

Lch

C

Barbie—

She smiled as she wrote her daughter's name. Barbie loved her apple cake—she'd make her take most of it home with her when she left. The smile faded as she wrote the next item.

F C

Pencil poised for the next entry, she hesitated. She stared thoughtfully at the shining expanse of yellow vinyl on the kitchen floor, and then wrote:

K F

Not much of a list, she thought as she glanced rapidly over it, but then I'll be back in stride soon. So. Get started on the bed and mirrors, then tackle the laundry and iron Frank's shirts. A waste of time—they were permanent press—but he refused to wear them unless they were absolutely wrinkle-free. So she'd do them as usual, disrupting the routine as little as possible.

By one o'clock she'd finished the last of the shirts and thought about lunch. Toast and tea, she decided. Invalid's fare, but then she was a semi-invalid, and the thought of a sandwich or soup had no appeal.

She settled at the table with her cup and plate and drew the memo pad to her. She drew lines through the first four items and then, draining her cup, crossed out "Lch." She smiled wryly. "Methodical Millie," Barbie called her, teasing her about being an inveterate list-maker and timetabler. Well, so be it, she thought—I'm too set in my ways to change now.

She set about assembling the cake ingredients. This particular chore was a labor of love. She mixed the batter and spread it in a flat Pyrex dish. She peeled and sliced the apples, splashed them with lemon juice, and distributed them thickly on top, sprinkling them liberally with white sugar, dusting them with cinnamon, and dotting the surface with butter. Lovely. She slid the dish into the warmed oven and set the timer. By the time she'd straightened up the kitchen and freshened herself up a bit, her beautiful girl would be here.

She crossed C off the list.

By three o'clock, when the doorbell rang, the house was redolent with the scent of apple and cinnamon. "Oh, heavenly," said Barbie, hugging her mother. "Mom, you shouldn't be baking—you shouldn't be on your feet at all. How does your ankle feel?"

"It feels fine, stop fussing." Mildred Burton hung her daughter's coat in the hall closet and led her into the kitchen. "Is this the sponge-rubber toweling?" She drew it out of the bag and set it on the counter top. "Primrose yellow. Nice—it matches the kitchen. Now sit down and we'll have some cake and coffee and a good long natter, as your grandma used to say."

Barbie took a bite of the warm cake and sighed with pleasure. "I never can get the top crisp and candied like that." She put down her fork. "Mom. You're not fooling me, you know. I don't buy that story about reaching for a can of peaches and falling off the stool. Pop did it, didn't he?"

"It happened the way I told you. I'm not one of those battered wives. It's just that your father drinks too much sometimes and doesn't know what he's doing—"

"Oh, he knows, all right. He doesn't have to be drunk to make your life miserable. He's been doing it for as long as I can remember. If I hadn't married Jack and moved out, I think I would have ended up killing him. As it is, I worry about you all the time."

"There's no need to, darling. I can look out for myself after all these years. What bothers me is what he did to Patty. How is she?"

"Miserable, Mom. It's been a week now, and she's still

huddled inside herself like a little snail. How did he know she was going out on her first date, anyway? You're always so careful talking to me on the phone—"

"I know. It was my fault. I thought he was down in the basement watching the Saturday game, but he must have come up for some more beer, heard me talking in the bedroom, and picked up the extension here in the kitchen. Has she heard from the boy again?"

"After that scene Pop made?" Barbie smiled bitterly. "He really did a hatchet job on that kid, jeering at him about his long hair, his clothes—and the boy's immaculate, Mom, a wonderful kid from a lovely family. And then all those filthy remarks about kids today 'making out' and 'shacking up.' By the time Jack threw him out, the damage was done. Patty dreads going to school every day—thinks the kids are laughing behind her back about her crazy drunken grandfather. She'll be a long time getting over it."

Mildred Burton's face hardened. "Whatever else he's done," she said, "I'll never forgive him for that. It won't happen again, Barbie, I promise you."

"No, it won't. Because he'll never set foot in our house again." She bent her head to hide the quick rush of tears.

"It's all right, darling. Come, have another cup of coffee and let's talk about something else."

Barbie looked at her watch. "Lord, yes. Another half hour and I'll have to leave." She glanced at the memo pad on the table and picked it up. "Good heavens, did you do all this today—you, the walking wounded?" She scanned the list. "I've gotten pretty good at translating this shorthand of yours. But what's FC?"

"Fix cane. That's why I asked you to pick up the toweling. The tip of the cane is making scuff marks on the vinyl here in the kitchen and I thought I'd pad it with the toweling—it'll cushion the jarring effect when I walk too."

"That's a good idea. But this floor is like a mirror. Mine's only a year old and it doesn't look half as good. Talking about the floor, I see it's on your list, and I absolutely forbid it, Mom.

You've done enough today. I'll run the polisher over it before I leave if you're dead set on getting it done."

"No, dear, I wouldn't think of it. You're right, it doesn't really need it. I'll let it go for a few days."

"Promise?"

"Promise."

"All right, then. But I can fix the cane for you before I go. Do you want to attach it with rubber bands?" Her mother nodded distractedly. "They're here in the drawer, right?"

Mildred watched as Barbie tore off a towel from the perforated roll, folded it, and fitted it to the bottom of the cane, fastening it securely with two heavy rubber bands from the drawer. "Gaudy if not neat. I think it'll do the job for you, though. Do you want to try it?"

Mildred took a few steps with the padded cane and smiled her approval.

"It's perfect," she said. "Like leaning on a marshmallow."

Barbie laughed as her mother drew a line through FC. "Well, I'm off," she said. She gave her mother a swift hug and kiss. "Don't tell his lordship I was here—the less he knows the better. I suppose he'll come in smelling like a brewery and you'll have cold beer and pretzels waiting."

"Old habits die hard, Barbie. Goodbye, say hello to Jack and Patty for me."

Mildred closed the door after her daughter and leaned heavily against it for a few moments, her head pressed against the frame. Then she straightened wearily and made her way back to the kitchen, turning on the lights as she went. Frank liked to come home to a well-lit house.

Within half an hour she had pork chops simmering in a tomato-and-pepper sauce, noodles ready to plunge into boiling water, and salad greens crisping in the refrigerator. She was sliding pretzels and potato chips into two bowls when she heard the key in the lock. Two tall cans of icy beer were standing beside the bowls when he walked into the kitchen.

He cocked his head toward the basement doorway.

"Why isn't the television on?"

"I still can't manage the stairs."

He snorted. "Boy, are you working this thing to death. Go ahead, keep throwing it in my face. It don't bother me *at all*, sister." His red-veined eyes glared at her. "The only thing I'm sorry for, I should of done a better job while I was at it." He scooped up the beer, jammed the bowl of chips on top of the pretzels, and headed for the stairs.

"Don't you want a tray?" She followed him, leaning heavily on the cane.

He twisted around, his face ugly with resentment.

"Don't do me no favors," he said and turned back to the stairs.

As he moved his foot for the first step, she lifted the padded end of the cane and gave him a violent shove that sent him plunging down the steep flight. He landed with a crash, his head smashing against the basement wall, his neck snapping with the impact. She knew with utmost certainty that he was dead.

She turned, her step firm and assured, and crossed to the phone to call Dr. Vincent, stopping at the table on the way to lean over the memo pad and draw a neat line through KF.

The Girl Friend

Morris Hershman

"Fourteen years old!" Banner's voice was hollow. He held up the pocket snapshot that had just been passed to him. "A face like a dream, pretty blonde hair and all."

Mill dropped his feet from the desk, swivelled back in his chair and nodded slowly. "An average case as far as I'm concerned. You're going to prosecute it, Mr. Assistant District Attorney, so you might as well get the facts straight."

"What did she do, this girl?"

Mill crossed one foot over the other and rubbed it with thumb and forefinger. "It's quite a story. We had to ask a lot of questions to get the real answers. We wanted to know *why* she did it. Maybe you'd like to know about the why, first." He sighed. "Being a cop is such a rough job on the nerves because a cop can't afford to have nerves."

Mill liked to make little speeches about what it took to be a cop. In the years that Banner had known him, four or five, it happened at least once whenever they met. They weren't close friends; Mill couldn't talk about much but a cop's job. He seemed to have no outside interests at all.

"If you look this over," Mill said, pointing to a number of typewritten sheets clipped together, "you'll get some idea. What you got to know about a girl like this is that it's not all her fault, no matter what kind of nasty thing she did."

Banner picked up the sheets and settled them in his lap. They were in question-and-answer form. The girl's name was Alice King.

Q: How old are you, honey?
A: Fourteen. Fourteen, last December.
Q: What school do you go to, Alice?
A: Marley Junior High.
Q: You get good grades?
A: B's and B-plusses.

Q: Do you have a lot of boy friends?

A: No!

Banner frowned at the pocket-size photograph. "Good-looking kid. Why's she so quick to say she hasn't got a lot of boy friends?"

Mill scratched his foot again, then the back of an ear. He lit a cigar and puffed until it was drawing nicely. "Nothing else she could say. Of course at the time I didn't know it, myself. Don't forget we had just picked her up a little while before."

It had grown dark, and Mill flicked on the desk lamp. In the building, on three sides of them, men scurried back and forth. Outside the window, a pink dot could be seen far away, apparently the bathroom of a private home. Close to it was a larger window with blinds down, and bright light glaring out through a wider slit at the top.

"That kid," Mill said suddenly. "She ought to have been having the time of her life, going to proms and things. At that age, a girl's just finding out that she *is* a girl, and she sure as hell likes the idea."

Banner shrugged, then looked down to the sheet that was now on top.

A: No!

Q: Did you ever have a job, Alice?

A: You mean a job where I worked outside my house?

Q: That's right.

A: Only part-time. I worked in a department store for a while, but the job didn't last.

Q: Why not?

A: They were stingy—cheap, you know—and they kept me working after hours and wouldn't pay me extra for that. My mother said it was practically white slavery. She told them off.

Q: And after your mother told them off, you left the job?

A: I was fired.

Q: What kind of a job did you get then, Alice?

Banner looked up, frowning. "The mother sounds like a louse. Alice doesn't want to talk about her."

"If you ask me," Mill shrugged, "the mother's a good-natured, hearty, heavy drinking, foolish woman. Maybe that's why the kid—go on reading, Ban, you'll see."

Q: What kind of a job did you get then, Alice?

A: In a dress shop, but just about the same thing happened. So my mother said I ought to work for her. She said she'd pay me ten dollars a week if I'd keep the house nice and clean before she—uh, worked.

Q: Sounds like a soft touch.

A: It was okay, for a while.

Q: What went sour?

A: I might as well tell you. Usually, mother kept me away from the house till half-past twelve at night. I'd stay over at a girl friend's place. But sometimes I had trouble with some of the customers. One of them, a Mr. Dail, sees mother twice a week. He happened to come in a little earlier once when I was cleaning. Mr. Dail took one look at me and said to mother: "I'd pay twenty dollars for just a half hour with her."

Q: What did your mother say?

A: She said no. She said she wouldn't let her kid do that. But Mr. Dail, he kept talking about it and after a few minutes, mother said that the rent was coming up in a few days and she was paying more than usual for protection. To the cops, I mean.

Q: So you went into the bedroom with Mr. Dail?

A: Mother said I wouldn't have any trouble. When Mr. Dail and I, the two of us, were finished, she was making jokes about it. All the time we were in there, though, she sat outside sobbing a little.

Banner, looking up, caught Mill's drily amused eyes. He avoided them, stood and walked to the window. The pinkish bathroom light far away had been put out. The sounds of routine police business had increased in tempo.

Finally, after swallowing quickly, Banner asked: "Did Alice King turn pro?"

The cop, openly pleased by Banner's interest, pointed to the sheets. "Read the q-and-a, you'll see." He added thoughtfully, "You know, I don't think you can imagine what the kid was like. Very refined, always smoothing down her skirt. When she asked for a glass of water she tacked on, 'please.' Never blamed her crime on circumstances or said she was victimized. In fact, a good kid. Like your daughter would be, if you had one."

Q: Did you do it with other men, Alice?

A: Sometimes. Mother always told them I was twelve and a virgin. She always charged more money for me than for herself. Up to twenty-five dollars. After it was over, she would give me five dollars for myself. Mother wouldn't let me do it more than twice a week.

Q: How many men would you say you've slept with, Alice?

A: I don't know.

Q: Ten? Is it that many?

A: I don't know.

Q: Twenty?

A: I don't know.

Q: Thirty? Forty? Fifty? Give me a number that's close to the truth, Alice.

A: Fifty, maybe.

Mill said, "You can skip the part where she gives names. The Vice Squad boys have picked up the ones she remembers, and they're in for a bad time. Your boss, the D.A., he'll see to that."

Banner said quietly: "At least I know now what you're holding the girl for. Delinquency. An easy case to prosecute. In her set-up, it could have been something worse."

"It was. It is." Mill looked intently at the tip of his cigar, talked slowly to it. "A hell of a lot worse."

In spite of himself, Banner lowered his head.

Mill added: "Alice King has good stuff in her, as a person. You take the average fourteen-year-old girl and put her in that spot and she becomes like the mother, you know—shiftless, lazy, vain, a stupid slob. Alice didn't."

Banner glanced at the snapshot.

"I don't mean just for looks," Mill said a little impatiently. "There's other things in a kid's life. Alice King kept up her grades at Marley Junior High, even improved them in one case.

She started to appreciate ballet and modern dance. She did some dating. Normal, in other words, except for what she did twice a week."

Banner looked a little sadly at the picture. Suddenly he stiffened and set it face down on the desk. He was flushed.

Mill smiled. "Thinking you'd like to jump the kid yourself, I bet!" More seriously he added, "One of the hard things about being a cop is that you can excuse the bad in most people because it's in you, too . . . Give me the sheets, will you, for a minute?"

Banner slowly handed them across. The cop turned four pages, his wet thumb driving a crease into every one, then a fifth.

"Here it is. Where she meets Ronald Hutchinson."

Banner's lip curled. "Another customer?"

"Another kid. Fifteen, in fact. I found out a lot about him. A big wheel at Marley Junior High: baseball team in summer and football in winter, editor of the school paper, member of Arista, student president of the G.O. And rich, too. Lot of dough in the family. Old man is president of a chain of supermarkets."

"The kid sounds like a snob."

"No." Mill shook his big head determinedly, and tapped a crown of ash off the cigar. "Nice, healthy kid with a lot of girl friends. A good-looking kid with nice manners."

Q: How did you come to meet Ronald Hutchinson?

A: I went out for the school paper.

Q: Oh, you volunteered to work for it.

A: That's right. I thought I wanted to be a reporter when I grow up, so I took a crack at it. Ron was the student editor. We hit it off, all right. We liked each other. We laughed at the same things and had a lot in common. I always think that's very important with a boy and girl.

Q: Tell me what happened between you two.

A: Nothing did, at the start. I knew he'd want to take me out, but I didn't rush him. He waited two weeks. There was going to be a dance in the gym at school on Saturday night and he asked me to go with him. I said I would.

Q: Did he call you at home?

A: No, I never want boys to call me at home. It can get confusing.

Q: How did your mother feel about your taking off Saturday night?

A: Mother said it was fine, because she wants me to have good times. She doesn't want to interfere with my social life.

Q: That's for sure. So you and Ron Hutchinson hit it off, I suppose.

A: The first date, at the dance, was very sweet. Ron couldn't samba, so a bunch of us showed him. It was a lot of fun. After that, I saw him in school. It got so that we used to hold hands over the lockers in our 'official' rooms. That means the rooms where students do things as a class, you know, according to what the principal wants.

Q: You were dating Ron pretty heavily?

A: We had a few cheap dates, first. We'd meet at the ice cream parlor and he'd buy me a soda and we'd sit and talk. We had an awful lot in common. Once in a while we'd go see a movie and hold hands. Then he'd walk home with me and say goodnight a block from the house. I never let boys call for me at the house.

Q: You didn't mind the cheap dates?

A: No, they were fun. Ron said that the whole town knew about his being rich, so he didn't have to impress girls by flashing a roll. A *bank*roll, he meant.

Q: In other words, you had nothing against Ron Hutchinson.

A: That's right, nothing.

Q: No grudge of any kind.

A: Of course not.

Q: Did you think you were in love with him?

A: I suppose so.

Q: You were serious about him, then?

A: Yes. Almost praying I could keep him interested till I was eighteen, so we could get married. That shows you what a fool I was!

Q: Why a fool?

A: On account of what happened.

Q: How many times a week did you see him?

A: Two, three.

Q: How did your mother feel about that?

A: At first she thought it was very nice and she told me not to give away anything, if you know what I mean. Then she said I ought to be home at nights, to work if I had to. She said expenses were going up and I ought to be paying a bigger share of my upkeep.

Q: How did you feel about that?

A: I wanted to get a job in a store, instead, but my mother didn't want that.

Q: The two of you argued?

A: Yes. I started to get sick when I had to use the bedroom with one of the customers. Sometimes I'd throw up or say that I had cramps.

Q: Tell me about last night—Saturday night.

A: Mother was a little under the weather. She wanted me to stay with one of our customers. The man came in, Mr. Cameron, and I just got sick when I saw him. I started to cry. Mother got angry, but when she saw she was licked anyhow, she told me to go.

Q: You had a date with Ron?

A: We were headed for a party over a friend of his' house.

Q: How about the knife, Alice? How come you took a pocketknife along with you on a date?

Banner caught his breath.

A: My mother thinks its a good idea to bring one, in case a girl gets into a spot where she needs a little help. Mother isn't like most people, you know, and she always tells me to be very careful when I go out on a date and never go beyond necking. When we're alone, she calls the customers animals. She always warns me that men are after one thing and a girl has to use any way possible to keep—well, you know.

Q: And you believe that?

A: Mother's had more experience than me.

Q: So you took a pocketknife along on every date?

A: Most of them. It came in handy for little things, you

know, like cutting open envelopes. I never had to use it to scare off a boy. Not till last night, that is.

Q: Ron made a pass at you?

A: We were at Baker's Lane. You know, a lot of cars stop there for couples to neck in peace and quiet. Ron had borrowed his dad's car for the date. He said to me. "What about it, honey?" He put a hand under my dress and started slowly unbuttoning it from behind. Like one of the customers does, Mr. Strawbridge, that is. Anyhow, I tried to stop Ron. I said: "I'm not one of those girls." And to make a joke out of it, to show I meant it for a joke, I pulled out the pocketknife and said: "Better not." Of course I said it in such a way he was sure it was a joke.

Q: He didn't give up trying, did he?

A: No. He was very calm, very patient, very sure of himself and sure what would happen. Like a customer. Any customer. I was sitting there with my knuckles in my mouth to keep from making a sound. Then Ron fumbled with something in his breast pocket and brought out a wallet and spread it open. He said very seriously: "I hope you'll let me buy things for you, and make life easier for you. A girl and her mother alone always have a rough time," he glanced down at my dress, my best dress, "and I'd be glad to help. The money doesn't mean a thing to me." And all the time he was running a thumb over the bills in his wallet just like one of the customers before he pays. Just like Mr. Dail. The exact same . . .

Q: All right, all right! We'll pick up the questioning later on. The way you're crying, a person would think I'd belted you one. Strike that!

Mill said thoughtfully: "She was in love with rich-boy Ron and, when he offered to buy her, just like one of the customers would, she acted blindly with the knife."

One of Mill's hands stiffened in a fist; he stuck out a forefinger and stabbed it suddenly against his heart.

Banner stared at the finger, then quickly looked away.

Double Jeopardy

Susan Dunlap

"Don't give me excuses. Do it right, damn it! What do you think I'm paying you for?" Wynne slammed down the phone.

I stood in the doorway, still amazed at my sister's authority, despite the fact that she had controlled situations for nearly forty years.

Even now, lying in the hospital, she continued to play the executive. But, after all, she was the first woman in the state to have become senior vice president of a major corporation. I wondered if it was Warren or some other harried assistant who had felt the sting of her tongue this time.

As she looked at me her expression changed from irritation to concern. "Lynne, why are you lurking in the doorway? You're shaking. Come in and tell me what's the matter."

I walked in, a bit unsteadily, and sat on the plastic chair next to the bed. "It happened again."

"What this time?"

I took a deep breath, holding my hands one on top of the other on my lap, trying to calm myself enough to be coherent.

The room was bare—hospital-green curtains pulled back against hospital-green walls. The flowers and plant arrangements had been sent to Wynne's apartment when she had first taken sick leave months ago, but by the time I arrived in the city, they were long dead. Funny how I hesitated to change anything in her apartment, where I, for however long it might be, was only a guest.

Wynne sat propped up on the hospital bed, her hair black and shining, with not a hint of gray.

I looked at her face, at the deceptively fragile smile that had always been strong. Our features were so similar, almost exact, yet no one had ever mixed us up. And Wynne's compact body had always looked forceful where mine had merely seemed small.

She'd changed suddenly when she'd become ill. It was as if her underpinnings had been jerked loose, and she had sped past me on the way to old age.

"Lynne, I'm really worried about you," she said with an anxiety in her voice I hadn't heard in ages. "What happened?"

"Another shot. It just missed my head. If I hadn't stumbled . . ." My hands were shaking.

Wynne leaned forward and reached out with her hands to my own, steadying mine with her own calm. "Have you notified the police?"

"They're no help They take a report and then—nothing. I don't think they believe me. Another hysterical middle-aged woman."

Wynne nodded. "Let's just go through the thing again. I'm used to handling problems—gives me something to think about when I'm on the dialysis machine."

It sounded cold, but that was the way she was now. We'd been apart since college, and emotionally longer than that. Really, I could hardly claim to know her anymore. Our twin-ness had never had that special affinity—secret baby language, intuitively shared joys and apprehensions. In us, the physical resemblance had merely served to point out our very different traits. I had wound up teaching in our home-town grammar school; she, more determined and ambitious, had made her way up in the world of business.

"So?" she said impatiently.

"Someone shot at me three times. If I weren't always tripping and turning my ankle . . ."

"And you have no idea who it might be?"

"None. Who would want to kill me? Why? Really, what difference would it make if I died? Who would care?"

"It would matter to me." She pressed my hands, then drew away. "You're all I have. I wouldn't have asked you to come if you weren't vital to me."

I bit my lip. "There are things . . . I want to say before . . ." But I couldn't say "you die," and Wynne, for all her lack of sentimentality, didn't seem to be able to supply the words for me.

Instead I said, "Wynne, you shouldn't cut yourself off like this."

"I have you. I need someone away from the company."

"But why? Why not let Warren come?"

"No." She spat out the words. "I can't let him see me like this."

She looked all right to me. Better than I was likely to look if I didn't find out who was shooting at me.

Wynne must have divined my thoughts, for she said irritably, "You don't show someone who's after your job how sick you are. I've never told any of them that I'm on the dialysis machine." She shook her head as if to dismiss the unacceptable thought. "I told them it was just one kidney that failed, that I was having it removed." Her face moved into a tenuous smile. "I know all the details from your own operation. So don't say that you never did anything for me."

I didn't know how to answer. Could Wynne really hide the fact that she was dying? Warren had been her assistant for ten years. He had taken over her job as acting senior vice president. I had assumed they were friends, but I guess I didn't understand the nature of friendship in business.

Brusquely, Wynne gestured for me to go on.

Swallowing my annoyance, I reminded myself that she was used to giving orders and now she had no one but me to boss around.

But before I could answer, a nurse came in and with an air of authority that dwarfed even Wynne's, motioned me away as she drew the green curtain in a half oval around the bed.

I walked to the window and looked out, but I didn't want to see the parking lot again. I didn't want to search each bush, behind every car, looking for a sniper. Instead, I turned back toward the room—this small private room, so very impersonal. Even Wynne, with all her power, hadn't the ability to stamp any image of herself onto it. It was merely a holding cell for the dying.

"Just another minute," the nurse called out.

I nodded, realizing as I did so that she couldn't see me behind the curtain.

I wondered if this room held the same horror for Wynne as it did for me. Or more? Or different? Would I ever see this mind-numbing green without thinking of the day I arrived in the city, unnerved by Wynne's sudden insistence that I come, after years of increasingly perfunctory letters. That first day. I sat down and she said she was dying. No, wait, not dying. She had never used that word. It was her doctor who said "dying."

It had been bright and clear that day, too. The sunlight had been cut by the venetian blinds so that pale ribbons sliced across the green wall. And when he told me, the light merged with the green and that numbing green shone and the wall seemed to jump out at me and I couldn't focus, couldn't think about anything but the wall.

Time softens things, but that moment remained hard and bright and brittle.

"Lynne, you keep staring off in the distance. Are you sure you're all right?" The nurse was gone. Wynne was looking at me, her lips turned up in the hint of a smile, but her eyes serious. "Are you still seeing the doctor?"

"Doctor? You mean the psychiatrist at home?"

"Yes."

"Wynne, I wasn't seeing him because I was crazy. It was just therapy. I needed some perspective."

"On?"

"Us," I answered. She looked truly surprised, and I couldn't help but feel stung to realize once more that she, who had influenced every part of my life, was so unaffected by me.

"You were saying, before the nurse came for my spit and polish, who might want to kill you? It's so hard to believe."

I shifted my mind gratefully. Still, where to begin? I was too ordinary—a middle-aged first-grade teacher—to make enemies. If it had been Wynne. . . .

"Well," she said, tightening her lips, "we'll have to examine the possibilities."

I shook my head. "I don't have any money, no insurance other than the teachers' association policy."

"And that goes to Michael?"

"Yes, but Michael's not going to come all the way from

Los Angeles to shoot his mother so he can inherit two thousand dollars and a clapboard house."

"I didn't mean that." She looked momentarily confused, and hurt. "I was just listing the possibilities. You have to do that. You can't let sentiment stand in the way of your goal. I had to learn that long ago. There are plenty of people who have wanted me out of the way."

"But they weren't trying to *murder* you!"

She shrugged. And she watched me.

"Wynne, I'm the one they're trying to kill. No one would kill you now. What would be the point? I mean . . ."

Her face turned white.

"Wynne, we don't have much time! Either of us. Maybe we can't find out who's shooting at me, but at least we can feel like sisters." I paused, then went on. "When you asked me to come here, after all these years, I thought you wanted to close the gap between us." I smiled, heard my voice breaking. "Frankly, I was surprised it mattered to you. It was a shock to realize how much it mattered to me. I . . ."

Her eyes were moist. She looked away. But when she turned back there was no sign of the emotion that had passed.

Startled, I began awkwardly brushing at my hair with my hand, rather than reaching toward my sister, as I'd instinctively wanted to do. I forced my attention back to the question under consideration. Suppose no one did know Wynne was dying. Warren at least had been kept in the dark, or so Wynne thought. I was beginning to wonder if she had accepted it herself. "You're not working," I said. "You don't have any connection with the company now. How could *you* be a threat to anyone?"

The lines in her face hardened. "I know things. When I get out of here, I'm going back. I'll see who's been out to get me. I'll take care of them! I'm too valuable for the company to just forget."

"You what!" I stared at the green wall. Wynne had shoved the death threat to me aside, finding it of less importance than interoffice grudges. I looked at her, wondering what we really meant to each other. In many ways we were so alike. I felt so helpless in the face of her bitterness.

"Who particularly," I asked, "would want to kill *you?*"

"Me?"

"I mean who might mistake me for you? An old lover?"

She half smiled, surprised. "What do you know about me?"

"Only what you've wanted me to know, like always. The lover was just a guess. After all, you're forty years old and single. There must have been men, maybe married . . ."

"You make it all rather melodramatic." She continued to look amused.

"Shooting is melodramatic!"

She didn't reply.

"What about Warren?" I persisted. "Would he kill to keep your job? Would he mistake me for you?"

She looked at me in amazement, as if the possibility were too fantastic to believe. "Lynne, anyone—Warren in particular —who would take the trouble and risk involved in murder, would be a bit more careful than that."

"Maybe they don't know you have an identical twin?"

She sighed, her jaw settling back in a tired frown. "They know. When you've held as important a position as I have, believe me, they know." She paused, then added, "But if you really think that someone is mistaking you for me, maybe you should move out of my apartment. Take a hotel room. I'll pay for it, of course."

I shook my head

Fingering the phone, she said, "Lynne, you haven't made much of a case for this death threat. I don't want to sound unsympathetic, but the truth is that you've always leaned on me. Are you sure that this death thing isn't just a reaction to my own condition? It does happen in twins."

"I think not," I snapped, finally exasperated. "I've been through years of therapy. Our bodies may be identical, but my mind is all my own."

She sat silent.

The awkwardness grew. "Listen Wynne, I know you've got business to take care of. I interrupted your phone call when I came in. I'll see you tomorrow."

She nodded, a tiredness showing in her eyes. But I wasn't out of the room before she picked up the phone.

As I walked down the hall, I thought again, what an amazing person she was. Dying from kidney failure, and she was still barking at subordinates. I wondered about Warren— did he allow her to run things from her hospital room? Did he believe Wynne's story about her condition? Could he think I was she, coming in for treatment? Not likely. If Warren were anything like Wynne, by now he would have a solid grip on the vice presidency. He would have removed any trace of Wynne, and she'd have to fight *him* for the job.

Still, I stopped by the door, afraid to go out.

If Wynne wasn't giving orders to Warren or some other subordinate, whom was she yelling at? "What do you think I'm paying you for?" she had demanded.

She wasn't paying anyone at the company. She wasn't paying any expenses—I was handling those. There was nothing she needed.

Or was there?

My hand went around back to my remaining kidney.

You Can't Be a Little Girl All Your Life

Stanley Ellin

It was the silence that woke her. Not suddenly—Tom had pointed out more than once with a sort of humorous envy that she slept like the dead—but slowly; drawing her up from a hundred fathoms of sleep so that she lay just on the surface of consciousness, eyes closed, listening to the familiar pattern of night sounds around her, wondering where it had been disarranged.

Then she heard the creak of a floorboard—the reassuring creak of a board under the step of a late-returning husband—and understood. Even while she was a hundred fathoms under, she must have known that Tom had come into the room, must have anticipated the click of the bed-light being switched on, the solid thump of footsteps from bed to closet, from closet to dresser—the unfailing routine which always culminated with his leaning over her and whispering, "Asleep?" and her small groan which said yes, she was asleep but glad he was home, and would he please not stay up all the rest of the night working at those papers.

So he was in the room now, she knew, but for some reason he was not going through the accustomed routine, and that was what had awakened her. Like the time they had the cricket, poor thing; for a week it had relentlessly chirped away the dark hours from some hidden corner of the house until she'd got used to it. The night it died, or went off to make a cocoon or whatever crickets do, she'd lain awake for an hour waiting to hear it, and then slept badly after that until she'd got used to living without it.

Poor thing, she thought drowsily, not really caring very much but waiting for the light to go on, the footsteps to move comfortably between bed and closet. Somehow the thought became a serpent crawling down her spine, winding tight around her chest. *Poor thing,* it said to her, *poor stupid thing—it isn't Tom at all!*

She opened her eyes at the moment the man's gloved hand brutally slammed over her mouth. In that moment she saw the towering shadow of him, heard the sob of breath in his throat, smelled the sour reek of liquor. Then she wildly bit down on the hand that gagged her, her teeth sinking into the glove, grinding at it. He smashed his other fist squarely into her face. She went limp, her head lolling half off the bed. He smashed his fist into her face again.

After that, blackness rushed in on her like a whirlwind.

She looked at the pale balloons hovering under the ceiling and saw with idle interest that they were turning into masks, but with features queerly reversed, mouths on top, eyes below. The masks moved and righted themselves. Became faces. Dr. Vaughn. And Tom. And a woman. Someone with a small white dunce cap perched on her head. A nurse.

The doctor leaned over her, lifted her eyelid with his thumb, and she discovered that her face was one throbbing bruise. He withdrew the thumb and grunted. From long acquaintance she recognized it as a grunt of satisfaction.

He said, "Know who I am, Julie?"

"Yes."

"Know what happened?"

"Yes."

"How do you feel?"

She considered that. "Funny. I mean, far away. And there's a buzzing in my ears."

"That was the needle. After we brought you around you went into a real sweet hysteria, and I gave you a needle. Remember that?"

"No."

"Just as well. Don't let it bother you."

It didn't bother her. What bothered her was not knowing the time. Things were so unreal when you didn't know the time. She tried to turn her head toward the clock on the night-table, and the doctor said, "It's a little after six. Almost sunrise. Probably be the first time you've ever seen it, I'll bet."

She smiled at him as much as her swollen mouth would permit. "Saw it last New Year's," she said.

Tom came around the other side of the bed. He sat down on it and took her hand tightly in his. "Julie," he said. "Julie, Julie, Julie," the words coming out in a rush as if they had been building up in him with explosive force.

She loved him and pitied him for that, and for the way he looked. He looked awful. Haggard, unshaven, his eyes sunk deep in his head, he looked as if he were running on nerve alone. Because of her, she thought unhappily, all because of her.

"I'm sorry," she said.

"Sorry!" He gripped her hand so hard that she winced. "Because some lunatic—some animal—!"

"Oh, please!"

"I know. I know you want to shut it out, darling, but you mustn't yet. Look, Julie, the police have been waiting all night to talk to you. They're sure they can find the man, but they need your help. You'll have to describe him, tell them whatever you can about him. Then you won't even have to think about it again. You understand, don't you?"

"Yes."

"I knew you would."

He started to get up but the doctor said, "No, you stay here with her. I'll tell them on my way out. Have to get along, anyhow—these all-night shifts are hard on an old man." He stood with his hand on the doorknob. "When they find him," he said in a hard voice, "I'd like the pleasure—" and let it go at that, knowing they understood.

The big, white-haired man with the rumpled suit was Lieutenant Christensen of the police department. The small, dapper man with the mustache was Mr. Dahl of the district attorney's office. Ordinarily, said Mr. Dahl, he did not take a personal part in criminal investigations, but when it came to—that is, in a case of this kind special measures were called for. Everyone must cooperate fully. Mrs. Barton must cooperate, too. Painful as it might be, she must answer Lieutenant Christensen's questions frankly and without embarrassment. Would she do that?

Julie saw Tom nodding encouragement to her. "Yes," she said.

She watched Lieutenant Christensen draw a notebook and pad from his pocket. His gesture, when he pressed the end of the pen to release its point, made him look as if he were stabbing at an insect.

He said, "First of all, I want you to tell me exactly what happened. Everything you can remember about it."

She told him, and he scribbled away in the notebook, the pen clicking at each stroke.

"What time was that?" he asked.

"I don't know."

"About what time? The closer we can pin it down, the better we can check on alibis. When did you go to bed?"

"At ten thirty."

"And Mr. Barton came home around twelve, so we know it happened between ten thirty and twelve." The lieutenant addressed himself to the notebook, then pursed his lips thoughtfully. "Now for something even more important."

"Yes?"

"Just this. Would you recognize the man if you saw him again?"

She closed her eyes, trying to make form out of that monstrous shadow, but feeling only the nauseous terror of it. "No," she said.

"You don't sound so sure about it."

"But I am."

"How can you be? Yes, I know the room was kind of dark and all that, but you said you were awake after you first heard him come in. That means you had time to get adjusted to the dark. And some light from the streetlamp outside hits your window shade here. You wouldn't see so well under the conditions, maybe, but you'd see something, wouldn't you? I mean, enough to point out the man if you had the chance. Isn't that right?"

She felt uneasily that he was right and she was wrong, but there didn't seem to be anything she could do about it. "Yes," she said, "but it wasn't like that."

Dahl, the man from the district attorney's office, shifted on his feet. "Mrs. Barton," he started to say, but Lieutenant Christensen silenced him with a curt gesture of the hand.

"Now look," the lieutenant said. "Let me put it this way. Suppose we had this man some place where you could see him close up, but he couldn't see you at all. Can you picture that? He'd be right up there in front of you, but he wouldn't even know you were looking at him. Don't you think it would be pretty easy to recognize him then?"

Julie found herself growing desperately anxious to give him the answer he wanted, to see what he wanted her to see; but no matter how hard she tried she could not. She shook her head hopelessly, and Lieutenant Christensen drew a long breath.

"All right," he said, "then is there anything you can tell me about him? How big was he? Tall, short, or medium."

The shadow towered over her. "Tall. No, I'm not sure. But I think he was."

"White or colored?"

"I don't know."

"About how old?"

"I don't know."

"Anything distinctive about his clothes? Anything you might have taken notice of?"

She started to shake her head again, then suddenly remembered. "Gloves," she said, pleased with herself. "He was wearing gloves."

"Leather or wool?"

"Leather." The sour taste of the leather was in her mouth now. It made her stomach turn over.

Click-click went the pen, and the lieutenant looked up from the notebook expectantly. "Anything else?"

"No."

The lieutenant frowned. "It doesn't add up to very much, does it? I mean, the way you tell it."

"I'm sorry," Julie said, and wondered why she was so ready with that phrase now. What was it that *she* had done to feel sorry about? She felt the tears of self-pity start to rise, and she drew Tom's hand to her breast, turning to look at him for comfort. She was shocked to see that he was regarding her with the same expression that the lieutenant wore.

The other man—Dahl—was saying something to her.

"Mrs. Barton," he said, and again, "Mrs. Barton," until she faced him. "I know how you feel, Mrs. Barton, but what I have to say is terribly important. Will you please listen to me?"

"Yes," she said numbly.

"When I talked to you at one o'clock this morning, Mrs. Barton, you were in a state—well, you do understand that I wasn't trying to badger you then. I was working on your behalf. On behalf of the whole community, in fact."

"I don't remember. I don't remember anything about it."

"I see. But you understand now, don't you? And you do know that there's been a series of these outrages in the community during recent years, and that the administration and the press have put a great deal of pressure—rightly, of course—on my office and on the police department to do something about it?"

Julie let her head fall back on the pillow, and closed her eyes. "Yes," she said. "If you say so."

"I do say so. I also say that we can't do very much unless the injured party—the victim—helps us in every way possible. And why won't she? Why does she so often refuse to identify the criminal or testify against him in cases like this? Because she might face some publicity? Because she might have started off by encouraging the man, and is afraid of what he'd say about her on the witness stand? I don't care what the reason is, that woman is guilty of turning a wild beast loose on her helpless neighbors!

"Look, Mrs. Barton. I'll guarantee that the man who did this has a police record, and the kind of offenses listed on it—

well, I wouldn't even want to name them in front of you. There's
a dozen people at headquarters right now looking through all
such records and when they find the right one it'll lead us
straight to him. But after that you're the only one who can help
us get rid of him for keeps. I want you to tell me right now that
you'll do that for us when the time comes. It's your duty. You
can't turn away from it."

"I know. But I didn't see him."

"You saw more than you realize, Mrs. Barton. Now, don't
get me wrong, because I'm not saying that you're deliberately
holding out, or anything like that. You've had a terrible shock.
You want to forget it, get it out of your mind completely. And
that's what'll happen, if you let yourself go this way. So, knowing that, and not letting yourself go, do you think you can describe the man more accurately now?"

Maybe she had been wrong about Tom, she thought, about
the way he had looked at her. She opened her eyes hopefully
and was bitterly sorry she had. His expression of angry bewilderment was unchanged, but now he was leaning forward,
staring at her as if he could draw the right answer from her
by force of will. And she knew he couldn't. The tears overflowed,
and she cried weakly; then magically a tissue was pressed into
her hand. She had forgotten the nurse. The upside-down face
bent over her from behind the bed, and she was strangely con-
soled by the sight of it. All these men in the room—even her
husband—had been made aliens by what had happened to her.
It was good to have a woman there.

"Mrs. Barton!" Dahl's voice was unexpectedly sharp, and
Tom turned abruptly toward him. Dahl must have caught the
warning in that, Julie realized with gratitude; when he spoke
again his voice was considerably softer. "Mrs. Barton, please
let me put the matter before you bluntly. Let me show you
what we're faced with here.

"A dangerous man is on the prowl. You seem to think he
was drunk, but he wasn't too drunk to know exactly where he
could find a victim who was alone and unprotected. He probably had this house staked out for weeks in advance, knowing
your husband's been working late at his office. And he knew

how to get into the house. He scraped this window sill here pretty badly, coming in over it.

"He wasn't here to rob the place—he had the opportunity but he wasn't interested in it. He was interested in one thing, and one thing only." Surprisingly, Dahl walked over to the dresser and lifted the framed wedding picture from it. "This is you, isn't it?"

"Yes," Julie said in bewilderment.

"You're a very pretty young woman, you know." Dahl put down the picture, lifted up her hand mirror, and approached her with it. "Now I want to show you how a pretty young woman looks after she's tried to resist a man like that." He suddenly flashed the mirror before her and she shrank in horror from its reflection.

"Oh, please!" she cried.

"You don't have to worry," Dahl said harshly. "According to the doctor you'll heal up fine in a while. But until then, won't you see that man as clear as day every time you look into this thing? Won't you be able to point him out, and lay your hand on the Bible, and swear he was the one?"

She wasn't sure any more. She looked at him wonderingly, and he threw wide his arms, summing up his case. "You'll know him when you see him again, won't you?" he demanded.

"Yes," she said.

She thought she would be left alone after that, but she was wrong. The world had business with her, and there was no way of shutting it out. The doorbell chimed incessantly. The telephone in the hall rang, was silent while someone took the call, then rang again. Men with hard faces—police officials—would be ushered into the room by Tom. They would duck their heads at her in embarrassment, would solemnly survey the room, then go off in a corner to whisper together. Tom would lead them out, and would return to her side. He had nothing to say. He would just sit there, taut with impatience, waiting for the doorbell or telephone to ring again.

He was seldom apart from her, and Julie, watching him, found herself increasingly troubled by that. She was keeping him from his work, distracting him from the thing that mattered most to him. She didn't know much about his business affairs, but she did know he had been working for months on some very big deal—the one that had been responsible for her solitary evenings at home—and what would happen to it while he was away from his office? She had only been married two years, but she was already well-versed in the creed of the businessman's wife. Troubles at home may come and go, it said, but Business abides. She used to find that idea repellent, but now it warmed her. Tom would go to the office, and she would lock the door against everybody, and there would be continuity.

But when she hesitantly broached the matter he shrugged it off. "The deal's all washed up, anyhow. It was a waste of time. That's what I was going to tell you about when I walked in and found you like that. It was quite a sight." He looked at her, his eyes glassy with fatigue. "Quite a sight," he said.

And sat there waiting for the doorbell or telephone to ring again.

When he was not there, one of the nurses was. Miss Shepherd, the night nurse, was taciturn. Miss Waldemar, the day nurse, talked.

She said, "Oh, it takes all kinds to make this little old world, I tell you. They slow their cars coming by the house, and they walk all over the lawn, and what they expect to see I'm sure I don't know. It's just evil minds, that's all it is, and wouldn't they be the first ones to call you a liar if you told them that to their faces? And children in the back seats! What is it, sweetie? You look as if you can't get comfy."

"I'm all right, thank you," Julie said. She quailed at the thought of telling Miss Waldemar to please keep quiet or go away. There were people who could do that, she knew, but evidently it didn't matter to them how anyone felt about you when you hurt their feelings. It mattered to Julie a great deal.

Miss Waldemar said, "But if you ask me who's really to blame I'll tell you right out it's the newspapers. Just as well the doctor won't let you look at them, sweetie, because they're having a party, all right. You'd think what with Russia and all, there's more worthwhile things for them to worry about, but no, there it is all over the front pages as big as they can make it. Anything for a nickel, that's their feeling about it. Money, money, money, and who cares if children stand there gawking at headlines and getting ideas at their age!

"Oh, I told that right to one of those reporters, face to face. No sooner did I put foot outside the house yesterday when he steps up, bold as brass, and asks me to get him a picture of you. Steal one, if you please! They're all using that picture from your high school yearbook now; I suppose they want something like that big one on the dresser. And I'm not being asked to do him any favors, mind you; he'll pay fifty dollars cash for it! Well, that was my chance to tell him a thing or two, and don't think I didn't. You are sleepy, aren't you, lamb? Would you like to take a little nap?"

"Yes," said Julie.

Her parents arrived. She had been eager to see them, but when Tom brought them into her room the eagerness faded. Tom had always despised her father's air of futility—the quality of helplessness that marked his every gesture—and never tried to conceal his contempt. Her mother, who had started off with the one objection that Tom was much too old for Julie—he was thirty to her eighteen when they married—had ultimately worked up to the point of telling him he was an outrageous bully, a charge which he regarded as a declaration of war.

That foolish business, Julie knew guiltily, had been her fault. Tom, who could be as finicking as an old maid about some things, had raged at her for not emptying the pockets of his jackets before sending them to the tailor, and since she still was, at the time, more her mother's daughter than her husband's wife, she had weepingly confided the episode to her mother over the telephone. She had not made that mistake again, but the damage was done. After that her husband and her parents made up openly hostile camps, while she served as futile emissary between them.

When they all came into the room now, Julie could feel their mutual enmity charging the air. She had wistfully hoped that what had happened would change that, and knew with a sinking heart that it had not. What it came to, she thought resignedly, is that they hated each other more than they loved her. And immediately she was ashamed of the thought.

Her father weakly fluttered his fingers at her in greeting, and stood at the foot of the bed looking at her like a lost spaniel. It was a relief when the doorbell rang and he trailed out after Tom to see who it was. Her mother's eyes were red and swollen; she kept a small, damp handkerchief pressed to her nose. She sat down beside Julie and patted her hand.

"It's awful, darling," she said. "It's just awful. Now you know why I was so much against your buying the house out here, way at the end of nowhere. How are you?"

"All right."

Her mother said, "We would have been here sooner except for grandma. We didn't want her to find out, but some busybody neighbor went and told her. And you know how she is. She was prostrated. Dr. Vaughn was with her for an hour."

"I'm sorry."

Her mother patted her hand again. "She'll be all right. You'll get a card from her when she's up and around."

Her grandmother always sent greeting cards on every possible occasion. Julie wondered mirthlessly what kind of card she would find to fit this occasion.

"Julie," her mother said, "would you like me to comb out your hair?"

"No, thank you, mother."

"But it's all knots. Don't those nurses ever do anything for their money? And where are your dark glasses, darling? The ones you use at the beach. It wouldn't hurt to wear them until that discoloration is gone, would it?"

Julie felt clouds of trivia swarming over her, like gnats. "Please, mother."

"It's all right, I'm not going to fuss about it. I'll make up a list for the nurses when I go. Anyhow, there's something much more serious I wanted to talk to you about, Julie, I mean, while Dad and Tom aren't here. Would it be all right if I did?"

"Yes."

Her mother leaned forward tensely. "It's about—well, it's about what happened. How it might make you feel about Tom now. Because, Julie, no matter how you might feel, he's your husband, and you've always got to remember that. I respect him for that, and you must, too, darling. There are certain things a wife owes a husband, and she still owes them to him even after something awful like this happens. She's duty bound. Why do you look like that, Julie? You do understand what I'm saying, don't you?"

"Yes," Julie said. She had been chilled by a sudden insight into her parents' life together. "But please don't talk about it. Everything will be all right."

"I know it will. If we aren't afraid to look our troubles right in the eye they can never hurt us, can they? And, Julie, before Tom gets back there's something else to clear up. It's about him."

Julie braced herself. "Yes?"

"It's something he said. When Dad and I came in we talked to him a while and when—well, you know what we were talking about, and right in the middle of it Tom said in the most casual way—I mean, just like he was talking about the weather or something—he said that when they caught that man he was going to kill him. Julie, he terrified me. You know his temper, but it wasn't temper or anything like that. It was just a calm statement of fact. He was going to kill the man, and that's all there was to it. But he meant it, Julie, and you've got to do something about it."

"Do what?" Julie said dazedly. "What can I do?"

"You can let him know he mustn't even talk like that. Everybody feels the way he does—we all want that monster dead and buried. But it isn't up to Tom to kill him. He could get into terrible trouble that way! Hasn't there been enough trouble for all of us already?"

Julie closed her eyes. "Yes," she said.

Dr. Vaughn came and watched her walk around the room. He said, "I'll have to admit you look mighty cute in those dark glasses, but what are they for? Eyes bother you any?"

"No," Julie said. "I just feel better wearing them."

"I thought so. They make you look better to people, and they make people look better to you. Say, that's an idea. Maybe the whole human race ought to take up wearing them permanently. Be a lot better for their livers than alcohol, wouldn't it?"

"I don't know," Julie said. She sat down on the edge of the bed, huddled in her robe, its sleeves covering her clasped hands, mandarin style. Her hands felt as if they would never be warm again. "I want to ask you something."

"All right, go ahead and ask."

"I shouldn't, because you'll probably laugh at me, but I won't mind. It's about Tom. He told mother that when they caught the man he was going to kill him. I suppose he was just—I mean, he wouldn't really try to do anything like that, would he?"

The doctor did not laugh. He said grimly, "I think he might try to do something exactly like that."

"To *kill* somebody?"

"Julie, I don't understand you. You've been married to Tom—how long is it now?"

"Two years."

"And in those two years did you ever know him to say he would do something that he didn't sooner or later do?"

"No."

"I would have bet on that. Not because I know Tom so well, mind you, but because I grew up with his father. Every time I look at Tom I see his father all over again. There was a man with Lucifer's own pride rammed into him like gunpowder, and a hair-trigger temper to set it off. And repressed. Definitely repressed. Tom is, too. It's hard not to be when you have to strain all the time, keeping the emotional finger off that trigger. I'll be blunt, Julie. None of the Bartons has ever impressed me as being exactly well-balanced. I have the feeling that if you gave any one of them enough motive for killing, he'd kill, all right. And Tom owns a gun, too, doesn't he?"

"Yes."

"Well, you don't have to look that scared about it," the doctor said. "It would have been a lot worse if we hadn't been warned. This way I can tell Christensen and he'll keep an eye on your precious husband until they've got the man strapped into the electric chair. A bullet's too good for that kind of animal, anyhow."

Julie turned her head away and the doctor placed his finger against her chin and gently turned it back. "Look," he said, "I'll do everything possible to see Tom doesn't get into trouble. Will you take my word for that?"

"Yes."

"Then what's bothering you? The way I talked about putting that man in the electric chair? Is that what it is?"

"Yes. I don't want to hear about it."

"But why? You of all people, Julie! Haven't you been praying for them to find him? Don't you hate him enough to want to see him dead?"

It was like turning the key that unlocked all her misery.

"I do!" she said despairingly. "Oh, yes, I do! But Tom doesn't believe it. That's what's wrong, don't you understand? He thinks it doesn't matter to me as much as it does to him. He thinks I just want to forget all about it, whether they catch the man or not. He doesn't say so, but I can tell. And that makes everything rotten; it makes me feel ashamed and guilty all the time. Nothing can change that. Even if they kill the man a hundred times over it'll always be that way!"

"It will not," the doctor said sternly. "Julie, why don't you use your head? Hasn't it dawned on you that Tom is suffering from an even deeper guilt than yours? That subconsciously he feels a sense of failure because he didn't protect you from what happened? Now he's reacting like any outraged male. He wants vengeance. He wants the account settled. And, Julie, it's his sense of guilt that's tearing you two apart.

"Do you know what that means, young lady? It means you've got a job to do for yourself. The dirtiest kind of job. When the police nail that man you'll have to identify him, testify against him, face cameras and newspapermen, walk through mobs of brainless people dying to get a close look at you. Yes, it's as bad as all that. You don't realize the excitement this mess has stirred up; you've been kept apart from it so far.

But you'll have a chance to see it for yourself very soon. That's your test. If you flinch from it you can probably write off your marriage then and there. That's what you've got to keep in mind, not all that nonsense about things never changing!"

Julie sat there viewing herself from a distance, while the cold in her hands moved up along her arms turning them to gooseflesh. She said, "When I was a little girl I cried if anybody even pointed at me."

"You can't be a little girl all your life," the doctor said.

When the time came, Julie fortified herself with that thought. Sitting in the official car between Tom and Lieutenant Christensen, shielded from the onlooking world by dark glasses and upturned coat collar, her eyes closed, her teeth set, she repeated it like a private *Hail Mary* over and over—until it became a soothing murmur circling endlessly through her mind.

Lieutenant Christensen said, "The man's a janitor in one of those old apartment houses a few blocks away from your place. A drunk and a degenerate. He's been up on morals charges before, but nothing like this. This time he put himself in a spot he'll never live to crawl away from. Not on grounds of insanity, or anything else. We've got him cold."

You can't be a little girl all your life, Julie thought.

The lieutenant said, "The one thing that stymied us was his alibi. He kept telling us he was on a drunk with this woman of his that night when it happened, and she kept backing up his story. It wasn't easy to get the truth out of her, but we finally did. Turns out she wasn't near him that night. Can you imagine lying for a specimen like that?"

You can't be a little girl all your life, Julie thought.

"We're here, Mrs. Barton," the lieutenant said.

The car had stopped before a side door of the headquarters building, and Tom pushed her through it just ahead of men with cameras who swarmed down on her, shouting her name, hammering at the door when it was closed against them. She clutched Tom's hand as the lieutenant led them through long institutional corridors, other men falling into step with them along the way, until they reached another door where Dahl was waiting.

He said, "This whole thing takes just one minute, Mrs. Barton, and we're over our big hurdle. All you have to do is look at the man and tell us yes or no. That's all there is to it. And it's arranged so that he can't possibly see you. You have nothing at all to fear from him. Do you understand that?"

"Yes," Julie said.

Again she sat between Tom and Lieutenant Christensen. The platform before her was brilliantly lighted; everything else was in darkness. Men were all around her in the darkness. They moved restlessly; one of them coughed. The outline of Dahl's sharp profile and narrow shoulders were suddenly etched black against the platform; then it disappeared as he took the seat in front of Julie's. She found that her breathing was becoming increasingly shallow; it was impossible to draw enough air out of the darkness to fill her lungs. She forced herself to breathe deeply, counting as she used to do during gym exercises at school. *In-one-two-three. Out-one-two-three—*

A door slammed nearby. Three men walked onto the platform and stood there facing her. Two of them were uniformed policemen. The third man—the one they flanked—towered over them tall and cadaverous, dressed in a torn sweater and soiled trousers. His face was slack, his huge hand moved back and forth in a vacant gesture across his mouth. Julie tried to take her eyes off that hand and couldn't. Back and forth it went, mesmerizing her with its blind, groping motion.

One of the uniformed policemen held up a piece of paper.

"Charles Brunner," he read loudly. "Age forty-one. Arrests—" and on and on until there was sudden silence. But the hand still went back and forth, growing enormous before her, and Julie knew, quite without concern, that she was going to faint. She swayed forward, her head drooping, and something cold and hard was pressed under her nose. Ammonia fumes stung her nostrils and she twisted away, gasping. When the lieutenant thrust the bottle at her again, she weakly pushed it aside.

"I'm all right," she said.

"But it was a jolt seeing him, wasn't it?"

"Yes."

"Because you recognized him, didn't you?"

She wondered vaguely if that were why. "I'm not sure."

Dahl leaned over her. "You can't mean that, Mrs. Barton! You gave me your word you'd know him when you saw him again. Why are you backing out of it now? What are you afraid of?"

"I'm not afraid."

"Yes, you are. You almost passed out when you saw him, didn't you? Because no matter how much you wanted to get him out of your mind your emotions wouldn't let you. Those emotions are telling the truth now, aren't they?"

"I don't know!"

"Then look at him again and see what happens. Go on, take a good look!"

Lieutenant Christensen said, "Mrs. Barton, if you let us down now, you'll go out and tell the newspapermen about it yourself. They've been on us like wolves about this thing, and for once in my life I want them to know what we're up against here!"

Tom's fingers gripped her shoulder. "I don't understand, Julie," he said. "Why don't you come out with it? He is the man isn't he?"

"Yes!" she said, and clapped her hands over her ears to shut out the angry, hateful voices clamoring at her out of the darkness. "Yes! Yes!"

"Thank God," said Lieutenant Christensen.

Then Tom moved. He stood up, something glinting metallically in his hand, and Julie screamed as the man behind her lunged at it. Light suddenly flooded the room. Other men leaped at Tom and chairs clattered over as the struggle eddied around and around him, flowing relentlessly toward the platform. There was no one on it when he was finally borne down to the floor by a crushing weight of bodies.

Two of the men, looking apologetic, pulled him to his feet, but kept their arms tightly locked around his. Another man handed the gun to Lieutenant Christensen, and Tom nodded at it. He was disheveled and breathing hard, but seemed strangely unruffled.

"I'd like that back, if you don't mind," he said.

"I do mind," said the lieutenant. He broke open the gun, tapped the bullets into his hand, and then, to Julie's quivering relief, dropped gun and bullets into his own pocket. "Mr. Barton, you're in a state right now where if I charged you with attempted murder you wouldn't even deny it, would you?"

"No."

"You see what I mean? Now why don't you just cool off and let us handle this job? We've done all right so far, haven't we? And after Mrs. Barton testifies at the trial Brunner is as good as dead, and you can forget all about him." The lieutenant looked at Julie. "That makes sense, doesn't it?" he asked her.

"Yes," Julie whispered prayerfully.

Tom smiled. "I'd like my gun, if you don't mind."

The lieutenant stood there speechless for the moment, and then laid his hand over the pocket containing the gun as if to assure himself that it was still there. "Some other time," he said with finality.

The men holding Tom released him and he lurched forward and caught at them for support. His face was suddenly deathly pale, but the smile was still fixed on it as he addressed the lieutenant.

"You'd better call a doctor," he said pleasantly. "I think your damn gorillas have broken my leg."

During the time he was in the hospital he was endlessly silent and withdrawn. The day he was brought home at his own insistence, his leg unwieldy in a cast from ankle to knee, Dr. Vaughn had a long talk with him, the two of them alone behind the closed doors of the living-room. The doctor must have expressed himself freely and forcefully. When he had gone, and Julie plucked up the courage to walk into the living-room, she saw her husband regarding her with the look of a man who has had a bitter dose of medicine forced down his throat and hasn't quite decided whether or not it will do him any good.

Then he patted the couch seat beside him. "There's just enough room for you and me and this leg," he said.

She obediently sat down, clasping her hands in her lap.

"Vaughn's been getting some things off his chest," Tom said abruptly. "I'm glad he did. You've been through a rotten experience, Julie, and I haven't been any help at all, have I? All I've done is make it worse. I've been lying to myself about it, too. Telling myself that everything I did since it happened was for your sake, and all along the only thing that really concerned me was my own feelings. Isn't that so?"

"I don't know," Julie said, "and I don't care. It doesn't matter as long as you talk to me about it. That's the only thing I can't stand, not having you talk to me."

"Has it been that bad?"

"Yes."

"But you understand why, don't you? It was something eating away inside of me. But it's gone now, I swear it is. You believe that, don't you, Julie?"

She hesitated. "Yes."

"I can't tell whether you mean it or not behind those dark glasses. Lift them up, and let's see."

Julie lifted the glasses and he gravely studied her face. "I think you do mean it," he said. "A face as pretty as that couldn't possibly tell a lie. But why do you still wear those things? There aren't any marks left."

She dropped the glasses into place and the world became its soothingly familiar, shaded self again. "I just like them," she said. "I'm used to them."

"Well, if the doctor doesn't mind, I don't. But if you're wearing them to make yourself look exotic and dangerous, you'll have to give up. You're too much like Sweet Alice. You can't escape it."

She smiled. "I don't tremble with fear at your frown. Not really."

"Yes, you do, but I like it. You're exactly what Sweet Alice must have been. Demure, that's the word, demure. My wife is the only demure married woman in the world. Yielding, yet cool and remote. A lovely lady wrapped in cellophane. How is it you never became a nun?"

She knew she must be visibly glowing with happiness. It had been so long since she had seen him in this mood. "I almost did. When I was in school I used to think about it a lot. There was this other girl—well, she was really a wonderful person, and she had already made up her mind about it. I guess that's where I got the idea."

"And then what happened?"

"You know what happened."

"Yes, it's all coming back now. You went to your first Country Club dance dressed in a beautiful white gown, with stardust in your hair—"

"It was sequins."

"No, stardust. And I saw you. And the next thing I remember, we were in Mexico on a honeymoon." He put his arm around her waist, and she relaxed in the hard circle of it. "Julie, when this whole bad dream is over we're going there again. We'll pack the car and go south of the border and forget everything. You'd like that, wouldn't you?"

"Oh, very much." She looked up at him hopefully, her head back against his shoulder. "But no bullfights, please. Not this time."

He laughed. "All right, when I'm at the bullfights you'll be sightseeing. The rest of the time we'll be together. Any time I look around I want to see you there. No more than this far away. That means I can reach out my hand and you'll always be there. Is that clear?"

"I'll be there," she said.

So she had found him again, she assured herself, and she used that knowledge to settle her qualms whenever she thought of Brunner and the impending trial. She never mentioned these occasional thoughts to Tom, and she came to see that there was a conspiracy among everyone who entered the house—her family and friends, the doctor, even strangers on business with Tom—which barred any reference to the subject of Brunner. Until one evening when, after she had coaxed Tom into a restless sleep, the doorbell rang again and again with maddening persistence.

Julie looked through the peephole and saw that the man standing outside was middle-aged and tired-looking and carried a worn leather portfolio under his arm. She opened the door with annoyance and said, "Please, don't do that. My husband's not well, and he's asleep. And there's nothing we want."

The man walked past her into the foyer before she could stop him. He took off his hat and faced her. "I'm not a salesman, Mrs. Barton. My name is Karlweiss. Dr. Lewis Karlweiss. Is it familiar to you?"

"No."

"It should be. Up to three o'clock this afternoon I was in charge of the City Hospital for Mental Disorders. Right now I'm a man without any job, and with a badly frayed reputation. And just angry enough and scared enough, Mrs. Barton, to want to do something about it. That's why I'm here."

"I don't see what it has to do with me."

"You will. Two years ago Charles Brunner was institutionalized in my care, and, after treatment, released on my say-so. Do you understand now? I am officially responsible for having turned him loose on you. I signed the document which certified that while he was not emotionally well, he was certainly not dangerous. And this afternoon I had that document shoved down my throat by a gang of ignorant politicians who are out to make hay of this case!"

Julie said incredulously, "And you want me to go and tell them they were wrong? Is that it?"

"Only if you know they *are* wrong, Mrs. Barton. I'm not asking you to perjure yourself for me. I don't even know what legal right I have to be here in the first place, and I certainly don't want to get into any more trouble than I'm already in." Karlweiss looked over her shoulder toward the living-room, and shifted his portfolio from one arm to the other. "Can we go inside and sit down while we talk this over? There's a lot to say."

"No."

"All right, then I'll explain it here, and I'll make it short and to the point. Mrs. Barton, I know more about Charles Brunner than anyone else in the world. I know more about him than he knows about himself. And that's what makes it so hard for me to believe that you identified the right man!"

Julie said, "I don't want to hear about it. Will you please go away?"

"No, I will not," Karlweiss said heatedly. "I insist on being heard. You see, Mrs. Barton, everything Brunner does fits a certain pattern. Every dirty little crime he has committed fits that pattern. It's a pattern of weakness, a constant manifestation of his failure to achieve full masculinity.

"But what he is now charged with is the absolute reverse of that pattern. It was a display of brute masculinity by an aggressive and sadistic personality. It was the act of someone who can only obtain emotional and physical release through violence. That's the secret of such a personality—the need for violence. Not lust, as the Victorians used to preach, but the need for release through violence. And that is a need totally alien to Brunner. It doesn't exist in him. It's a sickness, but it's not his sickness!

"Now do you see why your identification of him hit me and my co-workers at the hospital so hard? We don't know too much about various things in our science yet—I'm the first to admit it—but in a few cases we've been able to work out patterns of personality as accurately as mathematical equations. I thought we had done that successfully with Brunner. I would still think so, if you hadn't identified him. That's why I'm here. I wanted to meet you. I wanted to have you tell me directly if there was any doubt at all about Brunner being the man. Because if there is—"

"There isn't."

"But if there is," Karlweiss pleaded, "I'd take my oath that Brunner isn't guilty. It makes sense that way. If there's the shadow of a doubt—"

"There isn't!"

"Julie!" called Tom from the bedroom. "Who is that?"

Panic seized her. All she could envision then was Brunner as he would walk down the prison steps to the street, as he would stand there dazed in the sunlight while Tom, facing him, slowly drew the gun from his pocket. She clutched Karlweiss's sleeve and half-dragged him toward the door. "Please, go away!" she whispered fiercely. "There's nothing to talk about. Please, go away!"

She closed the door behind him and leaned back against it, her knees trembling.

"Julie, who is that?" Tom called. "Who are you talking to?"

She steadied herself and went into the bedroom. "It was a salesman," she said. "He was selling insurance. I told him we didn't want any."

"You know I don't want you to open the door to any strangers," Tom said. "Why'd you go and do a thing like that?"

Julie forced herself to smile. "He was perfectly harmless," she said.

But the terror had taken root in her now—and it thrived. It was fed by many things. The subpoena from Dahl which Tom had her put into his dresser drawer for safekeeping and which was there in full view every time she opened the drawer to get him somthing. The red circle around the trial date on the calendar in the kitchen which a line of black crosses inched toward, a little closer each day. And the picture in her mind's eye which took many forms, but which was always the same picture with the same ending: Brunner descending the prison steps, or Brunner entering the courtroom, or Brunner in the dank cellar she saw as his natural habitat, and then in the end Brunner standing there, blinking stupidly, his hand moving back and forth over his mouth, and Tom facing him, slowly drawing the gun from his pocket, the gun barrel glinting as it moved into line with Brunner's chest—

The picture came into even sharper focus when Dr. Vaughn brought the crutches for Tom. Julie loathed them at sight. She had never minded the heavy pressure of Tom's arm around her shoulders, his weight bearing her down as he lurched from one room to another, hobbled by the cast. The cast was a hobble, she knew, keeping him tied down to the house; he struggled with it and grumbled about it continually, as if the struggling and grumbling would somehow release him from it. But the crutches were a release. They would take him to wherever Brunner was.

She watched him as he practiced using the crutches that evening, not walking, but supporting himself on them to find his balance, and then she helped him sit down on the couch, the leg in its cast propped on a footstool before him.

He said, "Julie, you have no idea how fed up a man can get, living in pajamas and a robe. But it won't be long now, will it?"

"No."

"Which reminds me that you ought to give my stuff out to the tailor tomorrow. He's a slow man, and I'd like it all ready when I'm up and around."

"All right," Julie said. She went to the wardrobe in the hall and returned with an armful of clothing which she draped over the back of an armchair. She was mechanically going through the pockets of a jacket when Tom said, "Come here, Julie."

He caught her hand as she stood before him. "There's something on your mind," he said. "What is it?"

"Nothing."

"You were never any good at lying. What's wrong, Julie?"

"Still nothing."

"Oh, all right, if that's the way you want it." He released her hand and she went back to the pile of clothing on the armchair, sick with the feeling that he could see through her, that he knew exactly what she was thinking, and must hate her for it. She put aside the jacket and picked up the car coat he used only for driving. Which meant, she thought with a small shudder of realization, that he hadn't worn it since *that* night. She pulled the gloves from its pocket and tossed the coat on top of the jacket.

"These gloves," she said, holding them out to show him. "Where—?"

These gloves, an echo cried out to her. *These gloves,* said a smaller one behind it, and *these gloves, these gloves* ran away in a diminishing series of echoes until there was only deathly silence.

And a glove.

A gray suède glove clotted and crusted with dark-brown stains. Its index finger gouged and torn. Its bitter taste in her mouth. Its owner, a stranger, sitting on the couch, holding out his hand, saying something.

"Give that to me, Julie," Tom said.

She looked at him and knew there were no secrets between them any more. She watched the sweat starting from his forehead and trickling down the bloodless face. She saw his teeth show and his eyes stare as he tried to pull himself to his feet. He failed, and sank back panting.

"Listen to me, Julie," he said. "Now listen to me and take hold of yourself."

"You," she said drunkenly. "It was you."

"Julie, I love you!"

"But it was you. It's all crazy. I don't understand."

"I know. Because it was crazy. That's what it was, I went crazy for a minute. It was overwork. It was that deal. I was killing myself to put it across, and that night when they turned me down I don't know what happened. I got drunk, and when I came home I couldn't find the key. So I came through the window. That's when it happened. I don't know what it was, but it was something exploding in me. Something in my head. I saw you there, and all I wanted to do—I tell you I don't even know why! Don't *ask* me why! It was overwork, that's what it was. It gets to everybody nowadays. You read about it all the time. You know you do, Julie. You've got to be reasonable about this!"

Julie whispered, "If you had told me it was you. If you had only told me. But you didn't."

"Because I love you!"

"No, but you knew how I felt, and you turned that against me. You made me say it was Brunner. Everything you've been doing to me—it was just so I'd say it and say it, until I killed him. You never tried to kill him, at all. You knew I would do it for you. And I would have!"

"Julie, Julie, what does Brunner matter to anybody? You've seen what he's like. He's a degenerate. He's no good. Everybody is better off without people like that around."

She shook her head violently. "But you knew he didn't do it! Why couldn't you just let it be one of those times where they never find out who did it?"

"Because I wasn't sure! Everybody kept saying it was only the shock that let you blank it out of your mind. They kept saying if you tried hard enough to remember, it might all come back. So if Brunner—I mean, this way the record was all straight! You wouldn't have to think about it again!"

She saw that if he leaned forward enough he could touch her, and she backed away a step, surprised she had the strength to do it.

"Where are you going?" Tom said. "Don't be a fool, Julie. Nobody'll believe you. Think of everything that's been said and done, and you'll see nobody would even *want* to believe you. They'll say you're out of your mind!"

She wavered, then realized with horror that she was wavering. "They will believe me!" she cried, and ran blindly out of the house, sobbing as she ran, stumbling when she reached the sidewalk so that she fell on her hands and knees, feeling the sting of the scraped knee as she rose and staggered farther down the dark and empty street. It was only when she was at a distance that she stopped, her heart hammering, her legs barely able to support her, to look at the house. Not hers any more. Just his.

He—all of them—had made her a liar and an accomplice. Each of them for his own reason had done that, and she, because of the weakness in her, had let them. It was a terrible weakness, she thought with anguish—the need to have them always approve, the willingness to always say yes to them. It was like hiding yourself behind the dark glasses all the time, not caring that the world you saw through them was never the world you would see through the naked eye.

She turned and fled toward lights and people. The glasses lay in the street where she had flung them, and the night wind swept dust through their shattered frames.

Mrs. Norris Observes

Dorothy Salisbury Davis

If there was anything in the world Mrs. Norris liked as well as a nice cup of tea, it was to dip now and then into what she called "a comfortable novel." She found it no problem getting one when she and Mr. James Jarvis, for whom she kept house, were in the country. The ladies at the Nyack library both knew and approved her tastes, and while they always lamented that such books were not written any more, nonetheless they always managed to find a new one for her.

But the New York Public Library at Fifth Avenue and Forty-second Street was a house of different entrance. How could a person like Mrs. Norris climb those wide marble steps, pass muster with the uniformed guard, and then ask for her particular kind of book?

She had not yet managed it, but sometimes she got as far as the library steps and thought about it. And if the sun were out long enough to have warmed the stone bench, she sometimes sat a few moments and observed the faces of the people going in and coming out. As her friend Mr. Tully, the detective, said of her, she was a marvelous woman for observing. "And you can take that the way you like, love."

It was a pleasant morning, this one, and having time to spare, Mrs. Norris contemplated the stone bench. She also noticed that one of her shoelaces had come untied; you could not find a plain cotton lace these days, even on a blind man's tray. She locked her purse between her bosom and her arm and began to stoop.

"It's mine! I saw it first!"

A bunioned pump thumped down almost on her toe, and the woman who owned it slyly turned it over on her ankle so that she might retrieve whatever it was she had found. Mrs. Norris was of the distinct opinion that there had been nothing there at all.

"I was only about to tie my shoelace," Mrs. Norris said, pulling as much height as she could out of her dumpy shape.

A wizened, rouged face turned up at her. "Aw," the creature said, "you're a lady. I'll tie the lace for you."

As the woman fumbled at her foot, Mrs. Norris took time to observe the shaggy hair beneath a hat of many summers. Then she cried, "Get up from there! I'm perfectly able to tie my own shoelace."

The woman straightened, and she was no taller than Mrs. Norris. "Did I hear in your voice that you're Irish?"

"You did not! I'm Scots-born." Then remembering Mr. Tully, her detective friend, she added, "But I'm sometimes taken for North of Ireland."

"Isn't it strange, the places people will take you to be from! Where would you say I was born? Sit down for a moment. You're not in a hurry?"

Mrs. Norris thought the woman daft, but she spoke well and softly. "I haven't the faintest notion," she said, and allowed herself to be persuaded by a grubby hand.

"I was born right down there on Thirty-seventh Street, and not nearly as many years ago as you would think. But this town—oh, the things that have happened to it!" She sat a bit too close, and folded her hands over a beaded evening purse. "A friend of mine, an actress, gave this to me." She indicated the purse, having seen Mrs. Norris glance at it. "But there isn't much giving left in this city . . ."

Of course, Mrs. Norris thought. How foolish of her not to have realized what was coming. "What a dreadful noise the buses make," she commented by way of changing the subject.

"And they're all driven by Irishmen," the woman said quite venomously. "They've ruined New York, those people!"

"I have a gentleman friend who is Irish," Mrs. Norris said sharply, and wondered why she didn't get up and out of there.

"Oh, my dear," the woman said, pulling a long face of shock. "The actress of whom I just spoke, you know? She used to be with the Abbey Theatre. She was the first Cathleen Ni Houlihan. Or perhaps it was the second. But she sends me

two tickets for every opening night—and something to wear."
The woman opened her hand on the beaded purse and stroked
it lovingly. "She hasn't had a new play in such a long time."

Mrs. Norris was touched in spite of herself: it was a
beautiful gesture. "Were you ever in the theater yourself?" she
asked.

The old woman looked her full in the face. Tears came to
her eyes. Then she said, "No." She tumbled out a whole series
of no's as though to bury the matter. She's protesting too much,
Mrs. Norris thought. "But I have done many things in my life,"
she continued in her easy made-up-as-you-go fashion. "I have
a good mind for science. I can tell you the square feet of floor
space in a building from counting the windows. On Broadway,
that naked waterfall, you know . . ." Mrs. Norris nodded, remembering the display. "I have figured out how many times the
same water goes over it every night. Oh-h-h, and I've written
books—just lovely stories about the world when it was gracious,
and people could talk to each other even if one of them wasn't
one of those psychiatrists."

What an extraordinary woman!

"But who would read stories like that nowadays?" She cast
a sidelong glance at Mrs. Norris.

"I would!" Mrs. Norris said.

"Bless you, my dear, I knew that the moment I looked
into your face!" She cocked her head, as a bird does at a strange
sound. "Do you happen to know what time it is?"

Mrs. Norris looked at her wrist watch. The woman leaned
close to look also. "A Gruen is a lovely watch," she said. She
could see like a mantis.

"It's time I was going," Mrs. Norris said. "It's eleven-
thirty."

"Oh, and time for me, too. I've been promised a job
today."

"Where?" asked Mrs. Norris, which was quite unlike her,
but the word had spurted out in her surprise.

"It would degrade me to tell you," the stranger said, and
her eyes fluttered.

Mrs. Norris could feel the flush in her face. She almost toppled her new, flowered hat, fanning herself. "I'm sorry," she said. "It was rude of me to ask."

"Would you like to buy me a little lunch?" the woman asked brazenly.

Mrs. Norris got to her feet. "All right," she said, having been caught fairly at a vulnerable moment. "There's a cafeteria across the street. I often go there myself for a bowl of soup. Come along."

The woman had risen with her, but her face had gone awry. Mrs. Norris supposed that at this point she was always bought off—she was not the most appetizing of sights to share a luncheon table with. But Mrs. Norris led the way down the steps at a good pace. She did not begrudge the meal, but she would begrudge the price of it if it were not spent on a meal.

"Wait, madam. I can't keep up with you," the woman wailed.

Mrs. Norris had to stop anyway to tie the blessed shoelace.

Her guest picked at the food, both her taste and her gab dried up in captivity. "It's a bit rich for my stomach," she complained when Mrs. Norris chided her.

Mrs. Norris sipped her tea. Then something strange happened: the cup trembled in her hand. At the same instant there was a clatter of dishes, the crash of glass, the screams of women, and the sense almost, more than the sound, of an explosion. Mrs. Norris's eyes met those of the woman's across from her. They were aglow as a child's with excitement, and she grinned like a quarter moon.

Outside, people began to run across the street toward the library. Mrs. Norris could hear the blast of police whistles, and she stretched her neck, hoping to see better. "Eat up and we'll go," she urged.

"Oh, I couldn't eat now and with all this commotion."

"Then leave it."

Once in the street Mrs. Norris was instantly the prisoner of the crowd, running with it as if she were treading water, frighteningly, unable to turn aside or stem the tide. And lost at once her frail companion, cast apart either by weight or wisdom. Mrs. Norris took in enough breath for a scream which she let go with a piper's force. It made room for her where there had been none before, and from then on she screamed her way to the fore of the crowd.

"Stand back! There's nobody hurt but there will be!" a policeman shouted.

Sirens wailed the approach of police reinforcements. Meanwhile, two or three patrolmen were joined by a few able-bodied passers-by to make a human cordon across the library steps.

"It blew the stone bench fifty feet in the air," Mrs. Norris heard a man say.

"The stone bench?" she cried out. "Why, I was just sitting on it!"

"Then you've got a hard bottom, lady," a policeman growled. He and a companion were trying to hold on to a young man.

Their prisoner gave a twist and came face to face with Mrs. Norris. "That's the woman," he shouted. "That's the one I'm trying to tell you about. Let go of me and ask *her!*"

A policeman looked at her. "This one with the flowers on her hat?"

"That's the one! She looked at her watch, got up and left the package, then ran down the steps, and the next thing . . ."

"Got up and left what, young man?" Mrs. Norris interrupted.

"The box under the bench," the young man said, but to one of the officers.

"A box under the bench?" Mrs. Norris repeated.

"How come you were watching her?" the officer said.

"I wasn't especially. I was smoking a cigarette . . ."

"Do you work in the library?"

No doubt he answered, but Mrs. Norris's attention was suddenly distracted, and by what seemed like half the police force of New York City.

"I have a friend, Jasper Tully, in the District Attorney's office," she declared sternly.

"That's fine, lady," a big sergeant said. "We'll take a ride down there right now." Then he bellowed at the top of his lungs, "Keep the steps clear till the Bomb Squad gets here."

In Jasper Tully's office, Mrs. Norris tried to tell her interrogators about the strange little woman. But she knew from the start that they were going to pay very little attention to her story. Their long experience with panhandlers had run so true to pattern that they would not admit to any exception.

And yet Mrs. Norris felt sure she had encountered the exception. For example, she had been cleverly diverted by the woman when she might have seen the package. The woman had put her foot down on nothing—Mrs. Norris was sure of that. She remembered having looked down at her shoelace, and she would have seen a coin had there been one at her feet—Mrs. Norris was a woman who knew the color of money. Oh, it was a clever lass, that other one, and there was a fair amount of crazy hate in her. Mrs. Norris was unlikely to forget the venom she had been so ready to spew on the Irish.

She tried to tell them. But nobody had to button Annie Norris's lip twice. It was not long until they wished Jasper Tully a widower's luck with her, and went back themselves to the scene of the blast.

Mr. Tully offered to take her home.

"No, I think I'll walk and cogitate, thank you," she said.

"Jimmie gives you too much time off," Tully muttered. He was on close terms with her employer.

"He gives me the time I take."

"Is he in town now?"

"He is, or will be tonight. He'll be going full dress to the theater. It's an opening night."

"Aren't you going yourself?"

Mrs. Norris gave it a second's thought. "I might," she said.

The detective took a card from his pocket and wrote down a telephone number. "You can reach me through this at all hours," he said. "That's in case your cogitating gets you into any more trouble."

When he had taken her to the office door, Mrs. Norris

looked up to his melancholy face. "Who was Cathleen Ni Houlihan?"

Tully rubbed his chin. "She wasn't a saint exactly, but I think she was a living person . . . How the hell would I know? I was born in the Bronx!" A second later he added, "There was a play about her, wasn't there?"

"There was," said Mrs. Norris. "I'm glad to see you're not as ignorant as you make yourself out to be."

"Just be sure you're as smart as you think you are," Tully said, "if you're off to tackle a policeman's job again."

He had no faith in her, Mrs. Norris thought, or he wouldn't let her do it.

All afternoon she went over the morning's incidents in her mind. As soon as Mr. Jarvis left the apartment for dinner and the theater, she went downtown herself. The evening papers were full of the bombing, calling it the work of a madman. The mechanism had been made up of clock parts, and the detonating device was something as simple as a pin. It was thought possibly to have been a hatpin.

Well!

And there was not a mention of her in any account. The police were obviously ashamed of themselves.

Mrs. Norris took as her place of departure Forty-sixth Street and Seventh Avenue. Turning her back on the waterfall atop the Broadway building, she walked toward Shubert Alley. Anyone who could even guess at the number of times the same water went over the dam must have looked at it at least as often. And Cathleen Ni Houlihan—no stranger to the theater had plucked that name out of the air.

The beggars were out in droves: the blind, the lame, and the halt. And there were those with tin cups who could read the date in a dead man's eye.

Mrs. Norris was early, and a good thing she was. Sightseers were already congesting the sidewalk in front of the theater. New York might be the biggest city in the world, but to lovers of the stage a few square feet of it was world enough on an opening night.

She watched from across the street for five minutes, then ten, with the crowd swelling and her own hopes dwindling. Then down the street from Eighth Avenue, with a sort of unperturbed haste, came the little beggar-woman. She wore the same hat, the same ragged coat and carried the same beaded purse.

And she also carried a box about six inches by six which she carefully set down on the steps of a fire exit.

Mrs. Norris plunged across the street and paused again, watching the beggar, fascinated in spite of herself. Round and round one woman she walked, looking her up and down, and then she scouted another. The women themselves were well-dressed out-of-towners by their looks, who had come to gape at the celebrated first nighters now beginning to arrive. When the little panhandler had made her choice of victims, she said, and distinctly enough for Mrs. Norris to hear:

"That's Mrs. Vanderhoff arriving now. Lovely, isn't she? Oh, dear, that's not her husband with her. Why, that's Johnson Tree—the oil man! You're not from Texas, are you, dear?"

Mrs. Norris glanced at the arrivals. It was her own Mr. Jarvis and his friend. A Texas oil man indeed! The woman made up her stories to the fit of her victims! She was an artist at it.

Mrs. Norris edged close to the building and bent down to examine the box. She though she could hear a rhythmic sound. She could, she realized—her own heartbeat.

"Leave that box alone!"

Mrs. Norris obeyed, but not before she had touched, had actually moved, the box. It was empty, or at least as light as a dream, and the woman had not recognized her. She was too busy spinning a tale. Mrs. Norris waited it out. The woman finally asked for money and got it. She actually got paper money! Then she came for the box.

"Remember me?" Mrs. Norris said.

The woman cocked her head and looked at her. "Should I?"

"This morning on the Public Library steps," Mrs. Norris prompted.

The wizened face brightened. "But of course! Oh, and there's something I wanted to talk to you about. I saw you speaking to my young gentleman friend—you know, in all that excitement?"

"Oh, yes," Mrs. Norris said, remembering the young man who had pointed her out to the police.

"Isn't he a lovely young man? And to have had such misfortune."

"Lovely," Mrs. Norris agreed.

"You know, he had a scholarship to study atomic science and *those* people did him out of it."

"Those people?"

"All day long you can see them going in and out, in and out, carting books by the armful. Some of them have beards. False, you know. And those thick glasses—I ask you, who would be fooled by them? Spies! Traitors! And *they* can get as many books as they want."

"Oh, *those* people," Mrs. Norris said understandingly.

"And my poor young friend. They won't even give him a library card, and after I wrote him such a nice reference."

"Do you know where he lives?" Mrs. Norris said as casually as she could.

"No. But I know where he works. He fixes watches for a jeweler on Forty-seventh Street. I walked by there once and saw him working in the window. If you wait here for me, I'll walk over and show you the place tonight. He's not there now, of course, but I'm sure he'll be there in the morning. I hope you can help him."

"I'll try," Mrs. Norris said. A watchmaker.

The warning buzzer sounded within the theater. The lights flickered.

"Excuse me for a moment," the woman said, and picked up the box. "I've brought some violets for the leading lady. I want to take them in before curtain. Wouldn't it be nice if she invited us to see the play? I shan't accept unless she invites both of us."

Mrs. Norris followed the woman down the alleyway and then hung back as she handed the box in at the stage door. The woman waited and, observing Mrs. Norris, nodded to her confidently. Mrs. Norris was only reasonably sure the box was empty. She was beset by doubts and fears. Was there such a thing as a featherweight bomb? The doorman returned and put something in the woman's hand. She bowed and scraped and came along, tucking whatever she'd got into her purse.

With Mr. Jarvis in the theater, Mrs. Norris was not going to take any chances. "Wait for me out front," she said. "I want to have a look in there myself."

"Too late, too late," the woman crowed.

Mrs. Norris hurried.

"No one's allowed backstage now, ma'am," the doorman said.

"That box the old woman gave you . . ." It was sitting on a desk almost within her reach. "It could be dangerous."

"Naw. She's harmless, that old fraud. There's nothing in it but tissue paper. She comes round every opening night. 'Flowers for Miss Hayes,' or Miss Tandy or whoever. The company manager gives her a dollar for luck. I'm sorry, ma'am, but you'll have to go now."

Mrs. Norris beat a dignified retreat. The old woman was nowhere to be seen. But a watchmaker on Forty-seventh Street . . . Forty-seventh Street was also the diamond center of New York. What a lovely place for a leisurely walk-through with Mr. Tully!

Invitation
Josh Pachter **to a Murder**

The envelope was edged in black.

Curious, Branigan set the rest of his stack of mail aside and reached for the jeweled souvenir dagger he used as a letter opener. He slit the envelope open carefully, and slid out a square of heavy cream-colored notepaper.

It, too, was black-rimmed.

It was a formal, embossed announcement, and the raised letters read:

ELEANOR MADELINE ABBOTT
ANNOUNCES THE IMPENDING

MURDER

OF HER HUSBAND, GREGORY ELIOT ABBOTT,
AT THEIR HOME,
217A WEST 86TH STREET, NEW YORK CITY, NEW YORK,
BETWEEN THE HOURS OF
NINE THIRTY AND ELEVEN O'CLOCK
ON THE EVENING OF DECEMBER 16, 1971.
YOU ARE CORDIALLY INVITED TO ATTEND.

Branigan read through the invitation twice, then set it down on his desk and picked up the envelope it had arrived in. Heavy, cream-colored, black-bordered. Addressed in a precise feminine hand to *Chief Inspector Lawrence A. Branigan, New York Police Department, 240 Centre Street, New York, New York*. No zip code. No return address. Postmarked New York City.

Branigan picked up the announcement and read it again.

Eleanor Abbott, he mused. Mrs. Eleanor Madeline Abbott . . .

He reached for his telephone and began dialing.

It was still snowing when Branigan walked up the brownstone's eight steps and rang the bell. The door was opened almost immediately by a large man in butler's livery, black from head to toe except for the thin white triangle of his shirtfront.

"Inspector Branigan?" he asked, his voice surprisingly soft.

Branigan, nodding, pulled the black-rimmed invitation from his overcoat pocket and handed it over. Behind the butler, all he could see was a dimly lit corridor stretching back into darkness.

"Thank you, sir," the man said. "All the others have already arrived. Would you follow me, please?"

The others? Branigan thought, as he stepped into the house. *All the others?*

Halfway down the corridor, before a large wooden door, they stopped. The butler twisted the ornate brass knob and pushed the door open. "In here, sir," he said. "Mrs. Abbott is expecting you. May I take your coat?"

The room was dim, too. Like the corridor, like the butler, like the night. Thick damask curtains hid what might have been windows; subdued lighting trickled down from small panels set into the ceiling.

It was a large, plain room. No rugs or carpeting on the simple parquet floor, no paintings, nothing personal hanging from the dark, gloomy walls. There was nothing extra in the room, nothing decorative. Every item, every piece of furniture, was there because it was functional, because it was needed.

Like the double bed standing with its head flush to the far wall.

There was a man on the bed, propped up almost to a sitting position. His body was invisible, swathed to the neck in heavy blankets, but his wrinkled white face almost shone through the dimness.

Gregory Abbott.

At first Branigan thought he was too late, thought Abbott was already dead: the pale gray eyes, half covered by deeply creased lids, stared emptily across the room; the ravaged face, wreathed by wisps of snowy hair, was perfectly still. No smile of welcome, no frown of disapproval crossed the old man's thin, bloodless lips.

Then he noticed the slight rise and fall of the blankets, and separated the faint sound of labored breathing from the steady ticking of the clock that hung on the wall several feet above Abbott's head.

Branigan sighed with relief, and looked away.

To his right, a high-backed chair stood against the side wall. A young woman was poised lightly on the edge of the chair, her hands folded delicately in her lap. She wore a long black gown, simple and yet striking, set off by a single strand of pearls around her neck and a sparkling diamond on the fourth finger of her left hand. Branigan had learned that Eleanor Abbott was an attractive woman. He saw now that she was beautiful: as beautiful and, somehow, as cold as the December night outside.

Across the room from her, a dozen identical chairs stood side by side. The seat closest to Branigan was empty, obviously his, but each of the others was occupied. And, even in the dimness of the room, he recognized the eleven faces that were turned toward him, waiting.

Ryan was there, from the Los Angeles Police Department, and DiNapoli from San Francisco, both officers he had worked with in the past. There was Coszyck, who ran a local detective agency; Huber, an insurance investigator from Boston he had worked with once before; Braun, a private eye based in Cleveland, whose picture he had recently seen featured in a national news magazine. There was Devereaux, a Federal District Court justice from New Orleans; Gould, a St. Louis appellate court judge; even Walter Fox, "the old Fox," as he was known, just retired from the bench of the United States Supreme Court. Maunders, Detroit's crusading District Attorney, was there, and Szambel from Pittsburgh, and Carpenter, who had left Szambel's staff to become D.A. of Baltimore.

The eleven men looked at him closely, and Branigan could see that most of them recognized him, too.

They were fourteen people in all, lining the walls of the nearly dark, nearly quiet room, the silence broken only by Gregory Abbott's uneven breathing and by the inexorable ticking of the clock.

Finally, Branigan's eyes rested on the plain deal table in

the center of the room, and on the five objects that sat on its surface: a long-bladed kitchen knife, a thin strand of wire with a wooden grip attached to each end, a length of iron pipe, an amber bottle labeled with a grinning skull and crossbones, and a revolver that glinted dully in the dim light of the room.

It was Miss Scarlet, Branigan found himself thinking. *In the conservatory, with the candelabra.*

The image should have been funny, but it wasn't. It frightened him, frightened him deeply, and he was not sure why.

He looked back at the woman in the black gown.

She was smiling at him, and Branigan saw that she knew what he was thinking.

She's playing with us, he thought. *She set it up like this, and now she's playing with us. It's just a game to her.*

A game with the highest stakes imaginable. A game where the life of the old man in the double bed goes to the winner.

Okay, Branigan thought. *Okay, I'm ready.*

He took a step forward, into the room, and eased the door shut behind him.

Eleanor Abbott stood up. A lock of hair drifted down across her eyes as she rose, and she carelessly brushed it back with the tips of her fingers.

"Good evening, Inspector Branigan," she said. "If you'll take your seat, we can get started." She spoke softly, pleasantly, almost in a whisper, yet her voice carried firmly across the room.

It was a good voice, Branigan decided. It suited her.

He moved to the empty chair at the end of the row of twelve, and sat.

"Thank you," she said. "And thank you for coming. I want to thank *all* of you for being here tonight. I knew that *you* would come, Inspector, and you, Mr. Coszyck, since both of you live and work right here in New York. And I was confident that my invitation would pique your curiosities, Mr. Huber and Mr. Carpenter, enough to get you to make the trip to town. But most of the rest of you, though, I have to admit that your presence comes as a very welcome surprise. Some of you had to travel great distances to get here; your dedication to the protection of human life impresses me. And especially you, Mr. Justice Fox, I want to —"

"Come off it, young lady!" Fox said hoarsely. "Why I showed up here tonight doesn't make a damn bit of difference. What I want to know is why you sent me that—that incredible invitation!"

"Why did I invite you?" She smiled at him, the same warm smile she had already used once on Branigan. "I'm not a liar, sir. I invited you here—I invited all twelve of you gentlemen, twelve of this country's most eminent and respected legal and law-enforcement minds—I invited you here to witness a murder."

She paused, then—paused dramatically, Branigan realized with a start. He glanced down the row of his colleague's faces and saw eleven pairs of eyes fixed, unwavering, on Eleanor Abbott. Only the old man in the bed was not looking at her; his blank eyes never moved from an invisible spot on the door across the room.

"But first," the woman went on, "I want to give you just a little bit of personal history. I was born in Philadelphia in 1945, and—"

"You were born on *Thursday,* September the thirteenth, 1945," Braun broke in, "and not in Philadelphia, you were born in Essington, which is a few miles outside the city limits. I guarantee that every one of us has looked very carefully into your personal history, Mrs. Abbott, so why don't you cut the crap and get to the point?"

"The point," she said slowly. "I *am* getting to the point, Mr. Braun. I know that you've all done your homework, and I hope you'll all be willing to let me tell this in my own way."

She looked around her and smiled again. "You can see that this means quite a lot to me. I'll try not to take up more of your time than I have to."

That's one for her, Branigan thought. *This is her party, and she knows it.*

"Go ahead, Mrs. Abbott," he said. "Do it your way."

She turned to him and nodded and said "Thank you." Her leaving off the "Inspector" at the end of it made it a personal statement, and he thought for a moment that he would like to call her Eleanor.

And then she turned again, faced the old man in the bed and looked through him.

"I came to New York about five years ago," she said, "when I was twenty-one. The first two years I was here, I must have lived in half a dozen different tiny little apartments around town; I worked at three or four different silly little jobs. I made sandwiches in a delicatessen. I was a secretary for a few weeks, and not a very good one. I worked in a record store. One time I applied to a couple of the airlines, trying to get into stewardess school, but none of them were hiring.

"Three years ago, I was waiting tables at a little Italian restaurant down in the Village; Greenwich Village. One night—I can tell you what night it was; it was October nineteenth, 1968—that night, Gregory came in for dinner with some woman he'd been going out with and another couple."

She closed her eyes, and it was a moment before she went on. "I served them their dinner, they ate, they left, I never really noticed them. Then, a few hours later, I got off work, and Gregory was waiting for me outside. I don't know what he did with his girlfriend, but there he was. It was just like a movie: Gregory Abbott's got six million dollars in the bank, and he's leaning up against a parking meter with his grubby old hat on the back of his head and a beautiful bunch of flowers he'd picked up somewhere, at that hour, in his arms, and he's waiting for *me*. That was Gregory. That was the way he was.

"We got married six months later, a year and a half ago. It turned out he loved me." She opened her eyes and faced them. "It turned out I loved him, too."

"He was thirty-five years older than you were!"

"He still *is* thirty-five years older than I am. I thought it didn't matter." She let her eyes close again before going on. "I was wrong," she said. "It does matter. One year ago today, Gregory and I were staying with some friends in Aspen. I ski very badly, Gregory hadn't skied before at all, but they were very good friends and we were having a wonderful time. Late in the afternoon, Gregory said he felt practiced enough to try a run down one of the more advanced slopes. I—I remember thinking it wasn't a very good idea, but he was so full of energy, so full of life. . . ."

The room seemed subtly brighter, Branigan thought, and before he could wonder why he knew it was her face. *She looks as white as the snow must have been,* he told himself, and then was irritated by the thought.

"He fell," Eleanor Abbott said. "He lost his balance half-way down and fell. I was coming down behind him, I saw it happen, and there was nothing I could do. We got the ski patrol to bring him down the rest of the way. They had an ambulance waiting, and I rode to the hospital with him. The doctors said he had a massive coronary. He was in critical condition for more than a week.

"He pulled through, though. He survived." The color flushed back into her face, a violent red. "If you can call the way it left him survival. He's totally paralyzed. He can't see or hear. After it happened, I spent two hysterical months trying to get him to blink an *eye* for me, to show me it's just something gone wrong with his body, to tell me that somewhere in there *he* is okay. There was no response. The doctors tell me he is no longer able to think."

"Mrs. Abbott," Maunders said, softly.

She looked up. "It's been a year, now. He doesn't get any better or any worse. The doctors tell me there is no chance that he will ever recover, they hold out no hope at all. They *do* think, though, that with the proper medical care and treatment they can keep his *body* alive for ten more years, or even longer."

She said it bitterly, angrily, and for an instant Branigan found that he shared her anger.

"I'm not going to let them do that," she said. "Gregory Abbott is dead. That—that *thing* in the bed there is not my husband. My husband died a year ago today."

There was something new in her voice now, layered over the bitterness: something insistent, almost hypnotic. They stared at her, all of them, as motionless as the empty old man in the double bed.

"I loved my husband," she told them. "Out of my love for

him, I feel that there's one last thing I have to do for him. I have to put an end to that horror the doctors say is still alive, that terrible thing that *I* know is Gregory's corpse. I want to give him what the doctors have refused to let him have, this last year. I want to let him rest."

"And of course you don't give a damn about the six million dollars," Gould snapped at her. It was, somehow, a shocking statement, and it seemed natural for her just to gaze at him in silence, until he backed away from it and said, "No. No, I guess you don't. I'm sorry."

"The money is already mine, Mr. Gould," she said. "Gregory can't use it any more. And you're right, I don't give a damn about it. The only thing I give a damn about right now is my husband. That's why I'm going to kill him."

There, Branigan thought. *That's it. That's what I came to hear her say.* And then he frowned, asking himself why, now that he had heard her say it, the words surprised him.

"Just a minute, now," Ryan began, but she smiled at him and cut him off. "I know, Captain," she said gently. "I'm talking about murder, and murder is against the law. That's the *second* reason I invited the twelve of you here tonight: I wanted to give the law a fair chance to stop me. If you can, if you can keep what I intend to happen here from happening, then I give you my word that I'll never try anything like this again; I'll leave Gregory's body to his doctors and let them do what they like with it. But I want to warn you: you are not going to stop me. I am going to murder the miniscule amount of my husband the doctors have succeeded in keeping alive, tonight, in this room, within the next hour. It's now"—she turned her head to glance at the clock on the wall—"It is now ten o'clock. By eleven, in one hour, even the doctors will agree that Gregory Abbott is dead."

No one spoke. The woman in the long black gown sat down to silence, except for the whisper of her husband's breathing and the steady ticking of the clock hanging over his bed.

The twelve men looked at each other, at Eleanor Abbott, at the old man. They sat without speaking, spellbound, waiting, not quite sure what it was they should be doing, not at all sure there was anything they *could* do to prevent the murder they had been invited to witness.

They sat until ten minutes had passed, until Eleanor Abbott rose, walked quickly to the table of weapons in the center of the room, and picked up the amber bottle of poison.

Then they moved, and strong hands grabbed her from both sides before she could step away from the table. Branigan pulled the bottle away from her, and he and Coszyck led her back to her chair. She sat willingly, and they went back to their own seats without a word.

What the hell is she up to? Branigan thought. She *can't possibly imagine we'll let her get near him. What does she think is going on?*

At 10:20, she rose again. She was halfway to the table when Branigan and Coscyck stopped her, turned her around, and put her back in her chair.

This time they stayed with her, one on either side.

And still the old man's breathing and the ticking of the clock were the only sounds in the room. There was a moment when Carpenter put a hand to his mouth and coughed softly: Eleanor Abbott seemed not to notice and Gregory Abbott stared ahead vacantly; most of the rest of them glared at Carpenter, and he turned away, embarrassed.

At 10:30, Huber jumped up and moved impatiently to the old man's bedside. He went down to his hands and knees and carefully examined the floor beneath the bed and the bed itself. As he straightened up, dusting off the legs of his trousers, Braun and Devereaux looked at each other and got up and joined him. They ranged themselves around the three open sides of the bed, watching Abbott and his wife and the clock uneasily.

At 10:40, Eleanor Abbott suddenly stood, but Branigan and Coszyck clamped firm hands on her shoulders and forced her back into her chair.

Again, not a word was said.

The thin red second hand of the clock swept around and around as the minute hand labored slowly up the numbered face. DiNapoli glanced from the clock to his wrist, then quickly back at the clock. He scowled impatiently and adjusted his watch so the two timepieces were synchronized.

At 10:50 Maunders and Fox stood up together, grim-faced, and stepped to the table of weapons. The old Fox, his arthritic fingers quivering slightly, picked up the revolver. He broke open the cylinder, emptied out the cartridges and pocketed them, snapped the cylinder shut and placed the gun back on the table.

At 10:55, Branigan and Coszyck rested their hands lightly on Mrs. Abbott's shoulders.

Devereaux, at Abbott's bedside, pulled a handkerchief from his hip pocket and wiped beads of moisture from his forehead.

The old man on the bed breathed weakly, in and out, in and out, and the blankets piled over him rose and fell almost imperceptibly.

At 10:57 Gould stood up fitfully. He peered around the room and saw that there was nowhere left for him to go, and flung himself back into his chair.

It was 10:58. They tensed.

Huber and Braun and Devereaux inched closer to the old man's bed. Branigan and Coszyck tightened their grips on Eleanor Abbott's shoulders. Maunders and Fox braced themselves, leaning towards her as if defying her to seize one of the weapons on the table. Even the five men still seated—Szambel and Carpenter, DiNapoli, Gould, and Ryan—found themselves on the edges of their chairs, ready to spring into action.

But as the clock on the wall ticked loudly and its minute hand crawled closer and closer to the twelve, Eleanor Abbott sat calmly on her high-backed chair, and did not move.

Just before 10:59, Gregory Eliot Abbott's wrinkled eyelids flickered and closed, and his shallow breathing stopped.

"Gentlemen!" Eleanor Abbott's voice shot through the uproar. "If you'll go back to your seats and calm down, I'll explain."

They obeyed her.

She stood by the side of her chair, watching them, her full lips turned slightly upward.

"I warned you," she said. "I told you I was going to kill him, and I did."

"How?" Huber demanded.

Her smile broadened.

"Gregory's accident did serious damage to his heart, Mr. Huber, weakened it to a point where it was no longer strong enough to function normally by itself. What's kept it going all year has been medication, a heart stimulant that has to be administered at *very* regular intervals."

Branigan's eyes went wide. She waited, though, until Maunders saw it, and Szambel, and DiNapoli.

"The stimulant," she went on, pointing to the table of weapons, "is in that bottle. It's an incredibly powerful drug, which makes it incredibly dangerous if taken by a person with a normal heart. That's why the bottle is labeled with a skull and crossbones: even a small dose would make a healthy heart speed up so enormously that it could actually burn itself out. But Gregory needed that stimulant to make *his* heart beat normally, and he needed it frequently. He was due for a dose of it at ten minutes past ten this evening. I got up and tried to give it to him, but *you* stopped me."

"You said it was poison!" Coszyck rasped.

"I said no such thing. You *assumed* it was poison, and it *would* have been if *you* had swallowed it—but it was medicine for Gregory, and it was keeping him alive. I tried to give it to him, I tried three times, and each time I tried, you and Inspector Branigan chose to stop me. Without it, Gregory's heart just wasn't strong enough to go on beating, and so he died."

And so he died, Branigan thought. *I took the bottle out of her hands myself, and so he died.*

The twelve criminologists were silent.

Until, "Well?" Ryan said, his voice thick.

"Well," Eleanor Abbott told them, "you've got two choices. You can arrest me and accuse me of murdering my husband, but I'd like you to stop and think about that for a second. After all, gentlemen, *I* tried to give Gregory his medicine. *You* are the ones who stopped me, and caused his death. If you look at it that way, then *you* killed him, not me. I might get slapped on the wrist for not telling you what was in the bottle an hour ago, but once it gets out that you all sat back and let this happen, you men will be ruined. Your careers will be over."

"She's right," Braun said heavily. "With a story like this, there isn't a jury in the country that could convict her of murder."

"And we'd be sunk," Carpenter added. "I don't think anyone would *dare* to try and make out any kind of a case against us, but the publicity would rip us to pieces. It would destroy us."

The old Fox cleared his throat nervously.

"You said we had *two* possible choices," he reminded her.

"Yes, I did. I've gotten what I wanted, now: a release for Gregory. Is that such a terrible thing to have done? Do you really think he was better off the way he was, in that empty state that medicine and the law agreed was 'alive'? You can turn me in and see where it gets you, gentlemen—or you can work with me, and help me to get away with it."

"You're asking us to help you get away with murder!" Szambel protested.

She held up a hand.

"No, Mr. Szambel, I'm not *asking* you for anything. Arrest me and ruin yourselves, or help to protect me. The choice is entirely yours."

"I can't!" Devereaux cried. "I've spent forty years *upholding* the law. How can I turn around now and make a mockery of it?"

"We've got to," DiNapoli muttered. "She's got us over a barrel. There's no other way out."

"Forget it," Maunders grumbled. "Even if we wanted to, it'd be impossible. We'd never get away with it."

"The twelve of *us*?" Judge Gould chuckled grimly. "Don't be ridiculous! Who'd ever even *think* of challenging us?"

Branigan made the decision for them. "We'll *all* have to discuss it," he said.

She waved a hand at them and turned away.

They gathered in together and talked. Across the room, Eleanor Abbott was unable to make out individual voices or words, but she listened absently, confidently, to the meaningless hum, smiled at explosions of obvious protest, grinned at the eventual murmurs of agreement.

When they finally became silent, she turned to face them. They were staring at her.

"Gentlemen of the jury," she said, mocking them in her triumph, "have you reached a verdict?"

And Branigan stood up. There was a strange light in his eyes, a light that Eleanor Abbott could not have known, a light that had never been there before.

"We have," he said clearly.

And stopped, waiting.

For a moment she was confused, and then she realized what he wanted and completed the ritual: "How do you find?"

"We find the defendant guilty of murder in the first degree, as charged."

Her smile faded.

"What?" she asked him, not understanding it at first. "What do you mean?"

But when Branigan moved to the table of weapons in the center of the room and picked up the amber bottle and came toward her, she understood.

The Ransom
of Retta Chiefman
Stanley Cohen

They watched her get out of the taxi, pay the fare, and hurry into Bergdorf Goodman. They quickly told their own cabbie to stop and then climbed out. "You go in and keep an eye on her," Harry said. "I'll stay out here."

"Why don't you go in and let me take the outside watch? I don't know how to act in a place like that."

"Just act natural. Act like you might wanta buy something. But don't let her notice you. Now move!"

Bert walked uneasily across the street and into the store. He spotted her in the shoe department, trying on some sandals. A solicitous young salesman was waiting on her. When she held out her foot and shook her head decisively, the salesman jumped up and hurried into the back, reappearing a moment later with three more boxes. Bert circled the shoe department and came to a good vantage point by a rack of expensive blouses.

"Can I help you with anything?" An elderly woman, tall, slim, bluish gray hair, elegantly dressed. She looked at him disdainfully. He obviously didn't belong, despite his suit and tie.

"Just kinda shoppin' around," Bert said. He lifted a blouse off the rack and held it up by the hanger. After looking at it with great aplomb, he placed it back on the rack. "If I see somethin' I like, I'll let ya' know."

"Please do." She walked away.

Bert took another blouse off the rack. He delicately examined the hem of the fragile silken fabric with his rough fingers and nodded in appreciation. He fumbled with the tag and read the price. "Jesus H. Christ!" The words were practically a gasp.

Bert glanced back at the shoe department; she was gone! The heat of panic engulfed him. He began looking frantically in all directions but she was nowhere in sight. Had he blown it? Harry'd kill him. He whirled around and suddenly found himself face to face with her. Up close she seemed older than twenty-seven, middle thirties at least, and a little heavy.

As she glanced at him, her expression suggested that she wondered what he could be doing there. A Bergdorf's customer he wasn't. She took a blouse from the rack and studied it.

As Bert backed away, the elderly saleslady approached. "Mrs. Chiefman. So nice to see you. Can I help you with anything today?"

"Oh, hi. I'd like this blouse, please. And wrap it as a gift, it's for my mother. Be sure and take off the price, of course. And could you please hurry, I have an important appointment in ten minutes?" Her voice had a nasal whining quality. She took her charge card from her wallet and handed it to the saleslady.

Bert moved into handbags and leather goods and watched from there.

After the saleslady returned with the package, Mrs. Chiefman added it to the shopping bag with the two pairs of shoes. Then she left the store. Bert followed her out.

When she reached the sidewalk, she headed uptown. Bert crossed Fifth Avenue and returned to where Harry stood waiting. "There she goes," he said.

"Walk ahead of me. She notice you in there?"

"I don't think so. Like you told me, why should she?"

"Let's go," Harry said.

They walked up Fifth Avenue, watching her from a distance. She crossed Fifth at Fifty-eighth and went into the lower level of the GM Tower to Vidal Sassoon.

"What now?" Bert asked.

"We wait."

"You got any idea how long?"

"This should take about an hour," Harry answered.

"Here she comes now," Harry said. He nudged Bert, who was thoughtfully observing people and traffic and things.

"She looks a little different," Bert said.

"That's the idea," Harry said. "Let's go."

They followed her back across Fifth Avenue and into the Plaza. She went into the Palm Court and was led to a table.

"Now what?" Bert asked.

"We eat lunch."

"In here?"

"We gotta eat somewhere." They followed the maître d' between tables toward a far corner. As they moved across the area, Bert looked down at the food being eaten by people already served. Definitely not his idea of a good meal. Harry asked for the farthest table and they sat down, facing her back.

After the waiter had left them with their menus, Bert began studying it. "Jesus, look at these prices for this stuff!"

"Relax. It's an investment."

"There's nothin' to eat here."

"F' Crissakes, just pick somethin' and eat it!"

"What're you gonna have?"

They managed their finger sandwiches with fruit garnish and coffee and then trailed Henrietta Chiefman back down Fifth Avenue, taking turns following her into store after store. First it was Tiffany's, where she bought several pieces of expensive costume jewelry and dropped them into her shopping bag as casually as if she were buying groceries. She also bought a large sterling tea set and asked that it be delivered. Then off to Bendel's, where she found a blouse she liked and took one in every color. Then I. Miller for three more pairs of shoes, and finally Saks, where she made purchases on every floor.

They almost blew the whole thing when she left Saks by the side door and hailed a cab. Bert raced after her, heard her say Grand Central, and then ran to the front of the store to get Harry. They caught up with her as she was boarding the train for Scarsdale with her two shopping bags.

They sat a few seats behind her and when the train reached Scarsdale, they also got off. Then they trailed her Cadillac Seville in their panel truck and when she pulled into the long circular driveway, they were right behind.

As she was getting out of the car and the garage door was

descending, they dashed under it, wearing their rubber masks, each carrying a gun.

She threw up her hands. "What is this?"

"You're coming with us."

"You mean, you mean this is a kidnapping?"

"Call it what you want. Only, let's get moving." Harry grabbed her arm roughly and pulled her toward the door. He pressed the wall switch and the door began to rise.

"You'll live to regret this," she said. "My Harvey'll see to that."

"If we do, lady, at least we'll regret it with money. Now do as you're told and you won't get hurt. Let's go."

The apartment was small, the upper floor of a tiny duplex house, isolated, the lower floor vacant. Henrietta Chiefman sat on a sofa in the living room, a set of crude manacles fastened around her ankles. Another lengthy section of heavy chain went from the manacles to a radiator pipe. The whole business was fastened together with a couple of bulky padlocks and was sufficiently long to give her range to reach the bathroom. The chains made dreadful noises when she moved around. And so did she. She didn't like the arrangement at all.

Harry had been watching the Chiefman house, studying their habits for weeks. He'd seen Harvey Chiefman come and go each day in his Maserati. He had also observed that Thursday was the maid's day off. He'd even followed Henrietta Chiefman on some of her past shopping trips to the City, as well as other places she routinely went—her clubs, local shopping, her friends' homes.

He'd decided it was time for them to make their move. Since it was Thursday, she'd be home alone. They would speak to her through the intercom, getting her to open the door on the pretense that they were deliverymen, and would simply grab her when she opened the door, pulling on the rubber masks at the last possible moment. However, when they reached the house, she had already started driving out, a little earlier than usual, to go to the station. Harry chose to follow her rather than wait for her return. He didn't think it wise to have been parked in front of her house all day on the day she was taken.

"You'll pay dearly for this, I'll promise you that." She hadn't stopped since they picked her up. "You've done a stupid thing. A stupid thing. You're in big trouble."

Bert tried to ignore her as he sat across the room and watched television. Some of his favorite shows were on Thursday nights. He said to her finally, getting hot under his mask, "Look, why don'cha just knock it off and watch the TV, whatta'ya say?"

"You just call my Harvey so he can start arranging to have you put where you belong."

Harry checked his watch. "Now that she mentions it," he said to Bert, "I think it is about time for me to go and make the first call."

Bert glanced at Henrietta Chiefman. "Why don'cha stay here and let me go make the call?"

"Just take it easy. I'll only be a few minutes."

"Is this Harvey Chiefman?"

"Yes it is."

"We're holding your wife."

"What do you mean you're holding my wife? Holding her how? Who is this?"

"Chiefman, we grabbed your wife today and we're holding her for ransom."

"Retta? You're holding Retta for ransom? So that explains where she is."

Harry scratched his head in confusion over the tone of Chiefman's response. "Chiefman, your wife's safe return will cost exactly one million dollars."

"Well, you'll never get it from me!"

"Then don't expect to ever see her alive again!"

"Look, whoever you are, if you kill her, you're in a lot of trouble. As a matter of fact, you're already in a lot of trouble, you know? But don't expect to get any money out of me."

"Isn't she your wife?"

"She is at the moment. Listen, I might as well let you have it straight. I'm planning to leave Retta. And when I do, what you're asking could turn out to be peanuts compared to what she and some lawyer are liable to come up with."

"Chiefman, how much *are* you willing to pay?"

"I won't pay anything. I thought I said that."

"Chiefman, you won't get away with this!"

"What are you going to do, call the police?"

"Chiefman . . ."

"One thing, though," Chiefman said. "Whoever you are, do me a favor and don't tell her I'm leaving her. Okay? I think the least I can do is tell her myself. Wouldn't you agree?"

"We'll be in touch, Chiefman." Harry hung up the phone and left the booth. He drove back to their flat and called Bert into the kitchen. "I think we may have a problem, pal," he told Bert.

"How long do you expect to be holding me here?" Retta Chiefman demanded plaintively.

"It's hard to say for sure," Harry answered. "I'm trying to negotiate with your husband and frankly, he's not too . . . too cooperative."

"Well, if you plan to keep me in this, this place for another night, I'm going to need some things."

"What kinda things?" Bert asked.

"Some beauty aids. And some special foods. I cannot eat what you eat. I need certain special items."

"Such as?"

"Why don't I just write you a list?"

"Forget it. We can't be bothered."

"Don't tell me to forget it," she said with a raised voice. "I insist that you go and get what I ask for. I will not stay in this house another night unless I have the things I need!"

Bert scowled.

"Get her a pencil and some paper," Harry said quietly.

Bert went into the kitchen and rummaged around, returning with a stump of a pencil and a scrap of paper. He gave them to her.

She wrote industriously for several minutes, compiling a rather lengthy list. She handed it to Bert. "I made it very neat so that even you would have no trouble reading it. Please go right away as I'm already a day off schedule."

Bert studied the list for a moment and began to read it out loud. "Skim milk, dried prunes, brewer's yeast, raisins . . . raisins? Whadda'ya gonna do with raisins? Bake cookies?"

"I'm going to eat them," she snapped.

He glanced back at the list. "Unprocessed coarse bran? You're gonna eat that too? I thought that's what they fed to hogs. Perrier water?"

"You can get all of those things at the health food store on White Plains Road."

"And what about all these other things you got written here? Charles of the Ritz?"

"I do not intend to explain and defend my need for everything on that list. I simply will not be without them. You can get them all at Lord and Taylor in White Plains, or go to Bloomingdale's or Saks."

He looked at Harry. "I'm gonna feel like an idiot goin' in those places to buy all this stuff."

"Don't complain," she muttered. "Idiot would be a step up for you."

Harry held up a hand to tell Bert to restrain himself. "Just go get the stuff on the list. Maybe it'll keep her quiet. And take it easy."

After Bert had left, she turned to Harry. "Do you know how to play gin rummy?"

"Of course I know how to play gin rummy."

"We're apparently going to have lots of time to kill. Would you like to play some?"

He shrugged and smiled beneath the mask. "Why the hell not?"

"Why don't we play for money?"

"You don't have any. We took yours. Remember?"

"You'll be giving me a chance to win it back. If I lose, I'll have Harvey take care of it."

He shook his head. "What the hell. Let's see if I can find a deck o' cards."

Harry met Bert in the kitchen when he returned from his shopping trip. "She won all her money back," Harry said.

"She what?"

"We played gin rummy while you were gone and she won all her money back."

"You gonna let her keep it?"

"I don't know yet. I'm tryin' to decide what's the right thing to do."

"Harvey Chiefman?"

"Yes."

"I'm calling back to see if we can't do a little negotiating and come up with somethin' acceptable to both parties."

"'I've already told you I won't pay you one red cent."

"Have you called the police yet?"

"No. I'm hoping it's not going to be necessary. I'm a reasonable man. Look. You're in a lot of trouble. But if you just let Retta go, then we'll consider the case closed, no questions asked. Period. How does that sound?"

"Harvey, either you call the police or I'm gonna call 'em."

"You? Why would you call them?"

"I want 'em to know your wife's been kidnapped."

"I'll deny it."

"I'll warn 'em you'll probably deny it. Where are you gonna tell 'em she is, that they can check it out? What if they start thinkin' that maybe you're an accessory? And even if you convince the cops you're not in on it, how's it gonna look when the story gets into the papers and television that a man in your position and with your kind of dough isn't willing to put out a few bucks to determine whether your wife lives or dies? And I'll see to it that they know. And another thing, Harvey, how's this story gonna look when your case comes up in divorce court?"

Chiefman was quiet for a prolonged moment. Then, "I can see you've been doing a little thinking since the last time we talked."

"We're businessmen, just like you, Chiefman."

"Let me discuss it with my lawyer. Call me back tomorrow."

"Tomorrow morning, Harvey. And Harvey, we don't want to drag this thing on indefinitely. Understand?"

"Is she beginning to get to you a little?" There was a trace of knowing chuckle in his voice.

"Chiefman, I never said I didn't appreciate your position. But think of the newspapers and the divorce case and everything. Talk to your lawyer and come up with something reasonable. Okay?"

Bert was standing at the door when Harry returned from making the call. "She wants me to go shopping again," Bert said.

"What for this time?"

"She said she absolutely refuses to go another day without fresh underwear. And another thing. She says the chains have to come off."

"For what?"

"For one thing, to put on the underwear. And another thing, she wants to take a shower and she refuses to take a shower if she can't close the bathroom door all the way. And besides, she'd never be able to step over the edge of the tub with the chains on her legs."

"So take the chains off for a while. She ain't going nowhere."

"There's more."

"What else?"

"She's got to have clean towels."

"Anything else?"

"She says the tub's filthy. Says she wants us to scour it before she takes her shower."

"Give her the soap powder and let her do it herself."

"I already tried that. She said she's allergic to soap powders. She can't do it without rubber gloves."

"Then we'll get her rubber gloves. Go to the nearest store, get her a towel, a clean pair of pants and a pair of rubber gloves."

"Incidentally, did you do any good with Chiefman?"

"He says he wants to talk to his lawyer. I think I got him thinkin'."

"Hello?"

"Chiefman?"

"Yes."

"You talk to your lawyer?"

"Yes, I did. He agrees with me. Right down the line. You let Retta go and I won't call the police and we'll consider the case closed. You have my word on it. It'll have been a nice adventure for her to tell her children about some day . . . if she ever has any . . . which I frankly doubt. . . . I know one thing. If she ever does, they won't be mine. . . ."

"Chiefman," Harry said, trying to make his voice heavy with menace, "Let me tell you something. This is a negotiation. Hear what I said? A negotiation. We don't intend to just let you call the shots. Now you come up with something interesting or we put her away. And we go to the papers and TV and make it known you refused to talk to us."

"Listen, guy, I respect your threat as a good tactic. As you said yesterday, we're both businessmen. But face it. You've committed a federal offense. That's heavy stuff. And stupid. Don't you know the Feds'll find you? And I'm giving you a chance to walk from this with a whole skin. Besides, who will the media believe, me or you? Think it over, pal. Learn to recognize a sweet deal when you hear one. As a matter of fact, I should really make you pay me a little something."

Harry hesitated a moment. "We'll be in touch." He got back in the truck and returned to the apartment.

Bert met him as he entered the kitchen. "Well?"

"He says he's sticking to yesterday's offer."

"You're kidding?"

"But don't worry about it," Harry said resolutely. "He ain't gettin' away with it. I don't give up that easy."

Retta Chiefman called to them from the bathroom door. "Will one of you please do something? We just ran out of hot water."

Harry dropped in a dime and dialed. The light bulb was out in the phone booth and he needed a match to see the numbers on the dial.

"Hello?"

"Chiefman?"

"Yes."

"Chiefman, we've decided to go along with your deal."

"I think you're being smart. I really do. You're saving yourself a lot of grief. How do you want to handle it? Are you going to drop her off near the house, here, or what?"

"Jesus, come on, Chiefman. What do you take us for? Here's our side of the deal. Without callin' the cops, you have to go get her yourself where we left her. I promise you she's okay. We got a deal?"

Chiefman hesitated.

"Come on, Harvey. You're gettin' it your way. You're winnin' out. What more do you want?"

After a slight pause, "All right. Where is she?"

"There's this park in Darien, Connecticut that's completely deserted this time o' year and to get to it . . . ."

"Darien? You want me to go all the way to Darien? At this time of night?"

"It ain't that far, Chiefman. Go by the Merritt Parkway. Take Exit Thirty-six, North, go about two miles, you'll see a big stone archway on the right. You can't miss it. Follow the main road in and you'll see a big deserted house. Behind the house, there's a shed. She's in the shed. We left a little electric lantern burning in there but it won't burn too long so you oughta get moving. And take a knife or something. We left her tied up and gagged."

"I like the idea of my being the one to rescue her, but couldn't you put her a little closer to home? Besides, that's over a state line, you know."

"Chiefman, you were the one that set the deal. Right? How long's it gonna take you in that fancy sports car of yours?"

After another pause, "Okay."

Harry hung up the phone and stepped out of the booth, which was located at the intersection of Chiefman's street and the main road leading to it. He climbed into the truck where Bert was waiting. They sat in silence until they saw Chiefman speed by in his Maserati. Then they drove to Chiefman's house.

They pulled into the long driveway and backed the truck to the door. Using the keys from Retta Chiefman's purse, they went into the house, looked quickly around, and began loading the truck: five color television sets and a Betamax, some custom stereo equipment, a few antique pieces and some modern paintings, eight fur coats, lots of sterling, including matched service for thirty-six, all of Retta Chiefman's jewelry, some of her fancier-looking clothes and perfumes, Harvey's clothes, a dozen cases of liquor and another dozen of dusty-looking French wines. And of course they took the Seville, with the two shopping bags still in it. And they had the money out of Retta's handbag, or what was left after shopping for her. . . . What the hell! Everything considered, the caper didn't turn out all that bad.

Medicine Woman

Richard Deming

Jed Harmon, wearing his fishing clothes and carrying a tackle box, paused in the kitchen doorway to sniff the aroma of the spaghetti sauce simmering on the stove.

"You don't have much confidence in my fishing prowess, do you?" he said reproachfully.

Marcia Harmon, trim and neat in a starched gingham dress and apron, paused in her stirring of the sauce to smile at him. "You didn't have very much luck this morning."

From behind Jed, Sergeant Harry Cartwright said, "Late afternoon is when they hit best around here."

"You bring in a string of pike or bass and I'll stick the sauce and meatballs in the freezer," Marcia assured both men. "But in case you have your usual luck, we won't have to go hungry."

"Our usual luck?" her husband said. "What about those two nice bass we had for dinner last night?"

"What about the nice baloney we had the night before?" she countered.

"Just be prepared to freeze that stuff," Jed told her. Moving over to the stove, he bent to kiss her cheek. "Be back about six, hon."

Sergeant Cartwright said, "I'll take a look around outside before you walk out, Harmon. You wait here."

Jed Harmon's plain, pleasant face formed into a frown. "Flager couldn't know where I am, Sergeant. Why don't you relax?"

"I'll relax after you give your testimony tomorrow," the police officer said dryly. "Meanwhile my job is to make sure you stay alive to give it." His tone became definite. "Wait here."

With a resigned air, Jed Harmon set his tackle box on the

kitchen table. Sergeant Cartwright moved through the kitchen to the back door and went outside.

Placing a lid on the pot of simmering spaghetti sauce, Marcia went over to lean her head against her husband's broad chest. Her dark hair barely brushed his chin, for she was a foot shorter than his muscular six feet two.

"I'll be glad when this is over," she said. "It's a little nerve wracking having to wonder each morning if I'll be a widow by night."

"How could Flager's men possibly find me way out here?" he asked, stroking her hair. "I'll be kind of sorry when it's over. I'm enjoying the fishing."

She pulled back slightly in order to look up into his face. "It's not fair that a law-abiding citizen has to hide out from gangsters just because he did his civic duty. Mark Flager should be the hunted one. He's the one who tossed the bomb."

"He's not exactly running around free," Harmon said. "He's sitting in jail. And after I identify him from the stand tomorrow, he should be on his way to the death house."

"His army of gunmen are still free, though. I wish you hadn't seen it, Jed. Why did you have to be passing at that particular moment?"

"I'm glad I saw it. Do you think a man capable of tossing a bomb into a crowded restaurant should get away with it? He killed four people and injured ten. If he beats this rap, his crooked union will have a stranglehold on the whole restaurant industry. No one will dare oppose him."

Harry Cartwright came back in by the rear door. "No sign of anyone around," he announced.

Marcia drew away from her husband's arms. "I hope you have luck," she said. "But just in case, the spaghetti will be ready when you get back."

From the kitchen window she watched the two men walk down to the lake a bare hundred feet behind the house. They made an odd pair. Jed Harmon was tall and wide-shouldered, Harry Cartwright slim and wiry and no more than five feet eight. It seemed a little incongruous that the smaller man was the assigned protector of the larger. Of course, size and muscle meant nothing against bullets, and the district attorney had assured Jed and Marcia that Sergeant Harry Cartwright was the most adept man on the force with the pistol he wore holstered on his right hip.

The outboard skiff was a speck on the horizon when Marcia heard a car drive in the front way. Moving into the front room, she peered out the window to see a car parked before the front door where the gravel drive circled in front of the house. A tall, lean, dark-skinned man of about forty got out of the right side of the car. The driver, a plump blond man about ten years younger, got out the other side. Both were dressed neatly but inexpensively in light-weight summer suits and Panama hats.

As the men mounted the porch steps, Marcia slipped on the burglar chain and opened the door a bare crack. "Yes?" she said through the crack.

Both men removed their hats. The dark, lean man produced his wallet and opened it to show a badge.

"Sergeant John Minor of the district attorney's staff, ma'am," he said politely. "My partner here is Officer George Tobin. Are you Mrs. Harmon?"

"Yes," she said. "Just a moment, please."

Shutting the door so that she could slide the chain from its slot, she pulled the door open again and stood aside to let the men enter. "Has something happened, Sergeant?"

"Oh, no," the lean man said. "The D.A. just doesn't like to take chances. He wants us to tail your husband and his guard into town in the morning."

Both men moved into the front room and the lean man glanced around. "Do you have enough room to put us up overnight?"

"If you don't mind doubling up," Marcia said. "There are only two bedrooms, and my husband and I use one. Sergeant Cartwright's has a double bed, though, and one of you can use the front-room day bed."

"That'll be fine," the lean man said. "I know Cartwright pretty well, so I'll bunk with him. George, you can have the day bed."

His plump partner gave his head a jerky nod. He seemed to be uncomfortably warm; his face was beaded with sweat.

Marcia said, "Let me take your hats. Your coats too, if you'd like."

The lean man said, "I'm quite comfortable," and then surrendered only his hat.

The plump George Tobin decided to retain his coat too, though Marcia couldn't imagine why, because he obviously wasn't comfortable. She didn't urge him, deciding he was old enough to know his own mind. When she returned from placing the hats in the center hall closet, both had taken easy chairs. The plump man was wiping his face with a handkerchief.

"I think George is coming down with a cold," Minor said. "He's been having chills and fevers."

"Would you like some aspirin?" Marcia asked.

"No thanks," George Tobin said. "I'll be all right."

The lean man said, "We spotted a boat pulling out as we drove over the hump. Your husband and Cartwright fishing?"

"Yes. They'll be back at six. Excuse me a moment. I'm cooking spaghetti sauce and it's time to give it a stir."

When she returned from the kitchen, the plump man was still seated where she had left him, but the man who had introduced himself as Sergeant John Minor was nowhere in sight. Before Marcia could ask where he was, he appeared from the central hallway.

"Just washing my hands," he said with a smile. "You sure have a modern bath for so far from civilization."

"There's a deep well and an electric pump," she said. "We have all modern conveniences."

Minor reseated himself and Marcia sank into the center of the sofa. Glancing at her wristwatch, she saw it was only three-thirty and wondered how she could entertain her unexpected guests for two and a half hours.

"Would you like something to drink?" she asked. "I'm afraid all we have is beer."

"We don't drink on duty," the lean man said.

His plump partner blew his nose and said nothing. Marcia noted a slight tic in his left cheek.

There was a conversational lapse. Finally the lean man said, "How'd you and your husband ever find this place, Mrs. Harmon? It sure makes a wonderful hideout."

"It's the summer home of a doctor at the State Mental Hospital," Marcia said. "I'm connected with the hospital, you know."

"Oh?" Minor said interestedly. "You mean you work there?"

"Yes, I'm on the staff. Dr. Peterson, who owns this place, is my department head."

"It's sure a fine hideout. We had trouble finding it even with directions. I didn't know there was any place this isolated so close to the city."

"It's hardly close," Marcia said. "It's a good sixty miles and a little too isolated. We have to drive twenty miles for groceries."

"Well, your troubles will be over tomorrow," Minor said philosophically. Then he sniffed. "That spaghetti sauce sure smells good."

"It's only in case my husband and the sergeant fail to bring in any fish," Marcia said. "If they do, it goes into the freezer and I'll carry it home when we go in tomorrow. Unless you two don't like fish. I'll be glad to save enough out for you."

"I'm not crazy about fish," the lean man admitted. "I'd prefer spaghetti if it isn't too much trouble."

"No trouble at all," Marcia said. "How about you, Mr. Tobin?"

The younger man was looking too miserable to have much of an appetite for anything. Marcia began to suspect she might end up with a bed patient, for he seemed to be getting worse by the minute. However, he said in a high voice, "Spaghetti's about my favorite dish."

"Then I'd better stir it again, or you'll have burned sauce," Marcia said. "Excuse me a minute."

While she was in the kitchen stirring the sauce, the phone rang in the front room. Replacing the pot lid, she returned to the front room to find the lean man had answered it.

"Dr. Harmon?" he was saying into the phone. He glanced

at Marcia questioningly. "I didn't know your husband was a doctor."

"He isn't," Marcia said. "He's an architect. That's for me."

Moving over to him, she took the phone from his hand. The man remained standing next to her, obviously with the intention of eavesdropping. She didn't resent it, though. During the past few weeks she had become so accustomed to police supervision of her and her husband's every move that she accepted it as a matter of course. She even held the receiver slightly away from her ear so that he could hear both sides of the conversation.

"Dr. Harmon speaking," she said into the phone.

"Hi, Marcia," came the voice of Dr. Frank Peterson. "Just checking to see how you're making out. Who was that answering the phone?"

"Just one of the police officers. We have three protecting us now. Everything's under control, Frank. The place is lovely. It's actually more comfortable than our city apartment. We certainly appreciate your lending it to us."

"It was only standing vacant anyway," Dr. Peterson said. "With my blasted hospital schedule, I'm lucky if I can get down there two weeks out of the year. Jed testifies tomorrow, doesn't he?"

"Yes. At ten A.M."

"Then you'll be coming back to work?"

From the corner of her vision Marcia was conscious of the plump George Tobin rising from his chair and moving into the kitchen. Vaguely she wondered why, then dismissed it when she decided he probably was after a drink of water.

She said, "I'd like to hear Jed's testimony tomorrow. How about coming in the next day?"

"I guess we can manage without you one more day," Peterson said. "But work is piling up."

"I'll skip my vacation," she promised.

When she hung up, John Minor said, "So you're a lady doctor, huh? And you cook too."

"Not very neatly, I'm afraid," Marcia said, suddenly noticing that her white apron was freckled with brown spots where an exploding bubble of sauce had sprayed her.

"It looks as delicious as it smells," Minor said, grinning at the spots. "I don't know if I can hold out until six o'clock."

"I can serve you and Mr. Tobin early, if you like," Marcia said. "It won't be any more trouble."

"Well, it's kind of early yet. I'll see what George has to say."

Marcia ruefully examined her spotted apron again. "I'd better put this to soak, before the stains set."

She went up the central hall to the bathroom, tossed the apron into the tub and ran a couple of inches of water over it. Then she moved on to the bedroom she and her husband shared and donned a fresh apron.

The house was laid out with the combination front room and dining room running across its whole front. The central hall divided the rest of the house, the kitchen and bath being on one side of it, the two bedrooms on the other. There were two inside doors to the kitchen, one from the front room, the other from the hallway. Instead of returning to the front room, Marcia turned into the kitchen from the hallway, meaning to check her spaghetti sauce again.

Plump George Tobin apparently had just turned off one of the surface burners of the electric stove, for it still glowed with heat. His coat was laid across a chair, exposing a shoulder holster with a heavy automatic in it, and his right shirt sleeve was rolled past his elbow. He held a spoon containing liquid in one hand and was drawing the liquid into a hypodermic syringe. He gave her a startled look.

"Just having a shot of insulin," he said nervously. "I'm a diabetic."

"Oh?" she said in a calm voice. "Can I help you?"

"I'm used to doing it myself, thanks."

Setting the empty spoon on the table, he turned his back. Marcia watched quietly as he sank the needle into his forearm, her face suddenly pale, but her serene expression giving no indication of the thoughts which began flickering through her mind.

Opening one of the double doors beneath the sink, she

tilted a waste can forward, probed in the trash and drew out a small round tin with a removable lid. The curtains of the window over the sink were drawn back on each side. She placed the tin in the far right corner of the sill, so that the hanging edge of the curtain on that side concealed it.

After a glance at the plump man, whose back was still to her, she opened the spice cabinet and took down a small box. Lifting the lid of the pot on the stove, she liberally sprinkled from the box, set it back in the cabinet and stirred the sauce.

By then the plump man had completed his self-medication. Glancing over his shoulder at her, he laid the hypodermic syringe on the table, rolled down his sleeve and slipped back into his coat. He took a small oblong box from his coat pocket, placed the syringe in the box and dropped it back into his pocket. Then he turned to face Marcia.

She continued to stir the sauce, paying no attention to him. After a moment of contemplating her, he moved into the front room.

Marcia tasted the sauce, pursed her lips, gave it one more stir and replaced the lid. Moving toward the front room, she halted a foot or two back from the door when she heard the plump man whispering to his partner. She couldn't make out the whispered words, but she clearly heard the response.

"You damn fool!" the self-styled sergeant said in a low but carrying voice. "She's a doctor! She knows you weren't taking any insulin shot. Did you have to take a pop right now?"

Marcia moved into the room. Both men looked up at her. She gazed back at them steadily.

After a period of silence, the lean man said, "I guess you tumbled, huh?"

She nodded. "Insulin doesn't have to be heated in a spoon. Heroin does. I realize now that Mr. Tobin's perspiring and fidgeting were symptoms of addiction. It seems unlikely that a member of the district attorney's staff would be an addict, so I assume you're Mark Flager's men."

"You don't seem to be very scared by it," the man who called himself Sergeant Minor said slowly.

"I am," she assured him. "It just happens to be necessary in my work to control my emotions. May I ask what your plans are now?"

"We don't have any until six o'clock, Doc," the plump man said. "We'll just all sit around and wait until then." He was no longer sweating, his manner was relaxed, and he had a smile on his face.

Marcia said, "I assume you mean to kill my husband. Since you can hardly afford to leave witnesses, I suppose you mean to murder Sergeant Cartwright and me too."

The lean man said with a touch of regret, "We hoped to keep things friendly until the last minute. Now I guess we'll have to tie you up, unless you want to behave."

"How do you wish me to behave?" she asked.

"Well, if you sit down and stay quiet, we can still keep it more or less friendly."

Marcia seated herself on the sofa and primly folded her hands in her lap. Glancing at her watch, she saw it was now a quarter after four.

Fifteen minutes passed in total silence.

Eventually the lean man said, "Ain't it about time to give your sauce a stir?"

"Why should I bother?" Marcia asked. "Apparently none of us is going to live to eat it."

The younger man said, "Me and my buddy eat, Doc. How soon'll it be ready?"

"It's ready now. It gets better the longer it simmers, though. Providing it doesn't burn, which I'm hoping it does."

The lean man checked his watch. "No point in letting good spaghetti sauce go to waste. We'll have it about five. Go give it a stir, George. And look out the kitchen window while you're there. If the fish aren't hitting, they may come in early."

The plump man rose and entered the kitchen. He was gone about five minutes.

When he came back, he said, "There's a boat way out there, but it ain't heading this way. That sauce sure smells good. Full of meat balls too. I could eat any time."

"You know how to cook spaghetti?" the pseudo-sergeant asked.

"I think you just put it in water and boil it."

The lean man looked at Marcia. "Maybe we better let her cook it. How long's the spaghetti itself take, Doc?"

"About ten minutes," Marcia said. "The water has to be brought to a boil first, though, and that takes about ten minutes too. If you plan to eat at five, you had better start boiling water. You'll find pans in the lower cabinet to the left of the stove."

"You must not have heard me right, Doc. I said you were going to cook it." Marcia stared at him steadily until he smiled without humor. "You rather be tied up?"

"I suppose cooking for you two is the lesser of two evils," she said, rising. She moved into the kitchen and both men followed. As she bent to remove a small roasting pan from the cabinet to the left of the stove, the lean man looked out the window.

"That their boat?" he asked.

Marcia's heart leaped into her throat. But when she rose holding the pan, there was no visible emotion in her manner. Peering out the window, she saw a small boat in the distance slowly moving shoreward.

"I can't tell so far off," she said. "It's moving too slowly to be coming in anyway. Looks like it's trolling."

Carrying the pan to the sink, she ran it half full of water, set it on a burner and turned the control to high. She sprinkled salt into it. The lean man continued to gaze out the window. Finally he moved back to seat himself at the kitchen table, where his partner was already seated.

"They'll be a half hour to forty-five minutes getting in at that rate," he said. "I guess we can relax."

It was a quarter to five by Marcia's watch when the water boiled. Turning the burner control to simmer, she opened a package of thin spaghetti and dropped it into the water. The lean man rose to look out the window again.

"Still a good quarter mile out," he said. "I think they're heading in, but I guess they're gonna troll clear to shore. They'll be a long time yet."

He returned to his seat. Marcia got down two plates and set one before each man.

"You're not gonna eat with us?" the plump man asked.

"I hardly feel much appetite," Marcia said dryly.

"You're certainly a cool one," the lean man said admiringly. "Most women would be having the screaming-meemies by now."

Without answering, she placed silverware and paper napkins alongside the plates, set a dish of butter and a shaker of grated Parmesan cheese in the center of the table, and got a long loaf of Italian bread from the bread box and began to slice it.

"Some of that beer you mentioned earlier would go good with spaghetti," the plump man said.

After placing a plate of sliced bread on the table, Marcia silently got two cans of beer from the refrigerator, opened them and decanted them into tall, fourteen-ounce glasses. When she had served the beer, she tested the spaghetti with a fork, then turned off both the burner under it and the one under the sauce.

She let the spaghetti stand in its water while she lifted the sauce pot with a couple of pot holders and emptied it into a large bowl. She carried the bowl to the table and stuck a serving spoon into it. Then she placed a colander in the sink, dumped the cooked spaghetti in it and let it drain before transferring it to a second large bowl.

When she had placed the spaghetti bowl on the table with a serving spoon and fork in it, she asked sardonically, "Anything else?"

"I guess we're set," the lean man said. "Go ahead, George, while I take another look."

He rose to peer out the window again. When he reseated himself, he said, "Still trolling. They'll be a good half hour yet."

Marcia stood leaning against the sink as the men served themselves heaping portions of spaghetti and flooded it with the rich, dark brown sauce. Each helped himself to four thick meat balls.

"Umm," the lean man said after his first taste. "You make

it better than the Italians. But you sure make it hot. I don't mean just hot with heat. Hot with spice."

"My husband likes it heavily spiced," Marcia said. "He says if it doesn't make you sweat, it isn't good sauce."

There was silence for the next fifteen minutes as the men ate. The lean man was the first to finish. Draining his beer glass, he pushed back his chair and patted his stomach.

"I guess it was good sauce," he said. "I'm sweating like a pig."

Rising, he went over to look out the window. "We sure timed that right," he said. "They've given up trolling and are heading in wide open. They're only about a hundred yards out."

The plump man finished his beer, walked over to the window and looked out too. Then he looked at Marcia and drew his automatic from beneath his arm.

"Guess we better put her out," he suggested. "She might try to warn them by letting out a scream."

"It wouldn't be very wise to do that," Marcia said in a steady voice. "You would be committing suicide. I'm the only doctor within twenty miles, and you would be beyond help by the time you drove that far."

"What?" the lean man said with a frown. "What are you talking about?"

"Do you feel a slight burning in your stomachs?" Marcia asked. "And is your warm perspiration beginning to turn to cold sweat? Look at each other. That green cast to your skin is the first symptom of phosphorus poisoning."

Involuntarily the two men swung to stare at each other's face. Then, both glared at the woman.

"I don't see no green cast," the lean man said. "What you getting at, Doc? Spit it out fast."

Reaching behind her, Marcia pushed aside the righthand curtain and lifted the round tin from the sill. Opening it to show it was empty, she held up the label for them to see. In large red letters it said: RAT POISON.

"I realized that you were a couple of Mark Flager's hired killers the moment I saw George giving himself a shot," she said. "While he was explaining to you that I'd caught him in the act, I seasoned the spaghetti sauce with this."

The men gazed at the empty tin in horror. George began to bring up his gun.

"I can save your lives," Marcia said quickly. "Providing you let me give you the antidote at once. In another fifteen minutes no one will be able to save you."

George squeaked in his high voice, "Get up the antidote fast, or I'll blow your head off!"

Marcia's face was as pale as the two men's, but her voice remained serene. "You'll do nothing of the sort, because you're dead if you do. I'll give you the antidote the moment you lay your guns on the kitchen table."

The men stared at her. She said quietly, "The basic ingredient in rat poison is phosphorus, and every minute allows more of it to absorb into your bloodstream. By now your stomachs must be burning quite painfully and you're experiencing slight nausea. Feel how clammy your skins have become? You don't have time to quibble."

The men turned to gaze into each other's face, and what each saw in the other's reduced him to panic. Each clasped a hand to his stomach, as though acute pain had suddenly gripped him there. With one accord they tottered to the kitchen table. The plump man dropped his automatic upon it, the lean man dipped a hand beneath his arm and tossed a snub-nosed revolver next to it.

Marcia picked up both guns, quickly walked to the back door and tossed them outdoors.

Closing the door again, she said briskly, "The first step is to arrest the action of the phosphorus; then we'll have to clear your stomachs."

Opening the cabinet beneath the sink where the waste can was kept, she lifted out a quart bottle and poured about three ounces each into two glasses.

"This is nothing but turpentine," she said. "It will form a hard, solid mass with the phosphorus and prevent any further absorption into the bloodstream. Drink it down."

Both men obediently drank.

"You're not out of the woods yet," Marcia said in the same brisk tone. "Now you need an emetic."

Lifting down two large glasses of the same size she had served the beer in, she ran them nearly full of warm water. Spooning dried mustard into the water, she began stirring it.

"Hurry up, Doc," the lean man gasped. "My stomach's on fire."

"There's no hurry now," Marcia said. "We have to allow time for the turpentine to react with the phosphorus. You don't get this here anyway. Head for the bathroom and wait until I bring it to you. Quickly now!"

Ten minutes later, when Jed Harmon and Sergeant Cartwright entered the back door wearing sheepish expressions because they hadn't a single fish with them, Marcia said, "We have a couple of visitors, but it's nothing to get excited about. They're patients of mine."

She led them to the bathroom. The two gunmen were side-by-side on their knees, retching into the bathtub.

"Johnny Minor and George the Needle!" Sergeant Cartwright said in amazement. "Mark Flager's top hatchet men. What in the devil's the matter with them?"

"They ate some of my spaghetti sauce after I'd laced it rather liberally with cayenne pepper."

"That made them sick?" Jed asked with raised brows.

"Well, not exactly. It was more their imagination. They were under the impression that the can of rat poison you spread around in the woodshed had been emptied into the sauce."

When both men gazed at her, Marcia said, "They mistook me for a doctor of medicine. I didn't bother to explain that I'm really a doctor of psychology."

The People Across the Canyon

Margaret Millar

The first time the Bortons realized that someone had moved into the new house across the canyon was one night in May when they saw the rectangular light of a television set shining in the picture window. Marion Borton knew it had to happen eventually, but that didn't make it any easier to accept the idea of neighbors in a part of the country she and Paul had come to consider exclusively their own.

They had discovered the site, had bought six acres, and built the house over the objections of the bank, which didn't like to lend money on unimproved property, and of their friends who thought the Bortons were foolish to move so far out of town. Now other people were discovering the spot, and here and there through the eucalyptus trees and the live oaks, Marion could see half-finished houses.

But it was the house directly across the canyon that bothered her most; she had been dreading this moment ever since the site had been bulldozed the previous summer.

"There goes our privacy." Marion went over and snapped off the television set, a sign to Paul that she had something on her mind which she wanted to transfer to his. The transference, intended to halve the problem, often merely doubled it.

"Well, let's have it," Paul said, trying to conceal his annoyance.

"Have what?"

"Stop kidding around. You don't usually cut off Perry Mason in the middle of a sentence."

"All I said was, there goes our privacy."

"We have plenty left," Paul said.

"You know how sounds carry across the canyon."

"I don't hear any sounds."

"You will. They probably have ten or twelve children and a howling dog and a sports car."

"A couple of children wouldn't be so bad—at least, Cathy would have someone to play with."

Cathy was eight, in bed now, and ostensibly asleep, with the night light on and her bedroom door open just a crack.

"She has plenty of playmates at school," Marion said, pulling the drapes across the window so that she wouldn't have to look at the exasperating rectangle of light across the canyon. "Her teacher tells me Cathy gets along with everyone and never causes any trouble. You talk as if she's deprived or something."

"It would be nice if she had more interests, more children of her own age around."

"A lot of things would be nice *if*. I've done my best."

Paul knew it was true. He'd heard her issue dozens of weekend invitations to Cathy's schoolmates. Few of them came to anything. The mothers offered various excuses: poison oak, snakes, mosquitoes in the creek at the bottom of the canyon, the distance of the house from town in case something happened and a doctor was needed in a hurry . . . these excuses, sincere and valid as they were, embittered Marion. *"For heaven's sake, you'd think we lived on the moon or in the middle of a jungle."*

"I guess a couple of children would be all right," Marion said. "But please, no sports car."

"I'm afraid that's out of our hands."

"Actually, they might even be quite *nice* people."

"Why not? Most people are."

Both Marion and Paul had the comfortable feeling that something had been settled, though neither was quite sure what. Paul went over and turned the television set back on. As he had suspected, it was the doorman who'd killed the nightclub owner with a baseball bat, not the blonde dancer or her young husband or the jealous singer.

It was the following Monday that Cathy started to run away.

Marion, ironing in the kitchen and watching a quiz program on the portable set Paul had given her for Christmas, heard the school bus groan to a stop at the top of the driveway.

She waited for the front door to open and Cathy to announce in her high thin voice, "I'm home, Mommy."

The door didn't open.

From the kitchen window Marion saw the yellow bus round the sharp curve of the hill like a circus cage full of wild captive children screaming for release.

Marion waited until the end of the program, trying to convince herself that another bus had been added to the route and would come along shortly, or that Cathy had decided to stop off at a friend's house and would telephone any minute. But no other bus appeared, and the telephone remained silent.

Marion changed into her hiking boots and started off down the canyon, avoiding the scratchy clumps of chapparal and the creepers of poison oak that looked like loganberry vines.

She found Cathy sitting in the middle of the little bridge that Paul had made across the creek out of two fallen eucalyptus trees. Cathy's short plump legs hung over the logs until they almost touched the water. She was absolutely motionless, her face hidden by a straw curtain of hair. Then a single frog croaked a warning of Marion's presence and Cathy responded to the sound as if she was more intimate with nature than adults were, and more alert to its subtle communications of danger.

She stood up quickly, brushing off the back of her dress and drawing aside the curtain of hair to reveal eyes as blue as the periwinkles that hugged the banks of the creek.

"Cathy."

"I was only counting waterbugs while I was waiting. Forty-one."

"Waiting for what?"

"The ten or twelve children, and the dog."

"What ten or twelve chil—" Marion stopped. "I see. You were listening the other night when we thought you were asleep."

"I wasn't listening," Cathy said righteously. "My ears were hearing."

Marion restrained a smile. "Then I wish you'd tell those ears of yours to hear properly. I didn't say the new neighbors have ten or twelve children, I said they *might* have. Actually, it's very unlikely. Not many families are that big these days."

"Do you have to be old to have a big family?"

"Well, you certainly can't be very young."

"I bet people with big families have station wagons so they have room for all the children?"

"The lucky ones do."

Cathy stared down at the thin flow of water carrying fat little minnows down to the sea. Finally she said, "They're too young, and their car is too small."

In spite of her aversion to having new neighbors, Marion felt a quickening of interest. "Have you seen them?"

But the little girl seemed deaf, lost in a water world of minnows and dragonflies and tadpoles.

"I asked you a question, Cathy. Did you see the people who just moved in?"

"Yes."

"When?"

"Before you came. Their name is Smith."

"How do you know that?"

"I went up to the house to look at things and they said, hello, little girl, what's your name? And I said, Cathy, what's yours? And they said Smith. Then they drove off in the little car."

"You're not supposed to go poking around other people's houses," Marion said brusquely. "And while we're at it, you're not supposed to go anywhere after school without first telling me where you're going and when you'll be back. You know that perfectly well. Now why didn't you come in and report to me after you got off the school bus?"

"I didn't want to."

"That's not a satisfactory answer."

Satisfactory or not, it was the only answer Cathy had. She looked at her mother in silence, then she turned and darted back up the hill to her own house.

After a time Marion followed her, exasperated and a little confused. She hated to punish the child, but she knew she couldn't ignore the matter entirely—it was much too serious. While she gave Cathy her graham crackers and orange juice, she told her, reasonably and kindly, that she would have to stay in her room the following day after school by way of learning a lesson.

That night, after Cathy had been tucked in bed, Marion related the incident to Paul. He seemed to take a less serious view of it than Marion, a fact of which the listening child became well aware.

"I'm glad she's getting acquainted with the new people," Paul said. "It shows a certain degree of poise I didn't think she had. She's always been so shy."

"You're surely not condoning her running off without telling me?"

"She didn't run far. All kids do things like that once in a while."

"We don't want to spoil her."

"Cathy's always been so obedient I think she has *us* spoiled. Who knows, she might even teach us a thing or two about going out and making new friends." He realized, from past experience, that this was a very touchy subject. Marion had her house, her garden, her television sets; she didn't seem to want any more of the world than these, and she resented any implication that they were not enough. To ward off an argument he added, "You've done a good job with Cathy. Stop worrying . . . Smith, their name is?"

"Yes."

"Actually, I think it's an excellent sign that Cathy's getting acquainted."

At three the next afternoon the yellow circus cage arrived, released one captive, and rumbled on its way.

"I'm home, Mommy."

"Good girl."

Marion felt guilty at the sight of her: the child had been cooped up in school all day, the weather was so warm and lovely, and besides Paul hadn't thought the incident of the previous afternoon too important.

"I know what," Marion suggested, "let's you and I go down to the creek and count waterbugs."

The offer was a sacrifice for Marion because her favorite quiz program was on and she liked to answer the questions along with the contestants. "How about that?"

Cathy knew all about the quiz program; she'd seen it a hundred times, had watched the moving mouths claim her mother's eyes and ears and mind. "I counted the waterbugs yesterday."

"Well, minnows, then."

"You'll scare them away."

"Oh, will I?" Marion laughed self-consciously, rather relieved that Cathy had refused her offer and was clearly and definitely a little guilty about the relief. "Don't you scare them?"

"No. They think I'm another minnow because they're used to me."

"Maybe they could get used to me, too."

"I don't think so."

When Cathy went off down the canyon by herself Marion realized, in a vaguely disturbing way, that the child had politely but firmly rejected her mother's company. It wasn't until dinner time that she found out the reason why.

"The Smiths," Cathy said, "have an Austin-Healey."

Cathy, like most girls, had never shown any interest in cars, and her glib use of the name moved her parents to laughter.

The laughter encouraged Cathy to elaborate. "An Austin-Healey makes a lot of noise—like Daddy's lawn mower."

"I don't think the company would appreciate a commercial from you, young lady," Paul said. "Are the Smiths all moved in?"

"Oh, yes. I helped them."

"Is that a fact? And how did you help them?"

"I sang two songs. And then we danced and danced."

Paul looked half pleased, half puzzled. It wasn't like Cathy to perform willingly in front of people. During the last Christmas concert at the school she'd left the stage in tears and hidden in the cloak room. . . . Well, maybe her shyness was only a phase and she was finally getting over it.

"They must be very nice people," he said, "to take time out from getting settled in a new house to play games with a little girl."

Cathy shook her head. "It wasn't games. It was real dancing—like on Ed Sullivan."

"As good as that, eh?" Paul said, smiling. "Tell me about it."

"Mrs. Smith is a night-club dancer."

Paul's smile faded, and a pulse began to beat in his left temple like a small misplaced heart. "Oh? You're sure about that, Cathy?"

"Yes."

"And what does Mr. Smith do?"

"He's a baseball player."

"You mean that's what he does for a living?" Marion asked. "He doesn't work in an office like Daddy?"

"No, he just plays baseball. He always wears a baseball cap."

"I see. What position does he play on the team?" Paul's voice was low.

Cathy looked blank.

"Everybody on a ball team has a special thing to do. What does Mr. Smith do?"

"He's a batter."

"A batter, eh? Well, that's nice. Did he tell you this?"

"Yes."

"Cathy," Paul said, "I know you wouldn't deliberately lie to me, but sometimes you get your facts a little mixed up."

He went on in this vein for some time but Cathy's story remained unshaken: Mrs. Smith was a night-club dancer, Mr. Smith a professional baseball player, they loved children, and they never watched television.

"That, at least, must be a lie," Marion said to Paul later when she saw the rectangular light of the television set shining in the Smiths' picture window. "As for the rest of it, there isn't a night club within fifty miles, or a professional ball club within two hundred."

"She probably misunderstood. It's quite possible that at one time Mrs. Smith was a dancer of sorts and that he played a little baseball."

Cathy, in bed and teetering dizzily on the brink of sleep, wondered if she should tell her parents about the Smiths' child —the one who didn't go to school.

She didn't tell them; Marion found out for herself the next morning after Paul and Cathy had gone. When she pulled back the drapes in the living room and opened the windows she heard the sharp slam of a screen door from across the canyon and saw a small child come out on the patio of the new house. At that distance she couldn't tell whether it was a boy or a girl. Whichever it was, the child was quiet and well behaved; only the occasional slam of the door shook the warm, windless day.

The presence of the child, and the fact that Cathy hadn't mentioned it, gnawed at Marion's mind all day. She questioned Cathy about it as soon as she came home.

"You didn't tell me the Smiths have a child."

"No."

"Why not?"

"I don't know why not."

"Is it a boy or a girl?"

"Girl."

"How old?"

Cathy thought it over carefully, frowning up at the ceiling. "About ten."

"Doesn't she go to school?"

"No."

"Why not?"

"She doesn't want to."

"That's not a very good reason."

"It is her reason," Cathy said flatly. "Can I go out to play now?"

"I'm not sure you should. You look a little feverish. Come here and let me feel your forehead."

Cathy's forehead was cool and moist, but her cheeks and the bridge of her nose were very pink, almost as if she'd been sunburned.

"You'd better stay inside," Marion said, "and watch some cartoons."

"I don't like cartoons."

"You used to."

"I like real people."

She means the Smiths, of course, Marion thought as her mouth tightened. "People who dance and play baseball all the time?"

If the sarcasm had any effect on Cathy she didn't show it. After waiting until Marion had become engrossed in her quiz program, Cathy lined up all her dolls in her room and gave a concert for them, to thunderous applause.

"Where are your old Navy binoculars?" Marion asked Paul when she was getting ready for bed.

"Oh, somewhere in the sea chest, I imagine. Why?"

"I want them."

"Not thinking of spying on the neighbors, are you?"

"I'm thinking of just that," Marion said grimly.

The next morning, as soon as she saw the Smith child come out on the patio, Marion went downstairs to the storage room to search through the sea chest. She located the binoculars and was in the act of dusting them off when the telephone started to ring in the living room. She hurried upstairs and said breathlessly, "Hello?"

"Mrs. Borton?"

"Yes."

"This is Miss Park speaking, Cathy's teacher."

Marion had met Miss Park several times at P.T.A. meetings and report-card conferences. She was a large, ruddy-faced, and unfailingly cheerful young woman—the kind, as Paul said, you wouldn't want to live with but who'd be nice to have around in an emergency. "How are you, Miss Park?"

"Oh, fine, thank you, Mrs. Borton. I meant to call you yesterday but things were a bit out of hand around here, and I knew there was no great hurry to check on Cathy; she's such a well-behaved little girl."

Even Miss Park's loud, jovial voice couldn't cover up the

ominous sound of the word *check*. "I don't think I quite understand. Why should you check on Cathy?"

"Purely routine. The school doctor and the health department like to keep records on how many cases of measles or flu
or chicken pox are going the rounds. Right now it looks like
the season for mumps. Is Cathy all right?"

"She seemed a little feverish yesterday afternoon when she
got home from school, but she acted perfectly normal when
she left this morning."

Miss Park's silence was so protracted that Marion became
painfully conscious of things she wouldn't otherwise have
noticed—the weight of the binoculars in her lap, the thud of
her own heartbeat in her ears. Across the canyon the Smith
child was playing quietly and alone on the patio. *There is
definitely something the matter with that girl,* Marion thought.
*Perhaps I'd better not let Cathy go over there any more, she's
so imitative.* "Miss Park, are you still on the line? Hello?
Hello—"

"I'm here." Miss Park's voice seemed fainter than usual,
and less positive. "What time did Cathy leave the house this
morning?"

"Eight, as usual."

"Did she take the school bus?"

"Of course. She always does."

"Did you see her get on?"

"I kissed her goodbye at the front door," Marion said.
"What's this all about, Miss Park?"

"Cathy hasn't been at school for two days, Mrs. Borton."

"Why, that's absurd, impossible! You must be mistaken."
But even as she was speaking the words, Marion was raising
the binoculars to her eyes: the little girl on the Smiths' patio
had a straw curtain of hair and eyes as blue as the periwinkles
along the creek banks.

"Mrs. Borton, I'm not likely to be mistaken about which
of my children are in class or not."

"No. No, you're—you're not mistaken, Miss Park. I can
see Cathy from here—she's over at the neighbor's house."

"Good. That's a load off my mind."

"Off yours, yes," Marion said. "Not mine."

"Now we mustn't become excited, Mrs. Borton. Don't make too much of this incident before we've had a chance to confer. Suppose you come and talk to me during my lunch hour and bring Cathy along. We'll all have a friendly chat."

But it soon became apparent, even to the optimistic Miss Park, that Cathy didn't intend to take part in any friendly chat. She stood by the window in the classroom, blank-eyed, mute, unresponsive to the simplest questions, refusing to be drawn into any conversation even about her favorite topic, the Smiths. Miss Park finally decided to send Cathy out to play in the schoolyard while she talked to Marion alone.

"Obviously," Miss Park said, enunciating the word very distinctly because it was one of her favorites, "obviously, Cathy's got a crush on this young couple and has concocted a fantasy about belonging to them."

"It's not so obvious what my husband and I are going to do about it."

"Live through it, the same as other parents. Crushes like this are common at Cathy's age. Sometimes the object is a person, a whole family, even a horse. And, of course, to Cathy a night-club dancer and a baseball player must seem very glamorous indeed. Tell me, Mrs. Borton, does she watch television a great deal?"

Marion stiffened. "No more than any other child."

Oh, dear, Miss Park thought sadly, *they all do it; the most confirmed addicts are always the most defensive.* "I just wondered," she said. "Cathy likes to sing to herself and I've never heard such a repertoire of television commercials."

"She picks things up very fast."

"Yes. Yes, she does indeed." Miss Park studied her hands which were always a little pale from chalk dust and were even paler now because she was angry—at the child for deceiving her, at Mrs. Borton for brushing aside the television issue, at herself for not preventing, or at least anticipating, the current situation, and perhaps most of all at the Smiths who ought to have known better than to allow a child to hang around their house when she should obviously be in school.

"Don't put too much pressure on Cathy about this," she said finally, "until I talk the matter over with the school psychologist. By the way, have you met the Smiths, Mrs. Borton?"

"Not yet," Marion said grimly. "But believe me, I intend to."

"Yes, I think it would be a good idea for you to talk to them and make it clear that they're not to encourage Cathy in this fantasy."

The meeting came sooner than Marion expected.

She waited at the school until classes were dismissed, then she took Cathy into town to do some shopping. She had parked the car and she and Cathy were standing hand in hand at a corner waiting for a traffic light to change; Marion was worried and impatient, Cathy still silent, unresisting, inert, as she had been ever since Marion had called her home from the Smiths' patio.

Suddenly Marion felt the child's hand tighten in a spasm of excitement. Cathy's face had turned so pink it looked ready to explode and with her free hand she was waving violently at two people in a small cream-colored sports car—a very pretty young woman with blonde hair in the driver's seat, and beside her a young man wearing a wide friendly grin and a baseball cap. They both waved back at Cathy just before the lights changed and then the car roared through the intersection.

"The Smiths," Cathy shouted, jumping up and down in a frenzy. "That was the Smiths."

"Sssh, not so loud. People will—"

"But it was the *Smiths!*"

"Hurry up before the light changes."

The child didn't hear. She stood as if rooted to the curb, staring after the cream-colored car.

With a little grunt of impatience Marion picked her up, carried her across the road, and let her down quite roughly on the other side. "There. If you're going to act like a baby, I'll carry you like a baby."

"I saw the Smiths!"

"All right. What are you so excited about? It's not very unusual to meet someone in town whom you know."

"It's unusual to meet *them*."

"Why?"

"Because it is." The color was fading from Cathy's cheeks, but her eyes still looked bedazzled, quite as if they'd seen a miracle.

"I'm sure they're very unique people," Marion said coldly. "Nevertheless they must shop for groceries like everyone else."

Cathy's answer was a slight shake of her head and a whisper heard only by herself: "No, they don't, never."

When Paul came home from work Cathy was sent to play in the front yard while Marion explained matters to him. He listened with increasing irritation—not so much at Cathy's actions but at the manner in which Marion and Miss Park had handled things. There was too much talking, he said, and too little acting.

"The way you women beat around the bush instead of tackling the situation directly, meeting it head-on—fantasy life. Fantasy life, my foot! Now we're going over to the Smiths right this minute and talk to them and that will be that. End of fantasy. Period."

"We'd better wait until after dinner. Cathy missed her lunch."

Throughout the meal Cathy was pale and quiet. She ate nothing and spoke only when asked a direct question; but inside herself the conversation was very lively, the dinner a banquet with dancing, and afterward a wild, windy ride in the roofless car . . .

Although the footpath through the canyon provided a shorter route to the Smiths' house, the Bortons decided to go more formally, by car, and to take Cathy with them. Cathy, told to comb her hair and wash her face, protested: "I don't want to go over there."

"Why not?" Paul said. "You were so anxious to spend time with them that you played hooky for two days. Why don't you want to see them now?"

"Because they're not there."

"How do you know?"

"Mrs. Smith told me this morning that they wouldn't be home tonight because she's putting on a show."

"Indeed?" Paul was grim-faced. "Just where does she put on these shows of hers?"

"And Mr. Smith has to play baseball. And after that they're going to see a friend in the hospital who has leukemia."

"Leukemia, eh?" He didn't have to ask how Cathy had found out about such a thing; he'd watched a semi-documentary dealing with it a couple of nights ago. Cathy was supposed to have been sleeping.

"I wonder," he said to Marion when Cathy went to comb her hair, "just how many 'facts' about the Smiths have been borrowed from television."

"Well, I know for myself that they drive a sports car, and Mr. Smith was wearing a baseball cap. And they're both young and good-looking. Young and good-looking enough," she added wryly, "to make me feel—well, a little jealous."

"Jealous?"

"Cathy would rather belong to them than to us. It makes me wonder if it's something the Smiths have or something the Bortons don't have."

"Ask her."

"I can't very well—"

"Then I will, dammit," Paul said. And he did.

Cathy merely looked at him innocently. "I don't know. I don't know what you mean."

"Then listen again. Why did you pretend that you were the Smiths' little girl?"

"They asked me to be. They asked me to go with them."

"They actually said, Cathy, will you be our little girl?"

"Yes."

"Well, by heaven, I'll put an end to this nonsense," Paul said, and strode out to the car.

It was twilight when they reached the Smiths' house by way of the narrow, hilly road. The moon, just appearing above the horizon, was on the wane, a chunk bitten out of its side by some giant jaw. A warm dry wind, blowing down the mountain from the desert beyond, carried the sweet scent of pittosporum.

The Smiths' house was dark, and both the front door and the garage were locked. Out of defiance or desperation, Paul pressed the door chime anyway, several times. All three of them could hear it ringing inside, and it seemed to Marion to echo very curiously—as if the carpets and drapes were too thin to muffle the sound vibrations. She would have liked to peer in through the windows and see for herself, but the venetian blinds were closed.

"What's their furniture like?" she asked Cathy.

"Like everybody's."

"I mean, is it new? Does Mrs. Smith tell you not to put your feet on it?"

"No, she never tells me that," Cathy said truthfully. "I want to go home now. I'm tired."

It was while she was putting Cathy to bed that Marion heard Paul call to her from the living room in an urgent voice, "Marion, come here a minute."

She found him standing motionless in the middle of the room, staring across the canyon at the Smiths' place. The rectangular light of the Smiths' television set was shining in the picture window of the room that opened onto the patio at the back of the Smiths' house.

"Either they've come home within the past few minutes," he said, "or they were there all the time. My guess is that they were home when we went over but they didn't want to see us, so they just doused the lights and pretended to be out. Well, it won't work! Come on, we're going back."

"I can't leave Cathy alone. She's already got her pajamas on."

"Put a bathrobe on her and bring her along. This has gone beyond the point of observing such niceties as correct attire."

"Don't you think we should wait until tomorrow?"

"Hurry up and stop arguing with me."

Cathy, protesting that she was tired and that the Smiths weren't home anyway, was bundled into a bathrobe and carried to the car.

"They're home all right," Paul said. "And by heaven they'd better answer the door this time or I'll break it down."

"That's an absurd way to talk in front of a child," Marion said coldly. "She has enough ideas without hearing—"

"Absurd, is it? Wait and see."

Cathy, listening from the back seat, smiled sleepily. She knew how to get in without breaking anything: ever since the house had been built, the real estate man who'd been trying to sell it always hid the key on a nail underneath the window box.

The second trip seemed a nightmarish imitation of the first: the same moon hung in the sky but it looked smaller now, and paler. The scent of pittosporum was funereally sweet, and the hollow sound of the chimes from inside the house was like an echo in an empty tomb.

"They must be crazy to think they can get away with a trick like this twice in one night," Paul shouted. "Come on, we're going around to the back."

Marion looked a little frightened. "I don't like trespassing on someone else's property."

"They trespassed on our property first."

He glanced down at Cathy. Her eyes were half closed and her face was pearly in the moonlight. He pressed her hand to reassure her that everything was going to be all right and that his anger wasn't directed at her, but she drew away from him and started down the path that led to the back of the house.

Paul clicked on his flashlight and followed her, moving slowly along the unfamiliar terrain. By the time he turned the corner of the house and reached the patio, Cathy was out of sight.

"Cathy," he called. "Where are you? Come back here!"

Marion was looking at him accusingly. "You upset her with that silly threat about breaking down the door. She's probably on her way home through the canyon."

"I'd better go after her."

"She's less likely to get hurt than you are. She knows every inch of the way. Besides, you came here to break down doors. All right, start breaking."

But there was no need to break down anything. The back door opened as soon as Paul rapped on it with his knuckles, and he almost fell into the room.

It was empty except for a small girl wearing a blue bathrobe that matched her eyes.

Paul said, "Cathy. Cathy, what are you doing here?"

Marion stood with her hand pressed to her mouth to stifle the scream that was rising in her throat. There were no Smiths. The people in the sports car whom Cathy had waved at were just strangers responding to the friendly greeting of a child—had Cathy seen them before, on a previous trip to town? The television set was no more than a contraption rigged up by Cathy herself—an orange crate and an old mirror which caught and reflected the rays of the moon.

In front of it Cathy was standing, facing her own image. "Hello, Mrs. Smith. Here I am, all ready to go."

"Cathy," Marion said in a voice that sounded torn by claws. "What do you see in that mirror?"

"It's not a mirror. It's a television set."

"What—what program are you watching?"

"It's not a program, silly. It's real. It's the Smiths. I'm going away with them to dance and play baseball."

"There are no Smiths," Paul bellowed. "Will you get that through your head? *There are no Smiths!*"

"Yes, there are. I see them."

Marion knelt on the floor beside the child. "Listen to me, Cathy. This is a mirror—only a mirror. It came from Daddy's old bureau and I had it put away in the storage room. That's where you found it, isn't it? And you brought it here and decided to pretend it was a television set, isn't that right? But it's really just a mirror, and the people in it are us—you and Mommy and Daddy."

But even as she looked at her own reflection, Marion saw it beginning to change. She was growing younger, prettier; her hair was becoming lighter and her cotton suit was changing into a dancing dress. And beside her in the mirror, Paul was turning into a stranger, a laughing-eyed young man wearing a baseball cap.

"I'm ready to go now, Mr. Smith," Cathy said, and suddenly all three of them, the Smiths and their little girl, began walking away in the mirror. In a few moments they were no bigger than matchsticks—and then the three of them disappeared, and there was only the moonlight in the glass.

"Cathy," Marion cried. "Come back, Cathy! Please come back!"

Propped up against the door like a dummy, Paul imagined he could hear above his wife's cries the mocking muted roar of a sports car.

The Cost of Respectability

Kathleen Hershey

"Who says it never rains in southern California?" I grumbled to myself as I drew on my yellow slicker. January second, and my New Year's resolution to take a daily walk was going to be harder than I had anticipated. The sedentary life of a freelance writer, not to mention the ten pounds I had gained during the Christmas holidays, were reason enough to make my daily walk appear normal to my neighbors, unused to people outside of cars who weren't in elaborate jogging gear.

It was misting rain as I started up the steep hill. I was looking for something, some inspiration, to use in my writing.

The yards were consistently tidy, some edged in scalloped brick, and many flecked with junipers. Most of our neighbors had replaced their asphalt driveways with smooth concrete, a symbol of their continuing affluence despite inflation. It was lucky I had found a fresh approach to my writing that increased our total income enough to allow Jim and me to continue to live in this neighborhood.

There had been a time a little over a year ago when my husband had suggested my creative writing be put aside for something more lucrative.

"Even with my raise, I can't afford to keep up the payments on this place," he had said.

"Give me a little time, Jim. Maybe the novel will sell," I'd pleaded. However, soon after that I discovered a new market for my talent and was able to take the pressure off Jim.

I stopped to catch my breath by Mrs. Marshall's terraced rose garden. A persistent red blossom was leaning precariously with the weight of the unexpected rain. Only one of the Marshalls' Lincoln Continentals was parked in their driveway. A sodden cloth doll lay at the edge of the sidewalk. Getting careless, I thought in alarm. With a quick step, I kicked the wet toy out of sight into the ivy bordering the Marshalls' yard. Then I crossed the street and walked downhill.

At the bottom of La Terra Drive, a patrol car cruised by me. I turned on El Torro and walked past three Spanish-style homes, and noted with interest the helicopter now circling overhead. It appeared that another toddler had wandered off. Little else of consequence ever seemed to happen in our respectable neighborhood.

A second police car passed me and drove to the end of the street where the tract of houses ended and a lush green hillside began. Since my daughter Suzie was home from school today with a cold, I decided to retrace my steps and check on her.

The faster I walked, the harder and quicker the raindrops fell. By the time I reached the house, a red flare sputtered at our intersection and cordoned off La Terra. I hurried inside, closed and latched the heavy double door, then leaned against it in relief.

Suzie was watching television. She had a fire going in the fireplace. The gas logs were disappearing and reappearing in the flames as they remained impervious to the heat.

"I've locked us in, Suz. There are police cars outside."

"Helicopter?" she asked as she noticed the thud, thud, thud overhead.

"Yes."

"I hope it's not another little kid lost. Every time I babysit for the Williamses I have to rock Karen to sleep over and over again, because of her nightmares. Her mom seems really embarrassed about it."

"Is that so?" I asked.

"It's almost the same thing with the other two that wandered off. I guess it's really scary for a little kid to get lost on that hill."

"I suppose. You'd think their parents would watch them more carefully. You were never out of my sight when you were that small."

"Oh, Mom."

"A person can't be too careful these days. Be sure and call me if anyone comes to the door."

"Where are you going?"

"Upstairs."

I draped my slicker over a chair in the bedroom and sat down in my favorite chair by the window and scanned the neighborhood with my binoculars.

The drapes on the Dolans' second floor were closed. Alicia Dolan was probably due for another binge. Her friends in the exclusive woman's club she belonged to would be surprised if they knew she was a hidden alcoholic.

J. R. Travers was out of town again. What a shock it would be to Mrs. Travers if she were ever to discover old J. R. was a bigamist.

Inevitably I focused on the Marshalls' home, which backed on the hill. Sarah Marshall was the world's most impeccable housekeeper. Of course, they had no children to mess up their house. She kept her shoes by the front door and wore slippers all day to keep from spotting the floors. She was too busy with her charity work at the hospital to visit neighbors. Her husband, Randolph Marshall, was president of the Sanfield Bank and prominent in local politics. The Marshalls were frequently on the society page of our small-town newspaper. It meant a great deal to me to live near such well-known and affluent people.

I polished my binoculars with a tissue, then put them to my eyes again. The police car slowly rolled down the hill with a little child in the back seat. It did not slow or stop at the Marshalls' house. Writers need to be good observers, especially in a neighborhood that has a child molester.

I went to my typewriter. Self-discipline and daily writing is essential to a writer's success.

I pushed a clean sheet of twenty-pound rag content bond paper into my new Smith-Corona.

Marshall,

You got away with it again. If you want me to keep my mouth shut leave ten unmarked twenty-dollar bills at the usual place. . . .

A Matter of Pride

Richard A. Moore

Ed was in a lousy mood. It had been a bad week during a bad summer of a bad year. As he drove into view of his drought-parched lawn, a newscaster told of the breaking-off of crucial negotiations. While parking, he noticed the small round hole in the kitchen window, cursed the neighborhood kids, then turned the switch killing the radio explanation of the Dodgers' losing streak.

Inside, he mixed a dark Scotch and water, unfolded a newspaper and ignored the sound of the vacuum cleaner his wife was angrily scraping over the carpet ten feet away. A switch clicked and he sensed her stare.

"I think we need to talk."

"I can't think of anything I would rather avoid right now, Martha. Hold it until after supper," he said, not looking up from the newspaper.

A note of anger came into her voice. "I don't *want* to wait until after supper. I've been thinking about this for days and there will never be a convenient time for you to talk with me. There never is."

Ed kept the paper in front of him to avoid seeing the bandanna-framed red face. "What is it now? Are you going to gripe about your allowance again?"

"I want a divorce."

Ed reluctantly dropped the newspaper. "If you think a stupid threat like that is going to frighten me into an increase in your house-money, you're crazy. That's the dumbest thing I've ever heard."

Something about her deadpan look told him she was serious. "You just don't know when you're well off, Martha. You've got a nice home with no kids or job to worry about. All you have to do is keep the place clean and fix my meals. You've really got it easy."

"I work myself to death around here and you never even notice. I can almost live with your cheapness, but I can't stand being made to feel unwanted, unattractive and stupid."

Ed felt anger flush his face. "Einstein can rest easy in his grave and Cleopatra is fairly safe too. If you don't believe me, just check any mirror. If I hadn't made the mistake of marrying you, your parents would still have another mouth to feed."

"In three years of marriage, you almost convinced me that I really *am* stupid and unlovable. I have news for you, El Braino, I've been having an affair for three months and you haven't suspected a thing."

With the knowledge that she had finally gotten the last word in an argument, Martha marched from the room with an air of triumph. Ed was left with his crumpled newspaper, silent vacuum cleaner and black thoughts.

It was not the thought of losing Martha that outraged him. Life without her would not be a complete bed of nails. It was the thought of her in the arms of another man. Someone was possessing something that was rightfully his, and Ed found that the grossest of insults. Leave she might, but he would find out who the trespasser was and deal with him then.

He awoke the next morning with his mind as hard and lumpy as the sofa on which he had slept. He was staring into his second cup of instant coffee when Martha entered the kitchen, dressed in a very businesslike navy suit.

"I'm going to see a lawyer. You should probably begin making plans about moving out of the house."

The full force of his anger returned. "This is really *too* much. You are running around but I'm the one who has to move. You better talk to your shyster about how you can explain your dirty little affair to a judge."

Martha gave him a not-quite-smug smile. "I'm sure we can find grounds for action. As for infidelity? You have no proof, no proof at all. Next case please."

Now he had a second reason to find the lover. Without incriminating evidence, his wife could easily weep her way into a judge's heart and a fat settlement.

As soon as she left, Ed carefully searched for clues to the

identity of her lover. He found nothing. After a few brooding moments, he climbed into his car, drove downtown and rented a small sedan. He returned home and noted with satisfaction his wife's car in the driveway. He parked on a side street, out of easy view of the house but able to watch any departures or arrivals.

It wasn't a long wait. His wife soon appeared, dressed casually now in blouse and slacks after her formal visit to a lawyer. Ed dropped from view as her small car whirred past the street where he was parked. Quickly, he started his car and eased into the street, giving her about a two-block lead.

He discovered that tailing a car is not easy. Twice he almost had to stop to avoid pulling in directly behind her at stoplights. He made a mental note to buy some sort of disguise if he had to do much of this sort of thing.

Gradually, the two wound their way across town to a neighborhood that was very familiar to Ed. Martha confirmed his guess by parking in front of the two-story house owned by their friends, the Adamses. He resumed his vigil down the street and watched for hours while absolutely nothing happened.

He could easily imagine her crying on Joan's shoulder, spilling out her tawdry secrets. Joan would get a kick out of it all, he thought—she had always despised him. He shuddered at the certainty of Joan telling her husband, Frank, who sat across from him every Thursday at the poker table. He could see the smirk on Frank's face the next time they got together. He knew he would have to put an end to this situation and do it quickly.

It occurred to Ed that if he could get close to the house, he might overhear enough of the conversation within to be revealing. He scuttled along among the boxwood shrubbery listening for sounds and peeping in windows.

The peeping brought unsuspected results. He spotted his wife stepping across a hallway as naked as a marshmallow. He was still puzzling over the sight when he heard her voice faintly within.

"I'm out of the shower now, darling."

Darling? The certainty of the knowledge washed over him and with it came a bitter sense of betrayal. He sat on the dry earth under the bushes and tortured himself with lurid thoughts of his wife and his best friend.

Ed pushed aside the bushes and walked slowly back to the car. He now had all he needed to avoid a costly settlement, but the economics had suddenly lost importance.

Numbly, he drove without direction for a while before stopping at a bar. After several drinks, feeling began to return and it wasn't very nice. He tossed the liquor into his untasting mouth like an old fireman shoveling coal. His wife's lover was not his only shocking discovery. He *cared*. In some ways that bothered him more.

He drove back to his house and parked beside his wife's car. A look at his face caused her to stare in puzzlement as he walked past her to the bedroom. When he returned with a gun in his hand, the puzzlement turned to fear.

"Come along, Martha. We're going to visit your lover."

"Are you crazy, Ed? Put away that gun now and I'll forget you ever did this."

Ed waved the pistol in the direction of the door. "I don't plan to shoot you, but if you aren't through that door in two seconds, I'll kill you where you stand."

Martha walked quickly to the car. Ed drove but kept the revolver cocked and ready at his side.

After a few miles, Martha began to plead in a low earnest tone. "Think for a moment, Ed. You're throwing the rest of your life away. No matter what you feel now, you're sure to regret it later."

His silence frightened her all the more. "How do you know you aren't making a terrible mistake? What could you have found out in just one day? It's probably just some innocent . . ."

"I know what I know. I have the evidence of my own eyes."

Ed turned onto the side street that led to the Adams' house. Martha glanced around apprehensively and felt hope drain, leaving a mountain of fear in its wake.

They parked in front of the house. Ed slid across the seat and pushed her from the car. She tried to speak but had lost the power. They walked to the house and Ed rang the doorbell.

Frank opened the door and a look of surprise and annoyance crossed his face. He did not see the gun. "Well, hello guys. I wish you had called to let us know you were coming over."

There was an awkward silence. Ed knew he must speak, but his mind seemed blanked of all words and knowledge.

Frank suddenly noticed the gun. "What on God's earth is that for?"

Ed glanced at the gun as if he had forgotten it until the reminder. "I'm here to kill you, Frank."

The first shot pushed him back into the foyer. The second knocked him down. The third finished it.

Ed dropped the pistol into his pocket and sat in the nearest chair. He had accomplished his purpose and any other movement or thought seemed unnecessary.

Joan ran from the back of the house, almost tripping on the corpse of her husband. Martha disappeared, but somewhere he heard a phone being dialed.

When the police arrived, they had to shake him before he heard and obeyed orders. His only request was to speak to his wife before leaving for police headquarters. Someone nodded and he was escorted down the hall toward the back of the house. Just before he stepped into the room, he heard his wife speaking in a strange exultant tone.

"Just think, darling, now we are rid of both of the bastards."

"What a curious thing," remarked Mr. Warbasse, "auctioning off the entire contents of a single room."

"And what a room it must have been!" said his wife. "I wish I'd bid for that vanity."

"I wonder who the woman is. Or, perhaps, *was*. I suppose she may be dead."

"Not at all," declared Mrs. Warbasse, who fancied herself an authority on human conduct. "This is an act of total rejection, not of grief."

Her husband turned to her. "There you go, Sophie, building up a molehill again. Suppose she simply decided to redecorate her room and got rid of everything?"

"Oh, no. No woman would discard so very much of herself, right down to her books." A crate of books had been carried onto the platform.

"I won't go through all of these books," the auctioneer said. "There must be over a hundred."

"I suppose you mean divorce," said Mr. Warbasse. "Wouldn't she take her things with her?"

"Under some circumstances, no," declared his wife, and she tried to consider such circumstances.

Choosing six of the books, the auctioneer read off the titles. All were romantic novels, one a recent best-seller.

"For example, what circum—" began Mr. Warbasse. But his wife, within whose deceiving frame loitered a sense of romance, was leaning forward. "Shh!" she said with a gesture.

"Look at their condition," invited the auctioneer. "Like new. Most of them still have their dust jackets."

"Now, Sophie," whispered Mr. Warbasse, "you've probably read more than half of those books."

"Who'll offer twenty dollars for the pack of them?" asked the auctioneer. "That's less than twenty cents a book."

There was no response.

"Eighteen?" asked the man. "Sixteen?"

"One dollar!" cried Mrs. Warbasse, who was devoted to bargains. Many turned to glance at her but no one challenged. Her husband sat as though he longed to be elsewhere.

"One dollar?" the auctioneer asked, but not with great astonishment. "One dollar for all these fine volumes? Surely someone will bid higher. . . ."

Mrs. Warbasse looked about, evenly meeting every gaze that was directed at her. The hall became quiet.

"One small dollar," the man said, and he struck his gavel. "Lady, it's all yours."

"It'll probably cost ten dollars to have them carted home!" snapped Mr. Warbasse.

"Nonsense," replied his wife, who had a solution for all problems. "They'll fit into the trunk of a cab."

She stayed up late that night, going through the books. "Elizabeth Outwater Collins is her name," she announced immediately. "She has a fancy Ex Libris in all of them."

"I'm going to bed," said her husband, and he stood and left the room.

It was some time later, perhaps hours (at least, he was deeply asleep), when his wife's hand shaking his shoulder awoke him.

"For heaven's sake, Sophie, what is it?"

"Listen. I found a letter."

"A letter?"

"Yes, and what a letter! From Elizabeth to her husband. It was in one of the books."

"My God, did you have to wake me up for that?"

"Will you please shut up and listen? Her husband's a doctor, a Dr. Walter Collins on East 54th Street. The envelope's postmarked February 27th, only eight months ago, and it was mailed from Van Wert, Ohio. 'Dear Walter,' the letter says. 'You expected me home today but when I went to pack I found that I simply couldn't bring myself to return. It's not something I planned or thought out, it happened exactly that way. I guess this means that I'm leaving you.

" 'I think we've both known our marriage was a failure from really the first week and it would be kind of foolish to say that the magic has gone from it when there was never any at all—was there, Walter?—even during the honeymoon. I can't explain why after tolerating eleven years of this existence, why now that we've been apart for barely five weeks, I am suddenly unable to face the prospect of returning to this life. Look at my room, for example. We'd been married nine years, Walter, and I was twenty-nine when you suggested I move into a separate bedroom, and it has become to me, this room, a symbol of my total rejection. And another thing—I don't mean to hurt you, Walter (or do I? I'm not sure!)—but another thing I dread is going on through life listening to your stories. At just this moment I simply don't think I could sit through many more and preserve my sanity.' It's signed 'Elizabeth,' and then there's a P.S.: 'I keep wondering if it's a blessing or not that we never had children.'

"Well," demanded Mrs. Warbasse, "what do you think of that? 'Total rejection,' the identical words I used at the auction!" In speaking, she used a great deal of lower lip.

"I suppose it means they were divorced," conceded her husband.

"Of course it does! There's no other possible explanation!"

Her tone was difficult to accept without challenge. "Oh, I don't know. Suppose she regretted posting the letter and immediately flew home and intercepted it? After all, you did find it in one of *her* books!"

"Bah! Why would she open the envelope? And wouldn't she destroy the damn thing instead of slipping it into a book? And why, if she returned to him, were her things auctioned off?"

"Oh, I don't know!" Mr. Warbasse said testily. It was a disadvantage to argue in the recumbent position with someone who was upright and looking down with such cold triumph in her gaze. "I suppose you're right," he mumbled grudgingly and turned his back to his wife.

"Of course I am!" cried Mrs. Warbasse, who valued, above all, the final word. She returned to the living room and to the crate, now less than half filled with books.

Walter and Elizabeth were married in June, at the end of his internship.

It was on one of the medical wards at Bellevue that he first noticed her, a pretty young thing who always looked trim in the freshly starched white and blue of the student nurse's uniform. They began to go out, usually with other interns and nurses, and she always laughed at his stories—the humorous, sometimes poignant, never off-color incidents that he gleaned from the rich hospital supply.

"There was this enormous woman in the Out Patient Department" (this story was always a success and it kidded, in a disarming sort of way, the size of his nose), "a motherly type, *you* know. She was giving me her complaints and having a God-awful time with the language and all of a sudden she broke into Yiddish. 'Madam,' I said, 'I don't understand Yiddish.' 'Vot?' she cried" (here, he threw up his arms), " 'A nice young Jewish doctuh like you not spikking Yiddish?' " (He ran the *g* and *y* together; his simulated accent was good.) " 'But Madam,' I told her. 'I'm not Jewish.' Well, you should have seen her; you'd think her own son had disowned her. She slapped her forehead and turned up her eyes and she cried: 'Voise! He denies it!' " Everyone always laughed. "That one kills me," one of the girls sometimes said, and often: "You haven't heard the one about the woman in the O.P.D.? Walter, tell it to Martha. . . ."

There were many parties, late and spontaneous things whenever an excuse could be found, and Walter always had a central audience. "Walter has such a warm feeling for people," it was frequently said, usually in his hearing, although after a while most of them drifted away. Elizabeth remained at his side and met his glance with a smile, and later, often, they went to 11th Street for spaghetti or pizza. On the day she got her cap he proposed, and a week later she called him in his hospital room and accepted.

I love her, Walter told himself, and she loves me.

They took a two-week honeymoon on Cape Cod before leaving for his residency at the Boston City Hospital. A vacation counselor looked over their budget and into his files and came up with a cottage on the north shore, near Dennis. "A tiny thing," the man said, smiling, "ideal for honeymooners," and Walter found the remark faintly accusatory. "Very inexpensive," the man went on. "Pre-season."

It was indeed a small cottage, with two rooms and very little plumbing and an outhouse a few yards away. The beach was windy and the water cold—only once did Walter and Elizabeth test it. The two weeks passed in recurring daily patterns: their physical discoveries of each other, the periodic ceremonies of eating, the old radio from which nothing but a Rhode Island station could be heard, the magazines and newspapers they acquired, and strange little silences that even then began to form and congeal like something spilled and neglected. But with their new friends in Boston—the new doctors and nurses they later met and visited—Walter told of the honeymoon in droll and humorous terms, describing the shack as "two rooms and a path." Everyone laughed, just as everyone had back in New York. Bermuda, everyone was convinced, could not have been more fun.

Although they couldn't afford it, Walter insisted that he and Elizabeth go to Bachrach's on Newberry Street and sit in the clothes in which they were married. "We can't wait," he argued, "until we're wealthy to pose for a good wedding picture." He was proud of her even and photogenic features smiling, beside the not-too-bad likeness of himself. Framing it in white gold, he set it on a bookcase opposite the sofa-bed.

They had a sub-let on Beacon Street and Elizabeth worked that year. She did private-duty nursing at the Massachusetts General (it paid better, although she enjoyed ward duty more) and frequently she and Walter met in the evening at some midpoint between their hospitals. They went to Scollay Square one night to see the celebrated tassel dancer, and although they sipped their drinks and watched the show almost without conversation, another one of his stories sprang from this evening.

"There was this blonde," he explained, "pushing forty but quite attractive, and she came out between the acts and played the piano. Semi-classical stuff—you know, *Clair de Lune* and

Lieberstraum and once in a while *Tea for Two*—but no style or talent at all, like a good child playing for company. Anyway, we weren't paying much attention—" (*We*, he had begun to say, drawing Elizabeth into his stories and using the magnanimous *We* instead of the immodest *I*) "—until we noticed that she was *crying* while she played. Smiling, you know, at least with her lips, but crying too and trying to blink the tears from her eyes. There were some drunks at the bar and they kept laughing and calling out remarks and between her numbers there was no applause at all. Well, we were in the balcony, above her head but quite near to her, and we decided to send some requests and applaud and, do you know? she turned her face up to us and played straight to the balcony and never looked again toward the bar. Poor kid, we learned later that she was an English war bride stranded in this country with a child and trying to earn her passage back to England. I suppose the management took her on for peanuts."

"I've seen that girl, too," someone said. "I wondered about her." And another girl turned to her neighbor and said, "Friend of the downtrodden, that's Walter."

It was then—not more than seven months since their marriage—that his glance met Elizabeth's and he suddenly thought: Is that really the way it happened? He tried to remember but could not decide whether he had exaggerated or supplemented or distorted in order to help the story along. He raised his drink, thinking: I talk too damn much at parties.

He began to take care with his stories—particularly those about incidents shared with Elizabeth—and he began to watch her. He discovered that she had stopped laughing, or smiling, or responding at all. Once in a while he found himself distressingly less fluent, even stumbling in his delivery. A pool of new questions formed in his mind: Had Elizabeth stopped loving him? Why did she never complain? Why did they never quarrel; why had he never seen her cry? And one day, causing him remarkably little astonishment, another question surfaced in his thoughts: Did *he* love *her*? He had no desire to be divorced; did that not indicate love?

———

Sometimes awakening first, Walter watched Elizabeth from the bedside and remembered the courtship at Bellevue. He thought of the many women who considered him attractive and clever and he wondered why with this shy and simple girl from Van Wert, Ohio, this girl who should have been dazzled and devoted and immensely grateful, marriage was becoming colorless. They had acquired so many habits and short-cuts, the skilled pretenses that gave the appearance of happiness, but in the private morning stillness he saw himself and Elizabeth as disenchanted, overly polite, mute of even the normal marital grumblings. He wondered, then, if he called her "Dear" too much and too carefully, if he swept ahead too briskly to open doors for her, if there was not some effort made to include her in his life when it should have been something effortless. But I *do* love her, he told himself, looking over the form of her body as outlined by the counterpane, and once, closing his eyes and considering his emotion, he was surprised to find that his mind turned from Elizabeth and from any woman at all (and he remembered, just then, his childhood—the becoming aware of his awkwardness, the plainness of his features and the length of his nose, the first frustrations of inattainment—and his younger brother, nimble and muscular and with black wavy hair that looked good disorderly or combed, and of people saying: "He'll be a lady killer, that one!").

Once, as he watched, Elizabeth awoke and asked: "What's the matter?"

Impulsively, desperately, he held her close to him and whispered, "I love you, Elizabeth. I love you very much."

"And I love you too," she said.

When his training had been completed they returned to New York and Walter entered private practice. For a time Elizabeth continued to work but as his income grew he urged her to give it up. But she enjoyed it, she said, and he smiled and asked: didn't it look silly, her doing ward work at Bellevue with him in an air-conditioned Park Avenue office and paying a nurse more than Elizabeth earned herself? Besides, they liked to entertain and both of them couldn't be getting in late because of some emergency. And there were things that could occupy her at home: telephone messages, looking after his bag, the mail, his medical journals. Children, he might have added, but year followed year with no sign of pregnancy and Walter preferred to leave this undiscussed. "Shouldn't I be examined?" Elizabeth once asked, and he made some evasion. He found within him no great need for children, and was not anxious to learn which of them was sterile.

He tried to tell stories about Elizabeth that he thought would please her, stories that underscored her kindness and resourcefulness, but he came to realize that she felt no need for them. She seemed to take for granted that people liked her; she was content to sit silently among them, graciously seen but unheard. Not everyone is dynamic, Walter decided, and this is Elizabeth: gentle, bovine, utterly uncomplicated; and he drew no significance from the recent appearance of a snapshot of her father stuck into one edge of their wedding picture frame. Walter was particularly proud of her quiet dignity when his younger brother came east from California bringing that bleached frump of a wife of his, and Elizabeth sat beside the girl and smiled at her tales of Las Vegas and looked like a queen next to a harlot.

In time Walter developed one of those fabulously lucrative Manhattan practices for which medical acumen is not essential and of which wealthy, not very ill ladies are a mainstay. His ability to listen with undiminishing sympathy was absolute. "Your husband's the first doctor," a woman told Elizabeth, "who really *listened* to me, and for years everyone had been cutting me off and calling me neurotic!"

"But she is," Elizabeth later asked, "isn't she?"

He shrugged. "There are somatic considerations," he replied. Rarely did she inquire into his practice, and never did she persist.

In the ninth year of their marriage they moved into a cooperative apartment on East 54th Street. The rooms were many, and huge.

"What shall I do with this one?" Elizabeth asked. "Do you want a den?"

"It's got a bath; isn't it another bedroom? Why don't you fix it up for yourself?" She turned to him but he could read no expression from her face. "Now that we have the room," he went on, "there's no reason why you should suffer any longer from my irregular hours, the bedside phone . . ."

Elizabeth took over a year to completely furnish the room. She brought in brocaded drapes, a Chinese rug, mahogany polished to shine like tortoise shell. She canopied the bed and wrapped herself in matching cocoons of silk. She hid the lighting and silenced the switches and flanked herself with record albums, high fidelity, portable television. She subscribed to a book club and stacked her novels on shelves along the walls and, as they overflowed, into bookcases in every room.

"Elizabeth loves it," Walter told everyone, "her private little world into which nothing enters except by personal choice."

They came and looked into the room. "It's perfectly lovely," they said.

In the eleventh year of the marriage Elizabeth's father became ill and she flew to Ohio to nurse him. On the day she was to return Walter received, instead, a letter from her. *Dear Walter,* she wrote, . . . *I simply cannot bring myself to return . . .*

At first he felt nothing at all, or at least nothing that he could identify. While he was still seated with the letter in his hand, the phone rang.

"Walter? Did Elizabeth get back?"

"No; don't expect us tonight." (Just a second's hesitation.) "As a matter of fact, I have a letter from her. Her father's no better and she's staying on."

"Oh, what a shame! Why don't you come along anyway?"

"Thank you, but—well, I'd feel awkward . . ."

"Nonsense, come ahead. It'll do you good."

Walter went. For the first time in many years he told the story of the Jewish woman in the Bellevue Out Patient Department. It was new to this group and they laughed loud and long. He told other stories; he had never been so inventive or told some of them so well. Before leaving, he consented to attend two other parties.

Returning to the apartment, he read Elizabeth's letter once more. It was a first draft, he felt sure, impulsive, panicky. He would not write or call her, judging that with Elizabeth his total silence would be more eloquent than any appeal he might make. For a time he could let things rest, as long as he was not approached by an attorney or called into a court of law. Thinking of the cleaning lady, he put the letter into a book and returned the book to a shelf.

Thirty-four evenings later he returned to the apartment after supper and found Elizabeth sitting on the sofa in the living room, her bags on the floor beside her. She had lost weight, and seemed anemic.

"Hello, Elizabeth," he said.

For an instant she closed her eyes. "Walter, I don't know if you'll want me back—"

"My dear—"

"No, wait. I'm sick. I need an operation. That's why I returned."

She was badly frightened. He sat next to her. "Tell me about it," he said. "We'll get you the finest surgeon in New York."

She survived only four days following the surgery. During most of that time he sat at the bedside while the three shifts of special nurses read their magazines in the linen room.

"Walter," Elizabeth said hoarsely from time to time, "please give me something to drink . . ." Oxygen went by tube into one nostril and through the other another tube extended to her stomach.

"Darling, you know we have to keep your stomach empty."

"Walter, please. You've no idea how horrible it is to be so thirsty. Just a sip of something, Seven-Up . . ."

"I'll speed up the infusion." He adjusted the clamp that controlled the drop-by-drop flow of glucose and saline into her vein.

Sometimes for hours they did not speak. Her eyes remained closed—although he did not think from her breathing and from little sounds that she made, that she was continually asleep. And then: "Walter . . . Seven-Up . . ."

"Poor Elizabeth—my poor, dear, sweetheart Elizabeth. I wish I could . . ."

When he said this she turned and looked at him and at the crossword puzzle he was filling in. The special nurse returned from supper and Walter left to eat.

Elizabeth was very quiet on the day she died. Coma occurred late, and during one of the last lucid moments she said, "Walter, what story will you make out of this?"

He had never guessed that he would miss her so dreadfully, or carry so many memories that caused him to feel pain. He avoided speaking of Elizabeth, and of many things, and frequently long conversations terminated with no contribution from him. When unpacking the things that the hospital had returned he found a crossword puzzle on which he had been working and discovered in the margin, in a handwriting he could not recognize, the word *Hypocrite.* A marginal note, he told himself, anyone could have jotted it down while looking over the puzzle, and he searched the diagram itself for a possible application. *I don't ever want to see my bedroom again,* he remembered, *the symbol of my total rejection,* and he called an auction gallery and had them clear out Elizabeth's room— clothes, draperies, books, everything. The nights seemed to become longer and broken by restless, desultory dreams; he awoke each morning into the fresh taste of panic, convinced that the day faced him with problems with which he simply could not cope. New York traffic began to upset him and very often, as he drove his car, he felt his heart skip and stop, and he developed sensations of choking and dizziness. He discovered the brief comforts of sedatives during the day, sleeping pills at night.

One of the Bellevue nurses called him. "Walter," she said, "we heard about Elizabeth, we're all very sorry. There's a reunion, the old gang . . . we thought you might want to come, but if you don't, we'll understand . . ."

"Thank you for thinking of me. I'm not sure."

At the last moment, he went. He had found, also, that he could use alcohol as a crutch. He drank three highballs quickly and sat with the fourth, glad that he had come. These were their old friends—although he had seen so little of them in recent years—the people who had known him and Elizabeth from the beginning. Sitting silently and still, he felt their affection and sympathy flooding over him like sunlight.

A nurse, a former roommate of Elizabeth's, came and took Walter's hand and glanced at his black tie (still, after eight months). "Poor Walter," she said, "you miss Elizabeth terribly, don't you?"

At once, the room was quiet. This was the first mention of Elizabeth that had been made this evening. His heart was suddenly beating comfortably; he felt warm and pleasantly at ease. Like in the old days.

He smiled, and blinked. "You know," he said softly (it was so magnificently still; even on this carpeting a pin would have made a sound!) . . . "You know, I keep thinking of those four days in the hospital. She was on nothing by mouth—peritonitis, you know—it was her only chance. But she was so thirsty, and kept begging for some Seven-Up . . ." Lowering his head even more, he blinked again. He whispered the rest of it. *"The way it turned out anyway, I wish I'd sneaked one in and given it to her. I kept meaning to . . ."*

Walter, what story will you make of this? The words shot almost ballistically into his mind, so vividly that he looked up, not certain that they had not been spoken. And his brain and his eyes saw many things: a letter from Ohio, a crossword puzzle on the margin of which was scrawled a single word, a group of people who looked down at him and then slowly away. The girl's hands were now quite heavy on his own.

Walter's heart speeded up and began, again, to skip. His instinct had failed him. He had blundered beyond that dreadful limit at which displayed emotion becomes unsightly.

People began to speak again, in many separate conversations.

"Poor dear," murmured the girl, and drew her hands away.

Walter rose and moved across the room. Some turned as he passed but he was mindless of their words, and their smiles were like little gates being shut, little signs saying Beware Of The Dog.

He returned to his apartment and sat among the things he

owned and thought of the large empty room that must soon be made into a den. He took three sleeping pills and returned the vial to his bag, his hand brushing against the narcotics case. *No,* he whispered, closing his eyes, *no* . . .

He awoke late the next day. In addition to each morning's panic, he had a hangover. Deciding not to use the car, he left the building by the main entrance rather than through the garage. The mail had already arrived. Taking it, Walter headed for the subway.

"Sophie," called Mr. Warbasse, entering his apartment, "have you seen the newspaper?"

"No," said his wife, who preferred to glean the world's news from her television set.

"There's an item about that doctor, that Dr. Walter Collins."

"What about him?" demanded Mrs. Warbasse, interest plain in her voice.

Her husband lowered himself into the armchair. "Here, let me read it," he said, adjusting the reading lamp. " 'Physician Dies Under Subway' is the caption, and the article carries yesterday's date. 'A man identified as Dr. Walter Collins, 38, of 400 East 54th Street, fell into the path of an approaching Independent Subway train this morning at the East 53rd Street Station. Witnesses stated that prior to the fall, the physician had appeared to be ill, and that he had swayed on the platform as though he were dizzy. Because of the accident, service was—' Well, it goes on about how the line was delayed."

"My God!" said Mrs. Warbasse, and her husband looked up at her.

"I don't suppose he got the letter," she continued, "if he left early in the morning. You know how the mails are."

"What letter?"

Mrs. Warbasse shifted in her seat. "*His* letter," she said, taking a cigarette and striking a match. "The one his wife Elizabeth wrote to him, the letter he mislaid in that book. I thought he might be looking for it . . ."

"Sophie, do you mean to say that you returned that letter to him?"

"Well of course! Did you expect me to *keep* such a personal thing?"

"For heaven's sake, Sophie, why didn't you just destroy the damn thing? Why rake up—"

"Oh, what's the difference?" Mrs. Warbasse demanded in the strong, sure voice of the uncertain. "He couldn't have gotten it, anyway."

"It's interfering, that's what's the difference! It's meddling in something that doesn't concern you at all!" Rustling the newspaper, he raised it and held it rigidly before his face, cutting his wife from his view.

Mrs. Warbasse shrugged and stubbed out her cigarette. Standing, she walked to the door. "Kismet," said Mrs. Warbasse, who was—in her way—a philosopher.

The Prisoner of Zemu Island

Joan Richter

A needle of light pierced the white blaze of African sun and flickered high in the cloudless sky over Zemu Island. Ras Lazaar stood at the edge of the airfield, in the shade of a jacaranda tree, watching the gleaming splinter of steel sprout wings. A fusion of excitement and sadness held him, as he studied the plane's gradual descent. He had traveled to the mainland by boat many times, but he had never flown. He never would now. The new African government did not allow Indians to leave the island.

He pushed away the wave of self-pity. Unchecked it would engulf him in a deep sense of hopelessness.

Thirty passengers were on board the plane today—twenty-nine Germans on a tour of Africa, coming to spend the afternoon on Zemu Island, and one American woman traveling alone. Since Ras was the Director of Tourism they were all his responsibility, especially the American. The decision to grant her entry had not been reached without argument and threat. Except for newspapermen whose requests the new government automatically denied, it was a year since an American had sought to come to Zemu Island.

"If she is not what she says she is—if she brings trouble to the New Republic of Zemu Island—you, *Indian,* will pay for it!" Prime Minister Masaka's finger had pointed like a gun at Ras's head, firing the abbreviated Swahili with the slur of ethnic superiority. Only Ras's hatred of Masaka exceeded his fear.

When the plane touched the ground and streaked across the far runway, Ras stepped out of the shade of the tree. His stride showed only a bare trace of stiffness from the now year-old wound. He was taller than the average Indian, with the traditional olive skin and gleaming black hair. His frame was held together by pliant muscles developed by years of tennis and swimming. Since the political coup he had done neither, but at twenty-three his body did not show the year's absence from exercise. His mind, too, had survived the trauma of the two-day revolution in which the Indian population of Zemu Island had been decimated.

He had stopped asking why he had lived when so many had died, what instinct had sent him to the ground at the unfamiliar sound of gunfire, by what lucky accident a bullet had struck his leg and not his heart. The Africans had not killed him afterward, when they found him wounded and unconscious; instead they had put him in the care of the Cuban doctors who had come with the revolutionary force. Later, when he was given the position of Director of Tourism, he began to understand. The Africans needed him—he could read and write both Swahili and English.

It seemed without reason that Masaka should see a threat in the visit of the young American schoolteacher. Yet the attitude was in keeping with the Prime Minister's frequent rages and bursts of irrationality. The pressures of ruling a country were heavy on a man, even when he had the support of his people. Masaka had had that support for only a short time. Suspicion had quickly eaten at the edges of black unity when word spread that the revolution had been the organized effort of a foreign power which had chosen Masaka as its island leader, and not the spontaneous rebellion of Africans against a repressive Indian government.

Sober Africans began to ask questions. Some had begun to demand answers. Yukano was one of them.

Differences between Masaka and Yukano were evident even physically. Masaka was six feet tall, with a round head and enormous hands that were forever washing one another. Yukano was slight with a thin face and narrow shoulders, and he spoke softly.

At a meeting where Masaka had announced his opposition to the American teacher's visit, Yukano had risen and talked convincingly of Zemu Island's need to reinstate tourism as a source of revenue and prestige. Many were stirred by this argument, but others were unconvinced until Yukano spoke again. "The American June Hastings asks to come not just as a tourist but as a scientist interested in Zemu Island's marine life. Do you recall the prestige that came to Tanganyika when Dr. Louis Leakey made his excavations at Olduvai Gorge and found evidence of prehistoric man? How do we know what there is to be found in the waters of Zemu Island?"

Masaka had acceded to the majority, but Ras knew it was a defeat the Prime Minister was not likely to forget. Ras worried about the kind of action Masaka would take to soothe his wounded pride.

The plane came to a stop and the airfield sprouted life. Africans in ragged shorts and bare feet appeared to unload baggage. Airport officials of the same skin color, wearing starched uniforms and hats decorated with gold braid, stood at attention to some unseen authority. The sun streamed down and the concrete airfield glistened with the running of dry rivers and shimmering pools.

The first person to disembark was the German tour leader, with whom Ras shook hands. "Lunch is waiting for your group at the Manga Hotel," Ras said. "Afterwards the drivers will take you on a tour of the island." The balding pink-cheeked man mopped his forehead and managed a smile, then went off to tend his flock.

Ras's attention steadied on the young woman who appeared in the plane's doorway. A border of embroidery fluttered at the hem of her dress, the saffron-pink color of a ripe pomalo. A graceful sweep of bronze hair fell across her cheek. He was struck by the expression of expectancy in her eyes as she scanned the horizon of palm trees, then started down the steps.

"June Hastings?" he asked when she reached him.

She hesitated. "Yes."

"I am Rashid Lazaar. We have corresponded. I am with the Ministry of Tourism."

"I'm glad to meet you, Mr. Lazaar." She offered her hand. "Thank you for arranging for my entry permit."

"My pleasure," he said, a phrase he realized he had not

used with any real meaning in a long time. "I think if we go directly to immigration we will save time."

She fell in step beside him. "What about my luggage? Your customs people will want to check that."

"That will be delivered to another place—we must go there after we have finished here."

Though her eyes were veiled by sunglasses he could see that they were a pale brown, almost golden. There was a question in them. Her bronze head tossed. "Does someone from your office always meet a new arrival?"

"It is the policy of the new government."

"But I must be someone special to be entitled to the Director of Tourism himself."

The mischief in her voice was clear. It surprised him and reminded him of his sisters, and their playful jibes.

"You *are* special, Miss Hastings. You have not only chosen to visit Zemu Island, you have come for an unusual purpose. Zemu women and children have gathered shells for years and made necklaces of them, but no one has ever thought them of scientific interest."

"Maybe it's time someone did."

"Some in the government are doubtful, others are puzzled. Others still have suggested that you will give Zemu Island prominence by discovering something as important as what Dr. Leakey found at Olduvai Gorge."

She stopped and stared at him. "They don't really think that?"

"It is what has been said."

"By whom?"

Ras shrugged. "A man named Yukano." The name would mean nothing to her—Yukano had become prominent in island politics only a short time ago. But Ras thought he saw a flicker of recognition move across her face. "Have you heard of him?"

"The name sounds familiar, but maybe it's my Western ear. Even now many African names still sound alike to me."

He nodded, assuming she was referring to the last two years she had been teaching school in Kenya. "It is a funny thing. I have the same difficulties with British names—like your own. But Indian names are hard for Westerners, I think."

"Ignorance contributes to the confusion. People of one culture imagine those of another are all alike. Masaka and Yukano, for example. To a person unfamiliar with Africa they simply are both Africans. No thought is given to the possibility of great differences between them, that they are of different tribes and different persuasions—totally different personalities."

Her voice lowered as they approached the Immigration Building and fell silent when they reached the steps. Ras did not speak either, but his mind was churning. She was well informed, typical of the emancipated American women he had read about. He must be careful not to be guilty of the very thing she had just described. She was more than simply an American. She was an individual who had chosen to come to visit Zemu Island for a special reason. What that reason was he suspected he had yet to find out.

The immigration check was routine, even to the insolence of the African clerk who looked at Ras and yawned widely. In the past year Ras had learned to ignore such petty insults, but with the young woman at his side he found it difficult to hold back a rebuke. He was glad when they were outside again and he could lead her to the car he had left parked near the jacaranda tree. "Your luggage is being delivered to a building at the other end of the airport—it is just a minute's drive."

As he helped her into the front seat he thought of warning her that this would be no ordinary customs check. Two of the Prime Minister's own men would be in the banda and their instructions were to go through her belongings with exactness. If they found something they did not like, she would be put on the next plane leaving Zemu Island.

Ras decided to say nothing. A warning would serve no purpose but to alarm her. He hoped her luggage cleared. He wanted her to stay. There was very little he had wanted so much in a long time.

Perhaps he would even take her to Pwani Pwani—he had not been back since the day the guns had fired. He had thought he could never return, to walk over those sands where his mother and his sisters and the girl he had loved had played ball and gathered shells. How pretty they had looked, strolling along the beach, their brilliantly colored saris catching the breeze, like butterflies in flight. Sunday after Sunday they had gone to picnic at Pwani Pwani. One Sunday all of them had died . . .

"Tell me about the Manga Hotel," he heard June Hastings say. "Is it as nice as it used to be?"

He glanced at her quickly, torn from his reverie. "You know it?"

"I heard of it from someone who had been there years ago, when the Norberts owned it. They aren't still here, are they?"

Ras smiled. Anyone who had stayed at the Manga would remember the Norberts. "They're still here. They run the hotel for the government now." He was certain she was aware that the new regime had confiscated all private lands and possessions. "They have kept things up. It is a handsome building, white stone and coral, built around a courtyard that is always in bloom."

Purposely he did not mention the door. For some reason he wanted her to see it for herself, unprompted. He was tempted to add that a building, no matter how beautiful, did not make a hotel—only guests could give it life. There had been no guests for a year. The few boarders were foreign technicians who had come in the wake of the revolution, from Cuba and Russia and China. They had come to work, not to play. The lanterns that had always hung in the flame trees, lighting the terrace on Saturday nights, had not been lit in a year.

They had reached the end of the concrete runway where a wall of tropical forest faced them. Ras found the narrow dirt track that led to the banda and parked beside a car already there. It was Masaka's car. His heartbeat quickened, but in a moment resumed its even beat. How else would the two men assigned to check her luggage get to the airport, if not by car? But it was not like Masaka to let anyone use his.

The shade of the trees was deep and blinding after the brightness of the sun. Inside the banda it seemed darker still.

Two Africans in Army uniforms stood behind a table on which her luggage lay—a blue suitcase and one small metal trunk. Their black faces shone in the glow from a pressure lamp whose eerie light did not reach into the far corner to make distinguishable the figure standing there. But a familiar movement of hands washing one another told Ras who it was. A cold stillness touched his heart and did not go away.

June Hastings unlocked the blue suitcase, and the two men began to paw through the layers of pastel-colored clothes, looking into pockets, peering into the toes of shoes. Before opening the metal trunk she removed her sunglasses and put them in her purse. The glance with which she touched Ras was fleeting, but in the strange light her eyes looked to him like warm gold. Once before he had known someone with eyes of that color—in Dar es Salaam.

Several times he had gone there by dhow with his father, sailing first to Zanzibar and on to what was then Tanganyika. They would always stay two days—one to sell the copra they had brought from their plantation, another to visit a man named Benji, an old friend of his father. The two men would sit together in the shade of a mango tree, sipping tea, their voices hushed, their heads bent in serious talk. On the other side of the garden Ras would play with Benji's youngest son, named after his father. They drank orange fanta and stuffed themselves with sweet cakes and played marbles. Sometimes the girl who lived in the house on the other side of the garden wall would join them. Though she was the same age as they, rarely could she beat them in a marble game. Her hair was the color of dark honey, her eyes pale gold.

Each time they left Benji's house the packet of money his father had received from the sale of the copra would be smaller than when he had first received it, but the expression on his father's face would say that things had gone as he had wished. Ras was always tempted to ask what business his father had with Benji that took so much money, but he did not, knowing that when his father wanted him to know he would tell him. That time came. "Some day things will not be good on Zemu Island and you and your mother and your sisters will have to leave.

Benji is sending money for me to a bank in Switzerland. It is in my name and in yours. Should something ever happen to me, you will know what to do." Ras remembered how frightened those words had made him, and how little he had understood their full meaning.

Now he understood, but what good did it do? Those careful plans his father had made in Dar es Salaam, under the mango tree, while the sound of marbles clinked in the warm still air, had died on the beach at Pwani Pwani . . .

June Hastings turned the key in the lock and lifted the lid of the metal trunk. The two Army men looked up from the blue suitcase and turned to stare at the contents of the trunk, their eyes growing round and then narrow. They leaned closer and then straightened, muttering in Swahili to each other and to the man in the corner of the room.

Masaka left the shadowed security of the banda wall and moved to the table. She looked up but made no sign that his presence was a surprise to her. Ras felt his breath catch as he wondered if she knew who Masaka was.

The lid of the trunk held a collection of tools: files, tweezers, knives, hooks, brushes, a small rake and shovel. In the bottom of the trunk was a roll of netting, a half dozen litre-sized bottles filled with liquids, and several dozen clear plastic boxes of assorted sizes, separated by layers of cotton wool.

She spoke in a quiet fluent Swahili that surprised them all. "I have come to Zemu Island to gather specimens of seashells. These are tools I need to find the shells and to clean them." Her hand passed lightly over the contents of the lid and then moved to the items in the lower section. "The large bottles contain cleaning solutions—Clorox, alcohol, vinegar, formaldehyde. These plastic boxes are for the shells after they have been cleaned. Each will be wrapped in a piece of cotton, so it will not be crushed."

She had turned in the course of her explanation so that her glance touched each of them—the two Army men, Ras, and Masaka. Ras found it difficult to hide the rush of admiration he felt for her intuition. She might have guessed that Masaka would not understand a lengthy stream of English, but she could not have known how angry he would have become if his ignorance were revealed.

She withdrew a small blue-bound book from the trunk, with a colored photograph of shells on its cover. Ras read the title: *Shells of the East African Coast.* She opened to several pages. Each had some text accompanying the photograph of a shell.

"This book describes shells found along the coast of East Africa. I would like to do the same thing about shells in the waters of Zemu Island."

One of Masaka's large hands reached out for the book. He looked at its cover and turned to look inside. He snapped the book shut and thrust it at her. "You will make a book like this about Zemu Island?"

"I would like to."

"Where did you learn to speak Swahili?"

"In Kenya. I taught English in a school north of Nairobi. My pupils knew their own tribal languages and Swahili. I learned Swahili so that I could teach them English."

Masaka's hands had begun moving one over the other. Ras saw something building in him, but he did not know what it was, or its cause. His concern stirred. When Masaka spoke again, it would not be with an even voice, but with the beginning of some irrational anger. How would the girl react?

"Kenya has declared Swahili its national language! Why do they still teach English?"

Something in Masaka's expression had evidently prepared her for the attack. She only frowned thoughtfully. "English is just one of many subjects taught in Kenyan schools, like arithmetic and history and geography."

Masaka stared at her and then his face closed over. He motioned to the two men standing mute behind the table. The three of them marched out the door.

Ras stared through the open doorway after them. He was not certain whether to feel relief or worry. It was not like Masaka to give way so easily.

"Can we leave now?" Her voice took him from his thoughts.

"Yes, we can go," he said slowly, unable to free himself of the uneasiness he felt.

"Let's hurry then." She smiled at him, a mischievous smile. "I'm so hungry I could eat a horse!"

Her spirit was contagious. He grinned. "You will insult the Norberts with that kind of talk!" They were both suddenly laughing and he felt strangely free. He had to remind himself that his position had not changed. He was still a prisoner on Zemu Island. But the gloom of that realization was not as great as it usually was.

They put her suitcase and trunk into the compartment of his car. When they were driving off he turned to her and asked, "Did you know who he was?"

"Masaka? Not right away. It was so dark at first. After the revolution there were lots of photographs of him in newspapers and magazines, standing on the veranda of the old Sultan's palace with the new flag draped over the railing. I was scared stiff when I realized who he was."

"You did not show it."

"I felt it. I've never had a head of state come to the airport and check my luggage before."

"I told you that you were someone special."

"You didn't say *that* special." She leaned back, resting her head against the seat. "Ras, are we going to be seeing a lot of Masaka?"

The road from the airport to the Manga Hotel was narrow. He was behind a donkey cart laden with bananas, driving slowly. It was easy to turn and look at her. She had called him Ras, not Rashid. There were some things about her that were indeed puzzling—the easy comfort he felt, the strange sense of the familiar.

He shrugged. "I cannot speak for Masaka. He is not the most predictable of men."

"Or the most stable. I heard that on the mainland, but I thought it was just gossip, wishful rumor. But it's not. That man is cracking up. I'm not sure it's anything to rejoice about. Zemu

Island could be in for a lot of trouble with someone like him ruling."

"That is very dangerous talk."

"And I should know better. You might turn the car around and head straight back to the airport. Please don't. I'd be so disappointed. I've wanted to visit Zemu Island for a long time. I never thought I'd get the chance. It's a long way from Boston."

"Is that where you come from?"

"It's my mother's home. We went there to live after my father died ten years ago. He was a British doctor. We traveled a lot when I was small."

"You had been to Africa then—before the last two years teaching in Kenya?"

"Yes," was all she said.

The last turn brought them into the center of Zemu town with its narrow Arab alleys that twisted and cut back on each other. To a stranger they were a mysterious labyrinth, but to Ras they were home.

Some of the old pride stirred in him as he stopped the car in front of the hotel and waited for her reaction. The chalk-white walls appeared almost opalescent in the brilliance of the noonday sun. At intervals bougainvillaea clung and tumbled in scarlet cascades. The stairway entrance ascended to a wide arch embracing a massive double door carved of ebony. Spikes of polished brass were embedded in the oiled wood and gleamed in the equatorial sunlight.

She was silent beside him, staring, her profile still. After a while she turned. Her eyes were shining. "It's magnificent. I've never seen anything like it. And you were right—it would take an elephant to batter that door down."

He stared at her. "An elephant—I—"

Her soft brown-gold eyes gleamed with mischief. "You don't remember? How absolutely horrid of you!"

How absolutely horrid of you! Where had he heard those words?

Then he heard the clink of glass against glass. He saw the blue marble fly from his hand, hit the white one swirled with red, and split it in two. *How absolutely horrid of you!* she had cried, stamping her foot and running off, disappearing behind the garden wall.

The great double door swung open, splashing reflections of sun onto their faces. An eager young African in a starched white uniform and red velour fez came down the steps and opened the car door on her side. *"Jambo, Memsab. Jambo, Bwana.* Welcome to Manga Hotel."

Winky Norbert was waiting for them at the desk inside. He shook Ras's hand and smiled at the pretty girl with him. His wiry mustache twitched. "Good you didn't get here a while ago. Sheer bedlam with that tour. Couldn't please one of them, no less the lot. If they can't give Zemu more than four hours I'd rather they stayed away."

"That'll do with the complaining, Winky." Margaret Norbert appeared. "You know very well you loved every minute of it. You haven't been so chipper since the last tour. Twenty-nine lunches are twenty-nine lunches. Makes me feel we're still running a hotel."

She turned to June with a smile that deepened the wrinkles around her mouth and eyes. At fifty-five she was still an attractive woman. "Welcome to the Manga. I don't have to guess who you are. You're June Hastings, our first real guest in a long time."

June smiled. "Thank you. It's as lovely here as I heard it would be. Is there any chance you've given me a room overlooking the courtyard?"

"Take your pick. You can have one next to the Cubans or across from the Russians. The Chinese prefer the hotel down the street."

Winky patted his wife's arm. "Stop twigging the girl, Maggie." Then looking at June, "We've given you a second-floor room that looks right out onto a forest of bougainvillaea. I think you'll like it."

The road to Pwani Pwani wound along the edge of coconut plantations and through the ripening groves of clove trees. The warm humid air was heavy with the fragrance of an earlier crop, already harvested and drying in the sun. June had changed into a short blue dress that bared her suntanned arms. She was leaning back against the seat, her hair blowing in the breeze. It was the first time they had been alone since their arrival at the hotel.

"You've had time to remember," she said.

"I'd never forgotten. But it was better to pretend. If I had allowed myself to think, I could not have let you come. This way it has happened without my really knowing."

"It's that bad here then?"

"Why have you come?"

"Benji sent me."

"Benji? Benji died three years ago."

"I'm talking about Benji the son."

Ras thought of the small boy with the dark eyes with whom he had shot marbles and drunk orange fanta and gorged himself on sweet cakes—he was a man now. The last time Ras had been to Dar es Salaam young Benji had been at school in England.

"Where is Benji now?"

"I saw him in Nairobi, but he was leaving for New York."

Nairobi—New York—and he could not even go to Zanzibar. "Benji sent you. Why?"

"To find out what is happening on Zemu Island. No one on the outside really knows. Only a little has gotten out. I wasn't honest with you when I said I'd not heard of Yukano— I have heard of him. Some people think he is the man who should be ruling Zemu Island instead of Masaka. He would allow the British to return. He would seek American aid, not only Communist."

"What would he do for the Indians? Give them back their lives?" He'd spoken so bitterly that he knew she could make no reply. "Benji has a plan?" he asked softly.

"Not just Benji alone. There are others. But they need someone they can count on in Zemu. Benji wants to know if you will help."

"In what way? To make Yukano head of Zemu Island?"

"You mean he is an African," she said quietly.

He felt the bite of her words, the accusation in them and the challenge. She was no stranger to East African politics. She knew the deep animus that lay between African and Indian. She knew the tumult and bloodshed that had thrust the African into power. For those who had been born to the old way it would never be easy to accept black authority; but to fight it, or pretend that was not the way the tide ran, would be stupid.

"I know the differences between men," he said. "There is little likeness between Masaka and Yukano except for the color of their skin. Zemu will rot under the rule of a man like Masaka. I do not know that it will ever flourish as it once did, but with someone like Yukano there would at least be a chance." He fell silent.

"But how?" he asked after a while. "It would not be enough merely to get rid of Masaka. They would only put someone else like him in his place. And it would be dangerous— more dangerous than you can imagine. Masaka may be stupid, but those behind him are not. I do not think it was his own intelligence that made him suspicious of your visit. He was warned."

She smiled mischievously. "But after today no one will be suspicious."

"What makes you say so?"

"Today we are going shell gathering—and we'll be watched. After they see all the trouble we go to to get a few shells they will be convinced that shells are the sole reason for my visit."

"Then it is not a pretense?"

"It is, and it isn't. Marine biology is my field. I will write a book about the shells I find on Zemu Island. It will be published and copies will be sent to the government here. If any doubt over the purpose of my visit still lingers, it will disappear when copies of the book arrive. Yukano went a bit overboard when he talked of Olduvai Gorge—Africans are impressed by such things. They are impressed by books even when they can't read them.

"But Masaka will be reassured—and so will the Cubans and the Russians. Tours from Western nations will begin to come to Zemu Island and word will spread that Zemu Island is a lovely place. The government will become complacent and think that people have forgotten how Masaka came into power. It will assume there is no one interested enough in the welfare of this small piece of land floating in the Indian Ocean to plan a counterrevolution."

"Those are large words," he said. "The idea is larger still. You are talking about a long time—many months, perhaps years."

"I don't think Benji or the others involved with him have any illusions that it will be easy, that it will not take months of careful planning. They also know they cannot do it without help from someone here on the island—from you. Your position as Director of Tourism allows you to receive and send letters, a privilege others on Zemu are denied. It is a ready means of communication which cannot be duplicated with anyone else here."

"But every letter I receive or write is censored. They are not as naive as you think."

She shook her head. "I know. We would use a code."

He listened to her unfold a plan that could not work without him. It was a mad plan that had greater chance of failure than of success—but it offered hope, some hope. Ras realized that until she had come he had had no hope, no hope at all.

They had almost reached the place where he should turn off onto a narrow track that would take them to Pwani Pwani. He had slowed down, looking for it. It would be grown over now—perhaps they would have to leave the car and walk in— it would be difficult with the metal trunk. Ah, there it was—the place marked by a dead tree. The growth was not so thick that he could not drive through part of the way.

"Close your window so you will not get scratched," he said, rolling up his own. Branches strung with thorny vines and moss arched across the once open path. The perfume of ripening guavas had drifted into the car and touched his mind with memory—he had been picking guavas when the first shot came. Other shots followed, the bullets skipping like footsteps across the sand. Like dolls, his mother and the girls had fallen, brilliant piles of crumpled saris on the sand. Then his father, like a dervish, spinning, falling, coughing, dying on the sand. Ras was flattened in the underbrush of vines, the guavas he had picked and put in the front of his shirt squashed and wet and oozing against his chest, warm from the sun, warm like the blood in which his father lay. Pain exploded in his leg. Blackness passed over him but in his unconsciousness he strained to remember the familiar face among the bearded strangers, the African whose gun had aimed and with lust had killed— Masaka . . .

His hands were clenched around the steering wheel, whitening his knuckles and making the muscles of his forearms bulge. He stared through the windshield at the beach, at water glimmering through the suddenly denser tangle of green. He stopped the car, got out, and reached under the seat for the *panga* he kept there. The scent of guavas filled his nostrils as he struck at the vines that choked the path. The broad blade sliced through the ropy lengths as if they were bits of string. Sap oozed and trickled over his hands and arms.

When the path was clear, his arms fell to his sides, the point of the *panga* stuck in the sand beside his foot. His chest heaving, he turned and saw her standing by the car, watching him with her soft golden eyes, questioning, but not asking.

"We always came here to Pwani Pwani—my family. It was our special place. They all died here that first day of the revolution. I was picking guavas. They were walking along the sand. I have not been back, not until today." His dark eyes looked deep into hers. "It is time. I am ready."

She smiled gently and held out her hand. "Let's go then. There is lots to do."

They each took a handle of the metal trunk and carried it onto the beach where they placed it in the shade of a palm tree. He left her to open it while he returned for the two buckets she had borrowed from the Norberts.

Along the way he glanced on both sides into the dense tropical growth for a sign of anyone hiding there. They would be watched, but they would never know by whom or by how many. Once before the forest had camouflaged the presence of the enemy.

He started back toward the beach, carrying the buckets. He spied the tree where he had left her and saw the trunk as it had been, unopened. Then he saw her arm raised in the water, waving to him, splashing. He heard her voice and her laughter. He tore off his clothes and went racing into the waves. In a few moments he was shoveling and she was using the rake.

"Here's a beauty," she cried. "Look at it." She held a brown and white spiraled shell in the palm of her hand.

"There must be hundreds of them just like that all. over the beach."

"They'd be chipped or cracked. The shells I take back must be perfect." She dropped it into the bucket of formaldehyde solution and reached for a notebook. "Speckled Turret Shell," she said aloud, "otherwise known as *Terebra oculata.*"

"What about this one?" he said, extending his hand. She reached for it without looking.

"You don't take me seriously at all!" He could almost see her foot stamp.

"Oh, but I do," he said, tossing the small stone away and giving her a handful of shells he had been saving.

She grinned at him, and then set about recording the names in her notebook.

When the buckets were almost full she rose. "I want to set some traps in the rocks close to shore. Some shells are nocturnal. It won't take long. Then we can swim until the sun goes down, and come back tomorrow."

She cut squares from the roll of netting that had been in the trunk and with some thin wire gathered them into makeshift baskets. A small piece of the meat from the Norberts' kitchen served as bait. They laid the traps together, anchoring them with small stones. As they worked, their heads were close, almost touching. She spoke softly. "They're watching, I know. But they are stupid—we could be setting mines and they wouldn't know. Some day we will."

She looked up and her eyes held his for a moment, the

expression in them intent and serious. Then in the next instant her head tossed and she was running into the water.

The sun was low in the sky, a fiery orange ball that lit the surface of the transparent pale-green sea with strands of orange and gold. Between the breaking waves the water flowed like the soft folds of an iridescent sari. Ras raced after her and dove into the water, feeling the salt of it sting his eyes, blurring the memory that had begun of a girl he had once loved, a girl who had worn a sari of green threaded with bronze and gold on the last day of her life.

He swam alongside her. "Can you swim to those rocks out there? At the last one there is a deep pool and a cavern. If the light is right it is a wonderful sight."

Drops of water clinging to her eyelashes sparkled and flew away when she nodded and began an easy stroke beside him.

It was a long time since he'd made the dive and he wanted to be certain the passage was still clear, certain no rock had dislodged itself. He had warned her to let him lead the way. Her hand was in his as they swam underwater toward an archway of rock leading under a ledge in the rock ceiling.

It was the purple coral he wanted her to see, the sea anemones and the swaying ferns whose undulations were said to have teased love-starved sailors into thinking they were mermaids. It was a perfect time, the sun and tide were just right. There was a small space where they could rise to the surface and rest before they dove again.

"I've never seen purple coral before," she said.

"It is purple only in the water. It turns brown when it is in the air."

He was ready to dive again, anxious to show her more.

"Wait, Ras. The sun will set soon. This is a good place to talk. No one can hear us, no one can see. There are other things you must know—about Yukano and the money that is yours in Switzerland—and the code. It's important that you know the code right away. Should anything happen to me, then you could still get in touch with Benji."

"Nothing will happen to you."

She grinned. "I could drown."

He shook his head. "You swim too well." He smiled to himself, measuring the differences between them. She thought of setting mines in the sea and he saw saris in the sea. He wanted to show her the mysteries of an underwater grotto he had explored as a child and she wanted to plan a revolution. "This is not the place. The opening in the rocks above us is like a horn and our words would be carried across the island."

She looked at him, her eyes doubtful, but he knew she could not take the chance. She needed him. Benji needed him. He would be their tool, as Masaka had been the tool of the Cubans. Was there a difference? Would the people of Zemu Island feel any more loyalty to the man whom counterrevolutionaries would put in the Sultan's palace than they did to Masaka? How many people would die?—Africans this time.

Despite his questions he knew he would do what Benji asked. Not because he wanted revenge, or because success of the counterrevolution would make him free, but because it gave him hope. And without hope no man can live and stay whole.

He took her hand, wishing he could explain what her coming to Zemu Island meant to him. But even if he were able to say it, he was afraid she would think him sentimental and not ready for the task that lay ahead of him.

"We have time for one more dive and then we must go while there is still light."

They swam toward the shore in the sun's last golden path. In minutes night would fall. They left the water and felt the evening air was cool. She began to run, her wet hair streaming, calling to him, laughing, "Catch me if you can!"

A breeze stirred and furled the water's waves. Dark leaves fluttered and shadows moved at the forest's edge. Bearded men who looked like trees advanced across the sand. As if in a nightmare he stood immobile.

He heard shots, her one sharp cry, but he looked away so as not to see her body lying crumpled on the sand.

Cornell Woolrich

The Book That Squealed

The outside world never intruded into the sanctum where Prudence Roberts worked. Nothing violent or exciting ever happened there, or was ever likely to. Voices were never raised above a whisper, or at the most a discreet murmur. The most untoward thing that could possibly occur would be that some gentleman browser became so engrossed he forgot to remove his hat and had to be tactfully reminded. Once, it is true, a car backfired violently somewhere outside in the street and the whole staff gave a nervous start, including Prudence, who dropped her date stamp all the way out in the aisle in front of her desk; but that had never happened again after that one time.

Things that the papers printed, holdups, gang warfare, kidnapings, murders, remained just things that the papers printed. They never came past these portals behind which she worked.

Just books came in and went out again. Harmless, silent books.

Until, one bright June day—

The Book showed up around noon, shortly before Prudence Roberts was due to go off duty for lunch. She was on the Returned Books desk. She turned up her nose with unqualified inner disapproval at first sight of the volume. Her taste was severely classical; she had nothing against light reading in itself, but to her, light reading meant Dumas, Scott, Dickens. She could tell this thing before her was trash by the title alone, and the author's pen name: *Manuela Gets Her Man,* by Orchid Ollivant.

Furthermore it had a lurid orange dust cover that showed just what kind of claptrap might be expected within. She was surprised a city library had added such worthless tripe to its stock; it belonged more in a candy-store lending library than here. She supposed there had been a great many requests for it among a certain class of readers; that was why.

Date stamp poised in hand she glanced up, expecting to see one of these modern young hussies, all paint and boldness, or else a faded middle-aged blonde of the type that lounged around all day in a wrapper, reading such stuff and eating marshmallows. To her surprise the woman before her was drab, looked hard-working and anything but frivolous. She didn't seem to go with the book at all.

Prudence Roberts didn't say anything, looked down again, took the book's reference card out of the filing drawer just below her desk, compared them.

"You're two days overdue with this," she said; "it's a one-week book. That'll be four cents."

The woman fumbled timidly in an old-fashioned handbag, placed a nickel on the desk.

"My daughter's been reading it to me at nights," she explained, "but she goes to night school and some nights she couldn't; that's what delayed me. Oh, it was grand." She sighed. "It brings back all your dreams of romance."

"Humph," said Prudence Roberts, still disapproving as much as ever. She returned a penny change to the borrower, stamped both cards. That should have ended the trivial little transaction.

But the woman had lingered there by the desk, as though trying to summon up courage to ask something. "Please," she faltered timidly when Prudence had glanced up a second time, "I was wondering, could you tell me what happens on page forty-two? You know, that time when the rich man lures her on his yasht?"

"Yacht," Prudence corrected her firmly. "Didn't you read the book yourself?"

"Yes, my daughter read it to me, but pages forty-one and forty-two are missing, and we were wondering, we'd give anything to know, if Ronald got there in time to save her from that awful—"

Prudence had pricked up her official ears at that. "Just a minute," she interrupted, and retrieved the book from where she had just discarded it. She thumbed through it rapidly. At first glance it seemed in perfect condition; it was hard to tell anything was the matter with it. If the borrower hadn't given her the exact page number—but pages 41 and 42 were missing, as she had said. A telltale scalloping of torn paper ran down the seam between pages 40 and 43. The leaf had been plucked out bodily, torn out like a sheet in a notebook, not just become loosened and fallen out. Moreover, the condition of the book's spine showed that this could not have happened from wear and tear; it was still too new and firm. It was a case of out-and-out vandalism. Inexcusable destruction of the city's property.

"This book's been damaged," said Prudence ominously. "It's only been in use six weeks, it's still a new book, and this page was deliberately ripped out along its entire length. I'll have to ask you for your reader's card back. Wait here, please."

She took the book over to Miss Everett, the head librarian, and showed it to her. The latter was Prudence twenty years from now, if nothing happened in between to snap her out of it. She sailed back toward the culprit, steel-rimmed spectacles glittering balefully.

The woman was standing there cringing, her face as white as though she expected to be executed on the spot. She had the humble person's typical fear of anyone in authority. "Please, lady, I didn't do it," she whined.

"You should have reported it before taking it out," said the inexorable Miss Everett. "I'm sorry, but as the last borrower, we'll have to hold you responsible. Do you realize you could go to jail for this?"

The woman quailed. "It was that way when I took it home," she pleaded; "I didn't do it."

Prudence relented a little. "She did call my attention to it herself, Miss Everett," she remarked. "I wouldn't have noticed it otherwise."

"You know the rules as well as I do, Miss Roberts," said her flinty superior. She turned to the terrified drudge. "You will lose your card and all library privileges until you have paid the fine assessed against you for damaging this book." She turned and went careening off again.

The poor woman still hovered there, pathetically anxious. "Please don't make me do without my reading," she pleaded. "That's the only pleasure I got. I work hard all day. How much is it? Maybe I can pay a little something each week."

"Are you sure you didn't do it?" Prudence asked her searchingly. The lack of esteem in which she held this book was now beginning to incline her in the woman's favor. Of course, it was the principle of the thing, it didn't matter how trashy the book in question was. On the other hand, how could the woman have been expected to notice that a page was gone, in time to report it, *before* she had begun to read it?

"I swear I didn't," the woman protested. "I love books, I wouldn't want to hurt one of them."

"Tell you what I'll do," said Prudence, lowering her voice and looking around to make sure she wasn't overheard. "I'll pay the fine for you out of my own pocket, so you can go ahead using the library meanwhile. I think it's likely this was done by one of the former borrowers, ahead of you. If such proves not to be the case, however, then you'll simply have to repay me a little at a time."

The poor woman actually tried to take hold of her hand to kiss it. Prudence hastily withdrew it, marked the fine paid, and returned the card to her.

"And I suggest you try to read something a little more worth while in future," she couldn't help adding.

She didn't discover the additional damage until she had gone upstairs with the book, when she was relieved for lunch. It was no use sending it back to be rebound or repaired; with one entire page gone like that, there was nothing could be done with it; the book was worthless. Well, it had been that to begin with, she thought tartly.

She happened to flutter the leaves scornfully and light filtered through one of the pages, in dashes of varying length, like a sort of Morse code. She looked more closely, and it was the forty-third page, the one immediately after the missing leaf. It bore innumerable horizontal slashes scattered all over it from top to bottom, as though some moron had underlined the words on it, but with some sharp-edged instrument rather than the point of a pencil. They were so fine they were almost invisible when the leaf was lying flat against the others, white on white; it was only when it was up against the light that they stood revealed. The leaf was almost threadbare with them. The one after it had some too, but not nearly so distinct; they hadn't pierced the thickness of the paper, were just scratches on it.

She had heard of books being defaced with pencil, with ink, with crayon, something visible at least—but with an improvised stylus that just left slits? On the other hand, what was there in this junky novel important enough to be emphasized—if that was why it had been done?

She began to read the page, to try to get some connected meaning out of the words that had been underscored. It was just a lot of senseless drivel about the heroine who was being entertained on the villain's yacht. It couldn't have been done for emphasis, then, of that Prudence was positive.

But she had the type of mind that, once something aroused its curiosity, couldn't rest again until the matter had been solved. If she couldn't remember a certain name, for instance, the agonizing feeling of having it on the tip of her tongue but being unable to bring it out would keep her from getting any sleep until the name had come back to her.

This now took hold of her in the same way. Failing to get anything out of the entire text, she began to see if she could get something out of the gashed words in themselves. Maybe that was where the explanation lay. She took a pencil and paper and began to transcribe them one by one, in the same order in which they came in the book. She got:

hardly anyone going invited merrily

Before she could go any farther than that, the lunch period was over; it was time to report down at her desk again.

She decided she was going to take the book home with her that night and keep working on it until she got something out of it. This was simply a matter of self-defense; she wouldn't be getting any sleep until she did. She put it away in her locker, returned downstairs to duty, and put the money with which she was paying Mrs. Trasker's fine into the till. That was the woman's name, Mrs. Trasker.

The afternoon passed as uneventfully as a hundred others had before it, but her mind kept returning to the enigma at intervals. "There's a reason for everything in this world," she insisted to herself, "and I want to know the reason for this: why were certain words in this utterly unmemorable novel underscored by slashes as though they were Holy Writ or something? And I'm going to find out if it takes me all the rest of this summer!"

She smuggled the book out with her when she left for home, trying to keep it hidden so the other members of the staff wouldn't notice. Not that she would have been refused permission if she had asked for it, but she would have had to give her reasons for wanting to take it, and she was afraid they would all laugh at her or think she was becoming touched in the head if she told them. After all, she excused herself, if she could find out the meaning of what had been done, that might help the library to discover who the guilty party really was and recover damages, and she could get back her own money that she had put in for poor Mrs. Trasker.

Prudence hurried up her meal as much as possible, and returned to her room. She took a soft pencil and lightly went over the slits in the paper, to make them stand out more clearly. It would be easy enough to erase the pencil marks later. But almost as soon as she had finished and could get a comprehensive view of the whole page at a glance, she saw there was something wrong. The underscorings weren't flush with some of the words. Sometimes they only took in half a word, carried across the intervening space, and then took in half of the next. One of them even fell where there was absolutely no word at all over it, in the blank space between two paragraphs.

That gave her the answer; she saw in a flash what her mistake was. She'd been wasting her time on the wrong page. It was the leaf before, the missing page 41, that had held the real meaning of the slashed words. The sharp instrument used on it had simply carried through to the leaf under it, and even, very lightly, to the third one following. No wonder the scorings over-lapped and she hadn't been able to make sense out of them! Their real sense, if any, lay on the page that had been removed.

Well, she'd wasted enough time on it. It probably wasn't anything anyway. She tossed the book contemptuously aside, made up her mind that that was the end of it. A moment or so later her eyes strayed irresistibly, longingly over to it again. "I know how I *could* find out for sure," she tempted herself.

Suddenly she was putting on her things again to go out. To go out and do something she had never done before: buy a trashy, frothy novel. Her courage almost failed her outside the bookstore window, where she finally located a copy, along with bridge sets, ash trays, statuettes of Dopey, and other gew-gaws. If it had only had a less . . . er . . . compromising title. She set her chin, took a deep breath, and plunged in.

"I want a copy of *Manuela Gets Her Man,* please," she said, flushing a little.

The clerk was one of these brazen blondes painted up like an Iroquois. She took in Prudence's shell-rimmed glasses, knot of hair, drab clothing. She smirked a little, as if to say "So you're finally getting wise to yourself?" Prudence Roberts gave her two dollars, almost ran out of the store with her purchase, cheeks flaming with embarrassment.

She opened it the minute she got in and avidly scanned page 41. There wasn't anything on it, in itself, of more conse-quence than there had been on any of the other pages, but that wasn't stopping her this time. This thing had now cost her over three dollars of her hard-earned money, and she was going to get something out of it.

She committed an act of vandalism for the first time in her life, even though the book was her own property and not the city's. She ripped pages 41 and 42 neatly out of the binding, just as the leaf had been torn from the other book. Then she inserted it in the first book, the original one. Not *over* page 43, where it belonged, but under it. She found a piece of carbon paper, cut it down to size, and slipped that between the two. Then she fastened the three sheets together with paper clips, carefully seeing to it that the borders of the two printed pages didn't vary by a hair's breadth. Then she took her pencil and once more traced the gashes on page 43, but this time bore down heavily on them. When she had finished, she withdrew the loose page 41 from under the carbon and she had a haphazard array of underlined words sprinkled over the page. The original ones from the missing page. Her eye traveled over them excitedly. Then her face dropped again. They didn't make sense any more than before. She opened the lower half of the window, balanced the book in her hand, resisted an impulse to toss it out then and there. She gave herself a fight talk instead. "I'm a librarian. I have more brains than whoever did this to this book, I don't care who they are! I can get out whatever meaning they put into it, if I just keep cool and keep at it." She closed the window, sat down once more.

She studied the carbon-scored page intently, and presently a belated flash of enlightenment followed. The very arrangement of the dashes showed her what her mistake had been this time. They were too symmetrical; each one had its complement one line directly under it. In other words they were really double, not single lines. Their vertical alignment didn't vary in the slightest. She should have noticed that right away. She saw what it was now. The words hadn't been merely underlined, they had been cut out of the page bodily by four gashes around each required one, two vertical, two horizontal, forming an oblong that contained the wanted word. What she had mistaken for dashes had been the top and bottom lines of these "boxes." The faint side lines she had overlooked entirely.

She canceled out every alternate line, beginning with the top one, and that should have given her the real kernel of the message. But again she was confronted with a meaningless jumble, scant as the residue of words was. She held her head distractedly as she took it in:

cure
   wait
             poor
  honey   to

                        grand
    her
          health
                your
        fifty
                        instructions

"The text around them is what's distracting me," she decided after a futile five or ten minutes of poring over them. "Subconsciously I keep trying to read them in the order in which they appear on the page. Since they were taken bodily out of it, that arrangement was almost certainly not meant to be observed. It is, after all, the same principle as a jigsaw puzzle. I have the pieces now, all that remains is to put each one in the right place."

She took a small pair of nail scissors and carefully clipped out each boxed word, just as the unknown predecessor had whose footsteps she was trying to unearth. That done, she discarded the book entirely, in order to be hampered by it no longer. Then she took a blank piece of paper, placed all the little paper cut-outs on it, careful that they remained right side up, and milled them about with her finger, to be able to start from scratch.

"I'll begin with the word 'fifty' as the easiest entering wedge," she breathed absorbedly. "It is a numerical adjective, and therefore simply must modify one of those three nouns, according to all the rules of grammar." She separated it from the rest, set to work. Fifty health—no, the noun is in the singular. Fifty honey—no, again singular. Fifty instructions—yes, but it was an awkward combination, something about it didn't ring true, she wasn't quite satisfied with it. Fifty grand? That was it! It was grammatically incorrect, it wasn't a noun at all, but in slang it was used as one. She had often heard it herself, used by people who were slovenly in their speech. She set the two words apart, satisfied they belonged together.

"Now a noun, in any kind of a sentence at all," she murmured to herself, "has to be followed by a verb." There were only two to choose from. She tried them both. Fifty grand wait.

Fifty grand cure. Elliptical, both. But that form of the verb had to take a preposition, and there was one there at hand: "to." She tried it that way. Fifty grand to wait. Fifty grand to cure. She chose the latter, and the personal pronoun fell into place almost automatically after it. Fifty grand to cure her. That was almost certainly it.

She had five out of the eleven words now. She had a verb, two adjectives, and three nouns left: wait, your, poor, honey, health, instructions. But that personal pronoun already in place was a stumbling block, kept baffling her. It seemed to refer to some preceding proper name, it demanded one to make sense, and she didn't have any in her six remaining words. And then suddenly she saw that she did have. Honey. It was to be read as a term of endearment, not a substance made by bees.

The remaining words paired off almost as if magnetically drawn toward one another. Your honey, poor health, wait instructions. She shifted them about the basic nucleus she already had, trying them out before and after it, until, with a little minor rearranging, she had them satisfactorily in place.

your honey poor health fifty grand to cure her wait instructions

There it was at last. It couldn't be any more lucid than that. She had no mucilage at hand to paste the little paper oblongs down flat and hold them fast in the position she had so laboriously achieved. Instead she took a number of pins and skewered them to the blank sheets of paper. Then she sat back looking at them.

It was a ransom note. Even she, unworldly as she was, could tell that at a glance. Printed words cut bodily out of a book, to avoid the use of handwriting or typewriting that might be traced later. Then the telltale leaf with the gaps had been torn out and destroyed. But in their hurry they had overlooked one little thing, the slits had carried through to the next page. Or else they had thought it didn't matter, no one would be able to reconstruct the thing once the original page was gone. Well, she had.

There were still numerous questions left unanswered. To whom had the note been addressed? By whom? Whose "honey" was it? And why, with a heinous crime like kidnaping for ransom involved, had they taken the trouble to return the book at all? Why not just destroy it entirely and be done with it? The answer to that could very well be that the actual borrower—one of those names on the book's reference card—was someone who knew them, but wasn't aware what they were doing, what the book had been used for, hadn't been present when the message was concocted; had all unwittingly returned the book.

There was of course a question as to whether the message was genuine or simply some adolescent's practical joke, yet the trouble taken to evade the use of handwriting argued that it was anything but a joke. And the most important question of all was: should she go to the police about it? She answered that then and there, with a slow but determined *yes!*

It was well after eleven by now, and the thought of venturing out on the streets alone at such an hour, especially to and from a place like a police station, filled her timid soul with misgivings. She could ring up from here, but then they'd send someone around to question her, most likely, and that would be even worse. What would the landlady and the rest of the roomers think of her, receiving a gentleman caller at such an hour, even if he was from the police? It looked so . . . er . . . rowdy.

She steeled herself to go to them in person, and it required a good deal of steeling and even a cup of hot tea, but finally she set out, book and transcribed message under her arm, also a large umbrella with which to defend herself if she were insulted on the way.

She was ashamed to ask anyone where the nearest precinct house was, but luckily she saw a pair of policemen walking along as if they were going off duty, and by following them at a discreet distance, she finally saw them turn and go into a building that had a pair of green lights outside the entrance. She walked past it four times, twice in each direction, before she finally got up nerve enough to go in.

There was a uniformed man sitting at a desk near the entrance and she edged over and stood waiting for him to look up at her. He didn't, he was busy with some kind of report, so after standing there a minute or two, she cleared her throat timidly.

"Well, lady?" he said in a stentorian voice that made her jump and draw back.

"Could I speak to a . . . a detective, please?" she faltered.

"Any particular one?"

"A good one."

He said to a cop standing over by the door: "Go in and tell Murph there's a young lady out here wants to see him."

A square-shouldered, husky young man came out a minute later, hopefully straightening the knot of his tie and looking around as if he expected to see a Fifth Avenue model at the very least. His gaze fell on Prudence, skipped over her, came up against the blank walls beyond her, and then had to return to her again.

"You the one?" he asked a little disappointedly.

"Could I talk to you privately?" she said. "I believe I have made a discovery of the greatest importance."

"Why . . . uh . . . sure," he said, without too much enthusiasm. "Right this way." But as he turned to follow her inside, he slurred something out of the corner of his mouth at the smirking desk sergeant that sounded suspiciously like "I'll fix you for this, kibitzer. It couldn't have been Dolan instead, could it?"

He snapped on a cone light in a small office toward the back, motioned Prudence to a chair, leaned against the edge of the desk.

She was slightly flustered; she had never been in a police station before. "Has . . . er . . . anyone been kidnaped lately, that is to say within the past six weeks?" she blurted out.

He folded his arms, flipped his hands up and down against his own sides. "Why?" he asked noncommittally.

"Well, one of our books came back damaged today, and I think I've deciphered a kidnap message from its pages."

Put baldly like that, it did sound sort of far-fetched, she had to admit that herself. Still, he should have at least given her time to explain more fully, not acted like a jackass just because she was prim-looking and wore thick-lensed glasses.

His face reddened and his mouth started to quiver treacherously. He put one hand up over it to hide it from her, but he couldn't keep his shoulders from shaking. Finally he had to turn away altogether and stand in front of the water cooler a minute. Something that sounded like a strangled cough came from him.

"You're laughing at me!" she snapped accusingly. "I came here to help you, and that's the thanks I get."

He turned around again with a carefully straightened face. "No, ma'am," he lied cheerfully right to her face, "I'm not laughing at you. I . . . we . . . appreciate your co-operation. You leave this here and we . . . we'll check on it."

But Prudence Roberts was nobody's fool. Besides, he had ruffled her plumage now, and once that was done, it took a great deal to smooth it down again. She had a highly developed sense of her own dignity. "You haven't the slightest idea of doing anything of the kind!" she let him know. "I can tell that just by looking at you! I must say I'm very surprised that a member of the police department of this city—"

She was so steamed up and exasperated at his facetious attitude that she removed her glasses, in order to be able to give him a piece of her mind more clearly. A little thing like that shouldn't have made the slightest difference—after all this was police business, not a beauty contest—but to her surprise it seemed to.

He looked at her, blinked, looked at her again, suddenly began to show a great deal more interest in what she had come here to tell him. "What'd you say your name was again, miss?" he asked, and absently made that gesture to the knot of his tie again.

She hadn't said what it was in the first place. Why, this man was just a common—a common masher; he was a disgrace to the shield he wore. "I am Miss Roberts of the Hillcrest Branch of the Public Library," she said stiffly. "What has that to do with this?"

"Well . . . er . . . we have to know the source of our

information," he told her lamely. He picked up the book, thumbed through it, then he scanned the message she had deciphered. "Yeah"—Murphy nodded slowly—"that does read like a ransom note."

Mollified, she explained rapidly the process by which she had built up from the gashes on the succeeding leaf of the book.

"Just a minute, Miss Roberts," he said, when she had finished. "I'll take this in and show it to the lieutenant."

But when he came back, she could tell by his attitude that his superior didn't take any more stock in it than he had himself. "I tried to explain to him the process by which you extracted it out of the book, but . . . er . . . in his opinion it's just a coincidence, I mean the gashes may not have any meaning at all. F'r instance, someone may have been just cutting something out on top of the book, cookies or pie crust and—"

She snorted in outrage. "Cookies or pie crust! I got a coherent message. If you men can't see it there in front of your eyes—"

"But here's the thing, Miss Roberts," he tried to soothe her. "We haven't any case on deck right now that this could possibly fit into. No one's been reported missing. And we'd know, wouldn't we? I've heard of kidnap cases without ransom notes, but I never heard of a ransom note without a kidnap case to go with it."

"As a police officer doesn't it occur to you that in some instances a kidnaped persons' relatives would purposely refrain from notifying the authorities to avoid jeopardizing their loved ones? That may have happened in this case."

"I mentioned that to the lieutenant myself, but he claims it can't be done. There are cases where we purposely hold off at the request of the family until after the victim's been returned, but it's never because we haven't been informed what's going on. You see, a certain length of time always elapses between the snatch itself and the first contact between the kidnapers and the family, and no matter how short that is, the family has almost always reported the person missing in the meantime, before they know what's up themselves. I can check with Missing Persons if you want, but if it's anything more than just a straight disappearance, they always turn it over to us right away, anyway."

But Prudence didn't intend urging or begging them to look into it as a personal favor to her. She considered she'd done more than her duty. If they discredited it, they discredited it. *She* didn't, and she made up her mind to pursue the investigation, single-handed and without their help if necessary, until she had settled it one way or the other. "Very well," she said coldly, "I'll leave the transcribed message and the extra copy of the book here with you. I'm sorry I bothered you. Good evening." She stalked out, still having forgotten to replace her glasses.

Her indignation carried her as far as the station-house steps, and then her courage began to falter. It was past midnight by now, and the streets looked so lonely; suppose—suppose she met a drunk? While she was standing there trying to get up her nerve, this same Murphy came out behind her, evidently on his way home himself. She had put her glasses on again by now.

"You look a lot different without them," he remarked lamely, stopping a step below her and hanging around.

"Indeed," she said forbiddingly.

"I'm going off duty now. Could I . . . uh . . . see you to where you live?"

She would have preferred not to have to accept the offer, but those shadows down the street looked awfully deep and the light posts awfully far apart. "I *am* a little nervous about being out alone so late," she admitted, starting out beside him. "Once I met a drunk and he said, 'H'lo, babe.' I had to drink a cup of hot tea when I got home, I was so upset."

"Did you have your glasses on?" he asked cryptically.

"No. Come to think of it, that was the time I'd left them to be repaired."

He just nodded knowingly, as though that explained everything.

When they got to her door, he said: "Well, I'll do some more digging through the files on that thing, just to make sure. If I turn up anything . . . uh . . . suppose I drop around tomorrow night and let you know. And if I don't, I'll drop around and let you know that too. Just so you'll know what's what."

"That's very considerate of you."

"Gee, you're refined," he said wistfully. "You talk such good English."

He seemed not averse to lingering on here talking to her, but someone might have looked out of one of the windows and it would appear so unrefined to be seen dallying there at that hour, so she turned and hurried inside.

When she got to her room, she looked at herself in the mirror. Then she took her glasses off and tried it that way. "How peculiar," she murmured. "How very unaccountable!"

The following day at the library she got out the reference card on *Manuela Gets Her Man* and studied it carefully. It had been out six times in the six weeks it had been in stock. The record went like this:

Doyle, Helen (address)	Apr. 15–Apr. 22
Caine, Rose	Apr. 22–Apr. 29
Dermuth, Alvin	Apr. 29–May 6
Turner, Florence	May 6–May 18
Baumgarten, Lucille	May 18–May 25
Trasker, Sophie	May 25–June 3

Being a new book, it had had a quick turnover, had been taken out again each time the same day it had been brought back. Twice it had been kept out overtime, the first time nearly a whole week beyond the return limit. There might be something in that. All the borrowers but one, so far, were women; that was another noticeable fact. It was, after all, a woman's book. Her library experience had taught her that what is called a "man's book" will often be read by women, but a "woman's book" is absolutely never, and there are few exceptions to this rule, read by men. That might mean something, that lone male borrower. She must have seen him at the time, but so many faces passed her desk daily she couldn't remember what he was like any more, if she had. However, she decided not to jump to hasty conclusions, but investigate the list one by one in reverse order. She'd show that ignorant, skirt-chasing Murphy person that where there's smoke there's fire, if you only take the trouble to look for it!

At about eight-thirty, just as she was about to start out on her quest—she could only pursue it in the evenings, of course, after library hours—the doorbell rang and she found him standing there. He looked disappointed when he saw that she had her glasses on. He came in rather shyly and clumsily, tripping over the threshold and careening several steps down the hall.

"Were you able to find out anything?" she asked eagerly.

"Nope, I checked again, I went all the way back six months, and I also got in touch with Missing Persons. Nothing doing. I'm afraid it isn't a genuine message, Miss Roberts; just a fluke, like the lieutenant says."

"I'm sorry, but I don't agree with you. I've copied a list of the borrowers and I intend to investigate each one of them in turn. That message was not intended to be readily deciphered, or for that matter deciphered at all; therefore it is not a practical joke or some adolescent's prank. Yet it has a terrible coherence; therefore it is not a fluke or a haphazard scarring of the page, your lieutenant to the contrary. What remains? It is a genuine ransom note, sent in deadly earnest, and I should think you and your superiors would be the first to—"

"Miss Roberts," he said soulfully, "you're too refined to . . . to dabble in crime like this. Somehow it don't seem right for you to be talking shop, about kidnapings and—" He eased his collar. "I . . . uh . . . it's my night off and I was wondering if you'd like to go to the movies."

"So that's why you took the trouble of coming around!" she said indignantly. "I'm afraid your interest is entirely too personal and not nearly official enough!"

"Gee, even when you talk fast," he said admiringly, "you pronounce every word clear, like in a po-em."

"Well, you don't. It's poem, not po-em. I intend going ahead with this until I can find out just what the meaning of that message is, and who sent it! And I *don't* go to movies with people the second time I've met them!"

He didn't seem at all fazed. "Could I drop around sometime and find out how you're getting along?" he wanted to know, as he edged through the door backward.

"That will be entirely superfluous," she said icily. "If I uncover anything suspicious, I shall of course report it promptly. It is not my job, after all, but . . . ahem . . . other people's."

"Movies! The idea!" She frowned after she had closed the door on him. Then she dropped her eyes and pondered a minute. "It would have been sort of frisky, at that." She smiled.

She took the book along with her as an excuse for calling, and set out, very determined on the surface, as timid as usual underneath. However, she found it easier to get started because the first name on the list, the meek Mrs. Trasker, held no terror even for her. She was almost sure she was innocent, because it was she herself who had called the library's attention to the missing page in the first place, and a guilty person would hardly do that. Still there was always a possibility it was someone else in her family or household, and she meant to be thorough about this if nothing else.

Mrs. Trasker's address was a small old-fashioned apartment building of the pre-War variety. It was not expensive by any means, but still it did seem beyond the means of a person who had been unable to pay even a two-dollar fine, and for a moment Prudence thought she scented suspicion in this. But as soon as she entered the lobby and asked for Mrs. Trasker, the mystery was explained.

"You'll have to go to the basement for her," the elevator boy told her, "she's the janitress."

A young girl of seventeen admitted her at the basement entrance and led her down a bare brick passage past rows of empty trash cans to the living quarters in the back.

Mrs. Trasker was sitting propped up in bed, and again showed a little alarm at sight of the librarian, a person in authority. An open book on a chair beside her showed that her daughter had been reading aloud to her when they were interrupted.

"Don't be afraid," Prudence reassured them. "I just want to ask a few questions."

"Sure, anything, missis," said the janitress, clasping and unclasping her hands placatingly.

"Just the two of you live here? No father or brothers?"

"Just mom and me, nobody else," the girl answered.

"Now tell me, are you sure you didn't take the book out with you anywhere, to some friend's house, or lend it to someone else?"

"No, no, it stayed right here!" They both said it together and vehemently.

"Well, then, did anyone call on you down here, while it was in the rooms?"

The mother answered this. "No, no one. When the tenants want me for anything, they ring down for me from upstairs. And when I'm working around the house, I keep our place locked just like anyone does their apartment. So I know no one was near the book while we had it."

"I feel pretty sure of that myself," Prudence said, as she got up to go. She patted Mrs. Trasker's toil-worn hand reassuringly. "Just forget about my coming here like this. Your fine is paid and there's nothing to worry about. See you at the library."

The next name on the reference card was Lucille Baumgarten. Prudence was emboldened to stop in there because she noticed the address, though fairly nearby, in the same branch-library district, was in a higher-class neighborhood. Besides, she was beginning to forget her timidity in the newly awakened interest her quest was arousing in her. It occurred to her for the first time that detectives must lead fairly interesting lives.

A glance at the imposing, almost palatial apartment building Borrower Baumgarten lived in told her this place could probably be crossed off her list of suspects as well. Though she had heard vaguely somewhere or other that gangsters and criminals sometimes lived in luxurious surroundings, these were more than that. These spelled solid, substantial wealth and respectability that couldn't be faked. She had to state her name and business to a uniformed houseman in the lobby before she was even allowed to go up.

"Just tell Miss Baumgarten the librarian from her branch library would like to talk to her a minute."

A maid opened the upstairs door, but before she could open her mouth, a girl slightly younger than Mrs. Trasker's daughter had come skidding down the parquet hall, swept her aside, and displaced her. She was about fifteen at the most and really had no business borrowing from the adult department yet. Prudence vaguely recalled seeing her face before, although then it had been liberally rouged and lipsticked, whereas now it was properly without cosmetics.

She put a finger to her lips and whispered conspiratorially, "Sh! Don't tell my—"

Before she could get any further, there was a firm tread behind her and she was displaced in turn by a stout matronly lady wearing more diamonds than Prudence had ever seen before outside of a jewelry-store window.

"I've just come to check up on this book which was returned to us in a damaged condition," Prudence explained. "Our record shows that Miss Lucille Baumgarten had it out between—"

"Lucille?" gasped the bediamonded lady. "Lucille? There's no Lucille—" She broke off short and glanced at her daughter, who vainly tried to duck out between the two of them and shrink away unnoticed. "Oh, so that's it!" she said, suddenly enlightened. "So Leah isn't good enough for you any more!"

Prudence addressed her offspring, since it was obvious that the mother was in the dark about more things than just the book. "Miss Baumgarten, I'd like you to tell me whether there was a page missing when you brought the book home with you." And then she added craftily: "It was borrowed again afterward by several other subscribers, but I haven't got around to them yet." If the girl was guilty, she would use this as an out and claim the page had still been in, implying it had been taken out afterward by someone else. Prudence knew it hadn't, of course.

But Lucille-Leah admitted unhesitatingly: "Yes, there was a page or two missing, but it didn't spoil the fun much, because I could tell what happened after I read on a little bit." Nothing seemed to hold any terrors for her, compared to the parental wrath brewing in the heaving bosom that wedged her in inextricably.

"Did you lend it to anyone else, or take it out of the house with you at any time, while you were in possession of it?"

The girl rolled her eyes meaningly. "I should say not! I kept it hidden in the bottom drawer of my bureau the whole time; and now you had to come around here and give me away!"

"Thank you," said Prudence, and turned to go. This place was definitely off her list too, as she had felt it would be even before the interview. People who lived in such surroundings didn't send kidnap notes or associate with people who did.

The door had closed, but Mrs. Baumgarten's shrill, punitive tones sounded all too clearly through it while Prudence stood there waiting for the elevator to take her down. "I'll *give* you Lucille! Wait'll your father hears about this! I'll give you such a *frass,* you won't know whether you're Lucille or Gwendolyn!" punctuated by a loud, popping slap on youthful epidermis.

The next name on the list was Florence Turner. It was already well after ten by now, and for a moment Prudence was tempted to go home, and put off the next interview until the following night. She discarded the temptation resolutely. "Don't be such a 'fraid-cat," she lectured herself. "Nothing's happened to you so far, and nothing's likely to happen hereafter either." And then too, without knowing it, she was already prejudiced; in the back of her mind all along there lurked the suspicion that the lone male borrower, Dermuth, was the one to watch out for. He was next but one on the list, in reverse order. As long as she was out, she would interview Florence Turner, who was probably harmless, and then tackle Dermuth good and early tomorrow night—and see to it that a policeman waited for her outside his door so she'd be sure of getting out again unharmed.

The address listed for Library Member Turner was not at first sight exactly prepossessing, when she located it. It was a rooming house, or rather that newer variation of one called a "residence club," which has sprung up in the larger cities within the past few years, in which the rooms are grouped into detached little apartments. Possibly it was the sight of the chop-suey place that occupied the ground floor that gave it its unsavory aspect in her eyes; she had peculiar notions about some things.

Nevertheless, now that she had come this far, she wasn't going to let a chop-suey restaurant frighten her away without completing her mission. She tightened the book under her arm, took a good deep breath to ward off possible hatchet men and opium smokers, and marched into the building, whose entrance adjoined that of the restaurant.

She rang the manager's bell and a blowsy-looking, middle-aged woman came out and met her at the foot of the stairs. "Yes?" she said gruffly.

"Have you a Florence Turner living here?"

"No. We did have, but she left."

"Have you any idea where I could reach her?"

"She left very suddenly, didn't say where she was going."

"About how long ago did she leave, could you tell me?"

"Let's see now." The woman did some complicated mental calculation. "Two weeks ago Monday, I think it was. That would bring it to the seventeenth. Yes, that's it, May seventeenth."

Here was a small mystery already. The book hadn't been returned until the eighteenth. The woman's memory might be at fault, of course. "If you say she left in a hurry, how is it she found time to return this book to us?"

The woman glanced at it. "Oh, no, I was the one returned that for her," she explained. "My cleaning maid found it in her room the next morning after she was gone, along with a lot of other stuff she left behind her. I saw it was a liberry book, so I sent Beulah over with it, so's it wouldn't roll up a big fine for her. I'm economical that way. How'd you happen to get hold of it?" she asked in surprise.

"I work at the library," Prudence explained. "I wanted to see her about this book. One of the pages was torn out." She knew enough not to confide any more than that about what her real object was.

"Gee, aren't you people fussy," marveled the manager.

"Well, you see, it's taken out of my salary," prevaricated Prudence, trying to strike a note she felt the other might understand.

"Oh, that's different. No wonder you're anxious to locate her. Well, all I know is she didn't expect to go when she did; she even paid for her room ahead. I been holding it for her ever since, till the time's up. I'm conshenshus that way."

"That's strange," Prudence mused aloud. "I wonder what could have—"

"I think someone got took sick in her family," confided the manager. "Some friends or relatives, I don't know who they was, called for her in a car late at night and off she went in a rush. I just wanted to be sure it wasn't no one who hadn't paid up yet, so I opened my door and looked out."

Prudence pricked up her ears. That fatal curiosity of hers was driving her on like a spur. She had suddenly forgotten all about being leery of the nefarious chop-suey den on the premises. She was starting to tingle all over, and tried not to show it. Had she unearthed something at last, or wasn't it anything at all? "You say she left some belongings behind? Do you think she'll be back for them?"

"No, she won't be back herself, I don't believe. But she did ask me to keep them for her; she said she'd send someone around to get them as soon as she was able."

Prudence suddenly decided she'd give almost anything to be able to get a look at the things this Turner girl had left behind her; why, she wasn't quite sure herself. They might help her to form an idea of what their owner was like. She couldn't ask openly; the woman might suspect her of trying to steal something. "When will her room be available?" She asked offhandedly. "I'm thinking of moving, and as long as I'm here, I was wondering—"

"Come on up and I'll show it to you right now," offered the manager with alacrity. She evidently considered librarians superior to the average run of tenants she got.

Prudence followed her up the stairs, incredulous at her

own effrontery. This didn't seem a bit like her; she wondered what had come over her.

"Murphy should see me now!" she gloated.

The manager unlocked a door on the second floor.

"It's real nice in the daytime," she said. "And I can turn it over to you day after tomorrow."

"Is the closet good and deep?" asked Prudence, noting its locked doors.

"I'll show you." The woman took out a key, opened it unsuspectingly for her approval.

"My," said the subtle Prudence, "she left lots of things behind!"

"And some of them are real good too," agreed the landlady. "I don't know how they do it, on just a hat check girl's tips. And she even gave that up six months ago."

"Hm-m-m," said Prudence absently, deftly edging a silver slipper she noted standing on the floor up against one of another pair, with the tip of her own foot. She looked down covertly; with their heels in true with one another, there was an inch difference in the toes. Two different sizes! She absently fingered the lining of one of the frocks hanging up, noted its size tag. A 34. "Such exquisite things," she murmured, to cover up what she was doing. Three hangers over there was another frock. Size 28.

"Did she have anyone else living here with her?" she asked.

The manager locked the closet, pocketed the key once more. "No. These two men friends or relatives of hers used to visit with her a good deal, but they never made a sound and they never came one at a time, so I didn't raise any objections. Now, I have another room, nearly as nice, just down the hall I could show you."

"I wish there were some way in which you could notify me when someone does call for her things," said Prudence, who was getting better as she went along. "I'm terribly anxious to get in touch with her. You see, it's not only the fine, it might even cost me my job."

"Sure, I know how it is," said the manager sympathetically.

"Well, I could ask whoever she sends to leave word where you can reach her."

"No, don't do that!" said Prudence hastily. "I'm afraid they˅. . . er . . . I'd prefer if you didn't mention I was here asking about her at all."

"Anything you say," said the manager amenably. "If you'll leave your number with me, I could give you a ring and let you know whenever the person shows up."

"I'm afraid I wouldn't get over here in time; they might be gone by the time I got here."

The manager tapped her teeth helpfully. "Why don't you take one of my rooms, then? That way you'd be right on the spot when they do show up."

"Yes, but suppose they come in the daytime? I'd be at the library, and I can't leave my job."

"I don't think they'll come in the daytime. Most of her friends and the people she went with were up and around at night, more than in the daytime."

The idea appealed to Prudence, although only a short while before she would have been aghast at the thought of moving into such a place. She made up her mind quickly without giving herself time to stop and get cold feet. It might be a wild-goose chase, but she'd never yet heard of a woman who wore two different sizes in dresses like this Florence Turner seemed to. "All right, I will," she decided, "if you'll promise two things. To let me know without fail the minute someone comes to get her things, and not to say a word to them about my coming here and asking about her."

"Why not?" said the manager accommodatingly. "Anything to earn an honest dollar."

But when the door of her new abode closed on her, a good deal of her new-found courage evaporated. She sat down limply on the edge of the bed and stared in bewilderment at her reflection in the cheap dresser mirror. "I must be crazy to do a thing like this!" she gasped. "What's come over me anyway?" She didn't even have her teapot with her to brew a cup of the fortifying liquid. There was nothing the matter with the room in itself, but that sinister Oriental den downstairs had a lurid red tube sign just under her window and its glare winked malevolently in at her. She imagined felt-slippered hirelings of some Fu-Manchu creeping up the stairs to snatch her bodily from her bed. It was nearly daylight before she could close her eyes. But so far as the room across the hall was concerned, as might have been expected, no one showed up.

Next day at the library, between book returns, Prudence took out the reference card on *Manuela* and placed a neat red check next to Mrs. Trasker's name and Lucille Baumgarten's, to mark the progress of her investigation so far. But she didn't need this; it was easy enough to remember whom she had been to see and whom she hadn't, but she had the precise type of mind that liked everything neatly docketed and in order. Next to Florence Turner's name she placed a small red question mark.

She was strongly tempted to call up Murphy on her way home that evening, and tell him she already felt she was on the trail of something. But for one thing, nothing definite enough had developed yet. If he'd laughed at her about the original message itself, imagine how he'd roar if she told him the sum total of her suspicions was based on the fact that a certain party had two different-sized dresses in her clothes closet. And secondly, even in her new state of emancipation, it still seemed awfully forward to call a man up, even a detective. She would track down this Florence Turner first, and then she'd call Murphy up if her findings warranted it. "And if he says I'm good, and asks me to go to the movies with him," she threatened, "I'll . . . I'll make him ask two or three times before I do!"

She met the manager on her way in. "Did anyone come yet?" she asked in an undertone.

"No. I'll keep my promise. I'll let you know; don't worry."

A lot of the strangeness had already worn off her new surroundings, even after sleeping there just one night, and it occurred to her that maybe she had been in a rut, should have changed living quarters more often in the past. She went to bed shortly after ten, and even the Chinese restaurant sign had no power to keep her awake tonight; she fell asleep almost at once, tired from the night before.

About an hour or so later, she had no way of telling how long afterward it was, a surreptitious tapping outside her door woke her. "Yes?" she called out forgetfully, in a loud voice.

The manager stuck her tousled head in.

"Shh!" she warned. "Somebody's come for her things. You asked me to tell you, and I've been coughing out there in the hall, trying to attract your attention. He just went down with the first armful; he'll be up again in a minute. You'd better hurry if you want to catch him before he goes; he's working fast."

"Don't say anything to him," Prudence whispered back. "See if you can delay him a minute or two, give me time to get downstairs."

"Are you sure it's just a liberry book this is all about?" the manager asked searchingly. "Here he comes up again." She pulled her head back and swiftly closed the door.

Prudence had never dressed so fast in her life before. Even so, she managed to find time to dart a glance down at the street from her window. There was a black sedan drawn up in front of the house. "How am I ever going to—" she thought in dismay. She didn't let that hold her up any. She made sure she had shoes on and a coat over her and let the rest go hang. There was no time to phone Murphy, even if she had wanted to, but the thought didn't occur to her.

She eased her room door open, flitted out into the hall and down the stairs, glimpsing the open door of Florence Turner's room as she sneaked by. She couldn't see the man, whoever he was, but she could hear the landlady saying, "Wait a minute, until I make sure you haven't left anything behind."

Prudence slipped out of the street door downstairs, looked hopelessly up and down the street. He had evidently come alone in the car; there was no one else in it. He had piled the clothing on the back seat. For a moment she even thought of smuggling herself in and hiding under it, but that was too harebrained to be seriously considered. Then, just as she heard his tread start down the inside stairs behind her, the much-maligned chop-suey joint came to her aid. A cab drove up to it, stopped directly behind the first machine, and a young couple got out.

Prudence darted over, climbed in almost before they were out of the way.

"Where to, lady?" asked the driver.

She found it hard to come out with it, it sounded so unrespectable and fly-by-nightish. Detectives, she supposed, didn't think twice about giving an order like that, but with her it was different. "Er . . . would you mind just waiting a minute until that car in front of us leaves?" she said constrainedly. "Then take me wherever it goes."

He shot her a glance in his rear-sight mirror, but didn't say anything. He was probably used to getting stranger orders than that.

A man came out of the same doorway she had just left herself. She couldn't get a very good look at his face, but he had a batch of clothing slung over his arm. He dumped the apparel in the back of the sedan, got in himself, slammed the door closed, and started off. A moment later the cab was in motion as well.

"Moving out on ya, huh?" said the driver knowingly. "I don't blame ya for follying him."

"That will do," she said primly. This night life got you into more embarrassing situations! "Do you think you can manage it so he won't notice you coming after him?" she asked after a block or two.

"Leave it to me, lady," he promised, waving his hand at her. "I know this game backwards."

Presently they had turned into one of the circumferential express highways leading out of the city. "Now it's gonna be pie!" he exulted. "He won't be able to tell us from anyone else on here. Everyone going the same direction and no turning off."

The stream of traffic was fairly heavy for that hour of the night, homeward-bound suburbanites for the most part. But then, as the city limits were passed and branch road after branch road drained it off, it thinned to a mere trickle. The lead car finally turned off itself, and onto a practically deserted secondary highway.

"Now it's gonna be ticklish," the cabman admitted. "I'm gonna have to hang back as far as I can from him, or he'll tumble to us."

He let the other car pull away until it was merely a red dot in the distance. "You sure must be carryin' some torch," he said presently with a baffled shake of his head, "to come all the way out this far after him."

"Please confine yourself to your driving," was the haughty reproof.

The distant red pinpoint had suddenly snuffed out. "He must've turned off up ahead someplace," said the driver, alarmed. "I better step it up!"

When they had reached the approximate place, minutes later, an even less-traveled bypass than the one they were on was revealed, not only lightless but even unsurfaced. It obviously didn't lead anywhere that the general public would have wanted to go, or it would have been better maintained. They braked forthwith.

"What a lonely-looking road." Prudence shuddered involuntarily.

"Y'wanna chuck it and turn back?" he suggested, as though he would have been only too willing to himself.

She probably would have if she'd been alone, but she hated to admit defeat in his presence. He'd probably laugh at her all the way back. "No, now that I've come this far, I'm not going back until I find out exactly where he went. Don't stand here like this: you won't be able to catch up with him again!"

The driver gave his cap a defiant hitch. "The time has come to tell you I've got you clocked at seven bucks and eighty-five cents, and I didn't notice any pocketbook in your hand when you got in. Where's it coming from?" He tapped his fingers sardonically on the rim of his wheel.

Prudence froze. Her handbag was exactly twenty or thirty

miles away, back in her room at the residence club. She didn't have to answer; the driver was an old experienced hand at this sort of thing; he could read the signs.

"I thought so," he said, almost resignedly. He got down, opened the door: "Outside," he said. "If you was a man, I'd take it out of your jaw. Or if there was a cop anywhere within five miles, I'd have you run in. Take off that coat." He looked it over, slung it over his arm. "It'll have to do. Now if you want it back, you know what to do; just look me up with seven-eighty-five in your mitt. And for being so smart, you're gonna walk all the way back from here on your two little puppies."

"Don't leave me all alone, in the dark, in this God-forsaken place! I don't even know where I am!" she wailed after him.

"I'll tell you where you are," he called back remorselessly. "You're on your own!" The cab's taillight went streaking obliviously back the way they had just come.

She held the side of her head and looked helplessly all around her. Real detectives didn't run into these predicaments, she felt sure. It only happened to her! "Oh, why didn't I just mind my own business back at the library!" she lamented.

It was too cool out here in the wilds to stand still without a coat on, even though it was June. She might stand waiting here all night and no other machine would come along. The only thing to do was to keep walking until she came to a house, and then ask to use the telephone. There must be a house somewhere around here.

She started in along the bypath the first car had taken, gloomy and forbidding as it was, because it seemed more likely there was a house someplace farther along it than out on this other one. They hadn't passed a single dwelling the whole time the cab was on the road, and she didn't want to walk still farther out along it; no telling where it led to. The man she'd been following must have had *some* destination. Even if she struck the very house he had gone to, there wouldn't really be much harm to it, because he didn't know who she was, he'd never seen her before. Neither had this Florence Turner, if she was there with him. She could just say she'd lost her way or something. Anyone would have looked good to her just then, out here alone in the dark the way she was.

If she'd been skittish of shadows on the city streets, there was reason enough for her to have St. Vitus' dance here; it was nothing *but* shadows. Once she came in sight of a little clearing, with a scarecrow fluttering at the far side of it, and nearly had heart failure for a minute. Another time an owl went "Who-o-o" up in a tree over her, and she ran about twenty yards before she could pull herself together and stop again. "Oh, if I ever get back to the nice safe library after tonight, I'll never—" she sobbed nervously.

The only reason she kept going on now was because she was afraid to turn back any more. Maybe that hadn't been a scarecrow after all—

The place was so set back from the road, so half hidden amidst the shrubbery that she had almost passed it by before she even saw it there. She happened to glance to her right as she came to a break in the trees, and there was the unmistakable shadowy outline of a decrepit house. Not a chink of light showed from it, at least from where she was. Wheel ruts unmistakably led in toward it over the grass and weeds, but she wasn't much of a hand at this sort of lore, couldn't tell if they'd been made recently or long ago. The whole place had an appearance of not being lived in.

It took nearly as much courage to turn aside and start over toward it as it would have to continue on the road. It was anything but what she'd been hoping for, and she knew already it was useless to expect to find a telephone in such a ramshackle wreck.

The closer she got to it, the less inviting it became. True, it was two or three in the morning by now, and even if anyone had been living in it, they probably would have been fast asleep by this time, but it didn't seem possible such a forlorn, neglected-looking place could be inhabited. Going up onto that ink-black porch and knocking for admittance took more nerve than she could muster. Heaven knows what she was liable to bring out on her; bats or rats or maybe some horrible hobos.

She decided she'd walk all around the outside of it just once, and if it didn't look any better from the sides and rear than it did from the front, she'd go back to the road and take her own chances on that some more. The side was no better than the front when she picked her way cautiously along it. Twigs snapped under her feet and little stones shifted, and made her heart miss a beat each time. But when she got around to the back, she saw two things at once that showed her she had been mistaken, there was someone in there after all. One was the car, the same car that had driven away in front of the residence club, standing at a little distance behind the house, under some kind of warped toolshed or something. The other was a slit of light showing around three sides of a ground-floor window. It wasn't a brightly lighted pane by any means; the whole window still showed black under some kind of sacking or heavy covering; there was just this telltale yellow seam outlining three sides of it if you looked closely enough.

Before she could decide what to do about it, if anything, her gaze traveled a little higher up the side of the house and she saw something else that brought her heart up into her throat. She choked back an inadvertent scream just in time. It was a face. A round white face staring down at her from one of the upper windows, dimly visible behind the dusty pane.

Prudence Roberts started to back away apprehensively a step at a time, staring up at it spellbound as she did so, and ready at any moment to turn and run for her life, away from whoever or whatever that was up there. But before she could carry out the impulse, she saw something else that changed her mind, rooted her to the spot. Two wavering white hands had appeared, just under the ghost-like face. They were making signs to her, desperate, pleading signs. They beckoned her nearer, then they clasped together imploringly, as if trying to say, "Don't go away, don't leave me."

Prudence drew a little nearer again. The hands were warning her to silence now, one pointing downward toward the floor below, the other holding a cautioning finger to their owner's mouth.

It was a young girl; Prudence could make out that much, but most of the pantomime was lost through the blurred dust-caked pane. She gestured back to her with upcurved fingers, meaning, "Open the window so I can hear you."

It took the girl a long time. The window was either fastened in some way or warped from lack of use, or else it stuck just because she was trying to do it without making any noise. The sash finally jarred up a short distance, with an alarming creaking and grating in spite of her best efforts. Or at least it seemed so in the preternatural stillness that reigned about the place. They both held their breaths for a wary moment, as if by mutual understanding.

Then as Prudence moved in still closer under the window, a faint sibilance came down to her from the narrow opening.

"Please take me away from here. Oh, please help me to get away from here."

"What's the matter?" Prudence whispered back.

Both alike were afraid to use too much breath even to whisper, it was so quiet outside the house. It was hard for them to make themselves understood. She missed most of the other's answer, all but:

"They won't let me go. I think they're going to kill me. They haven't given me anything to eat in two whole days now."

Prudence inhaled fearfully. "Can you climb out through there and let yourself drop from the sill? I'll get a seat cover from that car and put it under you."

"I'm chained to the bed up here. I've pulled it over little by little to the window. Oh, please hurry and bring someone back with you; that's the only way—"

Prudence nodded in agreement, made hasty encouraging signs as she started to draw away. "I'll run all the way back to where the two roads meet, and stop the first car that comes al—"

Suddenly she froze, and at the same instant seemed to light up yellowly from head to foot, like a sort of living torch. A great fan of light spread out from the doorway before her, and in the middle of it a wavering shadow began to lengthen toward her along the ground.

"Come in, sweetheart, and stay a while," a man's voice said slurringly. He sauntered out toward her with lithe, springy determination. Behind him in the doorway were another man and a woman.

"Naw, don't be bashful," he went on, moving around in back of her and prodding her toward the house with his gun. "You ain't going on nowheres else from here. You've reached your final destination."

A well-dressed, middle-aged man was sitting beside the lieutenant's desk, forearm supporting his head, shading his eyes with outstretched fingers, when Murphy and every other man jack available came piling in, responding to the urgent summons.

The lieutenant had three desk phones going at once, and still found time to say, "Close that door, I don't want a word of this to get out," to the last man in. He hung up—*click, click, clack*—speared a shaking finger at the operatives forming into line before him.

"This is Mr. Martin Rapf, men," he said tensely. "I won't ask him to repeat what he's just said to me; he's not in any condition to talk right now. His young daughter, Virginia, left home on the night of May seventeenth and she hasn't been seen since. He and Mrs. Rapf received an anonymous telephone call that same night, before they'd even had time to become alarmed at her absence, informing them not to expect her back and warning them above all not to report her missing to us. Late the next day Mr. Rapf received a ransom note demanding fifty thousand dollars. This is it here."

Everyone in the room fastened their eyes on it as he spun it around on his desk to face them. At first sight it seemed to be a telegram. It was an actual telegraph blank form, taken from some office pad, with strips of paper containing printed words pasted on it.

"It wasn't filed, of course; it was slipped under the front door in an unaddressed envelope," the lieutenant went on. "The instructions didn't come for two more days, by telephone again.

Mr. Rapf had raised the amount and was waiting for them. They were rather amateurish, to say the least. And amateurs are more to be dreaded than professionals at this sort of thing, as you men well know. He was to bring the money along in a cigar box, he was to go all the way out to a certain seldom-used suburban crossroads and wait there. Then when a closed car with its rear windows down drove slowly by and sounded its horn three times, two short ones and a long one, he was to pitch the cigar box in the back of it through the open window and go home.

"In about a quarter of an hour a closed car with its windows down came along fairly slowly. Mr. Rapf was too concerned about his daughter's safety even to risk memorizing the numerals on its license plates, which were plainly exposed to view. A truck going crosswise to it threatened to block it at the intersection, and it gave three blasts of its horn, two short ones and a long one. Mr. Rapf threw the cigar box in through its rear window and watched it pick up speed and drive away. He was too excited and overwrought to start back immediately, and in less than five minutes, while he was still there, a second car came along with its windows down and its license plates removed. It gave three blasts of its horn, without there being any obstruction ahead. He ran out toward it to try and explain, but only succeeded in frightening it off. It put on speed and got away from him. I don't know whether it was actually a ghastly coincidence, or whether an unspeakable trick was perpetrated on him, to get twice the amount they had originally asked. Probably just a hideous coincidence, though, because he would have been just as willing to give them one hundred thousand from the beginning.

"At any rate, what it succeeded in doing was to throw a hitch into the negotiations, make them nervous and skittish. They contacted him again several days later, refused to believe his explanation, and breathed dire threats against the girl. He pleaded with them for another chance, and asked for more time to raise a second fifty thousand. He's been holding it in readiness for some time now, and they're apparently suffering from a bad case of fright; they cancel each set of new instructions as fast as they issue them to him. Wait'll I get through, please, will you, Murphy? It's five days since Mr. Rapf last heard from them, and he is convinced that—" He didn't finish it, out of consideration for the agonized man sitting there. Then he went ahead briskly: "Now here's Miss Rapf's description, and here's what our first move is going to be. Twenty years old, weight so-and-so, height so-and-so, light-brown hair—"

"She was wearing a pale-pink party dress and dancing shoes when she left the house," Rapf supplied forlornly.

"We don't pin any reliance on items of apparel in matters of this kind," the lieutenant explained to him in a kindly aside. "That's for amnesia cases or straight disappearances. They almost invariably discard the victim's clothes, to make accidental recognition harder. Some woman in the outfit will usually supply her with her own things."

"It's too late, lieutenant; it's too late," the man who sat facing him murmured grief-strickenly. "I know it; I'm sure of it."

"We have no proof that it is," the lieutenant replied reassuringly. "But if it is, Mr. Rapf, you have only yourself to blame for waiting this long to come to us. If you'd come to us sooner, you might have your daughter back by now—"

He broke off short. "What's the matter, Murphy?" he snapped. "What are you climbing halfway across the desk at me like that for?"

"Will you let me get a word in and tell you, lieutenant?" Murphy exclaimed with a fine show of exasperated insubordination. "I been trying to for the last five minutes! That librarian, that Miss Roberts that came in here the other night—It was this thing she stumbled over accidentally then already. It must have been! It's the same message."

The lieutenant's jaw dropped well below his collar button. "Ho-ly smoke!" he exhaled. "Say, she's a smart young woman all right!"

"Yeah, she's so smart we laughed her out of the place, book and all," Murphy said bitterly. "She practically hands it to us on a silver platter, and you and me, both, we think it's the funniest thing we ever heard of."

"Never mind that now! Go out and get hold of her! Bring her in here fast!"

"She's practically standing in front of you!" The door swung closed after Murphy.

Miss Everett, the hatchet-faced librarian, felt called upon to interfere at the commotion that started up less than five minutes later at the usually placid new-membership desk, which happened to be closest to the front door.

"Will you *kindly* keep your voice down, young man?" she said severely, sailing over. "This is a library, not a—"

"I haven't got time to keep my voice down! Where's Prudence Roberts? She's wanted at headquarters right away."

"She didn't come to work this morning. It's the first time she's ever missed a day since she's been with the library. What is it she's wanted—" But there was just a rush of outgoing air where he'd been standing until then. Miss Everett looked startledly at the other librarian. "What was that he just said?"

"It sounded to me like, 'Skip it, toots.' "

Miss Everett looked blankly over her shoulder to see if anyone else was standing there, but no one was.

In a matter of minutes Murphy had burst in on them again, looking a good deal more harried than the first time. "Something's happened to her. She hasn't been at her rooming house all night either, and that's the first time *that* happened too! Listen. There was a card went with that book she brought to us, showing who had it out and all that. Get it out quick; let me have it!"

He couldn't have remembered its name just then to save his life, and it might have taken them until closing time and after to wade through the library's filing system. But no matter how much of a battle-ax this Miss Everett both looked and was, one thing must be said in her favor: she had an uncanny memory when it came to damaged library property. "The reference card on *Manuela Gets Her Man,* by Ollivant," she snapped succinctly to her helpers. And in no time it was in his hands.

His face lighted. He brought his fist down on the counter with a bang that brought every nose in the place up out of its book, and for once Miss Everett forgot to remonstrate or even frown. "Thank God for her methodical mind!" he exulted. "Trasker, check; Baumgarten, check; Turner, question mark. It's as good as though she left full directions behind her!"

"What was it he said *that* time?" puzzled Miss Everett, as the doors flapped hectically to and fro behind him.

"It sounded to me like 'Keep your fingers crossed.' Only, I'm not sure if it was 'fingers' or—"

"It's getting dark again," Virginia Rapf whimpered frightenedly, dragging herself along the floor toward her fellow captive. "Each time night comes, I think they're going to . . . *you* know! Maybe tonight they *will.*"

Prudence Roberts was fully as frightened as the other girl, but simply because one of them had to keep the other's courage up, she wouldn't let herself show it. "No, they won't; they wouldn't dare!" she said with a confidence she was far from feeling.

She went ahead tinkering futilely with the small padlock and chain that secured her to the foot of the bed. It was the same type that is used to fasten bicycles to something in the owner's absence, only of course the chain had not been left in an open loop or she could simply have withdrawn her hand. It was fastened tight around her wrist by passing the clasp of the lock through two of the small links at once. It permitted her a radius of action of not more than three or four yards around the foot of the bed at most. Virginia Rapf was similarly attached to the opposite side.

"In books you read," Prudence remarked, "women prisoners always seem to be able to open anything from a strong box to a cell door with just a hairpin. I don't seem to have the knack, somehow. This is the last one I have left."

"If you couldn't do it before, while it was light, you'll never be able to do it in the dark."

"I guess you're right," Prudence sighed. "There it goes, out of shape like all the rest, anyway." She tossed it away with a little *plink.*

"Oh, if you'd only moved away from under that window a

minute sooner, they wouldn't have seen you out there, you might have been able to—"

"No use crying over spilt milk," Prudence said briskly.

Sounds reached them from outside presently, after they'd been lying silent on the floor for a while.

"Listen," Virginia Rapf breathed. "There's someone moving around down there, under the window. You can hear the ground crunch every once in a while."

Something crashed violently, and they both gave a start.

"What was that, their car?" asked Virginia Rapf.

"No, it sounded like a tin can of some kind; something he threw away."

A voice called out of the back door: "Have you got enough?"

The answer seemed to come from around the side of the house. "No, gimme the other one too."

A few moments later a second tinny clash reached their tense ears. They waited, hearts pounding furiously under their ribs. A sense of impending danger assailed Prudence.

"What's that funny smell?" Virginia Rapf whispered fearfully. "Do you notice it? Like—"

Prudence supplied the word before she realized its portent. "Gasoline." The frightful implication hit the two of them at once. The other girl gave a sob of convulsive terror, cringed against her. Prudence threw her arms about her, tried to calm her. "Shh! Don't be frightened. No, they wouldn't do that, they couldn't be that inhuman." But her own terror was half stifling her.

One of their captors' voices sounded directly under them, with a terrible clarity. "All right, get in the car, Flo. You too, Duke, I'm about ready."

They heard the woman answer him, and there was unmistakable horror even in her tones. "Oh, not *that* way, Eddie. You're going to finish them first, aren't you?"

He laughed coarsely. "What's the difference? The smoke'll finish them in a minute or two; they won't suffer none. All right, soft-hearted, have it your own way. I'll go up and give

'em a clip on the head apiece, if it makes you feel any better."
His tread started up the rickety stairs.

They were almost crazed with fear. Prudence fought to keep
her presence of mind.

"Get under the bed, quick!" she panted hoarsely.

But the other girl gave a convulsive heave in her arms,
then fell limp. She'd fainted dead away. The oncoming tread
was halfway up the stairs now. He was taking his time, no
hurry. Outside in the open she heard the woman's voice once
more, in sharp remonstrance.

"Wait a minute, you dope; not yet! Wait'll Eddie gets out
first!"

The man with her must have struck a match. "He can make
it; let's see him run for it," he answered jeeringly. "I still owe
him something for that hot-foot he gave me one time,
remember?"

Prudence had let the other girl roll lifelessly out of her
arms, and squirmed under the bed herself, not to try to save her
own skin but to do the little that could be done to try to save
both of them, futile as she knew it to be. She twisted like a
caterpillar, clawed at her own foot, got her right shoe off. She'd
never gone in for these stylish featherweight sandals with
spindly heels, and she was glad of that now. It was a good strong
substantial Oxford, nearly as heavy as a man's, with a club
heel. She got a grasp on it by the toe, then twisted her body
around so that her legs were toward the side the room door
gave onto. She reared one at the knee, held it poised, backed up
as far as the height of the bed would allow it to be.

The door opened and he came in, lightless. He didn't need
a light for a simple little job like this—stunning two helpless
girls chained to a bed. He started around toward the foot of it,
evidently thinking they were crouched there hiding from him.
Her left leg suddenly shot out between his two, like a spoke,
tripping him neatly.

He went floundering forward on his face with a muffled
curse. She had hoped he might hit his head, be dazed by the
impact if only for a second or two. He wasn't; he must have

broken the fall with his arm. She threshed her body madly around the other way again, to get her free arm in play with the shoe for a weapon. She began to rain blows on him with it, trying to get his head with the heel. That went wrong too. He'd fallen too far out along the floor, the chain wouldn't let her come out any farther after him. She couldn't reach any higher up than his muscular shoulders with the shoe, and its blows fell ineffectively there.

Raucous laughter was coming from somewhere outside, topped by warning screams. "Eddie, hurry up and get out, you fool! Duke's started it already!" They held no meaning for Prudence; she was too absorbed in this last despairing attempt to save herself and her fellow prisoner.

But he must have heard and understood them. The room was no longer as inky black as before. A strange wan light was beginning to peer up below the window, like a satanic moonrise. He jumped to his feet with a snarl, turned and fired down point-blank at Prudence as she tried to writhe hastily back undercover. The bullet hit the iron rim of the bedstead directly over her eyes and glanced aside. He was too yellow to linger and try again. Spurred by the screamed warnings and the increasing brightness, he bolted from the room and went crashing down the stairs three at a time.

A second shot went off just as he reached the back doorway, and she mistakenly thought he had fired at his fellow kidnaper in retaliation for the ghastly practical joke played on him. Then there was a whole volley of shots, more than just one gun could have fired. The car engine started up with an abortive flurry, then died down again where it was without moving. But her mind was too full of horror at the imminent doom that threatened to engulf both herself and Virginia Rapf to realize the meaning of anything she dimly heard going on below. Anything but that sullen hungry crackle, like bundles of twigs snapping, that kept growing louder from minute to minute. They had been left hopelessly chained, to be cremated alive!

She screamed her lungs out, and at the same time knew that screaming wasn't going to save her or the other girl. She began to hammer futilely with her shoe at the chain holding her, so slender yet so strong, and knew that wasn't going to save her either.

Heavy steps pounded up the staircase again, and for a moment she thought he'd come back to finish the two of them after all, and was glad of it. Anything was better than being roasted alive. She wouldn't try to hide this time.

The figure that came tearing through the thickening smoke haze toward her was already bending down above her before she looked and saw that it was Murphy. She'd seen some beautiful pictures in art galleries in her time, but he was more beautiful to her eyes than a Rubens portrait.

"All right, chin up, keep cool," he said briefly, so she wouldn't lose her head and impede him.

"Get the key to these locks! The short dark one has them."

"He's dead and there's no time. Lean back. Stretch it out tight and lean out of the way!" He fired and the small chain snapped in two. "Jump! You can't get down the stairs anymore." His second shot, freeing Virginia Rapf, punctuated the order.

Prudence flung up the window, climbed awkwardly across the sill, feet first, then clung there terrified as an intolerable haze of heat rose up under her from below. She glimpsed two men running up under her with a blanket or lap robe from the car stretched out between them.

"I can't; it's . . . it's right under me!"

He gave her an unceremonious shove in the middle of the back and she went hurtling out into space with a screech. The two with the blanket got there just about the same time she did. Murphy hadn't waited to make sure; a broken leg was preferable to being incinerated. She hit the ground through the lap robe and all, but at least it broke the direct force of the fall.

They cleared it for the next arrival by rolling her out at one side, and by the time she had picked herself dazedly to her feet, Virginia Rapf was already lying in it, thrown there by him from above.

"Hurry it up, Murph!" she heard one of them shout frightenedly, and instinctively caught at the other girl, dragged her off it to clear the way for him. He crouched with both feet on the sill, came sailing down, and even before he'd hit the blanket, there was a dull roar behind him as the roof caved in, and a great gush of sparks went shooting straight up into the dark night sky.

They were still too close; they all had to draw hurriedly back away from the unbearable heat beginning to radiate from it. Murphy came last, as might have been expected, dragging a very dead kidnaper—the one called Eddie—along the ground after him by the collar of his coat. Prudence saw the other one, Duke, slumped inertly over the wheel of the car he had never had time to make his getaway in, either already dead or rapidly dying. A disheveled blond scarecrow that had been Florence Turner was apparently the only survivor of the trio. She kept whimpering placatingly, "I didn't want to do *that* to them! I didn't want to do *that* to them!" over and over, as though she still didn't realize they had been saved in time.

Virginia Rapf was coming out of her long faint. It was kinder, Prudence thought, that she had been spared those last few horrible moments; she had been through enough without that.

"Rush her downtown with you, fellow!" Murphy said. "Her dad's waiting for her; he doesn't know yet. I shot out here so fast the minute I located that taxi driver outside the residence club, who remembered driving Miss Roberts out to this vicinity, that I didn't even have time to notify headquarters, just picked up whoever I could on the way."

He came over to where Prudence was standing, staring at the fire with horrified fascination.

"How do you feel? Are you O.K.?" he murmured, brow furrowed with a proprietary anxiety.

"Strange as it may be," she admitted in surprise, "I seem to feel perfectly all right; can't find a thing the matter with me."

Back at the library the following day—and what a world away it seemed from the scenes of violence she had just lived through—the acidulous Miss Everett came up to her just before closing time with, of all things, a twinkle in her eyes. Either that or there was a flaw in her glasses.

"You don't have to stay to the very last minute . . . er

. . . toots," she confided. "Your boy friend's waiting for you outside; I just saw him through the window."

There he was holding up the front of the library when Prudence Roberts emerged a moment or two later.

"The lieutenant would like to see you to personally convey his thanks on behalf of the department," he said. "And afterward I . . . uh . . . know where there's a real high-brow pitcher showing, awful refined."

Prudence pondered the invitation. "No," she said finally. "Make it a nice snappy gangster movie and you're on. I've got so used to excitement in the last few days, I'd feel sort of lost without it."